Warmonger's Wrath

The Wrecking Squad Book 3

Nick Snape

NICK SNAPE

Copyright © 2025 by Nick Snape

First Edition

First edition August 2025

Book Cover by Getcovers.com

www.nicksnape.com

Also by Nick Snape

Weapons of Choice Series
Hostile Contact
Return Protocol
Zuri's War
Finn's War
Alien Rebirth
Invasive Species
Legion Earth
Nemesis Earth
The Wrecking Squad Series
The Wrecking Squad
Butcher's Folly
Warmonger's Wrath
The Queen's Spawn
Emperor's Fall
Breaker's Ruin
The Scorching Standalones
The World in My Hands
Just Press Play
Warriors of Spirit and Bone
A Dragon of the Veil
A City of Ashes
A Queen in Blood

PRAISE FOR THE AUTHOR

'A masterful voice in modern sci-fi' **SPR**

'Nick Snape's creative storytelling, rich world-building, and engaging characters make this book an unforgettable journey.' **Literary Titan**

'Stunning series. Very highly recommended.' **Goodreads**

'Sci-fi with pace, heart and unafraid to tackle deeper questions of what it means to be human.' **Amazon Customer**

'Wildly creative' **Self-Publishing Review**

For Bryan

Thank you for the belief

CHAPTER 1

"Hooowwweeeeee. Are you seeing what I'm seeing?"

"Say that again, Schmid. Interference is a pain in your ass right now."

"I said, Lanik, can you see what I'm seeing?" replied Schmid. "Because I got my eyes on the prize right now and it's got 'fuck yeah' written all over it. That baby is a Navy cruiser. We're talking about the salvage find of the century."

Lanik sighed, rubbing his eyes with gloved hands. "Which part of 'no' did you not understand in the phrase 'no salvage', Schmid? You can look, but not steal, end of conversation, understand?"

"Come on, Lanik. They don't mean the ship. They want what's on the inside. That armour plating alone will have us on the beach sipping cocktails while fish eat the dead skin off our toes," Schmid's voice was almost wistful over comms.

Lanik felt a little nauseous at the image and checked the salvager's camera feed. Spinning gently in the distance was the central asteroid, their target, and somehow attached to it, a derelict Almaarian cruiser that looked as if it had lost numerous battles in its last few years. The rear warped, engines scorched, and as Lanik zoomed in, he suspected not all the damage was as old as it appeared.

"Thinking it's had a recent electrical fire," he mused, again rubbing his tired eyes, cold fingers inside his gloves numb as they squeezed. "Hey Candia, we getting the heating back on soon?"

"Ten minutes, Bossman," came Candia's reply. "Whoever serviced this last didn't have a fucking clue what they were doing. You should sack them and find someone new."

"That was you, darlin'," Lanik smirked. Same old, same old.

"It was? Damn, I need retraining. Start-up sequence initiated. Ten minutes on the nose, Lanik."

"Good to hear, because I ain't collecting pay cheques this big with frozen fingers."

"Or enjoying them with frozen balls. Yeah, yeah, yeah. Heard them all before. And no, I ain't warming them up for you. There's a water bottle in the galley. Candia is fucking out of here." The comms went dead to the sound of Lanik's gentle sigh.

One day.

He clicked on the comms, while scanning the data feed from the probes circling the asteroid field. "Schmid, how's the highway to hell? Is it clear?"

"Data says yes, but my gut says no," replied Schmid, his tone suddenly serious. "Riding these 'fields ain't all about the facts, Lanik. Sometimes you get the sense of it. Do you know what I mean? The way the rocks fly isn't all about the physics; some have a mind to go a-walkin' and then you is in the shit. One tear in the wrong place, and your soul gets sucked out along with your spirit-water."

Yeah, 'spirit'. The vodka kind, knowing Schmid.

"Roger that, Schmid. It's why we brought you. Keep me posted." Lanik signed off, but kept a close eye on the auto-works Schmid was overseeing.

The swirl of the shattered asteroids around the central target had set his bowels creaking when they'd first arrived. Schmid hadn't been confident either when they fired up the autoship intercepts and their additional shielding. But Lanik had to admit, the old bastard knew his stuff. Three days in, and he had devised a corridor through the battering rock and dust particles ready to allow the first probe safe entry. The additional data had made the next day a cascade of successes, leaving them looking at a safety corridor wide enough to send in a team.

He watched as the old soak guided the combination of autoships and mini-bots through the outer layers of the corridor, nudging a trajectory here and there, while leaving others stationed and continually micro-adjusting positions as they fed off shared predictive data.

"Lanik, you there?" Schmid said, transmitting the 'highway to hell' as the bossman had dubbed it, onto the cockpit's screen.

Lanik coughed, placing the coffee flask on the console. "Yeah, yeah."

"I think we're done. All signs are in the green, and my gut's stopped grumbling at me. Reckonin' your team can take a look-see whenever you're ready." Schmid flagged multiple data points, matching them with the highway. "These are stable for forty-eight hours. After that, I'm making no guarantees. The rest are good for seventy-two to eightyish. I can recalculate that if need be as we go. That enough time? Actually, fuck that, it's all you're getting."

Lanik took a sip, eyes running over the information. The team could be ready in an hour. Forty-seven hours would give them a chance to map the ship with auto-drones, take most, if not all, of the samples required and start the process of analysis. With a ship's map, they could leave some of the probes in combo with the drones to explore and work on any additional surveys they may need. Better to do that towards the end of the safe period.

"Senak, Timin, we're up. Good job, Schmid."

By the time Lanik was suited up, the rest of the survey team had prepped and stored the survey equipment inside a remote activated ship – a simple hollowed-out transport equipped with thrusters to save on their own fuel. With the cargo doors open, Senak directed the transport out of the hold with each of them tethered to three of the upper corners. Taking directives from Schmid's autoships and bots, they were soon entering the corridor.

"Hells' highway," said Lanik, watching while rocks flew by the outer reaches of the void Schmid had created. Just one of those could kill them in any number of ways. "Fucking space. Why the hell did I choose life in a vacuum that doesn't give a shit if you live or die?"

"Because it's better than Almaar, where society doesn't give a shit if a lowlife lives or dies, either. At least out here, you get to feel a little more free. More equal," replied Senak.

Timin snorted. "In space, no one can hear you philosophise. Except me, of course. Don't listen to him, Bossman. He's here because he's on the run from the Court police. I'm here because *he's* on the run and he'd be dead without me."

"Still free. Life might be a little shorter, but ... fuck, Bossman. Is that a Navy ship?" asked Senak. "Cos it's looking well worse for wear."

Lanik glanced up from the data stream in his HUD and eyed the cruiser. His first assessment appeared valid. It had suffered at the hands of the 'field, no doubt. But the scorch marks that spread outwards from the numerous breaches seemed recent. Space weathering had not taken its due yet. How recent, maybe the survey would be able to tell.

Senak directed them towards the stern, heading for the largest of the breaches where the ship had suffered most as it twisted and warped. As their transport slowed and redirected thrusters away from the detritus covering the asteroid, Lanik spotted something unusual.

"You got that. Senak?"

"What?" he replied.

"I do," said Timin. "Odd dust patterns near the rear engines. Want me to go look, Bossman?

After Lanik confirmed, Timin untethered and dropped towards the rear of the huge cruiser. His camera feed gave a poor view of where he was headed, the quality of the survey suits measured by robustness rather than the on-board systems. That was what the probes and drones were for. Even so, as the salvager landed, Lanik had enough of a view.

"Are those pinions?" he asked.

"Yes, and by the colouration of the impact hole, pretty recent. Take a look." Timmins dropped nearer, allowing the camera a better view. "Guessing, but those appear to be stock Karal kit."

"No fucking way anyone got in here," said Senak. "No way. This Rebekah Khan's shit? Did they get in? Victor said ..."

"Victor Goncho says a lot. Sometimes I even believe every third word," replied Lanik. He eyed the cruiser, judging the pinion's position against the ship itself and the breaches he could make out. Victor had hinted that whatever was inside the asteroid field had a value they should only measure by the contract. But information was power, and Goncho was after more than just money. He, and the creepy Sabier, wanted payback. Anything they could glean about Khan and the *Sunstar*, and the events around what happened to the original crew of the *Maverick* was fair game and added to his cut of the commission. The Incini hadn't stipulated any of that in the contract, so fuck 'em according to Goncho. "Senak, launch dual probes. Map the tail section; find us a way in. Keep me informed of anything that looks like another team was here first."

Schmid unclipped his magboots, left his lap belt on, and crossed his legs as he slapped them onto the galley table. The clear liquid in his flask sloshed a little, so he took a sip, ensuring none would go to waste. The bitter-sharp taste of the vodka flooded his senses, topping up the alcohol levels swirling about his blood.

"Ahhhh," he said, exhaling with contentment. "The first is always the best. Until the next one."

Candia eyed the older man, wisps of grey hair floating in the zero grav about his ears, dulled eyes rimmed in shadow with veins of red punctuating the dark.

"What you looking at, girl?" he said. It wasn't a question, more a fuck off and stop being so rude.

She tipped her own flask, letting the liquid moisten her lips. "An old sot, taking what could be his last drink."

"Every drink could be the last. Every breath, every mouthful of food. Live life however the hell you wanna. And I ain't living your life, I'm living *mine*." His legs dropped from the table, and Schmid leaned closer. "Remember that. Yeah? Live how you want, not some other sad fucker's way that you didn't choose."

Candia glared. Though she'd heard the same words uttered regularly from the old goat's mouth, they still rankled.

The alarm blared, shrieking at her and her drunken companion. Candia pushed herself up from the bench, and clomped to the junction, heading for the cockpit. Alarms were a mainstay of life aboard ship.

She dropped into the pilot's chair and swiped the console to reveal its source. If it was the heating system, she had plans on downing Schmid's entire bottle before tackling it.

It wasn't.

"What the fuck?" she said, and flicked over to the cameras. Alcoholic breath spewed over her shoulders as Schmid arrived at her side. She ignored it, flicking over the feed until she had a starboard view. Nothing appeared amiss until the light streaming into the camera cut off. A shadow. Exactly what the alarms had warned her of, but it was impossible.

Or at least, impossibly big.

"Is that ...?" The comms squawked, and she slipped the headset on.

"Do not attempt to run. We repeat: do not attempt to run. You are intruding on a war grave. Prepare to be boarded. I repeat, cut all engines."

Schmid gagged, thankfully turning away and preventing the contents of his stomach from making an appearance. Candia swore, flicking through more of the *Maverick*'s camera feeds. The ship, or at least parts of the Almaarian Battleship, came into view. Huge, ominous. Across its bow, the word *Segfi* was stencilled.

"Oh no," she said, and swiped through the menu, hand hovering over the engine controls. "Live your life."

The engines kicked in, thrusting the salvage ship into rapid acceleration. The hull thudded, as if rain splattered onto a window. Cannon rounds pierced the metal-skin, shattering wire and plexi-glass as they went. A round ripped through her elbow, severing her forearm, and in shock, she watched the errant limb float away. A second tore into her shoulder, a third smashed through her chest. Ribs parted; a heart exploded. A rag doll, lifeblood pouring into the ship to merge with Schmid's.

A last thought never completed.

The body was sprawled on the frozen deck. One hand, formed of dehydrated human, melded to the metal, fingers spread wide like the tentacles of an octopus. The forearm curved as if the bones had warped, leading to a shoulder that retained the semblance of a Navy uniform. Whoever they had been was lost as the face crumbled and wafted away at Lanik's gentle touch.

"Fuck," said Senak, stepping towards the crimson sac the once-human thing had apparently emerged from. He changed his mind, moving away with a sickened glance towards Timin, who stood stock still, his frosted visor locked onto the tangled mess emerging from the foul sac.

"On that we agree," said Timin, voice harsh, the words almost forced. He turned away, heading out of the cabin and back into the relative calm of the burnt-out corridor.

Lanik stood, brushing hybrid dust into the container, his stomach churning away with the horror of what he'd just done. In a second plas-glass container, he dropped a canine tooth.

The ship shook. A tremor that rattled the hull. Moans and groans reverberated through the metal, though no sound travelled the airless corridors. Ash rose amid the vibrations, shimmering in their lights as they all pounded towards the junction.

"Oh shit. Ship quake," said Timin, reaching the junction first, turning back to face Lanik. "Fucking horrors. Ship bloody shakes. What the f—" Timin exploded. His suit burst, blood and gristle splattering the junction walls, globules spiralling along the corridors. What remained of his body collapsed, half-floating in the low grav as more of him was drawn out to forge a briefly crimson mist.

Lanik's comms crackled. "Halt. Remain where you are. You are trespassing on a war grave."

Before he had a chance to respond, the deck reverberated, and a large armoured suit shoved Timin disdainfully aside. The visor defrosted, and the scarred face of a space marine stared back, carbine raised and aimed his way. On their sleeves sat the insignia of the 6th and High.

"On the word of Countess Segfi, you and your crew are judged and found guilty."

Chapter 2

Davina eased back into the plump couch, eyes feeling a little dreamy as she allowed the alcohol to soothe her mind. The three low echelon company executives were engaged in a slightly drunken debate about the future of Karal Mining. The consensus being that it would not be long before they would be forced to sell out their current mining rights and move the entire operation to ensure efficiency gains as they tapped into a new and currently unexploited outer section of the field. They were, as usual, debating the pros and cons of such a tactic, while occasionally seeking her views on some of the specifics around the survey she had dropped in their laps a few hours beforehand. Under Mr Duboit's – the *real* Mr Duboit's – guidance, she had manipulated – bribed – the results of several surveys from some of the smaller teams Karal had sent out a couple of years back. At the time, what they found had a medium-level wealth potential, and Karal had bought the rights. A sound investment, one whose worth was rising day-by-day as the resource-hungry Court spread their influence into the outer colonies, and quite possibly re-armed.

Of course, Mr Duboit had an angle. Unlike in the pre-Enforcer days when he would combine delicate scalpel cuts amid despicable acts of industrial terrorism, Duboit was being watched. However, the mundane industrial business practice of screwing over any company you could, remained in the noble's remit. Industrial terrorism? Not so much. Espionage, control of the flow of information, and under-the-table double dealings were all permissible. Refinement, in fact, of the skills needed to negotiate the political Court that served the Empire. Seeking out illegal tech on a derelict ship buried behind the human-created maelstrom of an asteroid family, however, was off the table. That was the remit of her single-minded new co-employer, Erikson.

Davina activated her wetware, taking the edge off the alcohol, and leaned in as the three executives reached a natural pause in their conversation. "Do we have any poignant thoughts to share with Mr Duboit? He is not one for minor detail, nor generalisations."

Heung-Sha leant forwards, hands clasped, elbows resting on his knees. He was young, ambitious and perfect fodder for Duboit's, and therefore Davina's, ambitions. "So, Duboit Holdings are willing to invest in such a move?"

"At negotiable rates, yes. I say yes, but Karal has a tendency to lack efficiency when dealing with the initial site preparation. Mr Duboit would want guarantees that the issues, with, say, R89 for example, won't be repeated. For that, I would be negotiating the contractual obligations that Karal would need to adhere to. That debacle cost millions in set-up costs, and nearly killed one of your best repair and recovery crews after its abandonment. Work to be done." She took a sip, ensuring the cocktail's alcohol would not impinge on where she needed the conversation to go.

"Mr Duboit," cut in Jenkra Tew. Astute, insightful, and a widower. Her husband lost as a result of a suit failure on M4 while servicing an autoship, "is not doing this out of kindness. He aims to squeeze as much money as possible out of us, out of Karal Mining."

"Of course," replied Davina, tilting her head and allowing the slightest of smiles to form.

"But your initial offer seems, how do I put this? *Softer* than we would have expected. Less harsh. I would suggest your Mr Duboit has something planned behind these generous terms." Jenkra didn't let her eyes waver, and Davina suspected the executive had been drinking a little less than her counterparts.

"You would be more worried if he didn't. Karal is in trouble, Ms Tew. Mr Duboit is offering to help, remembering, of course, that it is your operation that mines his current holdings. The costs associated with moving to one of the other companies have been taken into account in these terms. I will leave the survey with you. Be in touch if you decide to present any form of proposal to the Karal board." Davina stood, smoothing out her blouse and trouser suit. "I bid you goodnight."

She nodded once and left, weaving her way through the exclusive bar the Karal execs frequented towards the exit. A seed had been planted, one that may well not come to fruition, but there were secondary benefits. Mr Duboit's desire for Karal to survive was now evident in their minds, the willingness to help even if it wasn't on this project. All the while, sending out a second automated survey team to a single asteroid that had been part of the same inspection period. A mere brush with it had produced some interesting analysis, dismissed at the time and subsumed into the overall rights acquisition. Now if the hints were correct, Duboit wanted that asteroid, his ears in the weapons industry identifying a rising demand in the specific PMG combination it contained. A long game.

"Miss Connors."

The voice came from behind, polite, but strangely insistent. Not one of the execs. She had all their deets on file. Deets? Details. She slowed, painting a smile on her face despite the desire to get home and shower the day away.

"How may I ...?" she began, but cut herself short as she drank in the man's face. A small scar to the left of his nose drew her in first, and a slight bend to the nose. All eminently fixable, going by the cut of his grey suit and sharply collared white shirt. Her sensory wetware amplified the upwelling of fear in her stomach, providing a reason for it. One eye was an implant, beautifully done, and the hair above it and back across the scalp was false but fine work.

"I seem to have that effect," he said, his hands loose by his sides, eyes fully on hers without a hint of embarrassment. Confidence exuded from the man. The agent. He had to be an agent of some kind, Davina casting her mind back to her analysis of the video of Dricks fighting two of Victor's goons. He had that same wariness imbued in his body, his balance perfect to explode from at any time. "We need to talk, Miss Connors."

"I have nothing ..." He held up a single finger, a request for silence she felt compelled to adhere to.

"I understand. Incini, etc, etc. Let us say we should converse somewhere quieter. What I wish to speak of is for your ears only." He gestured towards the exit, the milieu outside of the bar much less than in the lower levels, but hardly quiet. He gave her a lopsided smile and eased in beside her. "Come, it would be better for you and me if we didn't create a scene in front of your curious gaggle of executives."

Davina forced herself not to look over, taking the agent's word for it. She nodded, turned away and headed for the cocktail bar's exit, the strange man at her side. As they passed the bar, she swallowed hard. A square-jawed supposed customer watched them all the way. Subtle, but obvious to the wary.

"Good. Makes things easier. I have a room booked a mere block down."

She glanced over. "You have a name?"

"Use Gerent if you wish. Names make things more comfortable, don't they?"

Davina didn't answer. Locking her eyes ahead, she scanned the thinning crowd while wondering who else Gerent had watching them. His pheromones hadn't altered, just an easy self-confidence in every stress indicator she could pick up. The rentable rooms off the main concourse began to appear. A venture for impromptu meetings that required a little more security, and discreetness, than the local bars. Used for whatever type of liaison that the denizens of M1 and 2 saw fit. Gerent palmed a door, not glancing around as he entered and held the door open for her. This room was set up as an office, with a convenient pull-out couch in the corner. The door closed behind her, and the green glow of the secure lock lit the room, soon replaced by the harsher room lights as they activated.

Gerent stepped past her, and slid a dampener from his inner pocket, which he engaged before setting it on the table.

"Better," he said, and sat opposite, hands resting on the table. No rings. Bare. He caught her looking, and his smile flattened a little. He held one set of fingers up. "Yes. No rings. I am not noble, nor do I have any status you would recognise."

"But an agent of some kind," she said, and pulled out the chair opposite to sit down.

"You could say that. Miss Connors, in a few minutes, your new employer is in for a shock. He will witness the outcome of his dabbling in affairs above his station. Dabblings that you have facilitated."

Davina kept quiet, pushing her hands down between her thighs to keep them still while the wetware infused her system. However much it helped, the agent was intently watching her eyes, looking for the tells she herself used when analysing others.

"And yes, as an Incini – and under the Directorate – you were and always will be acting under good faith. You may even believe *he* is searching for evidence of Duboit's possible sedition. Or perhaps, pushing the boundaries of what is acceptable in the eyes of the Emperor and the Court." He leaned forwards, his smile malicious but not a threat towards her. "And that is why I am here."

"I can't comment," she managed to say. Finding her Incini-indoctrinated confidence slipping away. He had, in one sentence, outlined her own concerns about the Enforcer's behaviour.

"I understand. I do. But what is about to happen stinks of conspiracy, and we are not yet sure whether," he paused, licking his lips, "your new employer is ingrained within it or not. However, a test is coming. And we need to follow the trail back to its source. And that is where you come in."

Davina blinked. The insecurity her wetware fought winning. The agent had made no threat, but somehow had unpicked the wounds she had been healing.

She coughed, hiding her feelings behind her hand. "I am not sure what you mean. If, by act, or deliberate omission of action, any of my employers swing close to treason, I am duty bound to report to the Directorate."

"That you are. Imagine, if you will, a mouse creeping up upon the cheese set in a baited trap. What happens if a guiding hand eases the mouse away? Wags its finger and sends the vermin on a different path?"

"I don't—"

That finger raised again, cutting her off. "What happens is it *breeds*. Its progeny more wary than the last, *fucking* and producing vermin until you are overrun. That is where you come in, Incini. I require your silence until such time *we* can burn out the infection running through the Court, even, dare I say it, the Enforcers. Kill the vermin at the source before they *breed* sedition."

"I am not sure that is within the tenets."

"I can assure you it is not. Deliberately so. They were set up in naivety by a past emperor whose view of treason was focused on the Court and its nobility. Not upon outside influences that sink their claws into our purest and steep them in poison." The agent slid a hand inside his jacket and placed a card on the table. Embossed, beautifully written in a florid style that drew her eye. He gently spun it, allowing her to read the embedded graphics via her implant. A dread set about her chest as the wetware translated.

"Sir," she began, again the single finger, staying her words as she tried to stand.

"I am the Minister's hand, no more than that. Nor a *sir*. I am the one who watches the watchers." He withdrew the card, eyes never leaving hers. "You understand now? I have your agreement? This conspiracy runs deep; the poison vicious. Stay by Erikson's side. Do as you are willed, but do not report to the Directorate. They will be compelled to act, and I will only have the puppets and not the puppet master by the end of it." He pushed his chair back, rising to place both hands on the table's edge. "Are we in agreement?"

Davina's mouth felt heavy, her tongue stuck to the roof as if paralysed. She nodded, the motion easing the inertia. "Yes, my ..." She struggled for the words, so many pressing in on her mind. An agent of the Court's Minister, the overseer of the nobility's political dance as they sought favour and status from the Emperor. This man will have been in the Minister's presence, possibly had sight of the Emperor himself. And he wanted her to break the tenets she had lived her life by for the last twenty years.

"Merely Gerent. That is the only name and title you require. Good. I have high hopes that I can put an end to this treachery with your help." He clasped the dampener and headed for the door. "Don't leave for half an hour and then seek Erikson. He may well be in contact, once realisation *hits*."

CHAPTER 3

"Flooding now," said Tremil.

A hiss rose in Rebekah's comms. "Good." She checked her visor for a progress report on the EM Tremil was bouncing off multiple probes. "We'll be on data packet only, Savvo. Yes?"

"Yes, Captain Khan," Savvo replied, bitterness dripping over comms. "Text only, short burst to cut through the jamming, ma'am, sir."

"Hope you're standing up and saluting too," cut in Arin, his words barely audible as the crackles increased.

"F—"

Savvo's comms cut off, but a data packet message soon followed, assigned to Arin only. A sneak peek showed a low-pixel picture of a middle finger salute.

"Don't bait him. That's an order," Rebekah said, suppressing the beginnings of a smile. That Savvo was alive and riled at being left on board the *Sunstar* was good enough news. The medbot in combination with that bastard Ormsk's venom analysis had kept him breathing and on the mend. She hadn't quite worked out the Bustan Lieutenant's intentions at providing the correct analysis. Perhaps he worked off keeping everyone off-balance until he was ready to strike. It certainly fit his tactics with the missile.

Rebekah snapped her rifle up to her visor, and as they synced, zoomed in on the complex sat amid the dust and brush of the Shema scrubland on its smallest continent. A high-end villa, walls and roof resplendent with state-of-the-art security systems to ensure no one got to see the viscount at play in his pool, jacuzzi or any other form of watery entertainment he appeared to relish. Safe, secure and normally filled by twenty armed guards with damn-fine security clearances. Only right now, the majority of those guards were protecting his cavalcade as they crossed the scrub and headed this way, blissfully unaware that any cries for help beyond the outer reaches of the dry desert would go unheard.

"You locked in, Arin?"

"Got a tracker beeping away. They'll be about an hour, max."

"Time to get heavy. Dricks, sit rep?"

"Lovin' being back on the ground, and in real armour. Not that shit-ass space stuff. I can see sky ... blue sky." Dricks cut herself off. "Got eyes on the rear entrance, Captain. No movement."

"Good. You're our eyes, Dricks. If the comms cut off ..."

"Use the burst code. It's not been that bloody long." Dricks added a chuckle, then cleared her throat.

Rebekah focused her carbine's additional sight. "Okay, on my mark ... 3, 2, 1, ... Mark." Her finger depressed the trigger, and the laser flared – a thin line of light that bore through the camera array stationed at the outer gate. As Arin's beam flared beneath hers to take out the secondary system, she switched target to the satellite dish, taking that down as Arin again followed suit, burning through the back-up systems.

"Now, ZZ3," she said. No need for the action codes and protocols anymore. A warbot with the beginnings of its own mind and a developing moral code. And thankfully, every sign it was on their side. She figured if they cut the bot in half, it'd have 'I am crew' written all the way through the middle. Didn't stop her nagging doubts, though they were little more than a trickle after the warbot had seared an AI-controlled Marauder in half on Scarva's ship.

Dust flew, caught upon the hot breeze as ZZ3 emerged from a camouflaged hole twenty metres from the gate. It powered across the scrub, feet reaching the sun-seared plas-crete of the driveway, and rammed into the double gates like a wrecking ball. Limbs tore at the ornate ironwork, bending, ripping until the dual lock combinations snapped. Gunports opened along the outer walls, and Arin needed no captain's order to protect the warbot. They both began to fire, the laser attachments rapidly destroying any targeting systems. Two brief clatters of machine gun rounds pinged off ZZ3's head, adding to the brutal scar where one eye remained missing.

"Shit. More repairs," stated Arin, as his laser burnt through the last of the targeting systems.

"Cover," said Rebekah, rising and running in one elegant movement. Well, as elegant as full Marine powered armour allowed you to be. The servos drove her forwards, compensating for the joys of planetary gravity and her current level of musculature to ensure her body wasn't taxed too much. One thing she knew, however, was that the crew's gym time was going to have to be upped. And when she said crew, she included hers.

The first human guard shot at ZZ3 as the warbot threw the gate aside, the combination of sculpted iron and armoured plate crashing into the dust beside the whitewashed walls. Bullets streamed across the bot's torso before Rebekah could intervene.

The first test.

ZZ3 strode towards the guard, whose panicked reaction to a hulking tank-bot Rebekah deemed appropriate. No one was paid enough to have their arms and legs ripped off, while their head was used as a bowling ball. A limb snaked from ZZ3's torso, catching the guard's lightly armoured ankle. He toppled over, head slamming into the plas-crete just inside the gates. A normal warbot would simply carry on, legs crushing the body underfoot, careless as to whether the human beneath died or not. Threat over. Move on. Next target.

ZZ3 dragged the guard towards it, then lifted him high, red eyes peering into his visor. They pulsed once, and the bot tossed the man aside and into the pool of the nearest water fountain. Another shot rang out, ricocheting off the warbot. Rebekah dropped to one knee just inside the gate and fired. It slammed into the second guard's shoulder, spinning them around on the first-floor balcony. Her second shot hit their armoured back. Blood bloomed. Despite her concern for ZZ3's actions, if you fired on crew, you made yourself a target.

She surveyed the front garden, her HUD mapping the expected layout – derived from their probes – over what she could see. Whatever role this viscount had, they could afford to project a false image of the villa for any passing spy satellites. That meant any identified auto-guards were likely fake, too. She had planned for ZZ3 to withdraw, but not now.

"Cover Arin's approach, ZZ3," she ordered.

"Yes, Captain," replied the bot, and its body reversed to stand by the mutilated gateway.

"On my way, Captain," said Arin.

A gunshot echoed beyond the walls, followed by a short burst of carbine fire. With the jamming, she couldn't get any signal from Dricks' camera feed, which gnawed at her, but it had been her choice to prevent any call for help.

"Dricks, sit rep." She eyed the driveway, particularly the overblown garage with its ridiculous fluted columns as she awaited a reply.

"Guards on the run. Two. One down, one decided I ain't lost it yet." There was a definite hiss to the comms.

"Copy that. Front garden clear," she replied. A check behind showed Arin had arrived, looking a little healthier than she felt after the run across. A second glance told her the guard immersed in the fountain's spray was zero threat.

"ZZ3, check the garage," she commanded. "Arin to the right, I'll take left."

"You got that itch?" asked Arin, carbine up and sweeping out to the side as ordered.

ZZ3 approached the garage door painted with a seascape. The driveway was perfectly clear of dust, as was the garden, and the warbot left no prints. Rebekah assumed some form of static charge was at play, perhaps connected with the false image they had from above.

"Yeah," she replied. The garage door bulged, the metal lats that made up its concertina-like construction extending towards them. The painted hues of blue warped, morphing into a large shape Rebekah vaguely recognised. Lats sprung open one-by-one, exposing the lower half of an auto-loader half-covered in a camo-net.

"Down, Arin!" she shouted, but he had already dropped as bullets poured, shredding the remaining garage door to reveal a mounted machine gun much like the Hammer Arin had used on the *Scourge*. The rounds tore into the driveway plas-crete, sweeping across Rebekah's hip plates. They resisted, for now, as two dual rotored drones burst from the hole in the door. ZZ3 sidestepped the multi-barrelled machine gun and crashed a motorised limb downwards, smashing the weapon into the floor. Rebekah rolled, bringing the carbine up to track the nearest drone. A single weapon was slung beneath, rotors spinning to keep it steady. But it didn't fire. Relieved, Rebekah rose to one knee, aimed and shot. The drone exploded; hull shattered by the burst of rounds with the second crashing to the driveway under Arin's hail of bullets.

Rebekah spun about to find ZZ3 had stomped the Hammer into pieces, red eyes pulsing until the warbot was satisfied the threat was over.

Arin huffed. "Okay, okay. Bonus points to the Captain. Jamming works despite it negating our own drones."

"Better believe it. Good job, ZZ3. Survey the garage and report."

"Yes, Captain." ZZ3 kicked aside the last of the mangled gun-barrels and entered the garage, the lights clicking on as they sensed a presence.

Rebekah caught a glimpse of the transports inside, sleek versions of both wheeled and flying vehicles that were designed for looks and speed over practicality. The temptation was to destroy them all, and leave a calling card. But the true target lay much deeper inside the villa, *if* Erikson's intel was correct.

"Threat assessment nil," said the bot. It raised hairs on Rebekah's arms. She shook it off.

"Guard the villa entrance, ZZ3. Make sure we have an exit. If you get sight of the convoy, I need to know as we're blind now." She made to climb the stone steps that led to the ornate entrance, before turning back. "Understood?"

"Affirmative," replied ZZ3. "Data burst may not get through so leave the doorways open. I detect the villa walls are EM sealed; vibration damped. I will find a way to contact you."

Rebekah reached the top, eyeing the double door entrance with its carved sea dragon motifs. The irony of someone obsessed with the sea and water having a hideaway in the scrubland was not lost on her. The projected image of a playful, sea sports loving viscount there for those that discovered his little oasis. While the truth lay hidden deep inside secure walls.

"Knock, knock, Arin."

Her sub-engineer and explosives expert didn't need any other invite. With the carbine at his feet, he clamped and wired in the four multi-directional mines he'd constructed from Davina's resources. With a grimace he stepped away, nudging his visor up a little to wipe away the sweat on his nose.

They both flattened against the wall, Arin raising his hand with the detonation remote ready. "In 3, 2, 1 ... M—"

The door opened, a guard sweeping the entranceway with a handgun and spotting Arin. She also spied the explosives, mouth forming an 'O' as Arin finished triggering the remote. The guard threw herself forwards, the blasted stone hammering against the thin armour about her legs and torso. Rebekah spun in, carbine ready, HUD analysing any heat signatures inside the hallway. It flagged a target, and she fired, the stream smashing a statue and rupturing the wooden stairway behind.

"Throw your weapon down." She fired again, the clatter of metal against stone her reward. "On the floor." The figure dropped, and as she entered, the hallway lit up. A male guard lay face down, a pistol still spinning against the polished marble where he'd thrown it, hands on the back of his neck. "Lay your hands out where I can see them. I find any weapon strapped to your upper back, I'll punch a bullet through your brain and wipe the smear on your dead arse."

She saw a tremble to his shoulder, and stepped inside, clicking the carbine trigger.

"Th-th-there's a knife."

"Remove it slowly and slide it over. I'm extra fucking twitchy today, just so you know." By the time she was at his side, the knife rested near his pistol. She pressed the muzzle of her weapon against the guard's neck. "Hands crossed against your back." He complied, and she wrapped a cable tie tight about his wrists. "Any other guards in here?"

"N-no," he stated, and she believed him. But belief didn't keep your squad alive.

"Arin, Sit rep." The hiss and crackle were louder, despite the open door.

"The other guard is a mess, but will live if …"

Yeah, if.

"They can wait. With me." She lifted the male guard by the tie, knowing the wrap would cut into his wrists. "Take point," she said, and Arin moved ahead. He didn't go far, checking then moving past the corner beneath the huge stairs to enter what appeared to be a uniform wood-panelled corridor. He stopped by the fourth set of panels and, glancing ahead to make sure it was clear, tapped the butt of his weapon against the wall. A hollow thud responded, a check with the next panel giving the expected dulled response of wood on stone.

She felt the guard tense, and leant in, her visor close to his ear. "Now. I'll ask again. Any more guards here?" His head shook. "But what about people? Hmmm. Any other *people* here?" The tension turned into a whimper, his body stiffening. He wanted to tell her, she knew. Wanted to blurt it all out, let someone know. But he was complicit, nearly as guilty as the fucker speeding through the desert towards them. Money. A root of evil that the nobility dangled before the lowlifes. A chance to buy some status when you were not fortunate enough to be born into it.

"Please," he said.

"Open it. If I have to break it open, I'll do it with your fucking head, understand?" He nodded in response, muscles relaxing as he leaned against the wraps, accepting the pain as they cut in.

"Second panel on the left. Retina scan behind it." He paused, as if accepting his fate. "I can access it."

Arin had the panel open, and she grabbed the back of the guard's neck, pressing him against the camera. He tensed again, but the panel clicked. Arin pushed the door wide, revealing an inky void thick with the chemical stink of fear and desperation. Wordless, Arin stepped in, cautious, with his movements deliberate as he scanned the stairs. A light blinked on, and the room beneath appeared in its stark white and scrubbed clean glory.

"Please. Don't make me ..." mumbled the guard.

Rebekah punched him on the back of the head, slamming his forehead into the panel. He dropped like a stone, and she stepped over him, following Arin down into the foul prospect of the sterile basement.

"Rebekah don't," dropped into her HUD, her comms now dead inside the room. She ignored Arin's plea and took each step with determination until she reached the bottom, and its chemically cleaned white tiles.

"Fucker," she said, knowing Arin was unlikely to hear her. Three cells, barely the size of a desk were strung across the far wall. Each occupied by whatever soul remained in the tortured, damaged humanity huddled in their corners. Scars, healed and unhealed, riddled their naked bodies. Waves. Patterns. Where the aesthetic didn't please, pieces sliced off or carved into new forms. At the far end, a mortuary slab and an array of sparkling tools. And above them, a myriad choice of water to wash away the blood on a viscount's hands.

"Record it," she sent, and drew out a small slate. Davina had been very specific. No use of HUDs, no recording other than via the slates. No copies other than those taken live.

When they were done, she peered at Arin. His visor was frosted as required, but the tremor in his jaw, the wetness either side of his lower cheeks betrayed his emotional state. For once, she knew why they were on this job, what the point of their intervention was. Though of course, the little shit would survive, unlike those who barely clung to life in the cells.

"Go," she sent, and as he turned to argue, shook her helmet. "Leave."

He clomped up the stairs, reaching the top as she turned back to the human sculptures in their personal hells. She shot them in turn, whispering a prayer for each. No one deserved to live like that.

The rules of engagement had been specific.

Fuck that.

On reaching the top of the stairwell, she turned about, removing two grenades from their pouches. She spun the timers and dropped them down the stairs. With a breath, she paused, and then picked up the male guard. Servos whirred as she threw him down the steps, slamming the door shut. She didn't look at Arin, she didn't have to. He'd be appalled, but the guard had known what was down there. Had allowed it. The explosions rocked the panel door, though she ignored them, walking through the entrance to find the female guard crawling across the slabs of the front entrance.

They had to know. They all did. But she couldn't prove it.

She could only imagine the bullet shattering the guard's skull as she walked on by, despite the call for revenge surging in her gut.

"Captain?" said ZZ3, head turning sideways to watch her and the approach road.

She blinked.

Captain?

Captain of the Wrecking Squad. A walking contradiction.

"Tear this fucking place apart."

Smoke curled, filling the once blue sky with a billowing blackness that roiled and bubbled into the atmosphere. Orange flames licked the scorched walls, their roar filling the viscount's ears as he stepped out from his sleek and expensive car. The blacked-out armoured transport at the front of his cavalcade had stopped diagonally across the road, armed guards sprouting from the roof, weapons trained on his burning villa.

Dexter swore, a dread sat heavy in the pit of his stomach.

A villa burned, but was that all?

A house can be rebuilt. But a reputation?

Viscount Lundstrom – Dexter to those within the nobility who knew him best – walked past the guards, ignoring their shouts and pleas but soon overtaken as they forged a ring around him. He walked on, eyes roaming across the mangled gates, the dried-up fountain, and the mix of broken bodies and restrained guards piled in the forecourt. Before the gate was a metal box.

"Miguel," he said. No other words were needed, and the guard strode over, passing a scanner over the box. With a nod, he flipped it open, re-scanning the contents before shutting the lid. The viscount clicked his fingers, and the guard hurried over, placing the box in his boss's hand. Dexter flicked the lid open, and dread rose to stifle his throat. A ring sat upon a slate. The mark of the Emperor's Enforcers.

Dexter removed the slate and ring, casting the box to the ground. Ensuring it was on silent, he watched as the recording played out, fingers quivering.

Marked.

Watched.

Still alive. But who talked?

He could only think of one recent dalliance. A man who liked to gamble. Erikson.

Chapter 4

"Take us in, Heki," Rebekah said, risking a glance over to check she had heard. The shock on her face indicated she had.

"Me?"

"You. Just link with the transponder, and it'll fly itself to the correct bay once you reach the set position." Rebekah waited, and eventually Heki nodded, swallowing as she did so. Only a tinge of the emotions crossed the distance between them, the symbiote gently entwined about the girl's neck apparently soothing the usual tempest.

"But not a word. You have no Karal approved licence, so if they call in, I take the lead. Okay?"

"Yes, Captain." A smile appeared, unconscious, not forced. Almost relaxed.

"Any news on the comms, Trem?" Rebekah asked, mindful of the need to keep both twins aware she regarded them as valued members of the crew. "Any patterns we need to be aware of?"

"If you mean from Shema, nothing so far. There has been encrypted traffic from the nobility, but that'll take a long time to decipher. On it, though." Tremil sounded positive, and Rebekah hoped things were on an even keel. Both girls now had their own cabin, Tremil keeping the captain's berth due to her modded console requirements. What hadn't surprised her in the few days since the move, was she still hadn't seen them apart when on downtime. Sometimes a space was just that, a sanctuary you could use if needed.

With Karal not calling in yet, she spun her chair and headed off to a showdown. The fun side of being a captain. She collected two flasks on the way, handing the herbal tea over when Savvo reluctantly opened his cabin door.

"Can I come in?" she asked, keeping her face as neutral as she could. Savvo nodded, stepping to the side, shutting the door as she passed.

"No stims, if that's what you're checking," he said, taking to his bed as Rebekah sat on the only chair.

She took a sip, eyeing him over the flask rim. "Not why I'm here, but pleased nevertheless. Any temptation? I mean, how did Dricks put it? You're as ornery as a constipated cow."

Savvo broke into a brief grin, leaning closer, one hand resting on his knee as he rubbed behind his ear. "About right I suppose. Yeah, there's been temptation. I'm not going to lie and say I haven't used the wetware. That fucking venom screwed up my dreams pretty bad."

She squeezed his knee, suddenly needing to reassure her second-in-command. To her surprise, his hand landed on hers, and squeezed back.

"I appreciate the support, Rebekah. Though, not being left behind from a mission."

"Left? We needed one of us in the sky, Savvo. And you were in no fit state to provide cover, never mind go in that fucking charnel house. You would have burned that scum and his enclave down to their bones and ground them for bread." Rebekah tried to avoid his eyes, the memories too painful. Leaving that fucker viscount alive hurt.

"Why didn't you?"

Yeah, why not?

"Because of this," she waved her hands about the cabin, "and you, and the twins. All of it. We did a job, stopped what was happening, and left the Enforcer's calling card. Yes, I could have killed him, but what then? The Enforcers would come for us, and that fucker's connected family. We made a difference. And perhaps for the first time one we can measure, rather than playing the Enforcer's games."

Savvo grinned at her.

"What the hell? This is not *my* therapy session we're having."

"Isn't it? Dricks said ..." he leant back, avoiding the slap on his arm.

"Dricks," Rebekah said, realisation she'd been played by her crew slotting home.

"Hey. It's a start. But you can't bottle this shit up either. Understand? This, Ormsk, what happened to Hanna or even Baja's gang. The *Scourge*'s crew. We all go through it together and bounce off each other. But you ..." he shook his head. "Nothing."

She stood, her purposeful glare fading into nothing. "Message received. And you?"

"Pissed off, but I'll live."

"We're not ready," said Tremil, her gaze falling on Heki who nodded in agreement. "Not yet, we know. But with the symbiotes, we could be soon. We just want you to think about that. We can't stay on board forever."

Rebekah paused at the airlock, turning in her basic suit to eye both girls. "I understand. But this is not the place ..." she trailed off. Where would be? Another Benetai?

The twins didn't react, and Rebekah knew they could sense the emotions pouring from her. The uncertainty. Maybe not the cause of it, but they were practised at making their educated guesses. Had moved beyond using ZZ3's imitation of the crew, their family, with the help of two alien symbiotes who appeared to redress the tumult of emotions they normally spewed out like active volcanoes.

"I'll see what I can do," she said. "Chocolate?"

"That won't work forever," stated Heki. "But please."

Rebekah entered the airlock, only Savvo and Arin joining her after they decided to maintain a watch on board. An adult presence for their peace of mind, as well as the two girls. So much was changing, and fast, but they couldn't take their eye off the threats from home base, the Minx asteroids, any more than they could from those their handler brought down upon them. They had added a viscount and his family to the list of those with a grudge. On top of Lieutenant Ormsk with the entire Bustan Navy, and whatever was left of the Butcher raging in his containment box. Then there was ZZ3. The bot's moral response to Rebekah's fury at the villa an interesting counterpoint. She had watched as the warbot used minimal force, using it as a test almost, and then ... well.

Was she really going to have a moral discussion with a fucking bot?

Apparently, according to Arin, yes.

The guard had sold his soul to the viscount. End of discussion. She had wanted to kill them all, taking her rage out on the villa instead. It still wasn't enough.

"You're quiet, Captain," Arin said as they finally sat in the transport shuttle to M2. "Something I said? I mean, I've kept silent, but there's a long list of things I could have said, or have said in the past, or thought about saying but didn't."

"You're rambling." Savvo punched Arin on the arm, then settled back in his seat. "Must drive Dricks crazy every time she wants some peace and quiet."

"Now there's a list. Arin's foibles, by Captain Hendricks. Foible number one, he breathes. Foible two, when not breathing, he talks too much."

"Foible," cut in Savvo, shaking his head. "Bloody dictionary on legs. Go on, explain."

Rebekah spared them both a glare, wishing she was in her suit and could shut off her comms link. Instead, she disappeared into her own head, musing over Tremil's statement. The answer lay in how to keep them hidden. They would need official ID on Karal. Obtainable on the underground market, but she was guessing Victor Goncho and his cronies would have fingers in that pie. The last thing she wanted was a connection to him, and the holo-masked weirdo he kept in tow. There was Trent Pike, but she suspected he was too rigid to bend any rules for them. That left Davina, and that opened a whole new can of space weevils. A no-go, even if she could persuade the Incini to help. The Directorate oversaw her actions, and one suspicious deal could lead them to the girls. At the moment, their futures hung on Davina categorising the events involving the twins as related to Duboit's contract. Anything else was fair game, and even that would be exposed should the horrors aboard the *Scourge* be discovered. Rebekah had little doubt there would be talk of sedition against the Court and Emperor. Like having a brain-patterned Butcher locked in a containment box, for instance.

And why was it still in the hold? And not floating in the depths of space?

Good question.

Do you throw away your ace in the hole even if it could kill you?

One of the officer-nobles, Major Ren for instance, and definitely that mega-shit Countess Segfi, would have kept such an ace hidden and sacrificed everything else first. And should it not prove as powerful as they thought, shrugged their shoulders and moved on to the next meat grinder. They were immune.

"Show me," said Tremil, shifting over to the other side of the cabin. ZZ3, at least the upper half of the hulking bot, sidled past, and dual limbs hovered above the adapted console.

"The Senti code has inherent links between algorithms that are woven in hidden patterns. The code is in three dimensions, but ..." ZZ3 said, a metal digit swiping across the screen to form what appeared to be an irregular cube made up of interlocking spider-webbed code.

"But ..." repeated Tremil, raising an eyebrow as she side-eyed the warbot. "You can't leave that hanging there. It kind of gets annoying."

"Annoying?" replied ZZ3. "Arin programmed it in deliberately. Why would he add something annoying to my architecture?"

Tremil snorted. "That's Arin. He looks for ways to, I dunno, prod and poke us out of the norm. Or make us think, react even. Make us feel ali—" She reddened, and Tremil found herself under the warbot's four-eyed regard.

"Yes," said ZZ3. "To fracture thinking, and stimulate your mind. That I can understand. I am the sum of many parts. They bounce off each other."

Tremil leant in, her head upon the bot's upper limb joint. "We all are, ZZ3. I am the part of me tortured in a lab – angry and vicious. And it comes bubbling out when I'm threatened. Another part was forged on the *Sunstar*. It loves, and feels love, but also frustration, a sense of loneliness amid a family, and in contradiction a feeling of belonging. It confuses and makes sense in equal measure. Among this emotional soup will be who I really am. And despite it all, I have to believe that someday I will simply be *me*." Her arms wrapped about the bot's metal limb.

"I find that comforting. I do not know why," replied the bot.

"Belief is a human trait I am only just beginning to understand. I would, and still do, swing from certainty to doubt within moments of each other. Savvo will tell you it's my biochemistry, Rebekah part of growing up, Dricks that time and patience are required, and Arin would tell a bad joke. Textbooks are no help. There is no one like me, except perhaps Hek, in this world. Nor anyone like you." Tremil pulled away from the bot, wiping a small tear though she didn't feel upset. Odd. "Now, what comes after that pause?"

ZZ3 returned its outward attention to the screen. "Senti visualise in a fourth dimension. According to Asham, the human mind struggles to perceive it, but once a mind is trained," the bot tapped and swiped at the screen, "the parts fold in together. This is a simulation; you will need to practise until such perception becomes natural. What I did back at Benetai was allow, within my parameters, Asham to guide me." On the screen the code reformed. What had been a spidery, disconnected algorithm became a wave of code. "Remember, this is simulation and translated by the Senti to infiltrate human computer systems. How it presents within a Senti system would be very different. But the principles ..."

Tremil filled in the pause. "Remain the same. I—" She cut herself off. Images of folded space seeped into her mind. Of Heki and her penetrating a malleable barrier, emerging to bask in the light of the Almaarian sun and thousands of light years from where they began. She had no doubt the two principles were not only connected, but inherent within each other. That the Senti were only one half of the puzzle. The other resting contented tentacles against her neck.

Four dimensions.

CHAPTER 5

Erikson gulped the water at his side. A small, uncharacteristic shake to his hand causing the liquid to spill upon his desk that sat central to the secure SCIF he prayed kept prying eyes from seeing what displayed on the screen. At first it had been a shadow, blocking out the vestiges of the Almaarian sun's light. And then, as the camera panned, the giant comms spike that pierced the void just as the huge bow of the battleship appeared. It's solidity against the backdrop of the sun had held Erikson in awe, before the reality of it struck home. A death knell sounded amid the silence of the black.

The warning, and the *Maverick*'s idiotic response, followed by the shimmer of Point Defence Cannon rounds that tore into the salvager's hull. The briefest of fireballs had filled the camera before it died. The vestige of oxygen within the tin can released as the cannon fire pierced the smaller ship's engines. That at least provided a little hope. Evidence of his involvement partially reduced by the deaths of the lowlifes inside, but he already had viewed the relayed footage of Lanik's penetration of the *Scourge*. The markings had been removed, but the correlation with his stored image left no doubt as to whose ship lay derelict on the asteroid. A conspiracy of some form uncovered, involving, he was sure, his handler at the very least.

He had received a few minutes recording from inside the *Scourge*. Enough to confirm the ship was dead, and according to Lanik, ripped apart from the inside out. A two-stage process of destruction, one recent, with additional bulkheads opened to enable a burn through of any residual oxygen. Why was a question he couldn't let go, but such thinking had led him to where he was now.

The house lights dropped, instantly ending as if snuffed out by the hands of the gods. The shake that had invaded his hand, rumbled through his body, and he let out a long, resigned sigh. A quick check showed the Enforcer SCIF had ceased to function, though his additional security was still active. He doubted its impact, but remained a spark of light in the ensuing dark. He hit the failsafe, praying that every scrap of data he held would be scrubbed, burned and eradicated from existence. Of course, that didn't mean it hadn't already been intercepted.

Erikson pushed himself away from the desk, and on standing, pulled back the bottom drawer. He removed the armoured vest, placing it over his head as the first crash of glass echoed along the hallway. He withdrew a handgun from its holster, checking the clip and pocketing several others. Supposedly bullets were old hat, kinetic weapons that threw a slug of metal vaguely in the direction of your assailant. Except they were deadly, reliable and hard to screw-up when no electronics were involved. Ten minutes of watching the Breakers at work taught you that.

But electronics had other benefits, and the cut-off scream from the hallway caused a shiver of satisfaction. While the HUD of whoever invaded his home warned of the laser trip, the pressure-triggered chem charge blew their foot off.

He dropped in beside his door, edging around to view the blood-spattered walls and the clearly dead black-clad violator of his temporary home.

Another poked their weapon through the side window, and Erikson fired, the flash of his gun lighting the hallway briefly before crashing into the assailant. They barely reacted, their weapon's sight alighting on Erikson. He threw himself to the side as the glare of laser fire threatened to burn into his retinas. More glass hit wooden floors, coming from the rear, and Erikson made for the upper level. A second laser flash streaked across the wall, singeing his vest, and he clattered up the stairs in hope a third wouldn't follow. Missing steps, his stuttering stride brought him to the top, and he let a small grenade bounce its way back behind him. The flash and bang that ensued dulled by his wetware as he headed for the first floor exit he had prepared.

The chemical smell of burning pursued him through the door. Erikson reached the window, and without pause, rammed the butt of his gun against a specific point in the pane. The window shattered, and as he leapt through, the pressure mines he had avoided on the stairs blew. Shoulders hit the low roof, and he rolled, missing his footing and dropping over the other side to hit the ground hard. With his hip dissenting, he rose to his feet only to be faced with a discordance of light that seared into his eyes.

"I suggest you duck, Mr Erikson," came a tremulous, female voice. "It's about to get *violent.*"

He did just that. Throwing himself to the ground, covering his head as the night burst into a cacophony of gunfire. Bullets hammered into his temporary home, tearing wood and brick, shattering the dark, yet silencing the voices within. It stopped as suddenly as it started, echoes disappearing into the night. He looked up, boots clomping either side of him to crash into what remained of the house. More shouts, sporadic gunfire, and his own weapon kicked away from where it lay.

"Get up, Mr Erikson. You are safe, for now."

He stood, brushing down his expensive trousers, re-tightening his tie. Releasing a breath, he tried to peer through the saturated light to catch sight of his supposed saviour. With his hand above his eyes, he blinked, making out a shadowed figure that any reasonable assassin would assume was a decoy. Somehow, he didn't feel it was. The figure took slow steps, smoke curling up into the night sky from a bright-ended cigarette sat within a simple yet beautiful cigarette holder. The hair wrapped about her head in a modest bun, grey against the harsh light, had no strand out of place. Another cloud of smoke rose, and the regard of the woman pinned him in place.

"You have made some powerful enemies, Mr Erikson. Dexter's family paid handsomely for the knowledge of where you currently reside, and I hated to disappoint." The harshest of lights cut out, revealing the rest of the elder woman, wisp thin, skin like aged paper, to his gaze. "Now, we need a little chat."

"Yes, Countess. I would like that," he responded. The building behind him began to collapse, his thoughts on the slate and the SCIF he had left inside.

"No, you wouldn't. But then, you have no choice." The last of the building caved inwards. "As you know, I can be rather *brutal* when ignored."

The limousine was a step above any Erikson had travelled in before. The leather soft, the metal burnished gold. But everything had a purpose. No ridiculous affectations the nobility so loved to show off their wealth or power. Functional elegance.

The silence had been stark. The Countess Segfi openly ignoring him as they slid smoothly away from the scene of his supposed rescue. All to make a point. A show of power he hadn't honestly needed. By reputation alone, he would have been cowed by her presence. He had considered breaking the silence, but decided this was a test among many others he might face as he tried to keep his skin attached to his body. Eventually, the limousine swept into a clearing beside the highway, and a shuttle lit up, engine mounts pointing to the ground, ready for vertical take-off.

Oh.

"Functional," said the Countess, her first words accompanied by a puff of smoke. "Just as you will need to be. A simple purpose in a much bigger mechanism."

"I don't understand," he replied as the limo came to a halt.

"Oh, part of you does. You have come across something distasteful, Mr Erikson. You have shown admirable tenacity in uncovering a conspiracy that goes far deeper than that idiot Stimpson. For that, I thank you. Now I know where the general was spirited away, I can start a real investigation into why, *and* what the Scourge of Almaar was actually doing hidden from mine and the Emperor's eyes."

Erikson restrained a cough, the smoke filling the rear of the limo scratching at his windpipe and lungs. "I—"

She turned to face him, tapping the cigarette holder into the ashtray, before meeting his eyes.

"Tell me what you think you know, and I will fill in any gaps I am at liberty to share. But have the mind, Mr Erikson, that I cannot share it all." The words came out a little rawer, emotion where her speech had been spattered with flat statements.

"I … I believe Baron Stimpson was likely acting selfishly. That the information he had bought flowered into a chance to extend any power base he may have. Perhaps, raise his status in the Court through the impact of financial gain."

The countess huffed quietly, closing her eyes a second. "A fool, you understand? No one achieves true status within the Court, or with the Emperor or gains his Minister's favour, through *money.*"

Erikson nodded once in agreement. "Yes. He employed a team to make an attempt on this asteroid family, field, whatever it is, and I was told to ..."

"Shut them down? Yes? Maintain their expected silence and retain their services at a guess. Useful until not." The countess tapped her cigarette again, though no ash fell off.

"Indeed. The rest ...," he did cough this time, hand to his mouth, "the rest is difficult."

The countess' features altered, an expression close to having a sour taste upon her tongue appearing. "I only have room for those with *balls*, Mr Erikson. The courage of their cause to the Court and the Emperor. Have I misjudged you? Wasted my time and resources on rescuing an Enforcer who is of no use to me? Perhaps I should have let Dexter have his fun with you in his pathetic dungeon."

Erikson railed at that. The words a stab to his pride and distaste for those nobles of Dexter's ilk. "Courage? Okay. I believe that General Asham had been hidden away, and if as you say, the Emperor is unaware, then for purposes against his mandate. My handler must be part of the conspiracy, or stupid. I think the former."

"And?"

"And that Asham had the battle AI aboard. That what he was working on was treasonous and whoever hid him away didn't want the AI to be found. I would go so far as saying they panicked, and destroyed the project including Asham. Perhaps, when someone talked, or their memory hadn't been perfectly wiped clean."

"Bravo, Mr Erikson. But I think you have a deeper suspicion locked away in that distrustful mind of yours. Something that involves an old squad of mine ..." She waited, taking a long drag of her cigarette and then stubbing it out, slowly lighting another.

"It's supposition," he replied.

"The Empire lives and breathes by supposition. The Court thrives on it," she replied.

He blinked away the new smoke, trying to avoid its pungency but forced to breathe it in. "Stimpson sent them to recover a containment box. Illegal tech he thought he could use. It's obvious the crew of the *Sunstar* got in, despite my handler's denials, and my change of role hid the fact they recovered the unit."

The countess grimaced, the lines around her mouth crinkling like parchment. "Convenient, don't you think? This sudden change of role. Taking on my old Breakers just after they may ... I say *may* ... have recovered the very containment unit they want hidden from prying eyes. Tell me, Mr Erikson. What was the previous mission they were sent on? Before Dexter."

"Err. You should know. Wetware. Recovering wetware. The hints were ..." He stared at her, slightly wide-eyed. Pieces dropped into place.

"That they were mine? From the *Scourge*? I told you this ran deep. Attempting to knock me out of the game."

"Your battleship. It was there, at the field. You *know* the unit was taken. That the Breakers have the battle AI. And now I'm knee deep in all of this. Tainted by conspiracy." He didn't think it possible, but his panic rose a little higher. Expendable wasn't the word. Scapegoat. He'd been set up to take the heat.

The countess nodded along, a slight smile creeping across her aged lips. "Now you might be useful to me. Yes, Mr Erikson. Set up, available to be discredited, and mistrust bred towards the one person who can give you a little hope in the dark. Me."

CHAPTER 6

The beer slid down her throat far too easily, the last dregs of glass number ...? She couldn't remember, and that was not a good sign. Savvo sat opposite, nursing his third, possibly only his second beer, with eyes on the bar's entrance.

"I'm just saying that more 'work' like that, you know, spanking noble arses, isn't so bad. Benetai was a stinking travesty. Wrong agency, if you know what I mean." Arin knocked back the whisky, cheeks redder than usual.

Rebekah glanced at him, recognising even in her drunken state that the former Private Enterman was trying to convince himself about their future prospects. The viscount's disturbing dungeon had been a shock to them both. A sign of just how divorced the nobility were from their subjects, the lowlifes, they lorded over. As if they were simply meat puppets to be played with and then tossed aside. No wonder those on Benetai had chosen a precarious life dependent on the thinnest of hulls and the mood of the gangs for an element of freedom. What had surprised her, was how the gangs operated. Baja's refusal to hurt Tensei more than necessary, the way those born and bred on the station treated them as a necessary part of daily life. It reminded her of M2 and 3 if she were honest. Freedom out on the asteroid field that made you forget just how controlled Almaarian society was by the whims of the nobility. The fucking Court, and their sense of honour steeped in their subjects' blood and tears.

Savvo scraped his chair along the floor, standing, eyes only for the woman walking through the open doorway. Nicky, her perfect skin glowing with the scrubbed health of a well-paid employee of Karal Mining. Maybe not the most prestigious job, overseeing the arrival and departure systems for the M4 space docks, but one of the happiest and snarkiest people they knew. Well, when Savvo let her anywhere near them, which by the look back over his shoulder, wasn't tonight.

Arin made to get up, and she grabbed his arm. "Leave him be. He's had it rough enough with that fucking toxin. Just give him some space."

"I was only going to mention the slave master thing, you know, see if she found it …" Her glare shut him up. Arin raised his hands, placating. "Okay, okay. Sheesh, what's a guy got to do for fun around here?"

"Not wind up the crew, just for once. Including me." She sighed, and scanned her wrist ID over the table pad, ordering another beer with a raised eyebrow towards Arin.

He shook his head. "Think I'm gonna go play some cards, you know. Let off some steam."

"You do that. I'm on next shift relieving Dricks, if that helps."

"Better get me some freedom time then." Arin shoved himself up from the table, nodding to Nicky who glanced over as she chatted excitedly to Savvo across the bar. Rebekah watched as he headed for the concourse, noting the hitch in his step when his brain had forced him to walk on by despite the temptation to intervene in Savvo's love life.

The beer arrived, though she began to wish it hadn't as a pair of suited legs appeared in her eyeline. A glance up, and her eyes met with a man's – Stig's father – who had peeled her off the corridor floor and guided her back to Savvo after she'd been attacked. The smile was genuine, warm, and beside him a quite stunning looking woman of similar age. She pegged them for early thirties, both with the same healthy glow as Nicky, their muscle mass a little more natural than her own. What had he said the last time they met? That he never got to see space? No, he was safe and by the look of it, happy. Basking in the grav, and the woman she took to be Stig's mother.

"Hi," Rebekah said, immediately regretting it as she detected a slight slur.

"Hello again," he said. "Just in from the 'field?"

She nodded. Tempted to mention the blood and gore, the killing. Her murder of a complicit but defenceless guard, or having to allow the scum who saw lowlifes as meat to carve to get away.

"Yeah," she said instead. "Washing out the dust." Rebekah raised the glass, forcing a smile. "Don't tell Stig, we'll both be in trouble."

"That is so true," replied the woman. Her teeth were perfect, the smile as genuine as Stig's father. "Michael was in so much trouble last time he got a little tipsy. Stig kept moving things out of the way."

"I'm a bad influence," Rebekah added. "Sorry."

"I'm Poppy, by the way. Pleasure to meet you ...?" That smile again.

Who was she today? The Breaker? The captain of a repair and recovery ship? A murderer? "Rebekah," she replied. "And likewise."

"Come on," said Michael, now she had a name for him. He took the crook of Poppy's arm. "Our reservation will be ready in ten minutes, and I haven't shown you this faux cocktail bar I found, yet. It's as about as far away from the one in Mesta as you could imagine."

"Enjoy," said Rebekah as they began to move away. Michael looked back at her, the smile and nod a goodbye. "Fuuuuck."

She downed the beer and looked around the bar. It was full of ships' crew, making the meeting with Michael and his plus one in this place a little odd. She shook it off. M2 was smaller than you first thought, and if you were honest, you probably passed the same faces every time you walked the corridors. It was just you didn't really *know* anyone. Passing spaceships in the night. She laughed at her own thought, and headed for her room, hoping beyond hope that she could hit the bed this time.

The punch took Arin by surprise, the second not so much as his wetware kicked in and he dodged to the side. His cheek bled where a ring had cut a thin line across the skin. He ignored it. Something to attend to later. The metal truncheon swung towards his knee, the aim, he was sure, to cripple him. Make him hit the floor so they could finish the job. Whether they were here to do some serious damage, or kill him, he hadn't ascertained. All he knew was the two bulked out assailants in their balaclavas had dragged him into the side corridor with violent intent. He raised his leg, the best he could manage, and the metal rod slammed into the side of his shin. It hurt like hell, but he was still up and lashed out towards its wielder who had sacrificed position for the attempt. He caught them on the back of the head, pummelling them to the ground and he skipped back, expecting the other to come in from the side.

The kick landed on his hip, and Arin slammed into the corridor wall. With his forehead taking most of the blow, dizziness spread, his wetware countering but not fast enough. He tried to slide away, but another blow hit him in the kidney, and then the snick of the metal truncheon signalled the next blow. Arin dropped and spun, wrist snapping back, and the knife tore through his skin and entered his assailant's thigh. The shout was male and pained, the truncheon released as he dropped his hands towards the wound. Arin ripped the knife across the muscle, and rolled away, up on his feet.

Arin had them both in his eyeline. One bled, howling, trying to staunch the blood, collapsing to the floor as his shredded muscle gave. The other was standing, but slightly off-balance after Arin's blow to the back of their head.

"I don't remember owing anyone money, so when did I piss you both off? I know my jokes are terrible, but a beating seems extreme." He spat on the floor, his own blood amid the spittle after the first blow. A tingle at the back of his mind had him spinning, but too late, and the taser slammed into his back, setting nerves on fire. Through a locked jaw, he grunted, and staggered against the wall. And then the blows came.

He curled up into a ball, accepting each hit, counting them one at a time while his wetware kept his mind from collapsing under the pain. Finally, it stopped, timed, he was sure, to coincide with the effects of the taser wearing off. The clatter of boots brought him out from the defensive ball, and he took in a pair of shoes. A woman's, though they were not elegant. Functional at best.

"Does it hurt?" she asked. "I do so hope it fucking hurts."

He tried to glance up, but could only move his head high enough to take in the chin. A holo mask flickered, his thoughts of Rebekah's encounters streaming in between his body's angry response to the beating.

"Lucky for you, I'm not allowed to kill you. Yet."

She knelt down, now in his vision, the mask flickering. Between the pain in his head, and the wetware, he could have sworn what stared through the image wasn't fully human. The eyes ... the eyes were coarse electronic implants.

"Tell that bitch that I'm still watching. You understand? Everyone she loves, one-by-one." The woman made a shooting action with her hand. "I'll have her eyes before I'm done."

She stood, feet turning to walk away when she stopped. "Tell Khan the *Maverick* hasn't returned. That I haven't had a transmission for over two weeks." She looked back then, the mask slipping. Two blue, electronic eyes narrowed amid the heart-shaped face, focusing on Arin. "If I find that you, and the rest of the *Sunstar* crew are involved in that, then no Incini or noble will stand in my way. You will beg for death."

Arin dropped his gaze, not wishing to feed the woman's wrath any more than he had to. As the feet moved out of his eyeline, he waited, slowing his breathing, trying to push away the pain in his body. A roll call of his bones came back more positive than he expected. Bruising. Whether that was by luck or by design was another matter. Eventually, he pushed himself up from the floor, the scrape of metal reminding him to re-engage his wrist blade. Once on his feet, the world spun, dizziness returning until the wetware compensated. A check of the time, and he decided against waking Rebekah, and used the walls as a guide towards the main concourse. From memory, he found himself at the med unit, ignoring the occasional offers of help from those staggering home from the all-night bars. He wrist scanned the lock and plonked himself down on a seat next to a clearly inebriated woman who had chosen the med unit to curl up and sleep inside.

The screen flickered into life, the simulated face staring back at him mouthing words he couldn't hear. Eventually, he worked out the drunken woman must have turned the volume down to sleep, and he swiped at the screen, adjusting the menu. A few presses and confirmations, and he paid for a basic body scan, with meds soon following. They kicked in after ten minutes, and with a great deal of stiffness, he stood and swore.

"Bloody grudges." Gaining access to the asteroid's comms, he left a message for Dricks, and headed for the sanctuary of his room. "She's gonna be pissed. And the Captain too. I wonder if Goncho and gang know how angry a hornet's nest they've stirred up."

CHAPTER 7

"It's too soon," stated Rebekah, her stare hard and focused on Davina.

Davina shuffled in her chair, sat behind the office desk and its combination of slates and old-fashioned paper Rebekah had not seen her use before. The sensor arrays were all up as usual, the room alive with monitoring electronics.

Today, Rebekah was alone. Savvo out on the asteroid somewhere with Nicky, blissful, she hoped. Arin back on board under Dricks' tender administrations after receiving a beating that wouldn't go unpunished. That particular itch needed scratching, and screw whatever the Enforcer had in mind.

"It's not up to me. I am the mouthpiece until Mr Duboit wishes to speak to you. He has bought out your service from Karal, from Pike, and you've been stood down from repair and recovery duties indefinitely. It is likely he'll speak with you tomorrow, but I understand it is dependent on acquiring specific information you'll be needing." Davina rested her hands on the desk, her back straight, eyes firmly on Rebekah.

"Too much," continued Rebekah, shaking her head. "Our consistent absence is going to be noticed by the other crews. Talk spreads. It won't make things easy."

"Agreed. I will pass that on."

Rebekah looked to the carpeted floor, aware that they were being recorded, and any conversation exposed to later analysis. But this one had to happen.

"You know about Arin?" She received a nod in response. "Then you need to know that I'm done with that. *I* am going to act, and this may have consequences for our future on Karal. I can't let these ongoing threats pass any longer."

Davina tilted her head slightly, the smallest of smiles alighting on her lips. "At this juncture, Mr Duboit has no issue with such a venture. We have no contracts with Goncho, the last is now null and void, though I believe they are not aware of that. Not yet."

"The *Maverick*?" Rebekah shot back.

"I am not at liberty to discuss previous contracts." Davina's finger tapped on her other hand twice, catching Rebekah's eye. "Recent or otherwise."

One of Davina's slates pinged, and she glanced down, lifting it so Rebekah couldn't see the screen. "Mr Duboit has set a time for 10am tomorrow morning. I suggest you attend without a headache hanging over you."

Rebekah blinked, trying to work out if there was a double-meaning to the Incini's words, and decided there probably always were.

"I'll be here. But please make my concerns known. No good having a cover role, if you're never here to fulfil it." She turned away, already at the door when another thought struck her.

Null and void.

The holo-masked woman had stated they'd had no comms traffic for two weeks, and if, as seemed likely, Davina had contracted them, the Incini knew something had happened. Possibly weeks ago. Why would Goncho and his crony believe the *Sunstar* was involved? Yes, they'd been away, sub-contracted as far as everyone on the Minx asteroids knew, but that had been by Duboit. For all intents and purposes, to the same employer. So which Duboit had contracted the *Maverick*? The real one? Or the Enforcer? And where did they send them?

"Fuck," she whispered. A stone formed in her stomach, forcing an engagement of her wetware in an effort to relax. She opened the door, her shoulders tense, an ominous feeling about the future weighing her down more than M1's gravity.

Had they sent them back to the *Scourge*?

"When will they know?" she said. "About the *Maverick*?"

"In about two hours."

Always comes down to violence. What would Michael and Poppy think, Stig too, if they knew what type of person I was? How far I would go to protect what was precious to me?

She left, heading for the shuttle bay, searching for a line out to contact the *Sunstar*.

"That look like them?" asked Savvo, tapping the galley screen showing an external camera feed.

Arin stood, as if he was looking closer at the images. He squinted. "How should I know? I can tell you what their fists look like, and that one won't be walking for a while."

Rebekah uncrossed her arms, eyes still locked on the screen, a shake to her head. A small squad of ex-soldiers were in the docking bay. They'd chosen the quietest time to enter, one at a time and suited up. Casual. But soldiers, the way they moved and signalled giving them away. Mercs. "I've got a bad feeling about this."

"They're going to do what, exactly?" said Hendricks. "They can't get in. Shoot a hole in the hull? Tremil has the door and navcom security tied down tighter than a duck's arse."

Rebekah lifted an eyebrow, unsure of what the hell Hendricks meant, but going with it. "If they have decent explosives, we could be in trouble. But this is something else."

Savvo flinched, then lifted his wrist and swore. "Gotta take this," he said, and walked off towards the cockpit.

Rebekah eyed him briefly, then looked back to the screen. The mercs weren't forming a squad, instead taking positions around the bay. They were watching the *Sunstar*. "Hendricks?"

"I see it," the ex-captain said. "Containment team. Every airlock and cargo door in their field of vision. Even the emergency escape hatch. They know the ship."

"No, no, no," echoed from the cockpit, followed by Savvo's concerned face as he strode back through. "Nicky. She's saying the power's down in her section of M2. The emergency doors have sealed."

Threatened to take everyone I love, and removing my eyes last.

"You got her address? Of course you've got Nicky's address. Send it to the twins."

"You want the residential schematics?" asked Tremil, standing and heading towards her cabin.

"I do, ASAP. Arin prep the suits, fire up ZZ3."

"And me?" asked Heki.

Rebekah's mind flipped over the possibilities. A plan forming. "I want the entry codes from VERT. Then the cameras down on the docks and on M2 on my mark. Can that be done?"

"Yes, but Tremil's the best at infiltrating systems. We'll sort it." Heki left and Rebekah turned to a clearly angry Savvo. There was a tremor to his hand that rested against the corridor wall and his eyes were narrowed, staring at her as if she was the source of all his troubles.

"If I can't trust you to act calmly, you can't come." She looked her second up and down, assessing every twitch and tell. Take him, and he may well lose it. Use more force than necessary, especially if the unthinkable had happened. Reveal who they were to everyone on M2 as he took retribution. If she didn't take him, they were at an end. The stress would break him, successful or not, and there would be no coming back. "Activate your wetware. Double it up if you have to, but I see you use a stim this'll be the last mission we do together. Understand?"

Savvo gave the briefest of nods, eyes flickering as his wetware flooded his system. Rebekah felt Hendricks' stare on her back; the judgement of her decision writ large on the engineer's face as she spun about. She wouldn't have taken that path, now or in the past. A soldier on the edge couldn't be trusted.

But they weren't Marines anymore.

"You and Arin," she said. "Defend the ship, the twins. Minimal force if possible," she ignored the grimace, "otherwise sweep up the bodies and we'll dump them like last time. Permission to use your initiative."

"Aye, Captain."

"Now HT. Doors and cameras," stated Rebekah, flexing her suit gloves and taking a final check that her carbine was maglocked in position. Motors hummed, and the cargo doors vibrated. She had no need to order ZZ3, the bot already in the air, with Savvo and her inside two sets of slaved Navy-issue suits that rose in unison. She couldn't help but think of the

Bustan Marauders. Mere meat inside their AI-controlled suits after extending their bodies beyond human limits in pursuit of her squad. And now, here she and Savvo were, under ZZ3's ultimate control. An errant algorithm, a spark of the Butcher's nature bubbling to the top of the bot's developing personality, and they could both be sucking vacuum in revenge for ripping the bastard's unit from the *Scourge*.

"I can take the cameras out, show a normal downtime like every other day and prevent any real-time recording," said Tremil.

"Copy that," replied Rebekah. "Arin, ZZ3. Now."

Arin discharged a grenade into the widening crack as the cargo doors opened. More effective in a closed, air-filled room, it erupted with a huge but ineffective bang in vacuum, but the desired chemical smoke erupted onto the deck amid a shower of metal foil. He fired another a few metres behind, then another.

ZZ3 sped straight for the slowly opening cargo doors, twisting at the last second to be sideways on. Savvo and Rebekah's slaved suits mimicked the bot's movements, and they flew onto the smoke-immersed docks where the warbot curved its flight, taking the fastest route out of both weapon and camera range as it ducked behind the *Sunstar*. Finally, the three of them dropped into the docking tunnel that kept ships' engines from frying the dockside on entry and exit.

A last check of Arin's feed by Rebekah showed the cargo doors were closing, gunfire pinging off the metal as the mercs fired blind but did their job. You sent a containment unit to do just that. Suppress any possible reinforcements, prevent any intervention from affecting your plans. If they just so happened to take down any of her crew, they'd regard it as a bonus. But the smoke hid the warbot, meaning she had fewer people on her kill list.

They swept around M4, and then, as expected, the forces on her body rose. The suit compensated as much as it could, but ZZ3 was acting on orders, accelerating as fast as possible. No need for the standard shuttle protocols, the soft take-off and landing with gentle burn and reverse thrust combining to make the journey to M3 and their destination, M2, as smooth as possible. They were going in hot.

"Second shot," said Savvo, cutting in to her thoughts, informing his captain he'd activated his wetware. The biochemical stress he was already under with the threat to Nicky was little different from the normal Breaker missions. More personal, but stress under the threat of violence was similar. The wetware would do its job, but that didn't prevent her worrying. Once an addict, the mind and circumstances had a tendency to draw you back, to dangle temptation. And yes, she had no doubts that were she a groundpounder, alcohol would sweep her up in the same cycle. Space keeps you sober, for it has no mercy.

Her brain hurt, eyes pressed against the back of her sockets, joints aching as the suit did its best to ease the physical impact of acceleration. A thought, and her own wetware swept her brain clear, flushing her mind of the pain responses because there was more to come.

"On approach. Coordinates set. Emergency airlock entrance identified," stated ZZ3. "Preparing slowdown. In 3, 2, 1 ... Mark."

The slowdown was rapid, her body screamed its defiance, mind a fugue until they slammed to a halt. All the suit's systems engaged at once, ZZ3 having prepared the safety protocols for the precise impact level. Rebekah sensed every muscle, joint and pissed-off bone in her body, and kicked in the wetware for a second time. By the time her mind cleared, ZZ3 had activated the airlock with Tremil's appropriated codes, swinging aside, maglocking to the hull of M2's main living quarters.

"Savvo, you with me?" she asked, clicking his feed and running over his vital signs. Amber, not because he had been damaged, but because his whole body had been through the same as hers. A glance to her own confirming they were both in the same condition. For a Breaker, amber was a normal operating level. But their bodies were no longer at their peak.

"On point," she said, snapping the order out. Savvo flinched, but reacted, and disengaged from ZZ3's slave program to ease next to the airlock. She was soon by his side, and they cycled in. "Tremil. Take M2 cameras down on my mark. 3,2,1 ... Mark."

"Wait, Captain. Three second delay ... in the green ... Mark," came the reply.

"Now, Savvo." He opened the inner airlock to flashing red lights and the blare of an alarm. They were one level down from Nicky's apartment. A slightly more salubrious area, the corridors filled with potted plants and printed pictures that broke up the monotony of uniform walls. There were no people, everyone sealed in their self-contained spaces after the power failure in case of breach. Somewhere, there may be a few workers roaming about. Those caught outside of their homes, bars or whatever, locked away in whichever corridor they were inhabiting at the time. If they came across them, there would be issues. But better that than the alternative.

Rebekah imagined the current panic running through Karal Mining control. Likely not Pike's remit, but he'd be in the mix and stressed. A brief smile flittered across her face as she followed behind Savvo, one hand on her sidearm but no weapon drawn.

They reached a bulkhead door, Savvo typing in the code via the battery-operated pad. It swung open, and they were met by a relieved look from a clearly drunk besuited office worker. She didn't even spare them a glance, unperturbed by their frosted visors as she stepped past and headed unsteadily towards her apartment.

Savvo ignored the drunk, reaching the stairwell and starting up. His body language remained wary, a good sign, and his vitals had relaxed a little. Not in the green, but close. On reaching the next level, he peered around the corner and signalled her up.

"Three doors down," he said, flagging the apartment on her HUD. "There's no one there. The door's sealed."

"When did you last check in with Nicky?"

"Before we took off. She was scared."

"She would be with your mood and the heavy warnings, Savvo. Fear spreads like a virus. Assess her door before calling her." She tapped him on the back, and her second moved, heading for the flagged door. His visuals appeared in the top corner of her HUD, but as Rebekah had started to suspect, there was no damage. No obvious attempt at forced entry. Savvo had his access kit out and wired up, and she turned to scan down the corridor as he ran through the systems.

Something nagged at the back of her mind. A feeling she had always trusted, though it had led to many avoidable scrapes. This wasn't a trap. They hadn't been drawn out to split the squad, but neither was Nicky the target. Nor was it a coincidence.

"Hendricks. Sit rep," she said.

A crackle of her comms signalled the reply. "They're just sitting there. Heki's trying to isolate their comms, see if she can pick out what they've been ordered to do. Nothing as yet, other than sit tight."

"Copy that. Keep me informed."

"Clear," said Savvo, the wires of his kit still attached. "No sign of any attempted entry. No failed password attempts since mine the other night. Shall I?"

"Yeah. Call her." Rebekah peered down the stairs, frustration spilling out as she smacked a hand against the wall. What was going on? Why M2? The holo-masked woman had threatened whoever she loved or cared about. The *Sunstar* was safe, Nicky was safe. Then who?

No. Had they been watching *her*? The notes. The bars.

"Tremil, you there?"

"Yes, Captain."

"I need a check on an office worker. I only have the first name, Michael. And a partner Poppy. Son named Stig. I need an address ASAP." She watched Savvo, his face animated by her HUD, wreathed in relieved smiles as he conversed with Nicky. Reassuring her she was fine, that there was no one there. To stay inside as the alert could be genuine and keep safe until it was switched off.

Would this stuff things up for him? Nicky getting an inkling of the type of work they were caught up in? How much had Savvo already let slip?

"I have three Michaels. No partners by the name of Poppy, but one has a son. Stickland."

"Has to be them. Where, what address?" It dropped into her HUD. The floor below, the one they'd entered from the airlock, but through the next bulkhead. Close. Too damn close.

"Savvo!" she shouted into comms, but didn't wait, taking the first half of the stairs in one bound. She leapt the next, her suit's servos soaking the impact as she reached the bulkhead. "Bulkhead code, now!"

Numbers streamed into her HUD, stressed fingers restarting the code but eventually getting it set. The door swung open, and she dropped, her hand upon the butt of her sidearm as she peered down the corridor. The alarm still blared, the emergency lights continuing to flash a warning. Six doors down, a guard stood. His thick neck and wide forehead turning to face her.

Brutish.

Not him. Her. What would she do?

She drew and fired, both bullets ramming into the man's chest. He toppled over, crashing to the corridor floor. Whether those inside heard was another matter, and she was already at the open door by the time Savvo tried to call her back. Too late.

She spun in. The hallway was long, at its end a living area, to the left a half-open door with the lights full on, shadows playing on the hallway carpet. Without thought, she was inside, foot clattering the door open. It was a bedroom, another doorway off to the right she ignored. A man of violence hunched over an occupied bed before her.

Her gun barked, the bullets shattering the skull of another besuited man. The gun in his hand struck the floor, and he toppled, blood spraying the edge of the bed. Michael was there; eyes wide with terror, hands wrapped in cable ties. Beneath him, shaking hands over his eyes lay a terrified Stig. She stuttered, heart-pounding.

"Captain," said Savvo, half-query, half reminder of who she was sounding in her comms.

Rebekah slammed the butt of her gun into the exposed neck. Instead of blood splattering Michael and Stig, the goon tumbled forwards. She hit him again, no remorse, ensuring he was out. Alive but unconscious.

She spun to find Savvo at the edge of the doorway. With a glance, he indicated along the corridor. She should have let him go, take the lead.

What a leader should do.

She shoved past, handgun up, pointing ahead as she reached the end of the corridor. The door again half-open. She entered, head full of the blaring alarm, mind tipped by violence and threat. The holo-masked woman was there, scalpel high, held against Poppy's throat. A thin cut had been started around the eye, blood seeping across the cheek. There was no smile there, just fear. Dread.

"Let me past, or I'll cut her," words slipped from painted lips. The face perfect, except for the eye implants. Rough cybernetics, a poor person's fix. Around them sat scar-tissue and a hint of old burns.

Rebekah had witnessed a hundred hostage situations. Had stood, gun ready in at least thirty last stands as desperate people used others as meat shields. None of them ended well.

And she had a Savvo.

Carbine synced; he blew a hole through one of the implants.

"Nobody threatens my people," she whispered.

Poppy shook and began to scream. Another wail rose from the bedroom. Another broken dream.

"Apologies," echoed her electronically muffled voice in the small living room. "Strike Team Delta, mission complete." It was the first thing that came into her head. Numb, she lifted the dead woman from the floor, turning away to face Savvo. "Get the others," she stated. "Major Ren wants them all." She kicked herself for using that name, but it spilled from her lips, and it was too late. Savvo had collected the other assailant, dragging him clear of the bedroom with frosted visor averted from Michael and his son after cutting their bonds.

Rebekah couldn't help but glance inside, Stig in his father's arms. Poppy alive but possibly traumatised back in the blood-spattered room. A boring life in space. Perhaps Michael would have a new view of his day-to-day world. Less violence, less blood than she could ever offer anyone.

In the corridor she took the still alive goon, spinning him around. Not Victor Goncho. One piece missing from the puzzle. Either way, he was about to be spaced. She hadn't promised to keep him alive, just prevent Stig and Michael from seeing the real her.

You don't fuck with Rebekah's dreams.

CHAPTER 8

“Good morning,” said the fake Mr Duboit. The holo's hair and mannerisms near perfect, but retaining that stiffness or perhaps the slightest of delays in the transmission.

"Uh-huh," replied Rebekah, who wasn't quite feeling in a good mood, her dreams plagued by the woman Davina had named Sabier on her way in. Her death played out on repeat, sometimes with the holo mask working, sometimes with Michael or Poppy being the one who died. The only sequence that never replayed was if Savvo hadn't killed her, or missed his shot. Those were the outcomes that kept you going. The 'what ifs' that the officer-nobles used to talk about. What if we don't attack first? What if the AI fleet comes back and strips your homes? The usual. Don't give them the chance, just like she and Savvo hadn't Sabier. Adding to the space debris milling about the Minx asteroids.

"A good night in the bars, I presume?" came his slimy reply, accompanied by a smile that didn't suit the face. A hint of who really lay behind the holo shield.

"Yeah. Something like that. Alarms go off, they seal a bunch of crews in a bar full of booze. For all we knew, the asteroid was about to dump us into the black. Stuff happens." She kept her face flat, feigning the odd eye flicker that would hint at a hangover as big as the *Sunstar*. The amount of coffee after the nightmares didn't make it too hard to fake.

"Yes. I've heard Karal might be engaging the fine print on their insurance."

She sniggered at that. Trent Pike, apparently, wasn't taking any calls while he investigated what the hell had happened on M2. Rumours were rife that a Court hit had taken place, or at the very least, a precision military strike team erasing an issue. Goncho had disappeared, likely gone to ground somewhere. She half-wondered whether this Duboit knew all this already, and didn't give a fuck about it. As long as his team were clean, and that came down to the twins' tech skills.

"You're sending us out again," Rebekah stated, wanting to get on with things. She engaged her wetware, cleared the caffeine headache and eyed the holo.

"Yes, I am. And though the issue is rather delicate, it appears you are the best we have for this role." Erikson leant in, fingers steepled below his chin. "However, after Benetai, I wonder if your tactics will fit what needs doing."

Wetware or not, that gnawed at Rebekah. "You blackmailed us, remember? Decided you wanted a team to crash through the mission window rather than delicately cut their way in. Riling the Bustan Navy was as much a surprise to us as to you, and we got away by luck when they switched their focus to Scarva. That was a lack of intelligence on your part."

"Was that a double-meaning thrown in there? How astute. Either way, you returned the kit, for which the noble involved is very grateful. Not that you care." His mood shifted, eyes narrowing. "You are my dogs to direct, Khan. It's your squad you are trying to keep out of the Countess Segfi's line of fire. However you do it, keep it up, or this agreement will end."

She tried to keep the anger in, lock the frustration down somehow. Her tongue dried in her mouth, the edge of her dream crawling back into her mind's eye, this time Duboit's eye was eviscerated. A knock at the door stopped her from making things worse.

"Come in, Connors," said Duboit, who had been watching her intently with a level of fascination that added to her list of reasons to space the fucker. Only he wasn't in space, and had more power in his ring than she had in a whole squad of ex-Marines.

Davina entered, slate in hand, her eyes cast to the floor rather than on Duboit. By the time the door had closed, she had taken the seat next to Rebekah, her eyes briefly on her before resting on the hologram.

"Connors will be your main contact as per usual. You know of Saim?"

"The largest moon around Palail? The gas giant."

"That's the one. We believe a noble has been recruiting ex-military for their own private army. Nothing unusual there. They all do it to some degree. A status symbol, if you will. Rumour is they are planning some type of war games." Erikson grimaced, as if finding that distasteful. "For honour and ... status in the lower echelons of the Court."

Rebekah somehow wasn't surprised. "I hope you're talking capture the flag type stuff. Infiltration runs. And without live ammunition."

"I couldn't say. Not in my remit. However, I never rule anything out. There is evidence connecting this Baron Winkal to other issues I am investigating, and the level of stealth tech being deployed to hide their activities is worrying. Of course it could all be part of the game, but I suspect not. Connors will provide the details. You are to get in, find out their level of deployment and equipment, their battle-ready status, and on my say, blow the place apart." Erikson sat back in his chair, a smile she wanted to knock down his throat on his lips. "Easy."

"I have prepped a mission brief," said Davina, turning to her. "And a run down on the tech we know they're using as well as expected strength. But those are estimates."

"My ship isn't built for stealth," said Rebekah. "But for strength. Before we even start, that's going to be a huge issue. The resourcing last time was pretty poor." She glanced at Davina, who didn't react. "I don't have to look at the brief to know we're going to need equipment not usually to hand on a mining station."

"You work with what we have. I have been considering one of the main issues, and may have a solution. But for now, assume everything is as it is," replied Davina.

"You mentioned yesterday about specific intelligence? Information."

"In the brief. Mr Duboit has obtained an initial scan of the satellite systems in place from a recent Navy bypass." Davina glanced over to Duboit, who nodded.

"Run through the mission data, come back to Connors with a plan. She'll relay my views on the proposal as I will be busy with other matters. But hold no doubts, Khan, this is not a request, however difficult it may appear."

Duboit cut out. Gone. Rebekah sure that she had seen the tiniest glimpse of the man behind the holo, but she was just fooling herself. Either way, the whole set up felt different. It had her on edge more than usual. Their last meeting about the viscount had been so different. Hands on and with a touch of emotion in there, as if it meant something to the Enforcer. A sliver of humanity confirmed by what she had witnessed at the villa. This time he had been just as insistent yet detached, distant. She couldn't put her finger on why.

Rebekah made to speak, but the look in Davina's eyes cut her short.

"Come through," she said, and stood, heading for the door.

Rebekah followed, a surly weight on her shoulders and more fire in her heart than she wanted. A clear mind was needed to get her through this. Savvo's presence would have calmed her down, but last night had been too emotional for him. Arin was a no-go whatever, and Hendricks? Rebekah was still caught up in the fallout from their last mission. How close that had been to going wrong, relying on a captain who couldn't be trusted to keep to the mission brief. Having her ex-captain here, discussing the next potential fuck-up didn't sit well with her.

"Sit," said Davina who closed the door to Duboit's office.

Rebekah did so, though it felt odd. As if she was back at the principal's office ready for a telling off. The Incini sat opposite, and handed over a slate.

"This is isolated. The brief outline is on there, but Mr Duboit wanted everything kept off any connected system. He thinks Baron Winkal has an extensive industrial espionage network that reaches into Karal. Nothing on this slate is to be transmitted, and once dissected and analysed, it is to be wiped clean post mission and returned. Understood?"

Rebekah stayed silent for a moment, eyeing the Incini before accepting the slate. "Agreed. Is that it?"

There was a slight shake to the Incini's head, the elegant hair hardly swaying. "No. I want you to read through the brief now and tell me what you think."

"Now?"

"Now."

Rebekah shrugged and leant back into her chair. Swiping, the slate opened and after a thumb print and retina scan, she began to read. The detail of the operation on the ground was scant, hidden under a cloud of tech that was the main issue. During the attack on the viscount's villa, they had the upper hand technology wise. Heki, and particularly Tremil, identifying weaknesses and though unable to overcome some of the difficult details, like false mapping, could at least say it was there. The jamming cloud had been key to the success of the mission, however. She wasn't an expert, but the hints amid the list of specs were worrying, and there were many.

"Long-range passive and active sensor arrays, extensive trip missile batteries, defence cannon platforms. Tighter than a duck's arse, as Dricks would say. You'd need a stealth ship to even approach the moon with any success, never mind land. So the alternative is to blow them out of the sky, which would be a calling card for ground defences. Or encouraging a complete system failure. Nigh on impossible for us, and even if it were, it would lead to a similar outcome. This is fucked up stuff, Davina."

That weight doubled down. They were being asked the impossible.

"I agree. I'm not an expert either, but a few enquiries in a different direction may provide an idea. The Baron is recruiting."

"Recruiting? You mean ...? Fuck Davina, you mean we infiltrate?" Rebekah stared back at the Incini, her mind a whirl. She needed to bounce this off the others, run through the deets together. "That'd require –"

"—new IDs, and time. I know. But it's an option to get someone on the ground. If this Winkal is as clued in as he sounds, I'm thinking we do something off the usual menu of Breaker tactics. And it has an added bonus ..."

"Like?" asked Rebekah.

"If your false ID is uncovered, what do they find? A Breaker on the run trying to hide who they are." Her face was almost smug, revelling in her deviousness. But the smile was genuine. She was trying to help, or if not, her Incini training needed an extra round of applause.

"If they're recruiting ex-Marines, there may well be some from our old units," added Rebekah, trying to run through the possibilities. Whoever went would be exposed again, naked to any retribution. No powered armour to keep the pain at arm's length. Davina made to cut in, but she got there first. "Yeah, yeah. Who may also be trying to hide, or know we are. Loyalty and all that shit. The difficult ones will be—"

"—those that are still loyal," finished Hendricks. "There's always some drugged up loyalist who believes the Emperor should have ignored the Senti and just carried on fighting. Who think deserters should have a bullet to the back of their heads."

"I get that. I'm not saying this is what we *should* do, only that it's an option we wouldn't have thought of," stated Rebekah, running her hand over her tightly shorn hair. "I've been through most of the deets. Just a glance, and I need you all to do the same. Find alternatives."

"We can look through the satellite tech," said Heki, glancing over to her sister.

"Yeah," started Tremil. "Some of the sensor info might give a clue to what software they're using. Maybe we can build a virus to take them down."

"But that'll have to be via physical integration," finished Heki. "Contact with the self-contained units. Unless you instigate via the directional laser comms they'll be using. That'll need codes."

"Or time, or both," added Tremil. "On first analysis that is. Decryption could be possible, but again, time."

"And that means getting close, and that'll lead to detection," said Savvo. "Most times we came up against this tech in the Breakers we just charged on through or blanket jammed. Planet wide if we could. I mean, we were just the battering ram."

"Like Bustan 7," said Arin, keeping his eyes to the floor and away from the twins. Those memories forever raw. "With no Battle AI, it was easier."

The jabber of noise echoed back and forth, and she left them to it until they'd worked through the initial tension.

She gently tapped at the table, face stony until she had their attention. "Okay. The slate is locked down tight so we can't share it around. Hek and Trem, you take it first. Copy down the specs of the defence and sensor system then pass it on to Arin and Dricks. You two need to think of what we would need if we go in hard. I'm guessing we take out their comms systems and linkage to the satellite shield first, then start looking for a data core of some form. But we'll be doing that on the fly, we know little about what's down there. So multi-purpose equipment needs are a priority."

"And me?" said Savvo.

"We're going to bounce around Davina's idea. See if we can make it work somehow."

"We?" he asked.

She assumed he was checking whether he was on ship-sitting duty again. After Nicky, and then Michael and Poppy's rescue, she had proof enough he was ready. "We," she replied.

Chapter 9

Davina examined the screen, running through the recruitment schedule as fast as she could, seeking a pattern that may well not be there. Erikson had set her the task, premeditating the method he suspected the Breakers would employ to get onto the moon and signifying his wish for a more subtle approach. He had fed her what to say, and she was contractually bound to follow through.

After spending time aboard the *Sunstar* with Rebekah and her crew, they were brighter and more cagey than Erikson assumed. He had taken the evidence of the *Maverick* and jumped to conclusions about how they approached each mission. The debrief from their successful recovery of the wetware should have proved otherwise. They hadn't gone in all guns blazing, instead attempting to fit in with an expected behavioural pattern for a bunch of lowlife scum. The fact they were strangers, and Scarva had meddled in there somewhere, set them apart and led to some form of gang retribution that had gone sour. But they had come through it, and survived the Bustan Navy somehow by using the decoy of an old navy cargo box she'd provided back when the *Scourge* wasn't even a consideration.

They deserved a little more credit.

However, Erikson was also likely right. All guns blazing against a well-protected viscount's villa had been appropriate though excessive. At least that's what she thought until Rebekah's hints at what lay buried beneath the rubble they had left behind. This time, they were facing a well-armed, and by the look of it, tech'd up noble with aspirations that were murkier than Duboit's. The hints were of something bigger, the implications wider. Was it linked to the treason the Minister's hand had been hinting at? The potential being a spider's web of connected small armies under the pretence of war gaming. As much as such frivolous and insensitive behaviour wouldn't surprise anyone less privileged than the noble class, Erikson's hints that they were in reality training armies for other purposes had her on edge.

Why? To what ends?

The Minister's hand required her silence while Erikson either dug himself into – or out of – a treasonous hole. This couldn't be a coincidence, but she had expected the hand's investigation to be related to recent events.

She opened her slate, bringing up the video of the *Maverick*'s demise, watching it back a second time. Erikson had denied her access to it. Nothing surprising in that, but Gerent had her on edge about what the Enforcer was really doing. His veiled threats of a deeper conspiracy. She watched the *Maverick* being opened up to the void, and the crew eviscerated by the callous violence of the PDCs. Sickened, Erikson was surely on dodgy ground. Seeing the battleship *Segfi* on her screen set Davina's bowels moving. What would the Directorate make of it? An Enforcer's mission destroyed by the Warmonger's flagship?

The countess? So why are you still working with the Enforcers, Erikson? Why hasn't the countess exposed you herself? In that lies what the Minister's hand seeks, I think.

To her mind the countess had Erikson by the balls, and he was therefore a pawn in her political game. Was that the hint Gerent was making? That it went so high that the Countess Segfi was caught up in all of this?

Impossible.

She was a steadfast servant of the Empire, a vigorous defender of the Court and the Emperor. A dead end as a conspirator, but if Erikson was under her direction, then maybe he was being manipulated elsewhere. Someone knowing he was about to be swamped by the countess' power and seizing an opportunity. It could explain how he'd been acting. That extra level of self-confidence he fronted when he had never needed to do so before. The slights, previously off-hand, now more blatant and delivered with greater venom, or perhaps the need to push others even further down.

Suppositions, and the only evidence she had were the mission parameters and subsequent destruction of the *Maverick*. A puzzle yet to be solved, and to decide whether she should hide the information from the Directorate, she had to understand not only the what, but the why. Denying the Directorate and serving the Emperor and his Minister blindly wasn't something that came easily. But if it was the countess, or more likely, someone willing to take her on, this was big. Huge.

Either way, she was caught in the middle between the Court, the Directorate and the ... the crew. Or at least the twins.

"Damn," she said, swiping away the vid and ensuring it was hidden. "Focus on what Rebekah needs."

She drew up her briefing from Erikson, reading through it once again. The deeper she went into the Enforcer's intelligence, the clearer it became. This Baron, or more likely those working for him, were pulling in any ex-army or navy they could find who had been discarded after the cessation. Soldiers whose contracts were up, deemed surplus to requirements and dumped back into society to sink or swim. And the shuttle runs to this moon went in waves, some from Almaar but quite a few were from Shema.

Davina pulled up a second file, one she had begun to build. After investigating a few backgrounds, it was apparent the Baron had wiped some of the passengers' cred histories and documentation and put in a few basic deets. Enough for a cursory glance if anyone was interested, but no depth. Birth town, marriage status, cred score, bank account. Enough to make them anonymous. No ex-soldier could afford even that basic ID wipe, so a shuttle half-full of similar anonymity was a little obvious. Each one passing through Palail's huge way station. After that, there were private shuttles with manifests she couldn't ascertain, but she had seen enough to know how the recruits to this private army were being funnelled. All that effort to hide the Baron's new pretend military and their capabilities from prying noble eyes, or as Erikson's thoughts indicated, to prevent the Court from seeing their fully armed and tech'd up private army with nefarious intentions. The type of thing the countess might well be interested in knowing more about.

Shema. Not where the crew would want to go back to after their encounter with Viscount Lundstrom, but the closest and the most obvious place to be recruited. All she needed were IDs with far greater depth than the Baron had doled out. And to know how many.

Of course, Rebekah had been right. There may well be ex-soldiers or even ex-Marines present that would know them. Not definite, the Breakers had eventually become a black ops team and out of sight for ninety-nine percent of the armed forces, but certainly in their previous roles. It still felt the best way to approach the mission, and begged the question why Erikson wanted the ex-Breakers instead of an Enforcer-lead team. Perhaps an in-system operation, close to a major hub like Palail's space station, was too obvious or too much for the Enforcers to contemplate. Or was it simpler than that? Perhaps Erikson wasn't certain what the Baron was doing, what if they found the Baron was loyal? Deniability was the purpose of blackmailing them in the first place.

Or was Countess Segfi pulling his strings? Or whoever Gerent was investigating?

Either way, she needed to lay the groundwork for the IDs.

"An Incini's work is never done."

"Six," stated Rebekah, a smile on her face.

"How am I going to convince Erikson that you need six IDs?" Davina took a sip of the cocktail, eyes wandering over to the large window and the concourse beyond. She felt the thrum of her dampener, and took a quick check to find it had reacted to another one operating in the vicinity. She doubted it was Rebekah, but a glance around the bar told her enough about whom it might be as she caught some form of office-cum-drinking session going on in the far corner.

"Simple. We need two burners. I was really thinking eight, one burner each, to make it more obvious but thought you'd choke on that. And if two just so happen to be modded a little," continued Rebekah. The zero-alcohol beer clearly clawed at her throat, a twist to her lips accompanied by a cough.

Davina paused at that, only a brief hitch as she placed her glass down, but noticeable. She didn't reply, just looked Rebekah straight in the eye for a second. From anyone else, she would have assumed she was being played. But despite their differences, the twins sat at the heart of all their dealings. That rock protruding from the smooth flow of her life.

Yeah right. A Minister's agent, a possible treasonous Enforcer and a pair of off-the-wall projective empath twins.

Smooth.

"Eight," she stated. "Possible, but there are no guarantees. It'll come down to how much interest there is in your resourcing. So, you're doing it my way?"

"That depends on other factors." Rebekah's eyes wandered over the bar as she took another drink, a sour expression accompanying her obvious distaste at the brew. "How many creds are on the line here? Because if the infiltration is a no-go, or we need pulling out, we will need a stealth ship to get past all the tech this Baron has circling his little fiefdom."

Davina smiled, a shake to her head before she suppressed the smirk completely. "Do you think Duboit values you that highly? Because I hate to break your heart, but he's an Enforcer through and through. He wants the job done. If you get burned, he just finds someone else. Another crew he can squeeze until they pop."

"So this infiltration is the cheapest way? A few IDs and smack the Breakers' arses on the way out the door? What a fucking surprise," Rebekah leaned back into her chair, ignoring the beer and staring at her hands, cracking both thumb knuckles. "I have a tech list. Some of which won't be readily available on Minx. If there's no ship, then we need that list fulfilling. I get that as a guarantee – on *your* word as an Incini that everything will be provided – then we'll start before you trace everything. Otherwise, there'll be a delay. Weeks."

"And if Duboit decides to wave your former lives in front of the countess as an incentive?" she asked, knowing what the answer would be.

"I don't need to answer that."

"No, you don't." She replaced her drink, trying not to look at the *Sunstar*'s captain. She felt a tinge of sympathy for the woman trying to protect her two young charges and ragged crew. Almost powerless to do anything other than what Erikson bid them to do, or else go on the run for as long as they could until the creds ran out or the ship fell apart. Or they did. "You got the list?"

Rebekah slid a hand inside her flight jacket and pulled out a battered slate, going through the security protocols before handing it over. A glance over the screen was sufficient for Davina to know that most of the tech was easily sourced, with only the odd quirky requirement in the mix. That, and one set of the old Navy base plans, and ...

"That's not exactly stealth, is it?"

"If you mean the schematics, no. But necessary if you're leaving us in the lurch. There're enough scrapped Navy ships that the base equipment is obtainable. After all, you managed to help out the *Maverick* with some tricksy stuff, no doubt, before their mission came to a final end. The *Sunstar*'s debris cannons are upgradeable, and it would take an Almaarian Navy engineer to recognise the difference. But if we need pulling out, then I want some firepower to take down the satellites and stealth platforms this baron has." Rebekah stood, turning to leave. "Keep the slate. I'm guessing he'll want a rundown on why we want them. But we get a 'yes', and your word on the schematics and the tech, we'll go in. No need to search for another crew with the time that'll take, or use one of his precious hit squads."

Davina nodded, finishing her drink. "I'll be in touch."

Rebekah left, leaving her beer and walking through the bar without a word to anyone else.

Sitting back into the plush sofa, Davina ran her eye over the resource requests. She had no idea what their purpose was, other than the stated need for stealth tech to approach the moon. Rebekah had gone in high, requesting the stealth ship knowing full well that wasn't going to happen, and that her ruse would be seen through. But the deflection had been subtler than that. In her opinion, she wanted the defence cannons, the PDCs, more than the resource list in her hands. That she could see a fight coming, or the need to run and the fight would find them.

"Not my problem," she said out loud.

Who am I fooling?

She rose, checking her dampener again and made to leave the bar. Her senses prickled, hairs rising on her neck and she kicked in her sensory wetware. An unease settled on her shoulders, the source of which her wetware couldn't help pick out. But she trusted her instincts and kept her dampener on as she swiftly exited into the concourse. She made no attempt to see if she was followed, a skill far from her training. But instead of heading home, she made for the transports across to M1. It was supposed to be her downtime, but right now the sanctuary of Duboit's, and therefore Erikson's, security system was calling her.

A couple of lifts and a small wait had her on the shuttle connection across to the main offices, with no hint of anyone on her tail. But a dread still sat there, a sliver of paranoia that wouldn't go away as she entered her office. One that passed as soon as her SCIF activated. The only oddness had been the thrum of her dampener back at the bar, and with that thought she took it out of her bag and dropped it into the secure box, and after cleansing it, blasted the tech into dust.

"Damn. No more meetings away from here." And with that she replayed the conversation in her mind. There was nothing there that specifically referred to the twins, nor the moon by name. A baron, yes, and the tech involved. The mission.

Sloppy.

Yet recoverable should the possibility her dampener had been cracked arise. But who would do that other than the hand of a Minister?

Who is he really watching?

CHAPTER 10

SENTO CITY, SHEMA

R ebekah took a last look over her shoulder, paranoia sitting at the back of her mind as she eyed the alleyway opposite. Since ZZ3 had flown her to the outskirts and returned with her suit to the *Sunstar*, she had an unerring feeling she was being watched. In part she was sure the local viscount they had 'dealt' with a few weeks back would have no knowledge of who blew up his villa, or her new identity or why she should even be here. Yet it nagged at her. People with power had the knack of finding things out, sick nobles with influence and a heavy dose of pathological sadism even more so in her book. But this had been her choice. The plan concocted with Savvo was sound except for one thing. Who went in alone?

Originally, they were going in as pairs, ZZ3 remaining on guard duty with the girls. But Davina had surprised them when she not only acquired all the components they had requested, but the location of an ageing and not quite functional set of PDCs. An opportunity they couldn't miss that required Hendricks' skills. So here she was alone, because there was no way Arin would be able to function without a partner, and she would have likely killed him herself if they were together more than a week.

In a way it was a boon. Hendricks was far too well known and would have been a beacon around which the nosier elements may have noticed the rest of the Breakers. She doubted word would have gone far, but it only took one ear, one disloyal and greedy ex-solider, to get the word out to the countess. Hendricks, of course, argued, but not as vociferously as she would have without a set of decent defence cannons to add to her beloved ship, and a pair of engrossed twins to keep an eye on. Stealth tech 101.

With her wetware engaged, she gave a final look to the alleyway. Nothing appeared in her enhanced sight, so with a last longing wish for the tech'd out glasses she used as part of a pilot's survival kit, stepped out. Pulling her faux leather coat in tight, and a ridiculous beanie hat close to her brow, she hunched her shoulders while walking down the street. The fizz and whirr of motors along the road gave her some reassurance, as did the increasing crowd heading in both directions about their daily business. She began to relax a little, suppressing the urge to keep looking over her shoulder. After a few minutes, she noted the bar Davina had provided, the dingy window with its neon lights proclaiming cold beer. Few people appeared interested in going in, so she had to adjust amid the flow to get herself to the doors and slide inside.

The air was thick with vaporous smoke whose mixed scent annoyed her nose. A cough and she was at the bar, the swipe of her wrist providing a small beer and a chance to talk to the server.

"Thanks," she said, taking a drink. It was surprisingly good considering the cleanliness of the front windows and the ageing sign. "Looking for Fenwick."

The woman nodded. Her hair tightly bound back revealing a set of cheap tattoos across her neck and shoulder. "Be an hour or so. You looking for work?"

After another sip, Rebekah smiled ruefully and nodded. "Yeah. Heard there's some off-world contracts going. Am I right?"

"Can't see why anyone would want to get off Shema," she said, finishing with a slight laugh. "But yeah. Fenwick is recruiting though not sure for how much longer." She picked up a glass from a lower shelf, examined it against the light and cleaned the rim before moving on to the next.

"Maybe I'm just in time then." Rebekah turned away, expecting to eye the other customers only to find she was alone. "Business not great?"

Another laugh. "It gets mighty busy later. When the miners come in on rotation."

Rebekah coughed again, wondering what the source of all the smoke was and deciding perhaps the bar was just soaked in the stuff. Four mines worked the mountains around Sento, digging out whatever ore they could find to fuel the economy. Thirsty work, and by the sound of it, a job the miners enjoyed drinking after to celebrate or forget.

The door shifted, and through it a man and a woman peered, their hands up to the glass. They were both dressed in similar styles, one she recognised. Under their clothes would be handguns, and either a badge or a noble's calling card. She turned away, facing the server.

"Know them?" she asked.

The woman looked over, eyes narrowing a little. "Not them, but their ilk. Either the Baron's security, or his fucking dickhead of a son's. Been harassing Fenwick about his recruits, just to warn you. Wanting to know numbers and names. Started a few weeks back. He was thinking they wanted to divert some their way, but he said it all seemed a bit random at first. Half-arsed, and then it became urgent. Fenwick's not so keen to get into bed with those shits."

The door opened, and Rebekah counted each footstep to the bar. Both had come in.

"Greta, is it?" said the man, his chin covered in a small black beard, hands resting on the bar top.

Rebekah didn't turn away, instead peering into her beer and leaning closer to the bar.

"It is. Beer, or something stronger?" asked Greta.

"Neither. Fenwick making an appearance today?" he continued.

Greta glanced Rebekah's way. It was a compulsion, a natural thing to do and about the last thing she needed at that moment. The regard shifted to her, eyes boring into the back of her neck.

Fuck.

Greta's almost pantomime look of regret didn't help.

The man turned Rebekah's way. "You looking for Fenwick too? A recruit? Which unit?"

The questions came out in an odd tumble, like a pressure valve had been released. It made her wonder just how hard the viscount was pushing his men to find whoever burnt his fucking torture palace down. Surely he could work out it was a top-of-the-line professional job. Or had something else happened?

"Just a groundpounder," Rebekah replied, downing the last dregs of the beer before placing the glass on the bar top.

"You wanting work?" the woman asked.

Rebekah tilted her head to look over. She had ice-blue eyes and the bleached hair and tanned skin of someone who spent too much time in the Shema sun.

"Not on Shema," she replied. "Would like to see a different world for a while. Less dust, less sun."

"Almaarian accent," said the woman. "Too hot for you here?"

Rebekah took that at face value, hoping there was no implied hint in there. "Yeah. And no miner, either. Heard Fenwick has some off-world ops going. Kind of think I fit the bill. Anyway, who's asking? Maybe I know others who might be interested."

"Viscount Lundstrom," said the woman, her eyes fading a little as she said the words. "Looking for some extra ... house security."

"Contracted? Cos that always makes the difference."

"Yeah. Short term." Her hand slipped inside her jacket, Rebekah trying not to react. Two fingers emerged with a chipped card. "Know anyone, then they can scan this."

Rebekah took it. An old trick, and her wetware sensed the subtle scan of her wrist ID by whatever device the viscount's security had activated. Tough. The only info on there was for her newly minted identity provided by Davina. A groundpounder who never settled on any world for more than a few months. She pocketed the card, and turned to Greta, glass out requesting another.

The man glanced over to Greta, who shrugged. "Fenwick'll be another hour or two. Sure you don't want that drink?"

"No. We'll be back. Tell that ingrate he needs to wait. Have an offer he'll want to hear." He headed for the door, sharing a few low but sharp words with his partner before they left.

"Arrogant bastards," said Greta.

"I'll drink to that," Rebekah replied, and the server took the glass and started to refill it. "What's the deal with this viscount? Not paid much mind to nobles and all their shit."

Greta sighed and poured her own beer after passing over Rebekah's. "Word is someone blew up the fuck's villa. Talk of it being the Baseborn, you know the resistance. I find it hard to believe, but by rep he's worse than his fucking dad. Runs the mines like a workhouse. Rules for this and that. Break 'em, and well, people disappear. You know how it is."

And she did. Too well. Though most of the nobility just acted as megalomaniac money makers, and their workers a means to a profitable end. Some went too far, and the worst brought down the Enforcers, and their Breakers. As for the Baseborn, the futility of their efforts was well known, the Court a behemoth, the nobility's power too ingrained. And there was no groundswell of support, just an acceptance their efforts were in vain. But with fucks like the viscount, you could see why some just had to fight back.

"Disappear?" she asked and leaned in closer. "You mean prison, or something worse?"

"Rumours is all. But something worse." She nodded towards the entrance. "Fenwick's early."

Rebekah pushed herself away from the bar, placing her glass down as the stick-thin middle-aged man entered. His suit was nearly as old as he was, with lines about his gaunt face where the Shema sun had etched its mark. But his eyes smiled to match his mouth, an obvious affection for Greta written there.

"How goes it Regreta?"

That laugh again. "Very funny. Like I've never heard that one before. Whiskey?"

"Naah. Just a cold water, thanks. Those Twat-strom's dogs I saw just leaving?" Fenwick glanced over to Rebekah who couldn't help but smile at the man's choice of name.

"One and the same. They are definitely recruiting. Tried to take this one from under your nose." Greta handed over the water, nodding towards Rebekah.

Rebekah held out her hand, at which Fenwick looked blankly before he broke out in another smile and shook it. "Cassie," she said. "Cassie Henstridge. Groundpounder looking to get off this too fucking hot planet and somewhere that pays."

Fenwick looked her up and down. Not like someone examining a piece of meat. An appraisal, yes. But different. She couldn't help but like the man.

"Pleasure. I have a full roster, but maybe I can squeeze you in. Heard of Saim?" he said.

"One of Palail's moons. There's an old base up there, if I remember. Navy," she replied, standing a little taller.

"That's right. Now in the hands of Winkal, and he's playing some kind of political bollocks and recruiting for a private military. I can't guarantee how above the line they are, or know much about whatever crap he's playing at. But the pay's good, and I've heard from the first lot I sent out who are on leave. All positive." Fenwick stood back having collected his water. "Shall we sit?"

Rebekah nodded, taking a seat when an ominous shadow appeared at the entrance. The door swung open as the viscount's security detail returned. Fenwick swore under his breath, eyes to the sky as he painted a smile on his lips and turned about.

"Fenwick," said the male security guard. "About time. Got an answer for us?"

Fenwick coughed, then shook his head. "Not the one your viscount wants to hear. I'm moving on. I was just saying to Cassie here that it's about time I tried somewhere else."

"Fuck that, Fenwick," said the bleached blonde woman as she entered the bar. "You don't get to say *no* to the viscount. He speaks, you fucking wag your tail."

Fenwick paused and shrugged his shoulders. "I am under no contract or obligation to any of the Lundstroms. I am free to do as I wish."

The man slapped Fenwick across the face, a cut lacing his cheek that splattered blood onto their shared table. He staggered, collapsing to the floor as the woman moved in. Her foot, intended for his balls, never connected as Rebekah placed herself in the way, blocking the blow with her raised leg.

"Fuck off, bitch," spilled from the blonde's mouth.

Rebekah found she had punched her to the ground sometime after the last syllable. She then raised both hands, backing towards the crawling Fenwick. "Hey. You can't just beat some fucker up because you get an answer you don't like."

The man went for something strapped to his back. A mistake. She lashed out, grabbing his arm and continuing to twist the limb beyond its capabilities. He was forced to spin about as his shoulder screamed in pain. At the same time, she slid the extending baton from its sleeve on his back. With a shove, she sent him into the blonde, the tumble of legs and arms greeted by the tip of the baton clattering against the floor as it reached its full length.

"Now I've not used one of these in a while." She twirled the baton. "But I reckon I can remember enough. And yes, your viscount definitely needs some new security staff."

The woman reached under her shoulder, and with no regret at all, Rebekah lashed out. The snap reverberated around the room; the woman's eyes wide as pain crashed in. Her handgun clattered to the floor amid howls about her broken wrist.

"Enough. Now fuck off." She kicked the gun away. They both stood, Rebekah wary as they backed towards the door. "Greta here will look after your gun until we're gone."

For a moment, she worried that the thought of having to inform the viscount of their failure would lead to them trying again. And if they pushed things much further, she'd be forced to seriously injure them, and the mission was done. Possibly more than done if they began to investigate beyond the wrist ident. Their indecision came to an end, and they both clattered out of the door, threats ringing but ignored.

"Shit," said Greta, who had pocketed the gun and was lifting Fenwick from the dirty floor. He bled from the cheek, but it was nothing serious.

"Well, that's me finished," he said, and using Greta's arm, steadied himself a little. "I don't know whether to say thanks, or 'what in all the gods' hells have you done to me?' I'm now marked."

"I know their type. So do you. You were either finished, or working for them. Room on that last shuttle for two?" Rebekah looked him up and down this time.

"Yeah. Maybe three, eh Greta? You fancy a new start somewhere?"

CHAPTER 11

SAIM

Savvo jostled the burly woman in front, the recurrent growl she had used on board the shuttle repeated as she turned to face him. Old scars marred her cheek and ran across her nose, likely shrapnel by its ragged nature, adding menace to her consistently bad mood.

"You're off the bloody shuttle, now. Surely you can perk the fuck up," he stated, twisting his own features into some form of humorous pleading that scored exactly zero points by the glare he received.

"What's your problem?" she asked. Or stated. Fuck it, he wasn't sure which.

"The constant bitchin'." He wasn't convinced he'd hit on the right reply as she spun around to face him. Her brow rippled with deep furrows, and her biceps twitched beneath the thin shirt she wore over a cut-off t-shirt. He'd seen those muscles on the shuttle run. Honed in the gym, no doubt, but originating on a battlefield somewhere.

She laid out the threat front and centre. "I do hope we're in the same barracks, shitface. Cos me and you, we're gonna have some fun if we are."

He smiled back, refusing to back down but not making the situation any worse. He dropped the eye contact, giving her an excuse to turn away with the win but no more than that. Enough for him to make his mark in the annoying queue. Being quiet wasn't going to cut it. He'd worked that out on the final shuttle from the way station. His initial passage from Shema had been sprinkled with ex-soldiers, their presence probably only noticeable because he was one of them and looking. Wary of any that he may know, and in return may blow his cover. Those he picked out were disinterested in him, or anyone else. Just living their lives and ever-so slightly on edge among the crowd. Few who'd experienced army life felt comfortable again amid the civvies. Especially those who had experienced direct combat. That dependence on the soldier next to you unrepeatable in the world outside of war. Rarely ever able to fit in, with the memories of screams no longer dulled by the drugs, or later in combination with the wetware to numb thought and mind.

It was on the shuttle from Palail that they had come together. A feeling of being at home, back amid people who knew what it was like, and on the hunt for someone to depend upon as the usual hierarchies appeared.

Vanessa, the burly female soldier, had marked him for that role. Unfortunately, he had already made his choice. A certain shaven-headed, pale-skinned individual with distinctive red eyebrows who occasionally glanced his way from the front of the queue. Hence, the need to push the woman away. Mark himself as an arsehole. Well, more of an arsehole.

A hurray echoed down the line, and the doors of the terminal opened to allow the thirty or so soldiers enter the next chamber. Inside was a row of three makeshift desks, waiting behind them those army admin clerks every Marine wanted to snap in half. The disinterested type, barely a second of eye contact as they ran through your details. Admittedly, Savvo had missed a final encounter with their surly attitude by deserting. A bit extreme, but likely worth it. After all, it meant his wetware remained active.

Arin had reached the first desk, and by his posture and the clerk's reaction, was neck deep in his usual jokey banter that would cut zero ice. He watched as the male clerk ran over a checklist on his slate, then scanned Arin's wrist with barely a glance his way before gesturing towards a set of benches behind him. Arin wandered off, chipping in on someone else's conversation as he spread himself in a space big enough for two.

His new frenemy, Vanessa, was up and the change in demeanour came as a surprise. Gone was the surly façade. She was almost deferential, passive, in her interaction.

Broken.

Fuck.

He followed on.

"Name," came the bored request.

Savvo eyed the clerk, wisps of her long blonde hair sticking out from under a cap bearing the baron's coat of arms. Too long for space, that was for sure. Anyone who spent enough time in zero-g just cut the annoying stuff off and out of the way.

"Burghard. Stan Burghard," he proffered his wrist, and the electric prickle of the scanner passed over his ID chip. Davina had arranged their reprogramming; the twins having confirmed the quality of the changes on their return.

"Two years service, six months on the frontline, three in reserves. That right?"

"Close enough. Got my ship licence too. Basic type 2. Shuttle runs," he added.

"Interesting," she replied, but wasn't really listening. "Barracks assignment S4. Take a seat."

He grimaced. "What about the pay? You know accounts, and all that?"

Without looking, she waggled the scanner at him. "Take a seat. You have to pass the physical and, um, mental acumen tests before payment confirmation."

"Uh-huh," he said, and moved on. Vanessa, fortunately, was in conversation with someone else. A glimmer of a smile there, the passiveness hidden away again behind her veil. Arin chose that moment to shift on the bench, and a space appeared which he took full opportunity of.

"Thanks," he muttered, dropping his kitbag on the floor next to Arin's. He waited for a gap in the sub-engineer's conversation with the man next to him before offering his hand. "Stan, 37th Groundpounders."

Arin grimaced, a twitch to his eyes as he took the hand. "Sparks, 4th Sappers."

"And you're still alive? Fuck man, no wonder you look twitchy." Savvo released his grip.

"Hey, even I'm surprised I'm still alive. This is Shoddy, so named, he tells me, because everything he made fell apart. He's with the 3rd Engineers. Segfi's ground crew."

"*Was*," said Shoddy, a rim of grey hair cut close around a bald pate. "Definitely was. Looking forward to a warm bed, decent grav and some good grub. Hate space."

"With you there, brother," replied Arin. "With you there. Can't trust anyone in the black. Always putting you down when you're locked in a tin can for days on end. Eh, Stan?" Arin didn't look over, but Savvo had no need to see Arin's face to know he was wearing a stupid grin.

Savvo left them to their conversation and eyed the terminal. It was a multi-use area bereft of any form of windows because there was exactly nothing to see out there. A barren rock, pitted with ancient craters in one of which the base had been built. The cliff-like sides rose all around, blocking out any other view after the shuttle had dropped inside. It was thankfully clear of dust, a fact Savvo put down to multiple shuttles' engines blowing much of it clear. There were two regolith covered hangars to one side of the terminal, both fronted by huge doors set inside concrete which he again took to be constituted from the local rock debris. A thick and functional rad barrier, he had seen many similar buildings on the major asteroids of the belt.

The base itself was another klick to the north. He had only managed a glimpse as the shuttle came in for a runway landing to save fuel in the thin and mainly carbon dioxide atmosphere. Hunched beneath the rising slope of the crater, it gave the impression of a giant egg yolk rising slightly off centre from a lower level that spread in a circle to peter out where dual train tracks and smoothed roadways began. Around these sprawled various roughly built buildings he took to be storage and garages. Nothing exposed to space, even in a thin atmosphere, stayed shiny long. Functional, sealed and rad free were the key elements.

"Okay, up and at 'em!" The voice was familiar by its attitude. The tone of a unit commander, not the officer-noble. The hands on, day-to-day manager who kept you in line. His last had been Hendricks, though she'd gone by a different name back then. Solid, dependable and the wall between you and the officer who didn't give a flying shit if you lived or died as long as you won. The speaker wore the same cap with the baron's coat of arms and adorned with a bar that marked him out as a captain. At least it would in the Almaarian forces. "Through the central doors, boys and girls, you'll find your ride across the beautiful landscape of Saim. A wondrous rock of joy and love. The moment you step on that train you are mine, understand? Captain Trenchard's the name. Captain, understand. Pass the medical, physical and mental tests and you will be commissioned into our beloved Baron Winkal's private military, and then you are *his* as well. Any questions? Nope? Get your arses aboard then."

Savvo stood, taking his kitbag and glancing around. Vanessa had attached herself to another, and mentally wishing her luck, he sidled in behind Shoddy with Arin at the engineer's side. He kept his eyes on the thirty or so recruits around them, and knew Arin, despite his constant spew of inane conversation, would be doing the same. So far there had been no faces he recognised. Good news. Just a room full of ex-forces all down on their luck and desperate to be needed. Some had been broken by life amid an uncaring society just by trying to survive their day-to-day lives, and even here may fall by the wayside. Nature was cruel. A noble-controlled, hierarchical society, even more so.

The train was modern, clean and robust. Savvo was reminded of the auto-trains that rolled about some of the mining asteroids collecting ore for later transport. No windows, as that added a cost, and also pointless when the journey was a mere ten minutes. Seated a row behind Arin, he sank into the chair, almost lulled to sleep when the carriage slowed and the captain piped up again, ordering them off.

They passed through a simple airlock out of a tunnel-like structure where the train parked, and then on into a concourse. It was well-lit, the light as close to natural as any Savvo had been in, and airy. He assumed this was the 'yolk', the dual levelled centre of the base. There were even some plants growing inside sectioned areas and a running fountain before a set of stairs next to a large lift.

"Just need some ducks," said Arin with a cheesy grin. Shoddy laughed. Savvo didn't.

"This, boys and girls, is the main thoroughfare. Suck it up. Your quarters are not so salubrious, but each has a common area that does the job." The slightly greying scalp of the captain reflected the light as he lifted his cap to replace it centrally on his head. He nodded to a passerby, a woman in a well-cut suit in her middle years. She returned the nod, and glanced over the recruits with a smile before walking on. "Right, over here." He led them fifteen metres around the circumference to a doorway marked with an S4. "This will be your section until you pass the testing. This door will remain locked and the rest of the base out of bounds until then. Each corridor has a set of self-sealing doors. Should they engage, they can be reopened using that same coding twice. If there is a breach, the lockpad will tell you where to go. Once barracks are allocated, that's where you sleep, shit and eat until you're accepted in. *If* that happens, you'll be moved onto new accommodation."

The captain thumbed the lockpad and wafted his wrist over. The screen turned green, and the door sprung open.

"In you go. Sergeant Mereda is waiting for you. Don't piss her off, I still have the scars."

By the time Savvo was through the door and into the wide corridor, names were being called out in groups of six. He swore under his breath when he heard his.

"Burghard, get your arse down here!" bellowed a frustrated voice. He pushed past Arin and Shoddy, and joined the group of five that included Vanessa and her new best bud. A giant of a man in his late thirties with a sneer the same size as the attitude he gave off amid the sweat. A brief glance caught Vanessa's eye who returned his look with a raised eyebrow and a smirk.

The sergeant shook her head. "Hope the rest of you is better than your bloody hearing, Burghard. Section D, in there. Take a bunk and a locker for your kit. In the canteen in one hour. Gear will only be allocated once you are contracted, but wear something loose."

Mereda turned away, while Savvo stared at her back. Her name wasn't Mereda, at least it hadn't been when they had a short fling before he joined the Breakers.

Jinny. That was it. Jinny Long.

Shit.

By the time he'd entered the allocated section, the only spot available was a top bunk nearest the shower room. Below him was Vanessa, who sat with her kitbag half open but looking into the distance. Lost.

Broken.

All an act, and his sudden need to help had to be locked down. The Wrecking Squad came first. And the mission, such as it was.

CHAPTER 12

TWEEM

"Bring her in smooth, Heki," said Hendricks, eyes on the monitor and the small moon that orbited Shema. "There's grav, only about 0.2 standard, but you go with the navcom."

Heki side-eyed the engineer who was currently acting as the ship's co-pilot. She forced a smile, her symbiote's tentacles shuffling to reposition as her emotions shifted from contrite to acceptance. She knew what she was doing, and probably Dricks knew that, but just couldn't help chipping in with something. Perhaps it was her need to be in control resurfacing based on their age difference or Heki's inexperience. It certainly couldn't be because of her skill level, could it?

Heki adjusted for the combination of moon rotation and the increasing grav, with one eye on the intricate platform that wrapped half the moon. Dricks had said it looked complex and weak, but it was far from that. Yeah, a spaceship giving it a whack wouldn't go down well, but the shipyard had churned out some of the finest ships in the Navy fleet over the years. Currently on a thirty-year licence to some noble's company since the cessation, it mainly built private ships with the shift in the war, while forty percent of the yard was dedicated to repairs and refits.

"Calling Tweem moon dock. This is the *Solar Flame*, requesting berth at the repair docks, come back," said Hendricks the comms briefly crackling in response before a voice cut in.

"This is Tweem. Are we expecting you, *Solar Flame*?"

Heki knew they had been on the shipyard's sensors since they left Shema's orbit, and that they had run a passive scan and queried the transponder. But then, you could never be too sure who you're dealing with. They could after all be space pirates, rather than a bunch of ex-Marines using a false ship's ID with their eyes on a pair of defence cannons. Not the most legal refit for a private ship unconnected to the nobility.

"Yes you are, Tweem. Look under *special* projects," replied Hendricks, tipping a wink Heki's way. She rolled her eyes.

"Aha. Special you say ... mmm ... sending docking link. Careful flying *Solar Flame*, that's a tight berth."

The voice cut off, and the dock's transponder signal blinked through to Heki's console. She accepted the request, and casting an eye over the code nodded as their ship's pseudonym was accepted. As the manoeuvring thrusters engaged, she lifted her hands away from the controls under Hendricks' watchful eyes.

"You not trust me?" she asked, meaning to lighten the mood a little, but it came out surlier than she meant. Heki sent what she hoped looked like an apologetic smile, that seemed to ease the engineer's sour wince. "Sorry. Came out wrong."

"Lots to be learning. You're doing great, and you know me well enough. I can find it hard to let a little slack slide by." Hendricks patted her arm as she rose. "I'll be in the cargo bay, okay?"

"Okay." Heki returned to the console and began a visual sweep of the ships within the yard. Partially due to curiosity, but also to a deep mistrust rooted in her gut after the encounter with the crew of the *Maverick*. Not to mention the Bustan Navy.

"Trem, do we know what's out there?" she asked, knowing her sister had the same level of inquisitive paranoia.

Her twin's voice sounded in the comms, "Cataloguing now. Rebekah said not to intrude on their systems, so I can only pull from what surface data there is and the transponders."

"Let me know when you're done," she replied, and clicked off, guiding the external cameras to take in those ships berthed for refit or repair. There was a number of them, from small shuttles having their shielding resurfaced for atmospheric entry, to a Navy patrol ship that had a collection of autobots crawling over its outer hull. She watched them for a little while, marvelling at the sheer number of bots who appeared to be working on the sensor arrays and linked systems that were embedded in the hull. Everything from their PDCs, the single missile tube, to the camera systems was getting some form of overhaul.

The ship's thrusters brought the *Solar Flame* to a halt, proceeding to shift them gently sideways. Metal scraping metal reverberated through the hull as the docking struts wrapped the ship and locked them into place. The engines tuned down to a low rumble before switching off.

"We in?" said Hendricks.

"We are," said Heki. "Want me to bring you back some chocolate?"

"Har bloody har."

External comms engaged, and the same voice sounded in Heki's ears. "This is Tweem control. Please link your port airlock to the docking struts. Your oversight engineer is Yena Snow, when she comes knocking, please do the courtesy of letting her in. Tweem works on cooperation and speed. Berths are expensive, and we start charging your owner from the moment contracts are exceeded. Control out."

"Wow," said Trem, cutting in. "Pushy."

"The norm away from the belt," said Hendricks. "Time is money, always paying out into some noble or other's pocket. This place is run by Baroness Lundstrom, and has been making her and her family a pretty penny since she acquired the Navy's licence. Coffee time."

Heki chuckled. When wasn't it time for coffee? She eased her hand about her neck, and her symbiote wrapped small alien tentacles around her fingers before crawling onto her forearm where it settled to feed. Both appeared to need very little food, with Trem suggesting that perhaps they were taking in more than what they physically saw. Their integration with their biochemistry, brain activity and electromagnetic field perhaps tying into some form of complex feeding. Either way, the difference to their joint emotional state had changed their lives, and she never wanted to go back.

"You need a name," she said as she walked through to the galley.

Hendricks already had her flask prepared and eyed the symbiote as it nuzzled against Heki's forearm. "Going to have to hide those two away, you know. And you can't forget, understand? They get seen, and we may as well put a flashing sign on the side of the ship: 'Weird shit going on here'. The only people that talk more than Arin are bored dock workers."

"But then ... you know ..." said Tremil as she entered the galley and mimed her head exploding. "They'll get a head full of our other issues."

Heki twisted her lips as she thought, tongue poking at one corner. "How about we lock ourselves into the cargo hold? ZZ3 is in there, and the Butcher. Move the printer through while you use engineering and the work bay. None of the PDC schematics show any need for internal access to that hold."

"We can put the symbiote tanks in there, too," added Tremil. "We're here for what? Two days?"

Hendricks nodded. "Three twelve-hour shifts, fifty-two hours of contracted time when you include breaks. After that, Davina will have to intervene. But doable. You okay with that?"

Heki rubbed her shoulder, a sigh slipping from her as she ran over the reworked schematics displaying on the console. The printer had proved its worth, despite the complexity and difficulty with bonds that meant thirty percent of the components it built were rejected on testing. Still far better than not having what it produced.

She spun on the chair, getting to her feet and collecting the newly printed sensor board. The advantage they had as a new ship's sub-engineering team was a certain warbot.

"Try this one," she said, and handed ZZ3 the board.

"That the third one?" asked Tremil, working on a basket of wires and components at a cobbled together table of cargo boxes and an old shelf.

Heki knew she wasn't looking for an answer, just a distraction from whatever puzzle she was working on.

"Yes," replied ZZ3, and the bot connected a set of wires and links extruding from a hip plate to the array board. A hum ensued, the bot's four working lights spinning in a circle. "This one is sound, but will degrade more rapidly than a constructed board."

"As will they all," replied Heki. "We'll set up a testing algorithm, it'll put an extra strain on each component, but may help us catch potential issues before they arise. Compile a list of the most needed replacement parts."

"A sound concept," said ZZ3. "Your planned effect is interesting. Creating a shadow of the *Sunstar*, rather than trying to hide completely."

"That's the hope. We don't have the Senti metal, or understand how it works to absorb all that EM. But producing a shadow on an active sensor sweep gives us a fighting chance with any weaponry aimed our way and may confuse missile locks. We can use the same system to disperse our signal when we're pinged at distance. Of course, not much chance on a rapid slowdown with all that heat facing where we're heading."

"Only need rapid, if going at speed," said the warbot, almost absent-mindedly. "Not always necessary. But useful to think about. If time, you may wish to consider how effective the probes were. Asham applauded the efforts made, and suggested small ships could use false signatures that way."

Trem stopped what she was doing, her eyes lighting up as she stared over at ZZ3. "Now I like that—" she stopped in mid flow, turning about to eye the boxed probes Arin had been stockpiling ever since they said goodbye to Scarva's ship. "I like that a lot."

"Pity such a great mind ..." began Heki, but ZZ3's limbs quivered, and she managed to reel in the next words. Somewhere in there was a pacified part of Asham. The containment unit retaining the dark, shadowed version that had devised monsters they were not allowed to see, despite looking into the mirror and seeing one every morning.

ZZ3 said nothing, but the aura surrounding the bot shifted. Neither she nor Tremil could really define what they saw. Like an emotional cloud they sensed among the crew, that in ZZ3 felt real. No, real was the wrong word, but just as emotions couldn't be 'seen' by other humans, you knew they were there. Some were sensitive to them, and others who had been discovered and enhanced in a lab, poured them forth like a tsunami.

Tangible. That's as near as I can describe it.

"Heki, Trem," stated Hendricks over comms. "I've got to go and check on some issues with the gimbal configurations. Apparently not as easy a switch as we thought with the current provision. Snow has an option on a scrapped ship I can check out."

"Aren't we due some down time?" said Tremil, checking her slate.

"Yeah. That's why I need to get this sorted now before the restart otherwise we're looking at an additional shift," replied Hendricks. "I'll see if I can do some extra shopping while I'm there. Any requests?"

"I have a new list," stated Tremil, a smile creeping across her face as she eyed the probes.

Chapter 13

TWEEM

Activate.

Sleep mode negated.

Sensory sweep of hold initiated.

ZZ3 adjusted, limbs gently syncing and repeating the pattern that mirrored its eyes. The tremors subsided, and the warbot remained still, wary.

Unusual vibration patterns detected. External maglock compromised. Deadlock activated.

'We're under attack?'

Unknown. Engineering works may have interfered with systems.

'Yeah, right. And look what happened to me last time I trusted supposition. A hundredth of me swirling about your chips while the rest sits festering in a box.'

That hundredth is worth a thousand times the foul thing inside the containment unit.

'... agreed.'

Sweep maintained. Uncertain analysis. Conflict.

'Jamming.'

Possibilities defined. 70% certainty someone is attempting entry.

ZZ3 rose, gathering the tarpaulin Heki had left by the warbot's side. It strode past the adapted console and the printer, shifting the cargo boxes of the nearly depleted raw materials for the printer to find a position at an angle to the hold doors. Ensuring it covered the airlock that led into the main ship, the warbot settled down into position.

Attack possibilities increasing. Parameters near 85% certainty. Heat rising.

'Cutting through ...'

"Heki, Tremil. Come back, emergency channel HT," stated ZZ3, connecting with the internal comms. "I rep—" The comms system died.

Engaging protection protocol crew. Heki and Tremil are crew. I am crew.

The click of limb panels opening up echoed through the hold, and the gentle whirr of servos. Heat flare rose, red then a brilliant white as the plasma torch cut through the deadlock. ZZ3 waited, a memory rising from its bank of a hit team assaulting the same bay. Under HT protocols, two fear-filled and desperate twins had ordered the destruction of each member. Now the choice lay with the bot, but the girls' needs remained the same. Survival.

I am crew.

Protect crew. At what cost is the enemy's choice.

Air whooshed through the doors, coalescing briefly into a thin mist before disappearing into the vacuum. A drone flew in, zero-g and with multiple LADAR lasers flaring red as it scanned the hold. The picture it built would be drawn in the HUDs of whoever waited outside. ZZ3 passive and beneath the disruptive surface of the tarpaulin, waited. Impatient. Setting a simple algorithm to calm the judders reverberating through its servos.

'You are changing.'

Is this really the time?

'Is 'evolution' in your lexicon?'

Is 'be quiet' in yours? Suppressing interaction.

The drone spun about, rising towards the top of the hold. ZZ3 knew it would take station, and have some form of weaponry on board should it be required. It didn't recognise the model, only its intent. The warbot marked the machine as a secondary target and shifted the tarpaulin so it had a visual on the open doors with dulled electronic eyes.

The first of the assault team entered, rifle up, black against black in their armoured spacesuit. The HUD frosted, but the person inside would have a full representation of the hold, and any suspicious signals flagged. Something would leak from Arin's tarpaulin, nearly as fast as ZZ3's opportunity to end this speedily.

Mission parameters conflict with protection protocol.

Keep hidden, stay quiet, don't draw attention.

Conflict.

Wait.

A third and fourth member of the team entered, splitting to move about the hold. ZZ3 desperately wanted to access their comms, hear what they were communicating. To know their intent. Whether it needed to deter or kill.

The last member slid the doors to.

Four.

Five with the drone.

Intent unclear. Protection variables increased.

Activate.

ZZ3 rose, the tarpaulin sliding away to expose the warbot to the assault team. They fired simultaneously.

Deterrent failed. Protect crew. The enemy has chosen the cost.

One limb lifted and shot back, the spray of bullets cutting across the fourth member who had closed the doors. Plates cracked, and the combatant slammed into the hull, weapon flying away in a lazy arc towards the deck. Lifting a second limb, ZZ3 aimed for the third intruder when bullets rained in, clattering against the bot's armour from the other two members. The warbot marked their positions and opened fire at the first target, concentrating on one place. The visor. Pummelling the weak spot as they ducked for cover.

A final volley shattered the upper part of the helm. Dead, be it by the void or by a bullet. ZZ3 strode out from behind the boxes as another panicked volley hammered into its hull, aiming both arm weapons towards the shooter. Too late, ZZ3 realised the intent was to draw it out, and a grenade crunched into the warbot's lower limbs. The explosion rocked the hold, staggering ZZ3 who was forced to use three limbs to prevent flying back. A second grenade spun in, and the warbot lashed out with its other arm to swat the explosive against an inner wall. Shrapnel peppered the bot, but it ignored the danger, sweeping bullets across the hold to force the remaining assailants to duck. Sensors detected movement behind, and ZZ3 kicked backwards, a leg limb splitting the suit's chest in two and shattering the ribcage behind. Blood filled globules spilled into the hold, but ZZ3's eyes were on the two remaining members of the assault team. They had taken position next to the Butcher's containment box, heads moving back and forth, sensors informing the bot that comms chatter was flowing in both directions.

End threat, deal with next threat.

Their rifles pointed the warbot's way, bullets pinging off its armour. They both had a grenade left but had already seen the bot shrug them off.

'They know you.'

Bullets rained in, all directed on a single spot, and ZZ3 moved, pounding to one side, bringing in to play one of the hold's struts to block their field of fire.

Agreed within 90% parameters.

A pulse hit. A wave of EM designed to knock a warbot out. Achievable on an unmodified AD unit if you knew the codes, just like on the *Scourge*. Of course, ZZ3 was far from unmodified anymore.

100%.

ZZ3 fired, the underarm grenade smashing into the source of the pulse, the drone, which briefly erupted before pieces of its shell filled the upper hold.

Evolution. Such EM weapons no longer work thanks to our glorious leader. Targets acquired.

ZZ3 leapt, three limbs launching the bot from the deck where it had been maglocked, dual grenades destroying whatever had been behind it. The arm mounted gun tore into an assailant, visor shattering, blood spraying across the final member of the assault team who threw themselves aside. By the time they had their weapon ready, the last thing they saw were four angry spinning eyes.

ZZ3 spun the airlock, entering the main corridor to find the air thankfully still present.

70% probability a single assault on the hold. Possibility of entry through main outer airlock doors remains. Assessing.

The warbot stopped next to the monitor near the cargo hold, drawing out the combination of physical wires and connection pads it had procured in its battle to keep the Butcher well and truly inside the containment box. These ZZ3 carefully placed on the control panel, and on connecting, began a swift search through the camera systems. They were all down, nothing worked, along with the comms the bot assumed had been jammed. Whoever had gained entry knew their business, and coupled with the attempt to down the warbot with an EMP surge, indicated they were dealing with the Almaarian armed forces.

Not space pirates or scavengers.

'We're on a private shipbuilding yard. The security will be extremely tight.'

Agreed.

'You know who this is. They came for me on my asteroid, and now they come for the part of me in the containment box. You can't …'

I am crew. Protect crew.

'If someone harnesses what lies in there. That which was me fused with a Battle AI … their plans go beyond just the crew.'

Images of alien hybrids poured from the bot's memory banks. The evil the Butcher carried out, be it from petulance or fear. Imploring hands, eyes open in silent agony as they realised what had been done to them. Terror.

Stop.

The corridor reverberated, the clank of magboots on metal echoing through the air. ZZ3 withdrew the wires, turning to face towards the cockpit, arm weapons ready.

53% ammo left. Two grenades.

'Two sisters and their symbiotes.'

The warbot started down the corridor, not using any stealth, well aware of the likelihood that comms traffic from the team in the hold would have got through. Jamming or silencing ship communications left them in control of the flow of information, ZZ3 left with its parameters and protocols and the pacified ghost of a psychopath general.

A muzzle protruded around the galley corner. A sight attached that would stream a feed directly into the HUD of the soldier – yes, a soldier, or a Marine – and protected by the metal walls. But to a warbot, such things were trivial. Able to crash through, take the hits, destroy the threat.

Except I am crew.

"This is warbot AD3 of the battleship *Segfi*. Reprogrammed to protect the crew of the *Solar Flame*. I have eliminated the threats to my ship's hold."

'Subtle. I like it.'

"You mean you killed them, you fucking traitorous piece of metal. Right?" The sound that followed was like the tapping of a helmet.

80% probability they heard or saw the battle.

"Withdraw and leave the crew fit and well, and the set protocols dictate you will be allowed to leave ... alive." ZZ3 kept the tone steady, and on point. How a warbot may respond.

"No way are we turning our back on you. We're here for the containment unit in your hold. We have two of your ... crew ... as hostages. We will not hesitate to kill them."

Voice analysis detects 90% probability of fear.

Fear is a killer in humans. Isn't that right, Asham?

'Mistakes are made.'

Shots are fired, people die, often everyone.

"I state again, leave the crew, leave the *Solar Flame*, and all shall live." ZZ3's limbs adjusted, arms up, weapons ready. It did not trust the soldier to act appropriately. "Do not make me act in deference to my protocols."

ZZ3 detected an electronic chatter, infuriated that it could not hear what was being said. Standard Marine assault teams operated in sixes or eights. That meant the possibility of two inside, and two outside. They had attacked when the ship was at its lowest compliment, possibly only expecting Hendricks to be aboard.

They want the Butcher, not the twins.

"Let us take the containment unit, and we will return these girls. Your crew," said the soldier, the gun barrel bobbing a little as he spoke.

100% certainty acting on new orders.

'Lie.'

Lie?

'Tell them you are programmed not to allow the box to leave the ship at any cost, including destroying the Solar Flame *and yourself. Lie.'*

Lie.

I calculate a 65% certainty they will attempt to leave with the girls. Meat shields.

'Bargaining power. But alive.'

Protect crew.

"My protocols will not allow it. I have been ordered to destroy the ship, the crew and myself before allowing the containment unit to be removed. Acting now." ZZ3 slammed a metal leg into the deck. "Engaging AD protocol ..."

"No, no. Wait," said the soldier. "Wait."

Again, the comms chatter that ZZ3 was so near to detecting. Frustration bubbled, a new thought, one Asham didn't help with as he filled the bot's mind with some of his own.

"We're leaving, understand AD3 of the *Segfi*? We're going."

The muzzle remained where it was, but more noises rattled along the deck. Scrapes of metal upon metal, followed by muffled cries.

"Leave the crew," stated the warbot.

"No," said the soldier, and Heki appeared at the far end near the cockpit, a handgun to the back of her head and a chain of metal balls around her neck.

'I designed those.'

Helpful. I have no knowledge.

'They are proximity explosives with a twist. Kill the soldier, his suit triggers the explosive ring.'

You have issues. What about wounding?

'That was also an option I added.'

Tremil appeared next, guarded by a third soldier. There must be one more outside, not two as expected. She again wore the explosive necklace, her eyes wide with what ZZ3's memories labelled as fear at 100% certainty. Yet no one was dead or committing suicide. The opposite in fact, very much in control. However, there was a shimmer, an oddness to its sensor data the bot didn't recognise, placing ZZ3's system on high alert – flagging both girls as their hands reached for each other. The gap between them morphed into a void, suddenly empty of data. Whatever they were doing, the soldiers seemed unaware, and lay beyond the warbot's direct experiences. Only understanding that it felt displaced. Odd. With a ghost of a memory haunting the periphery of ZZ3's thoughts – just out of reach.

'You know what these are?' said the soldier. "Neck bombs."

The shimmers stopped instantly. Like a curtain had dropped, negating the weird sensor data. The only certainty, the two symbiotes that had dropped softly and unseen to the deck from beneath the girls' clothes immediately afterwards.

The talkative soldier stepped out. "They die, then boom."

"They? But not you." ZZ3 rose an arm, and eviscerated the soldier. Bullets tearing the body into shreds, before turning the weapon on the other two. "Harm them in any way, and my programming dictates I hunt you down. Kill you, and then whoever gave you the orders."

'Another lie?'

No.

ZZ3 backed away, the two soldiers pushing Heki and Tremil ahead as they headed for the airlock. They remained silent, shaking, biting their lips hard enough that blood flowed. On reaching the junction, ZZ3 turned away from the airlock and back towards the cargo hold, eyes always looking ahead, always on the twins and running analysis after analysis as they were forced onwards. The warbot couldn't detect emotions, but having seen the feed of what happened upon the *Maverick*, remained startled at their apparent control as the soldiers refrained from any attack on the girls or themselves. Perhaps the need to survive restrained them, or the symbiotes had drained enough emotion to allow a modicum of control.

When they reached the junction, both soldiers backed away, keeping Heki and Tremil between them and ZZ3. Young eyes leaked tears, and blood remained on their lips, but no sounds except whimpers left the girls' mouths.

'They'll have told them they'll die if they talk.'

How do you know?

'It's what I would have done. In case they could warn someone.'

"Wait," growled one of the soldiers, his voice electronic and harsh from their frosted helmet. He flipped open the emergency store, and using one hand at a time, handed each of the twins an emergency suit. Ones the Incini had provided. "Put them on."

The Incini.

Who knew where they would be and when.

ZZ3 fidgeted on the spot, limbs trembling while the girls quickly slipped on the suits. A last pleading look fell the bot's way as the helmets dropped into place, a ding signalling the seal.

"Stay there, or we engage the explosive, understand."

"Kill them, and my programming enables your death," replied the warbot. A swirl of red eyes emphasised the point. More comms chatter, and the inner airlock door sprung open, the soldiers and their prisoners squeezing in.

I am crew ...

ZZ3 reversed itself and spurted down the corridor, entering the hold airlock and back into the death scene it had left behind. Blood and the dead floated about the Butcher's coffin, the hold doors still closed. A small win the warbot found dissatisfying. Crew were in danger, and it had failed to save them.

Yet.

The warbot reattached to the internal systems, and began reworking the hold and airlock doors, seeking the methods the assault team had employed to enter. By the time the airlock responded to Hendricks' code and scans, ZZ3 knew they had simply bricked the system. An all-out attack that left the ship paralysed so they could cut through the deadlock.

"Heki, Tremil?" crackled over the comms. "What in all the hells is going on?"

CHAPTER 14

PALAIL WAY STATION

Rebekah collected her kitbag, swinging the lies she had been sowing for the past week onto her back. With a last look at the ex-storage cupboard she'd spent seven days sleeping in with three others, she sighed, and headed past the foul toilet-cum-shower room they had shared with another room full of ex-soldiers all pretending to be someone they weren't. Trust was a curious thing, and by the time they had transferred to the shuttle via Palail's way station, she expected a few truer bonds to form with the usual shake and nods of the heads when comrades-in-arms began to put faces together with the reality of their situation. Getting past the false trails they had all laid. Of the three she had shared the extremely cheap berth with, two were definite armed forces. The tells obvious. Routines, cleanliness amid the squalid conditions. Making do, and able to fill the boredom they were used to between missions. The third she suspected had clocked them all and had spun whatever tale came to mind. The one thing they weren't, was any form of spy or informer.

She said her goodbyes, expecting to see most of them again on the shuttle to Saim, and headed along the freighter's busy and sweat-filled corridor towards the cargo doors. There she exited, and made her way along the concourse to find the information board for her next stop. Fenwick had loaded the deets onto her wrist ID before he and Greta had said their goodbyes above Shema, and taken berths well away from her own. Guilt by association, he had called it. The shuttle run had been quiet, no sign of the viscount's cronies, but then Fenwick had contacts everywhere and had cleared their way aboard the first flight in return for a few favours owed.

The board flickered into life, and she found herself surrounded by familiar faces all gazing up at the list of departures with a sense of purpose. Just a very different one to hers.

Her slate buzzed against her thigh, and she eased her hand inside her pocket while reading the information board. An hour to kill, and as if as one, twenty of her fellow passengers all moved off towards the nearest bar. She hoped they were aware of the prices on a way station.

She thumbed the slate and wished she hadn't as Dricks' urgent message request appeared.

A glance around led her to walk over to a more secluded corner, and with her back to the wall, she slid down to the floor. She pushed in an earpiece and stared at Hendricks' face.

"Something wrong?" Rebekah asked. Of course there was. This wasn't part of the plan, unless Savvo and Arin had already discovered what they needed.

Hendricks was silent for a touch too long. "It's all gone to fuck," the engineer said, her words barely a whisper as she leant against the console in the *Sunstar's* cockpit.

"Savvo, Arin?" were her first voiced thoughts. Hendricks shook her head.

"No. At the shipyard. There was an assault team. Had to be Marines of some form. They came for the containment unit. They knew it was on board." Hendricks wiped away tears.

Rebekah's thoughts were of the twins. Only a threat to Arin or the girls would lead to such a display on screen. She swore.

"Heki and Tremil? Tell me, Dricks. No bullshit."

"They took them. ZZ3 fought off the raiders who entered the hold, but ... shit, Rebekah. They took the twins. Wrapped them in explosive necklaces. Fuck ..."

She blinked, resting the slate on her knees. An assault team there for the Butcher. Boarding the ship when it was in a guaranteed dock – an *ex*-Navy shipyard supposedly – with her crew dispersed across the fucking system carrying out a mission for Duboit. One Davina had almost led them by the nose into being an infiltration run, splitting them up. Negating any perceived chance of failing to recover their prime target. Not a baron and his pretend army, but whatever remnant of the Butcher and the battle AI they could make use of.

Assuming, that is, that the Enforcer was knee-dip in this shit. But why now? Why not beforehand?

The *Maverick*. They had sent the salvage ship to investigate the *Scourge*, and that problem had been negated. Removed. Davina had said as much, and the holo-masked freak's attack on Michael and family had confirmed it.

Everything had changed at that moment. Pivoted. They must know that the containment unit had been taken, and in their stupidity, likely removed by a crew of ex-Breakers and their dumb-as-fuck captain who thought they had some advanced tech and a dead general as leverage. Instead, they had a fucking Bustan battle AI and whatever psychotic remnant of Asham's brain patterning lay inside. One that had terrified an awakening warbot.

So was this their Enforcer? Everything pointed that way. Perhaps the bastard had even blown up the *Maverick* himself, stopped them from blabbing about whatever they had found. And Davina, of course, had sold them out. Helped split them up, arranged the refit for the PDCs. A coincidence perhaps, but a convenience they had used.

The certainty that they were fucked loomed large, and whoever contacted them about the twins would be after a swap on their terms. Urge them to give up something extremely dangerous, in return for something even more fucking dangerous. If they were alive. If they hadn't lost control and forced their kidnappers to put them down like rabid dogs.

Her head hurt, and she refused herself the luxury of the wetware. This was her pot of shit, created by short-sightedness. They should have left that thing aboard and blown it up with the rest. Except it wouldn't have been the end. The unit built from the Senti metal that ZZ3 and his ghost passenger didn't even know the limits of.

And the casualties of such a plan were her two charges, in the hands of whatever noble or Enforcer had sanctioned the assault. Surely by now they would have worked out what they had in their hands?

"Where are you?" She prayed the answer would be close. Time was not on her side.

"In the outer dock. Berth 23A."

"On my way," she clicked off, and stared at the blank screen for a while, before making up her mind. She swiped the slate, keying in a secondary code and waited until it lit up again. "Fenwick. Want to make some money?"

She stood before the warbot, the lumbering metal-limbed machine staring at the floor, eyes whirling.

Almost as if it was alive. Human even.

"Hendricks has shared your camera feed with me. What happened, how you responded," she said. The bot shuffled position, eyes still locked to the deck.

"You stopped one half of the assault team from getting the Butcher or whatever monstrosity he has become now," she continued.

"I am crew. I failed to stop them taking the twins. I am supposed to protect crew ... I did not," said the warbot. It looked up, the swirl of lights became a maelstrom. Was it confusion? Worry. More human traits.

"What would they have done if it was Hendricks, or me, in their way?" she asked, realising she was gently prodding a fucking warbot because it needed her to do that.

The bot fidgeted again. "Humans work on certainties; I work on probabilities. Within 90% probability, they would have killed you and taken the Butcher. There is a 50% possibility with more time they could have recognised Heki and Tremil's abilities, and discovered the symbiotes, perhaps both, and taken them anyway."

"And the action you took?" asked Hendricks, her face drawn, eyes swollen.

"65% until ..."

"You lied," she finished, impatient with the pause in his explanation. "However that has been achieved in a warbot ruled by logic. And after that lie the odds were much greater. Nearer one hundred percent, close to certainty that they, or whatever fucker was commanding them, could see the girls were valued and may be used for negotiation."

"Or as bait," added Hendricks.

"I know what you're trying to do. I am a warbot, governed by protocols and code. I understand I am not to blame," stated ZZ3.

"No. You don't," Rebekah replied, stepping closer, laying a hand on ZZ3 for the first time since the *Scourge*. "Now you care. You care that you are crew, and are concerned you let us, yourself, and above all else the twins, down. Even if you don't understand what is happening, or it is not present in your code, *we* see it."

"Asham does not understand the concept. You try; you either succeed or fail."

"You are not Asham," stated Hendricks. "But you told me it was his idea to lie."

"He showed me the logic. And his past experiences using such a verbal trick. It had the desired effect. I can use such an action again." The bot's eyes focused on Rebekah. "I will analyse what you say. I know an urgency to recover Heki and Tremil. That as time passes, their chances diminish due to their nature. If that is caring, then I care."

"And the soldier. The one you killed when it was not required?" Rebekah asked, adjusting her hips and resting a hand below her chin. "What was that act for?"

The bot's eyes paused. "That was not Asham. That was solely my choice. It may have increased the possibility that they are more careful around the twins."

Rebekah removed her hand, but kept her eyes on the warbot. "I'll give you that. It's what I would have done, but perhaps for different reasons. Okay. We need Savvo and Arin out of there."

"And how do we manage that?" asked Hendricks. "It's a bloody big moon and the skies are tech'd out." She slammed a fist on the container next to her.

Rebekah sighed, sitting back on a low cargo box to eye her ex-captain. "I have a plan, with a little help from a new friend. How far did Heki and Tremil get with their modifications?"

"A long way, but I can't make head nor tail of the schematics to finish the job," replied Hendricks, shaking her head.

ZZ3 spoke up, "Nor Asham. The ideas are there, but not the ways all the pieces fit together. *They* are in the containment box." It looked over to the black unit and its deep shadow, a tremor running through the warbot. The source of half their problems, the rest somewhere unknown.

Hendricks sucked at her lips, while rubbing the back of her neck. "But not his idea about the probes giving a false signal. I'm thinking Arin might have more success with that. He discussed a few concepts before he left. And ZZ3 finished the PDC additions, after we left in a fucking hurry."

"That is a start. If I could get Arin and Savvo to a specific spot, and identify an entry point, what then? Do we have another way to get in short of using the PD cannons? There must be something," stated Rebekah. "Jamming? A virus?"

ZZ3 rose to its feet, limbs stretching out. "Senti code," it stated. "I have been teaching the twins how to work with it. It confuses systems."

"Satellites are programmed to send, only receiving with predefined encryption from specified sources," said Rebekah.

"Not if I have direct contact," said the warbot. "And if that does not work, I could carry one of our glorious leader's newly explosive probes."

"Start subtle, finish as a Breaker. As crew. I like it." Rebekah took out her slate, opening it and waiting as she made a call. Fenwick answered. "Are you up for a few creds?"

"Your request seems a little weird, but hey, figure I owe you something. Yes, I have a proxy who will do what you ask for the agreed price." Fenwick leant in a little closer. "Going to cause a predicament though."

"They love predicaments, don't you worry. My crew are experts on them."

CHAPTER 15

SAIM

"Remind me again why I signed up for this shit?" said Arin, his newly shorn scalp red and sweaty from effort as he pounded across the exercise yard.

Wrapped about his legs were the same weights as Savvo wore, with the addition of another set around his hips due to a particularly lacklustre display of fitness the previous day. May have been the effect of the moonshine Shoddy had procured for them. The taste was still at the back of Savvo's mouth every time he swallowed.

"Because," replied Savvo, a wheeze between each word, "the alternative was to blast our way in." He stopped, his heart deciding that residing in his throat was a better option than his heaving chest.

Arin doubled over, the clank of the weights inside their pouches finally stopping as he knelt down to rest his hands on the concrete floor. "Shit, we have a warbot. We could have just ripped this place a new hole."

"And risk scratching your true love?" Savvo stood, head woozy. The exercise yard swirled for a second before settling down. Ten metres away, Sergeant Mereda grinned back at him, and twirled her finger once round.

"Fuck me," he said and slapped Arin on the back.

"What?"

"Again. We have to go around again." Savvo stretched out his back, and adjusted the straps on his leg weights. An addition to increase their fitness for those who required extra 'attention'. The same attention Mereda had been applying to every drill and task pushed his way. At first, he assumed she was punishing him for whatever perceived faux pas he had done in the past. But the more he thought about it, and suffered, the more it appeared she was making sure there was no obvious favouritism. There were plenty more than just her here under a false name, and cliques and past acquaintances were frowned upon. Or drilled out of them, at least.

He yanked up Arin, who choked, then staggered into a half-jog, half-stumble. Eventually he hit a rhythm and Savvo managed to join him. Side by side they carried on pounding the smoothed regolith floor surrounded by four others who had been singled out for the sergeant's *special* attention. Ten minutes, and they collapsed at her perfectly shined boots, chests tight, before staggering to their feet to stand at ease.

She shook her head, the ever-present grin below eyes that swept over everyone before settling on Savvo. "Spacers," she said, using the word almost as an expletive. "Got no stamina and need help opening a soda bottle. Pathetic. Wash up, food, rest and back at 07:30 sharp. And Sparks," she pointed at Arin's legs, "bring the weights. You, my friend, are the unfittest of them all. Dismissed you shower of shit."

Savvo started to move away only to realise Arin hadn't joined him. He turned back to find him sprawled on the concrete, one hand holding a weight he'd obviously tried to remove.

"Leave me here to die." He coughed into the dusty floor.

"Tempting. But Mereda would only jump start your heart in the morning and set you on another run." Savvo undid his own weights, then collected those about Arin's hips as he rolled onto his knees. After helping him up, he handed them back. "She is right though. When we get back, more gym time, fewer Danishes with extra sprinkles."

"Torture me some more, why don't you. I bet those girls have been pigging out on my stash. And Dricks. Bastards, all of them." He brushed down his legs and eased his back before staggering over to join Savvo as they headed back to barracks. "And where's the Captain? Ain't she supposed to be here by now?"

"Definitely soon, unless she got made in Shema, in which case this is your future, Marine, and you'd better get used to it." Savvo grinned, though worry did sit in his chest, likely taking up the space his heart had vacated before the last run. Rebekah was late, and from what he'd heard, the last shuttle run was exactly that. The last for a while. Rumour was once the latest recruits were through basic testing, they would be on their way for some training exercises with another noble's army. One that was six months ahead of them. This was the type of information they were here to pick up, before cracking the admin data core and making a run for it.

Not that Savvo had any indication this private army had any treasonous intentions. All the talk was of regaining the skills from the war, not *going* to war. The whole thing was beyond a noble's 'show pony' as Hendricks would call it. There appeared far more purpose than that, a greater level of professionalism than a noble's plaything. But they had seen no live ammo training. Even the shooting range had used simulation. Odd. An enigma, and to his mind one that wouldn't be answered anytime soon.

They both staggered into the barracks, and on to their allotted rooms. After passing testing, they had been assigned their own private space. Small, but appreciated. No more than a bed and a desk, but after being crammed into the small bunkhouses, very welcome.

Savvo stripped down, grabbed his towel and headed for the showers. They'd be cold, those receiving less of Mereda's extra love sessions would have used the allotted heated water, but right now, he did not care.

As he entered the corridor, shouts echoed from further down, nearer the common room and the canteen. Familiar ones, punctuated with the odd threat of retribution. Arin. Towel gripped about his waist, he ran towards the kerfuffle, finding Arin underneath a burly-looking newbie who was throwing punches.

"You fucking bastard," the newbie was shouting, his accent Shema between the swear words. "You left my mates to fucking die." He slapped Arin either side of his head, aiming for the ears. A move designed to disorientate that Arin saw coming. He swivelled his head, and while the newbie was low, headbutted him in the chest. Air wheezed from the man's lungs, but he still managed an elbow into Arin's nose, blood flying.

Torn between nakedness and intervening, Savvo let the towel go, aiming to grab Arin's attacker before it got really messy. Except he missed, finding himself falling from a rabbit punch to the side of the neck. Mind swirling, he realised he was on the floor when another punch landed, slamming his forehead into the concrete again.

"And this fucker. In it together. Bastards."

Amid the uproar, a kick landed in his chest. Savvo curled into a ball, and rolled away, gaining his feet to find himself face-to-face with an almost exact copy of Arin's attacker. Brothers, had to be. His chest was sore, ribs thankfully not broken nor his lungs constricted. He was, however, naked and unready for a fight. Body near done after the drills. A glance told him Arin had shoved off his attacker, and a sudden fear hit his mind as the ex-Breakers wrist flexed in anger.

No.

He lashed out at the brother, missing the kick deliberately, but releasing an almighty scream of anger that rippled down the corridor. The man punched him low, and he went down, wrapping about himself and releasing another shout, this one of exaggerated agony. Arin had turned, eyeing him, his wrist stilled as Savvo mouthed 'no' between the waves of pain.

Orders barked along the corridor, soon joined by the stomp of feet and eventually the polished boots of Sergeant Mereda in his eyeline. More scuffles, and swearing, ensued while he quietly threw up on the floor.

"Why are you messing up my barracks, you little shit?" barked Mereda, the comment thrown at the now restrained Shema newbie. She had always had a way with words.

"This fucker, and that fucker," replied the attacker's brother, "left our mates to die back on Bustan 8."

Savvo, head swimming, pushed himself up onto all fours, coughing out the last of his vomit. "No way," he managed to say.

"Jumped me," spat Arin, standing up, his shirt torn and blood splattered across his face. "When I opened my bloody door."

"Did not, sarge. He took one look at me and knew who I was. Fucker was going to turn rabbit, so I grabbed his shirt and then he went all in. Except he's a fucking wimp as well as a coward." The Shema spat at Arin, the brother growling which appeared to be the limit of his vocabulary.

What the hell was going on?

The grin had left Mereda, her eyes glassy. "I'm not having ill-discipline in the ranks, you hear me? None. You signed your contracts, and know the outcome. Five days behind fucking bars, punishment detail all round for two weeks. And Sparks, bring your weights. And Stan, some clothes. Sheesh, you're fucking ugly naked."

Savvo activated his wetware, clearing his head as he stared up at the regolith concrete ceiling. His chest hurt like shit, his thoughts all over the place while the rock-hard supposed bed, caused his muscles to stiffen.

"I didn't."

"I know," he replied, a sigh leaving his lips first.

"I never hit the bastard first. He asked if I was Sparks, grabbed me and threw me to the floor when I said I was," continued Arin.

"I know. You've told me a hundred times already. I get it. But you were going for ..." Savvo left it there. They'd been over and over it, trying to work out what the hell was happening. If anything, being recognised as Breakers had been the greatest risk. Deserters, and likely, once exposed, imprisoned to await transportation to an Imperial Prison, or worse, to Countess Segfi. But being accused of something they had never – and for that matter – could never have done, was simply weird.

He stood up, the wetware doing just enough to retain his balance as his body complained. He staggered over to the bars of the cell. Leaning against them, he tried to peer around the corner. Unlike a normal prison, they weren't in a room. An open cell, bars sunk into the floor and ceiling with two hard beds and a bucket in the corner. Keeping it simple.

"Hey. Shema bastards," he shouted. "You there?"

Arin arrived next to him, a medpad across his nose similar to the ones Savvo wore on his chest and lower abdomen. Bruising swelled below both eyes. "What you doing? Aren't we in deep enough?"

"I want to know what's going on. It's all wrong. Think, Arin," he gestured around the cell, signalling it was clear. His wetware gave no indication there was much in the way of electronics in the walls or ceiling. Why would you need such things for a grunt's cell? "This isn't right. In fact, it's all wrong. Odd. But we can't risk being questioned any further. They find the wetware we're sporting, then questions start about why it's still active. A dig here and there, and we could be on Segfi's extra special guest list."

He turned away, eyeing the bars. He clattered his hand against it. "Oi, Shema grunts. What the fuck was that all about?"

A shuffle and scrape of boot on floor rolled down the short corridor. "Heh. Mistaken identity, I think. My brother gets very excited very quickly." The tone was remorseful, almost apologetic. Yet there was a hint of humour there.

Savvo waited for the explosion to come.

"Are you shitting me?" shouted Arin, sliding his arm through the bar. "Are you on the level? Mistaken identity? You said my bloody name."

"Lots of sappers called Sparks, you know. Common mistake." There it was again, humour amid the apology. "With that ugly fucking face you got, it was an easy mistake to make."

"You piece of shit," shouted Arin. "I've got a broken nose and five days in the bloody brig followed by more fucking punishment, because my name is Sparks and you've a bad fucking memory."

There was a short chuckle. "That's about it. A shitty memory, and a few extra creds."

Savvo flinched. A glance from Arin confirmed he'd heard the same thing. He shook his head when Arin went to speak again. "Leave it."

Extra creds. A set up. But why?

An alarm went up, and an explosion rocked the building.

CHAPTER 16

SAIM

Rebekah scanned the data pouring into her HUD. Telemetry, atmospheric data, likelihood of death if ZZ3 didn't slow bloody down soon.

"I have access to your life signs in slave mode, Captain. Am I affecting your bodily health?"

"I think it's the potential lack of bodily health, ZZ3," she replied, her stomach heaving as the bot lurched to avoid a rock formation, before swinging past another a mere few centimetres from its blunt, grey edges. There, amid the life sign data, came a big adrenaline spike.

"This is how our glorious leader likes to fly."

"Why am I not the fuck surprised?" she engaged the wetware, saving whatever chems the suit could provide for the landing. At least, she hoped it was a landing. That was the thing with being a pilot. Scaring the shit out of your fellow Marines was fun. Your hands were on the controls, you knew the limits you could push, how close you could hug the ground, how many Gs you could pull swinging around the next bend. The limits. Until someone else was in control, then it got kind of funky. Pilots, the worse passengers ever.

Control freak.

"The hills ahead were formed by the meteor impact, Captain. Beyond those sits the crater, and we will need to dip ... sharply."

Our glorious leader and his pauses.

"I'll be ready," she said, and cracked dual thumbs.

ZZ3 swerved, aiming for a saddle between the regolith hills. The bot kept extremely low, not fifty centimetres above the ground, its movements sudden as it jagged between the rubble. The base's radar and LADAR systems were operational, and logically, keyed in for fast moving missiles as the most likely form of attack. The long-range systems were scattered around the circumference, and they had woven a path slowly at first, only to speed up as they neared the edge for when secondary systems would kick in. Their aim was for speed and shock, to be on the base and negate any missile response by being too close before they could respond. Of course, anti-missile and emplacement guns were still an option.

"Dricks. Reaching the edge in 5, 4, 3, 2, 1 ... Mark," she said into the comms. High above them, the *Sunstar* would be trying out its not-so new point defence cannons on a set of satellites. ZZ3 had infested two outer facing satellites to allow them entry, and in so doing ascertained there were some systems linked into the base defences. They would be guiding at least part of any active response, so an obvious target and potential distraction. "Shoot, destroy and run to the agreed meet."

"Dipping," said ZZ3.

That was an understatement. They hit vertical, straight down the crater face for a few seconds, only Rebekah's training and wetware keeping her conscious as they dived along the rock wall, entering a lazy curve as they neared the crater floor. If they'd flown straight out, they would have been in the meat grinder the noble-officers so loved throwing them into during the Bustan war. Tech then had been the most valued, and the meat inside the suits the diversion.

"I detect a response," stated ZZ3, and data poured into Rebekah's HUD. Alarms, weapons fire – but no actual bullets fired, or missiles released.

"What's happening, ZZ3? Why such a strange response?"

"Deciphering comms," the warbot replied. The base was using an Almaarian code variant Heki and Tremil had cracked a few months back. "That is strange."

"Assessment," she said, heart thudding as the bot jerked to the left then right before lowering into a crack in the rocky surface.

"They are confused by the attack on the satellites. A real attack. Physical damage."

"They think we're one of their pretend bloody armies?" she asked, knowing the answer. "That we're another bloody noble playing silly fucking games. They're in for a shock."

"They are," replied the warbot. Somehow there was an edge of uncertainty to its voice. Rebekah understood. Any attack on the base would be targeting allies. Soldiers they had fought side by side with against the Bustan. Most would have laid down their lives for the colleague next to them, and that could so easily have been her or one of her squad.

"They are hailing."

"Maintain silence. We minimise casualties, ZZ3. This we already agreed. But we need them out. The girls," she left in her own pause, "are crew."

"Incoming," ZZ3 said, and yanked to the right, out of the crack and wove between rock piles that Rebekah instinctively knew were range markers. Cannon fire tore into the ground, dust rising in a streak across the crater. They were near, and she had a full view of the base in her visor. Suited soldiers were running towards their stations, some of the parked transports were beginning to move, their weaponry adjusting. Whether they were full of real ammunition was another matter.

"Actioning switchover in 3, 2, 1 … Mark." Bullets strafed across her suit, pinging off the armoured plate, leaving a scar. More rapped against the warbot as it angled away from the base, heading for one of the train tracks, and beyond that, a lone building. Even the warbot and her suit were no match for half the potential firepower of the base. But they weren't heading for the base.

Rebekah checked over the two other slaved suits, each flagging minor damage as more rounds flew around them. Nothing to worry about. Yet.

"On approach. Releasing slave program in 3, 2, 1 … Mark."

Rebekah sensed the change, and her suit automatically adjusted, immediately entering slowdown as she speared towards the prison walls. A glance at her HUD showed ZZ3 hitting the ground, rolling to its feet and pounding towards the single set of machine guns that hadn't as yet responded to their presence.

She swung about the prison walls, her HUD flagging two incarcerated Marines on the northern side. She adjusted the suit's thrust, slowing down to land on her feet and on the run. By her side, the two other suits mimicked her actions, and they reached the lee of the wall, clear of any potential weapons fire. She removed the charges from a pack, and commanded the suits to wait. She then placed the explosives swiftly against the main doors, setting the timer rather than risking any electronic signal before heading back around the corner.

"Set," she said. "Sit rep, ZZ3." She eyed her HUD, the image of a mangled, multi-barrelled machine gun entering her visor as the bot's limbs tore another apart. On the smooth concrete floor of the gun emplacement there lay a suited soldier, scrabbling to get away from the warbot, fear and recognition on her face.

"Pacified."

"Better believe it," she said. "Fire in the hole."

Her suit's mic muffled the explosion, and she spun in, carbine up. The secondary airlock door had also been blown away, and the dust inside hung in the air, the lower grav taking its time to pull the rock particles towards the ground. Coughing and shouts reverberated within the room, and she broke through the cloud to enter. Two guards were sprawled in opposite corners. Dust lined their faces, hands clawed at their throats as the oxygenated air mixed with the foul carbon dioxide atmosphere.

"No risk," she said to herself, and the butt of her carbine crashed into the first guard. A yell pulled her around, and she fired without hesitation. The low-powered bullet cracked into the man's chest, missing where she had aimed. A rib would likely give out, but hopefully they'd live as they were thrown back into the corner. She commanded the slaved suits inside, and took a mask from a pack, and collected another. After securing the first guard's survival as they lay unconscious, Rebekah strode over to the second, her visor still frosted, and pulled the struggling soldier from the floor and attached the mask. A brief estimate from her HUD gave them a good chance of recovery, and she stepped away, collecting the soldier's handgun. A quick check confirmed her suspicion. Low-powered ammo like hers.

This is really some type of noble game? Fuck.

ZZ3 lurched into view, standing by the entrance, arm guns exposed and ready. "We have multiple transports approaching. In weapons' range in two minutes."

"Copy that. We'll go out the back way. Keep them occupied," she replied. She checked the lockpad, which was a simple card key slot. Logical when the guards were all on rotation. A quick search of the unconscious guard elicited said key, and with a swipe the door spun open. She sent in the slaved units, following afterwards to find a corridor of six cells. The first of which had a couple of dubious looking brothers inside, hands up and against the wall after seeing her carbine and powered armour. Ignoring them, she reached the end cell and two peeved looking crew who eyed her armour with trepidation.

"Knock, knock," she said. "Prisoner transfer."

"You have got to be kidding me," said Arin. "What did we do this time?"

Rebekah unfrosted her visor, but hid her face from the imprisoned brothers. "You mean apart from being an arsehole with verbal diarrhoea? No time, the base is up in arms and heading this way."

"What the hell?" he said, but stepped back at his captain's glare.

She swiped the card, and the cell door slid back. Ordering the slaved suits inside, she checked on ZZ3's feed to find the warbot engaged in a stand-off with the transports. At least one was carrying live ammo, and dust filled the atmosphere around the bot's defensive position behind a concrete wall.

"Couldn't you just have requested a chat? A negation of contract and kind of collected us with some candy for the journey?" said Arin, half-inside the navy suit.

"You actually read those contracts? Short of selling your soul, you are here until the terms are up. No. And we're in a hurry," she replied.

"Hurry?" asked Savvo, attaching his helmet with a click. The systems fired up, and his voice entered her comms. "What's happened?"

"Long story, no time. They took the twins," she said the bare minimum, even thinking about it would tie her emotions up in knots. Lead her to lash out at those outside who were not involved in creating her turmoil.

"Took? How? Who?" Arin's words tumbled into her comms as his helmet engaged.

Arin's evident anxiety, the stress threaded into his words, threatened to trigger her own. Rebekah's second-in-command came to her rescue.

"Shut the fuck up," ordered Savvo, a hard edge to his voice. "Focus on getting out."

"Savvo, give your new friends the last mask. They'll have to share. Arin," she threw him the pack of remaining explosive. "Do what you do second best and blow us a new door."

Savvo nodded, his face, as shown by her suit's systems, twisted into a worried frown. Knowing about the twins was a double-edged sword, but she needed them to be swift, at their peak. Not questioning. Arin attached the explosives.

"Hey, you two," Arin pointed back to the other cell. "Next time we meet, I get to break your ugly noses. And I was a sapper, remember? So Sparks is out of here. Fire in the bloody hole. Duck you fuckers!" The wall shattered outwards, dulling only briefly the sharp chatter of gunfire. Savvo was out first, on point as always, carbine up and synced. Rebekah followed, signalling ZZ3 while Arin flipped a middle finger and followed behind.

"We need to hurry," stated ZZ3, rounding the corner at pace, ricochets pinging. "Permission to slave suits."

"Granted," replied all three in unison, confirming within their HUDs with an eye-click.

"This is going to be close," said the warbot. Whether it meant the pursuit, or to the ground was a moot point. Apparently, it was both, as they started off steady, keeping the prison building between them and the transport weapons. "Drones incoming."

Chapter 17

SAIM

"Closing within thirty metres," said ZZ3. "Down to 25% fuel capacity. I must attempt to leave the moon in the next sixty seconds if I am to have enough to reach escape velocity."

Rebekah flicked through her menu. "Dricks, come back. Urgent."

"Here, captain. *Solar Flare* transponder engaged."

Relief at her ex-captain's voice slithered along her spine. "Activate intercept protocol 3C. It will link the ship to my suit and manoeuvre into position to collect us. PDCs active."

"PDCs? But ..." There was a crack in her voice. No one wanted to harm their ex-allies.

"Drones, Dricks. Just drones, but we're screwed if they lock on – and they're close. Too fucking close." She checked her HUD again, noting the connection protocol had completed between the suit and ship, communicating their position. "Take us up when ready, ZZ3."

"Now," the warbot replied and pulled up sharply. The stress on their bodies compensated to some degree by their suits, the rest by wetware as they were forced to engage their chips. The warbot kept the curve steep, and accelerated away from the planet, while the weak grav resisted its efforts. Rebekah's mind numbed, fog rising despite the chem stimulus and drew in as much help from the suit as it would allow. Her stress monitor hit orange, and flickered back and forth into the red as they breached the edge of the thin atmosphere.

Gunfire spewed around them, the pursuit drones releasing full payloads as they reached the upper limits of their flight capability. Every jolt the warbot made at this speed rattled them about until their suits compressed to hold them still. Rounds pinged off the warbot.

"Warning," stated the bot, and that was all they got. The slave program suddenly ended, and the bot pulled them in, wrapping arms around as it spun about. Squashed in against the warbot's chest, they felt every strike as ZZ3's back armour reverberated under heavy calibre gunfire. "Fuel expenditure critical. Back armour at 20%."

"Throw us wide," said Rebekah. "Before the next volley."

"I—"

"That's an order," she shouted.

"1 and mark," replied the bot, and they spun away as the robotic limbs flung them to the sides.

She didn't have the time to check on the others, engaging her suit's orientation program with the moon. The drones flagged below, the distance probably at the extremes of their weaponry, except they were on the edge of space and the forces at play less. She could see the flare of their guns, and the swift flight of the cannon rounds as they hurtled their way.

An alarm sounded. A proximity warning, and the *Sunstar* appeared in the corner of her visor, the aft guns staring her way, while the upper emplacement pummelled the drones. A welcome sight, with most of the drones' weapons fire rattling against the thicker plate of their ship.

But not all.

Her HUD flagged, but it was Arin that caught her attention.

"Noooo."

Rebekah dropped into the cockpit chair, her short, sweat-stained hair plastered against her scalp. With the top half of her suit discarded, she activated the navcom, eyes roaming over the data feed.

"Engaging half-burn," she said. The baron had maintained a single combat ship's presence, a refitted patrol ship that would have taken them down in seconds if it had been in position. They had timed their run for its sweep of the transport lanes to the way station. The distance enough to give them a head start. The other two craft in orbit were for supply and transport. She suspected the latter had more powerful PDCs than on the manifest, but they were far from combat ready and slow to react.

"We clear?" asked Savvo, dropping in by her side and running over the sensor data. He nodded as he did so.

"Clear. We hardly did enough to warrant a pursuit," she replied, a crack to a single thumb expressing her worry. "Hopefully this baron cares about protecting what he has more than what he's lost. Track the patrol ship, see what it does."

"Will do. You'd better check in on ZZ3." Savvo looked her way. "Took a beating at the end. Arin's in a mess."

She pursed her lips, then rubbed at her nose, trying to hide her mood. "For all his words, it's the twins he'll be in a fucking mess about. As will we all." She stood, squeezing his shoulder on the way past. "That and we just screwed up our cover. At least we won't have an Enforcer to worry about. Just a countess." She left him with that, feeling bad about piling it all on. But that's what second-in-commands were for. To take the shit off her shoulders when the weight got too much. Except it hadn't. Just made it worse, in fact, knowing they all suffered.

"The *Winkal* is heading for the moon, to Saim. Course adjustments indicate they either haven't seen us, or have been ordered there," said Savvo, his voice dry. Hoarse.

"Then we have some time. Plot a course for the asteroid belt. For Karal. Not direct, but keep us moving that way." She left, heart heavy as she passed Tremil's cabin and then Heki's. Unable to do much beyond praying they were safe, and in a semblance of control. Once whoever had them realised their prize, there may be no way to get them back. Butcher or not, why would you risk letting such potential go? After four years, they were now 'assets' once again. Tools. Weapons.

How to mount a rescue when we don't know who took them, or where they are?

By asking those who do.

We were set up.

They knew about the Butcher, or at the very least the AI, and came for it. Only ZZ3 stood in their way, a surprise when they were probably expecting Hendricks at most.

She walked into the workshop bay, the 3D printer humming away in the corner, piles of shiny metal and armour plate to one side that Hendricks was sorting through. Arin was on his knees, the upper half of ZZ3 lying face down on the deck, back exposed, its hull ragged.

"That tickle?" asked Arin.

"Define tickle. It is not in Asham's experience," replied the warbot.

"Why am I not surprised?" a chuckle left Arin's lips, though there seemed little heart in it. He glanced up as Rebekah's magboots clicked and released as she approached.

With a sigh she glanced at some of the complex exposed innards of what was essentially a tank on legs. Except this one had a mind of its own. An evolving one she couldn't help feel they had abused beyond its limits.

"Is it bad?" she asked, wincing at how poor the words sounded. Not 'is our beloved warbot going to be okay'.

Arin's lips quivered a little, but she had been right, his worries lay beyond just the warbot. "ZZ3 reports minimal internal damage that if I touch will probably make things a little worse. All systems are operational, and I can tweak the software as workarounds for some of the minor damaged parts. One limb has sheered off, but we recovered that, and I can make a new joint system using the others as an example."

"Tell the captain," said Hendricks, and held up the stiff metal plate he was holding.

Arin shrugged. "ZZ3 has suggested we adapt his outer hull. Use thicker plating to replace the damaged armour, rather than try to match what's there. I'd struggle anyway."

"Why's that an issue?"

ZZ3's lights glowed, and the head shifted to face her. "Our glorious leader is worried it would look mismatched and ugly," Arin guffawed slightly in the background, "in reality it would be weightier and use more energy and fuel under gravity. I would be a little slower, though my servos are graded for the extra strain. However, as a shield, it would have additional benefits."

"ZZ3 means we seem to be getting shot at a lot," said Hendricks.

"Running away a lot more than we used to," added Arin. He looked over to Rebekah, his eyes red raw. "And when we go get the girls, that's likely to go up a notch. I've listened to Dricks. There's no way that was a militia assault. Not pirates, either, or salvagers with no idea who they were up against."

"What makes you think we're going in gun blazing?" she asked, her heart straining as the sub-engineer laid out his willingness to step into whatever dangers lay ahead for the sake of two girls.

"Cos that's what we do. We break things, and whoever has Heki and Tremil, they're going to need a microscope to put them back together." Arin glanced over to Hendricks whose face was set grim, her eyes locked on the deck as she nodded. "And tweezers. Those really small ones with the needle point ends. Probably a dustpan and brush just in case."

Rebekah turned to Hendricks; her fingers balled tight into a fist to try to keep all her roiling emotions at bay. Her ex-captain lifted the armour plate up off the deck, and looked at her straight, the hardness back in her eyes from her old days as a squadron officer.

"We're all in. All the way, whatever the cost. Duty, loyalty. They are part of us, and us them. As much members of the Wrecking Squad as any other. No one gets left behind." Muscles straining, she dropped the plate at Arin's side. "So no pussy-footing around thinking you're doing whatever needs to be done alone."

ZZ3's lights pulsed. "They are crew."

"How far would you go, though?" she said. "Because they have what we prize the most, and want the Butcher and the fucking battle AI he's melded with. They want what it knows. What it can do. Whether that's to make a freak-show out of their own soldiers, or reprogram them with his fucking bastardised wetware, or to fight a fucking ..."

The hold went silent. Arin, Hendricks, even ZZ3 staring at her.

"... war."

The shock of her words reverberated about her mind. War. A battle AI, illegal tech, treasonous. The Enforcers would be seeking it to suppress the AI under the direction of the Court and the Emperor. If the mysterious Mr Duboit had known they had it, then he had every opportunity to take it when they were docked in Karal. So why not? Yes, the Enforcers liked to act behind the scenes, draw the least attention from the lowlifes. Subtle strikes that brought nobles to heel without too much fuss, or attention on the political games of the Court.

Instead, they had been lured onto a mission with parameters and tactics dictated by their handler. Dividing the squad, leaving the ship, barely protected as far as the assault team knew. The fact they were refitting with the PDCs was a happy coincidence, with Davina conjuring up an old set in next to no time to facilitate the attack.

But why not on Karal? To keep his pretence as Duboit in place?

Or to hide the identity of whoever came for the Butcher. War. What nobles love the most. More honour in real blood and conquest than the war games Savvo and Arin had just been extricated from.

"War," she said again, looking to each of her crew present. "Fuck."

CHAPTER 18

Erikson sucked in a long breath, thumb fiddling with the Enforcer's ring, spinning it about as he stared at the blank screen. Life had taken a sharp left turn. Sudden, unexpected, though if he were honest, he had pushed so hard investigating the Breakers and what turned out to be the *Scourge*, something was bound to have happened. Though being under the countess' wing was perhaps not where he expected to be. Nor in the middle of what looked like high treason. Not only a powerful noble, or some group within the Court, hiding the *Scourge* away, but now desperately trying to recover the AI while shifting the evidence to point Segfi's way.

"Damn," he whispered, fingers now rapping on the desk. The flight back to Almaar had been filled with tension. His handler had taken badly to the attack on his safe house. Accusations flying about poor security, potential leaks, and basically how useless Erikson must be to allow himself to be nearly caught like that. The countess had instigated a clean up of her interference, the condition of his house put down to a combination of deliberate gas leak and high explosives. Helped by the traces of chem charges, and the Enforcer's need to keep the attack quiet and out of the ears of other nobles.

Perhaps he shouldn't have asked about retribution for the Lundstroms. That, apparently, was a step too far. The androgynous electronic tirade switched to threatening his downfall, something he'd already assumed was in the offing. But his bargain with Countess Segfi was clear. He was to maintain his decorum, keep his role as long as he could, and deflect any flak coming her way when possible. All the while, arranging for the Breakers to be on mission and separated from their ship so she could acquire the AI containment unit. That would keep it out of treasonous hands and give her team chance to investigate and hopefully discover any clues as to who hid the *Scourge* and enabled General Asham's work.

All went well, until it didn't. A hint that something had gone wrong lay in the time lag between the assault team's attack, and this conversation. Days that left him on edge.

He spun his ring again, and with a sigh eyed the slate, waiting. The singed but functional Senti comms was attached to the back. Some good news at least.

The slate lit up and shimmered before an unfamiliar face appeared. Young, eyes sparkling, blonde hair swept back and completely false. On the other end was the countess, or her proxy, and taking no risks.

The voice was disguised too. "A failure," stated the holo.

"What? They were on board with the mission. I had confirmation that two of the four had been recruited and were on Saim. And Khan was en route to Shema." He frowned, unable to quite work out what could have gone wrong. Segfi's assault teams were ruthless and efficient, he had witnessed that firsthand. The best.

"All true. But they had a warbot. One from the old days. You know, a battle tank on legs that we were not prepared for. I have to say, Mr Erikson, it was quite impressive. I must remember to pass on our thanks to the research and development team." The holo's smile was tight, no amusement there despite the comment.

"So, what now? They still have the containment unit? The AI? Blow them out of space, perhaps, to make sure no one else gets it?" Erikson raked through his mind, trying to think of what would come next. He didn't put much store by the crew's intelligence other than Khan. Would she put together the pieces and work out they had been duped, and that he was complicit? Of course she would. He had set the parameters tight. The where and the how of the mission.

Once the assault team had confirmed the AI was present, they were to question the one they called Hendricks. Strip any memories from her mind, rip out any knowledge she may have had of the *Scourge*, any clue as to who had hidden the ship, before disposing of her and eventually the rest of the crew. Burned.

Of course, if the containment unit hadn't been there, the same would have happened. Only seeking who they had sold it to, or where it was hidden. Either way, they were disposable. Their link to Segfi, the stolen wetware and the *Scourge* a black mark against the countess' name that needed eradicating before it muddied her search for treason amid the Court.

But now?

"Well, I have *you*, Mr Erikson. An Enforcer with *balls*. Apparently, these Breakers like surprises. Squirrelling away secrets, which, as you know, I do not like. On board were two girls of Bustan origin. Let us assume they are precious to this Captain Khan, shall we? Why else would they be aboard, after all. Now we need to find out just how desperate they are to get them back." The blonde hair flicked to the side, swishing about the slate's screen. An odd gesture, but Erikson assumed it was the holo's attempt to hide the intake of a cigarette and the subsequent billow of smoke.

"An exchange?" He paused, thinking through the consequences of what the holo had said. There was more between the words, he was certain. But either way, things had gone badly. "Are you proposing I get involved in this?

If they have any common sense, they will already know they were set up. And by me."

The strange hair flick happened again. "Exactly. You remain useful to me, and therefore the Court, as we root out treason. What an Enforcer should be doing. Yes, they will know. But that gives you power, Mr Erikson. It means there's no other way forward for them. If they want those children, then the means is through you. And, of course, the only thing we want in exchange is the containment unit. The battle AI. A bonus would be any knowledge they scoured from the *Scourge* about who may be involved, but I can live without that as long as I know we have that foul Bustan tech under lock and key."

He thought on that, his ring spinning, skin raw beneath. There would be zero trust. But then he had an Incini. And pulling the countess out of this crisis situation would raise his standing, and from there huge potential to be centre stage when the Court and the Emperor got wind of what the countess had achieved.

"Agreed. I will need to use my Incini as a go-between. To set the terms. If she is aware I am rooting out treason by acquiring the unit, the Directorate would agree with my actions." At least, that's what should happen.

"Connors?" said the holo, the faintest of smiles on the false lips. Erikson nodded. "Yes, yes. I can see your reasoning, though keep my name from her ears, Mr Erikson. Loose lips could bring down my investigation and let such scum go free from the Emperor's wrath. Understand?" Again, the hair flick. One that took some time to resolve.

"Where and when?" he asked, trying to work out where the *Sunstar* could be by now.

"I'm thinking somewhere remote, so if we have to act a little more forcefully to retrieve the AI, there are fewer places to run." She deployed a flat smile, one the holo mimicked well. A viciousness there.

And fewer witnesses. Less chance whoever hid the Scourge *gets wind.*

"So, I'm thinking one of the moons about Trazor. Empty. Perhaps Daphene would suffice? As for the when, negotiate that with Khan. Within the next two weeks, though. Any longer risks the discovery of our plans. And do not take a *no*, Mr Erikson. Understand? Explain the weight of the Enforcers, your reach and that of the noble who has their precious girls. Should they choose to run, I may have to blow them up and all the evidence with it. That will not do. I have worked hard to put an end to this ... this sedition." More smoke blowing, he assumed, and then the eyes peered straight at him, demanding his agreement. Expecting it.

"I understand," was all he managed under that gaze.

"I have a breadcrumb tracker on their ship, left by my assault team in case an opportunity arose, or they decided to offload the containment unit. After breaking the rest of the crew out from Saim, they were heading to Karal when the signal stopped. I'm guessing they may have something stashed about Minx they want. I can't for a moment consider they would be heading there to question your Incini about a failed mission and two missing girls."

"Ah."

Davina rolled over, hand coming down on the alarm to shut off its incessant demand she wake up. With a yawn, last night's dreams fluttered into her mind. The void, blood-speckled on her helmet visor. Hendricks' lifeline tugging at her back while her lungs and throat begged for mercy. Then the girls' voices echoing in her ear, offering hope. Those moments when she could have cut Hendricks free, increased her own chances of survival.

A shiver ran down her spine, accompanied by an involuntary cough. Ghost pain wracked her chest, pain where there wasn't any. Just a memory.

Heki's sallow face and blue lips.

She padded across the room, used the bathroom, brushed her teeth and ignored the face in the mirror. It would reveal her true self, the one she was hiding, possibly running from in her daily routine. With a desperate need to feel clean, she chose to shower. Usually that was saved for after work. Washing off her sins, the taint of both the real Mr Duboit and the fake one who now dictated her life.

Tremil's sunken eyes, arms forced into a spacesuit, helmet locked home.

After scrubbing herself, she towelled dry and extricated her hair from the safety of a shower cap. With a shake of the head, she let it fall naturally before gripping the side of the wash bowl.

Her eyes rose to the mirror.

Blue-lipped, blood running down her chin, she stared back. The faint sheen of a visor between her and the glass. Over her shoulders two young girls desperate to be loved, to be needed. Overpowering in their intent.

"Damn," she said, blinking the image away. Rubbing her eyes. "Damn Erikson. And all of this."

What he'd asked was to negotiate for the AI the Breakers had stashed in their hold. He had made no play about it being 'illegal tech', no hiding what he knew. She had almost expected to be played, but the bluntness he had shown when delivering the last mission for Rebekah and her crew had become a bludgeon.

And this was it. That moment described by the Minister's agent, Gerent. She had first thought Erikson to be seeking evidence on Duboit. Attempting to access the *Scourge,* find what was on board. And the *Maverick*'s demise had not put an end to it. Whatever had happened on the next mission had left the girls in his hands, or those of whoever he was working with, and the desire for that containment unit even greater. More desperate. A red flag that should be passed by the Directorate. Except she had been asked not to. Asked? Does an agent of the Minister ask?

"Damn," she repeated, resting her head against the mirror's surface, the voice of the *Maverick*'s *bastardo* ringing in her ears. Enjoying the moment as he abandoned an Incini to her death.

Abandoned.

Was there still some hope? Could she find a way to save the girls if not the crew? The silence could help that, at least until Gerent lifted the embargo on her evidence.

Her slate pinged and with a sigh she pushed herself from the mirror, refusing to look into its depths. The message was from Erikson in the guise of Duboit. A date and time. Rebekah was coming, riding a tide of anger and anguish.

"Fuck."

CHAPTER 19

Fear.
Dread.
Hunger.
Thirst.
Rage.
Sickness.
Lonely. Lonely. Lonely.
Empty.
Help me.
Rebekah?

Footsteps rang along the corridor, echoing against the polished concrete as if they were the only steps on the moon. Purposeful, urgent, expectant. Functional shoes, metal soled that gently gripped and released the magnetised floor when just enough force was applied. But still tiring. Exhausting for those who were old, ill, yet determined to keep up appearances. A suck upon the elegant cigarette stick that contained her medication, a gentle release of billowing smoke the moon's scrubbers would endure removing from the atmosphere beneath the regolith dome.

Letting the pain ease, though it would swiftly return, she stopped beside the sealed doorway, eyes glancing over the sign above the door. It glowed green. Entry allowed. Of course, they knew she was coming, so it had better be. The words written in LEDs declared the room as Clone Development Room 2. The countess cricked her neck, the pop of ligaments loud in her ears and either ignored by her entourage or unheard.

"Well?" she said, the word forceful despite the pain in her lungs.

The white-coated scientist stepped in at her side. Professor Irons B.Sc., M.Sc., blah, blah, blah. A man with the morals of a warbot and the curiosity of a small child. Tear it apart, see what it does, repeat just in case you missed something. Just the type of inhuman bastard who would work for her hidden away at the fringes of the settled system. Him, and twenty others just as amoral, though most were enjoying the creds as well as the breaking of rules that restricted the limits of their research.

Irons' retina and wrist scanned the lockpad, the metal door sliding open to reveal the lab. It was dark, the lights inside providing a soft green illumination. She knew better than to ask for the harsh lights her old eyes preferred and let the scientist lead the way. Inside were twelve clear bulbous tubes, and in those clear sacs that pulsed softly in a manner she found simultaneously fascinating and repulsive as they mimicked human wombs.

"This batch is developing well," said Irons, striding over to stand between the two end tubes. One hand rested on each. "Sample 2.7 shows promise, and we believe we have upped the longevity to within acceptable parameters."

"Acceptable?" she asked.

"Four years as estimated via previous empirical data. And 2.8 possibly fifty percent longer than that after applying the refined splicing." In the glow of the sickly green light, the scientist's face beamed. She found it horrifying. The Court named her Warmonger for all her efforts to win the Bustan war, and gain revenge for their initial attack. Yet here stood a true monster. One she had nurtured in the shadow of Asham. A purveyor of freaks at her call. If only she didn't need to do so.

"And how long to grow each batch?" she enquired, ignoring the man's consternation as she drew on her cigarette and emitted a stream of smoke.

With a barely concealed sneer, he strode over and upped the atmosphere scrubbers while answering. "Six months."

Countess Segfi chose to ignore his insolence, and approached the two containers, scanning the thin wombs and curled forms inside. Both were women, naked, innocent. Their minds empty of thought other than the base impulses for survival. Nutrition, induced sleep, oxygen, growth. Now, fight or flight? That pathway to survival was a completely different matter.

"So, we cull the other batches and focus on these, professor," she stated, nostrils flaring as the infuriating scientist glowered. He had the good sense to do so while staring at the clones, but it was there.

"I would prefer not to," he said through gritted teeth. "I have only just got to grips with Asham's adapted wetware. The recovered batch has some interesting tweaks I would like to *test*."

She let out another pillow of smoke, drawing the moment out, enjoying his distaste. "Agreed," she finally said suppressing the phlegm rising in her throat and the incessant need to cough. "But these new clones are a priority. I want the factory up and running. And your side project ...?"

"The resourcing is minimal, Countess. The results are admittedly poor, but it all adds to the research." He looked away, and then towards his feet, unbonding the soles over and over.

Countess Segfi allowed herself a predatory smile. Her spies had told of his obsession with Asham's failed hybrid research, but the time spent was tolerable and kept him and his team on a short leash. Side projects fed academia when the boredom set in. A motivation to keep going. Besides, if he succeeded in breeding a sane hybrid, well …

"Okay Irons. I won't initiate a kill order. But I want my clones in the growth chambers ASAP, and the wetware ready for initiation. Understand? Six months I want specialised units at my beck and call, and if not, it will be you I will hold responsible."

Irons managed a nod having finally got control of his ridiculous emotions. She turned away, leaving behind a trail of smoke and rejoined her entourage. Her elite guards, the 1st and High, awaited her with steely eyes behind their visors. And, of course, the new specialist scientist she had brought along for a first visit to his dual charges.

Without a word they walked on, entering the automated factory Irons would soon be ramping up to full capacity. Rows and rows of bulbous but mostly empty tubes, autobot nursemaids, integrated medbots, synth-skin printers. Everywhere but the nearest corner waiting to grow a huge batch of humans, clones. Blank and ready for programming.

She gripped the balustrade overlooking the human growth factory and chuckled, smoke slipping between her teeth. Asham had seen her vision and found it distasteful. But it was efficient, eradicated doubt, reduced the uncertainty of command. No longer requiring drugs and the suppressive elements of the wetware that blunted the edge of combat, numbed the soldier to the repetitive death. They would die at her command. But more than that. Their minds programmed how she wished. No more square pegs in round mission parameters. Now she could shape their skills and send the perfect soldier to carry out her orders. The possibilities were endless, *if* they had a war to fight.

"I do so like this," she said, the comment pointedly ignored by her entourage as she moved further along the walkway to the waiting lift. They dropped through two floors, emerging into a carbon copy corridor. Lights blinked on as her elite disembarked, and she followed behind, enjoying the silence. Like a catacomb, her long-dead husband would have said. A tomb.

Of course, it had to be.

They reached the strange, discoloured wall straddled on either side by newly embedded doors coated in what she hoped was an effective barrier. Otherwise, this may be a short visit. For all of them.

The clatter of metal-soled shoes echoed behind, and another white-coated minion ran to meet with her group. Her guards didn't flinch, they knew this technician. The only one still standing after a case of base stupidity coated the walls of the cell in torn skin, blood and saliva.

"Countess," puffed the middle-aged woman, her lungs heaving after her rush down the corridor. "I wasn't expecting you so soon."

"No, Illiana. I keep my schedule quiet for obvious reasons. How are our new guests?"

"Pacified. Drugged. The screaming ..." she tailed off, clear distaste on her face. Normally it would annoy the countess, but this woman had steel running through her spine. She could allow a little leeway, even though the children were an asset. No longer human from the moment she had been made aware of them. Tools she needed. Had long wanted and thought lost.

"I understand. Can I see them?"

Illiana nodded, and wrist scanned a sensor by the nearest embedded door. One section of the discoloured wall phased into a pseudo-screen. The cell was mainly clean, except for the patches of blood and gore dotted around that the cleaning bots had missed. Two beds stood at opposite sides of the room, and strapped to them a pair of girls in striped skinsuits. Emerging from them were multiple tubes, two for food and hydration, the others for the waste they would produce. Encased about their heads some of the most illegal tech in Almaar outside of the Emperor's Imperial Prisons. A psionic suppressant. Illegal because it meant you had some form of psionic who required suppressing. Rare and coveted, and so few survived beyond the first week of captivity without the tech. The bastard Bustans had begun to breed their own, hence her intervention on Bustan 7 when the intelligence came her way.

The Breakers.

"Why the drugs?" the countess asked, stepping closer, drawing on her cigarette stick as she peered at one of the girls.

"They are strong. Before she died, Dr Trequan believed their potential was beyond anything we've met before. The pacifiers, the psionic masks, barely contain their projected emotions and if they sense a presence ... Well, Dr Trequan clawed her own throat out, and the other technicians, hmm, they were utterly unprepared." Illiana shrugged her shoulders. "I know of no other way until the new doctor arrives."

Segfi raised an eyebrow to her companion who stood watching the girls with a bland expression. As if deciding what to have as a snack, rather than feast on the banquet of possibilities she was presenting.

"This is Dr Henshaw. He will be leading any further work with the Bustan twins. However, he has a job to do first. If you will open up for us, Illiana, please."

The technician blinked. "Are you sure, Countess? I don't mean to be rude but ..."

"Oh, not me. I'm here for what happens afterwards."

"Open up," stated the doctor, clearly impatient. He collected a metal-lined box from one of the elite soldiers. "You are delaying the work. Much to do. Give me a rundown of the drugs you used, the timings and I need an analysis on the latest brain pattern, especially Gamma and Beta cycles, understand?"

Illiana nodded and fished into her lab pocket to produce a well-used slate. She swiped and handed it over after selecting the up-to-date information. The countess smiled, smoke slipping out between her lips. As they talked through the girls' current state, she eyed the two other members of her entourage. Two young females waited below the mess of hair and blank expressions. Clones. Experiments with no soul or functioning thought other than base instinct. They wore striped skinsuits and would soon be sporting the latest in human designed wetware inside their skulls. Soon.

The doctor and Illiana entered the room, their conversation now muted as they moved between the twin Bustan girls. Henshaw kept referring to the slate, and back to each of the empaths, his blank face registering the barest flicker of a smile as reality knocked down the walls of disbelief he had built over years of experimentation.

Yes. We can't risk losing them.

Far too valuable

Henshaw started an animated conversation with the technician, and it wasn't long before they had his box of scientific tricks open and were discussing its contents. Illiana's worries were quickly allayed, and they both peered back at the countess. They gave a brief nod and went back to work.

Fear.

Loneliness.

Pain. So much pain.

Hate and pain.

And blood.

I see flesh, hear screams, taste dread.

Rebekah ... don't abandon me.

I need your arms.

Your touch.
My mind ... slips.

CHAPTER 20

Rebekah sucked in a breath, holding it, counting to ten. It was no good, she needed the release. The habitual stress reliever. She cracked both thumbs, the ritual pops helping her calm.

Karal loomed. M4 and the docks waiting for them. Inside, a multitude of repair autobots and dock workers scurried to ensure the next mining ship or recovery run was prepped and ready. Part of their routine, as it had been for three years. She doubted she would ever get to see this view again. And it hurt. In a way, the Minx asteroid family was her home from home. A place to escape the pressure of keeping her additional crew hidden and their secrets close.

Thoughts of chocolate impinged on her mind. The fierceness of love. Of being needed.

She blinked away the errant tear, said nothing. Just stared as the *Sunstar* slid between the multitudinous scaffolding nested about M4. The platforms that awaited the next expensive shipment of PMG from the 'field ready to fill the cargo holds of the Karal autoships.

Savvo said nothing. He was undoubtedly experiencing the same emotions behind a stony expression. His thoughts likely on Nicky, what could have been. She had listened to his words, sensed his emotions, his anguish. That chance she had wanted to offer all of them, a new life, now lost under the hound master's whip and subsequent betrayal.

"Fuck," she whispered. Best word she could come up with.

"Agreed," said Savvo, his voice barely a whisper.

"You ready for this?" crackled over the internal comms. Hendricks' voice stern, expectant. "Because if you're not …"

"Tough shit," they all replied.

"Docking now," she said. "Provision up. Whatever we can food and water wise. Scrubbers, filters, the lot. Dried mushrooms if you have to, but I want this ship ready for the long haul, you understand? We're getting them back, and after that … after that I'm dropping you useless bastards off and finding a nice quite hole to hunker down in. You listening to me, Wrecking Squad? I can't fucking hear you."

"Sorry, El Capitaine. You're breaking up. Right after 'we're getting them back' it all went kind of crackly," said Arin.

"Fuzzy," interjected Hendricks.

Savvo nodded by her side. "All I got was a load of captain's bullshit. Nothing new there."

"Dickheads," she said, suppressing the smile that threatened to bubble to the surface among the love she had for her crew. "All of you, you hear? D-I-C-K-H-E-A-D-S. Dickheads." She spun the chair, avoiding Savvo's gaze, unable to meet his eyes. Was it guilt, or love? That deep well of friendship that wanted to erupt, kick him and the rest off the ship while she rode out alone to rescue the girls and then off into the supernova sunset.

"What you going to say?" he asked, almost, but not quite, grabbing her arm.

She stopped, thumb cracks echoing in the small cockpit. "She warned us. Warned me. Blatantly said she can't be trusted with keeping us safe. If she had spoken of the containment unit to the Enforcer beforehand, I think all this would have ended months ago. They knew because of the *Maverick*, their second sortie. And yes, Davina's complicit in setting us up. But we can't be surprised at that. Won't stop me from ripping her wetware out through her ears, however."

"I didn't think it would."

She looked back then, glancing over her shoulder at Savvo's sullen eyes and lips. "I'm not sure how long we can stay. When I'm back, take the chance to see Nicky. Kick those two lovebirds off the ship and make sure they have a good night."

"It could be our last chance," he stated, glancing at the deck. "Better make it a good one."

Hands shaking, she engaged the wetware, taking full advantage of the induced neurotransmitters despite the long-term effects of prolonged use having never been fully tested.

Life is full of risk. For some more than others.

She palmed the lock, waiting for a response from the screen. It would be Davina, she had no doubt. Duboit's efforts would be meaningless to her. The trust, the little there was, shattered. With Davina the written, contractual phrases would have purpose, and in there lay the Incini trap.

Perfect hair, a calm face and sharp eyes appeared on the screen. No words passed. A silence that hung heavy between them, but the door clicked open. Rebekah entered, senses heightened, noting the arrays and usual preparations were in place. Even the expensive robo guard disguised as a lamp was on duty. Every word they spoke would be recorded, analysed and shared with their handler.

And she was fucked if she was going to be careful about it.

Rebekah threw herself into the chair before the Incini's desk, legs flung over one side, sideways on and refusing to look the witch in the eye.

Again, the silence. And she refused to break that, too. An irony, some would say. Fuck them.

Davina shoved her slate aside, clasping hands on the desk, a stylus between them. "I—" she began.

Rebekah smashed her foot into the arm of the chair, shattering the wood. She stood, picked up what remained and threw it against the office door. It refused to break, so she sauntered over to hurl it again against Mr Duboit's wall until only firewood remained. She tossed the remaining pieces onto the luxuriant carpet, and crossed her arms, eyes locked onto the Incini with a furious curl to her lips.

"Let me finish that sentence for you," she growled. "*I* am a traitorous, selfish bitch who destroys the lives of others when the Directorate and their tenets dictate. That about fucking right?" Rebekah squeezed her arms in tight, finger pulsing against her biceps.

"In your eyes, that's a fair assessment." Davina coughed, gathering a tissue from a box and repeating the involuntary reflex. "I'll give you that. This," she gestured to the pile of firewood, "won't solve anything."

"Solves my first problem. Keeping you alive long enough to hear the next pile of lies."

Davina snorted, half-a-laugh in there somewhere. "That's appreciated. Are you ready to listen? Your missing crew are alive. I am tasked with ensuring they remain alive and returned to the *Sunstar*."

Rebekah didn't trust herself to answer. Of course they were alive. Assets were no good dead. What state they were in was another matter. She shifted her standing position enough to hint she was listening, her head now tilted, the scowl still present.

"In return for the containment unit you apparently took from the *Scourge*," finished Davina.

"Go on."

"Nothing more to say. I am to draw up the conditions of the exchange. Safety guarantees inked under Incini tenets." Rebekah made to speak, a snide remark upon her lips when Davina raised her hands to quieten her. "He, Duboit, doesn't want to risk the unit being damaged. Therefore, a safe exchange, away from any other interested parties and under Incini tenets could see both parties reach a satisfactory conclusion."

"Fuck," said Rebekah, releasing the grip on her arms and running sweaty fingers through her short hair. She released a glare at the Incini, only to receive a tight, unflinching smile in return. "What's to say they aren't breaking into the *Sunstar* as we speak?"

"I am unaware of why, but my own supposition based on analysis of the Breaker's past behaviour, current situation and aggressive tendencies, would hint that you have rigged the unit, and likely the ship, to blow."

Rebekah had to admit she was right.

"Only what we had to hand. Enough to destroy the entire docks and if we time it right, M1 with it. Debris is a swine in space." She mimed an explosion, Sabier's shocked face coming to mind as Savvo drilled a bullet into her brain. She wondered what he'd have done at this point.

"My problem is *you*. Davina Connors. Incini. I don't trust you, despite your title. And that makes all this so much harder." She pushed her tongue up to the roof of her mouth, suppressing the words desperate to pour out. "I won't agree to anything that puts my remaining crew at risk, understand?"

"And you understand, that should you or your crew break the agreement, your rights are forfeit."

Rebekah nodded, then spat on the floor, walking away. "I'll be in touch."

The beer eased down her throat, soothing the rawness of the flesh but not her mind. A glance at her slate screen reflected a face equally as raw. Eyes red-rimmed below sweat-stained hair, dark bags sagging, wrinkles about her mouth she couldn't remember having. She shoved it away. Right now, the captain should be back on board her ship, reassuring her crew everything would work out.

Fuck.

She slurped the last dregs, and slammed the glass down, heading for the exit. She reached the doorway when a familiar face passed through the concourse crowd. Bald-headed and clearly unaware his nemesis was behind. Anger welled up, and she had no intention of suppressing it. She charged into the crowd, eyes on Victor Goncho's back, lava running through her veins, reasons sweating from her pores. A glance behind and he had her in his sights, the initial anger quickly switching to fear as he drank in her intent. He sped up, shoving those in front out of his way.

A flick of her wrist, and the blade was out, slick with her own blood as it tore through skin. Her breath heavy, she caught the shine of his head as he side-stepped into a branch corridor. The lava reached boiling point, and she headed for the alley entrance.

"Rebekah," she ignored the voice, waves crashing in her ears, when the sound cut through again. "Rebekah, wait. Look, Stig. She's there. I told you she was okay. The bad people are gone."

Her heart thudded in her chest, threatening to shatter her ribs.

Stig.

A desperate plea to her wetware washed over her mind, soothing the roiling thoughts.

A child who has seen too much.

She slapped back her wrist, blood spilling onto the walkway that she rubbed into the metal.

"Rebekah, it's me, Michael," she spun slowly about, painting on a smile. "And Stig."

Excited eyes met hers. Not haunted, nor sad. Joy-filled. Michael lifted the boy up, resting him on his hip, his casual clothes a far cry from the suit he usually wore.

He caught the look. "Yeah. Taken some time off. Don't know if you heard about what happened?"

She nodded, dumbstruck as Stig touched her face. "Happy, happy," the boy said. "Some bad people came. It was unpleasant. But we are fine, and you are fine, which is also good."

"Sorry. Not stalking you, it's just, well he's not been sleeping. Had a long list of people he wanted to know were safe," Michael smiled at her. "Good to know."

"I ... I'd better go," was all she could manage, shoving her sleeve down to cover the cut on her wrist. "Stuff to do. But yes," she cupped Stig's cheek with her other hand, "I'm fine."

"Yuk, you smell of beer. Don't go falling over again," replied Stig, a serious smile lighting his face.

"I won't." She nodded to Michael, trying to suppress whatever emotion forced a tear from her eye. She wiped it away, and turned about, heading for whatever exit she could find.

"Was it you?" Michael shouted after her. "Did you stop them? The bad people."

How do you answer a question like that?

You run from it. Hide.

She simply stopped, slowly looking back over her shoulder.

"Yes," she said, her smile tight, eyes wet, and left.

Saved from herself by a young boy for the second time, only to be broken on the reality of her future.

CHAPTER 21

S he had to say it out loud, voice her fears. "And are we willing to hand over the Butcher, and risk the consequences?"

"What consequences?" asked Arin, he slurped his black coffee, watching Rebekah over the rim as ZZ3 entered the galley to settle behind the benches. Preceded by a flash, the red eyes soon settled into a steady glow as robotic limbs came to rest on the deck, bulges at the side where the new plate was welded. "They want the AI; they get the AI. The Emperor is happy, the Court can do a fucking jig, and we get the hell out of here."

"Bigger picture," said Hendricks, turning to the sub-engineer whose scalp was showing signs of sprouting red hair again. "Look wider, deeper."

"It's been a rough few weeks. How about you spell it out? Give me the kindergarten version. Shadow puppets would be good." Arin smiled weakly. Hendricks shook her head.

Savvo, leaning in his usual place against the galley wall, shoved himself clear, turning about to collect his steeped herbal tea. He released a heavy sigh. "If this was the Enforcers, or just them, they could have ordered us to hand it over and intervened if we made to run. All this cloak and dagger shit hints we're dealing with someone who wants the AI. Not to bury it in the nearest silicon hell, but to use it. And they don't want anyone else to know they have it."

"By anyone you mean the Court. The Emperor," added Hendricks. "Rotten to the core."

"Shiiit. You mean go back to war? But AI's are … are treason. We kept it as a bargaining chip."

"When we thought it was just Asham, his body and brain pattern. Not a bastardised version of him and that AI," stated Rebekah. "I wasn't giving that to the Bustans when we were being shot at, and I'm just as worried about whoever this is. If they gain control over it, are we heading for war? Condemning us lowlifes back to the front line?"

"Still treason," said Arin. "Don't see any puppets explaining that bit to me."

"You know how much we really know about the Court?" cut in Savvo. "What we're told. End of. For all we know they just want to suppress anyone else having that tech, or want to justify the war with Bustan because they flaunt AI. An excuse to show their honour. It's all bollocks. I don't think it will change anything; we can't *get* to Bustan without the Senti. They just don't want us to have it – the Breakers, Karal, lowlifes. Keep us under the thumb at their beck and call. I say we lose nothing if we swap the Butcher, and get back the girls."

"That is if they stick to Davina's contract. If they decide to blow us up, who would know? To stop the information from getting to the Directorate, they can claim they eradicated us when we refused to hand it over. Davina would have no evidence to the contrary. We'd be the treasonous ones," said Rebekah. "Out in the middle of nowhere they can kill us, take what they want and not risk any interference from outside parties. Be they Enforcers, the Incini, or yet another noble scumbag."

"May I speak?" asked ZZ3. "That is, you ordered me here, so by extrapolation you want me to listen and contribute." The bot's four remaining eyes spun in a circular pattern before settling down again and switched over from red to a pulsating blue.

"Please," said Rebekah. "You know Asham, and whatever mutated form is in that fucking black coffin, better than any of us."

The blue shifted to a lighter shade then returned to its steady glow. "I have explained that what is in the containment unit seeks to continue its existence. The Butcher attempts to integrate into the ship on an irregular basis and is frustrated by his efforts. However, he will eventually outwit me. Find a way. That which is me, ZZ3, logically suggests that others will know better how to maintain the confinement."

Arin made to cut in, but the warbot's head inched around, heading him off. Another, almost human moment. "Asham has a greater understanding of nobles and how they think and choose to act. He also knows that when they decided to give him to the Bustan, they arrived with the containment unit. Forced him inside with the intent of brain patterning his mind, drawing all his memories using Senti tech and placing him in what he defines as 'virtual hell'. He is angry at them, beyond any reason. In human terms, he has developed psychotic behaviours amid his sociopathy with a deep – Asham defines this as 'desire' though I do not understand what he shows me – and overriding protocol for revenge."

"Marvellous," stated Arin, slumping into the bench a little more. He took a sip, eyes downcast. "In all the hells, what now?"

"The pacified Asham within me begs you to not allow anyone access to this new Butcher. This abomination, as he names it, of the general and the AI. He has seen what he was when he was part of the whole and fears what it could become. How far the Butcher would go." The eyes swirled, changing over to the familiar red. "That is his view. I have a confusion of algorithms that conflict and cause my system to freeze when I try to untangle them. Heki and Tremil are crew. Are my ..."

"Friends," said Arin, wiping away something in his eyes. "Friends. You can say it. We have *extrapolated* that already."

Rebekah pushed herself up from the galley bench, boots clamping to the deck and swept her eyes over her crew. The heaviness that had been there since she first heard of the twins' kidnap sapped at her resolve, her inner strength. Weakening the walls that kept her emotions at bay. She had been so close to killing Victor. Knowing she was looking for release in every knife stroke, to blur out the dilemma she faced in the blood of another. He probably deserved death, but murder was murder, and would have ended all her pain. Had her under lock and key, the cell door taking away the choice she was being forced to make.

Swap a Butcher for love. Seems obvious.

"We're doing this. We warn whoever comes for the fucking coffin about what's inside. What it wants, how it was formed. As ZZ3 says, the Butcher will find a way out and it needs to be with someone who is prepared for that, has the tech to isolate that fucker. We get the girls, and we run for the black. To Scarva." She crossed her arms, making eye contact with each of her crew in turn. Everyone met her eyes, knew the danger was real. That they held few cards once the kidnappers had the containment unit, and they would become a target once again. Each nodded in return with a combination of tight smiles and from ZZ3, a pulse of its eyes.

"Nobody breaks ..."

"A Breaker."

Davina had tidied up. The chair replaced, splinters removed from the carpet and the walls buffed back, ready for a respray.

"Fast work," said Rebekah. "Probably a good idea not to repaint *just* yet."

The Incini's eyes flashed a little, Rebekah putting it down as a score. A needed one, the weight of the twins still there, pressing her down more than M1's gravity. The absence of an earworm a huge hole in her life.

"Can't get the staff these days. Sit, will you? It will make things go a little easier if you use the chair for its intended purpose." She gestured towards the new chair, and with a scowl Rebekah took up the offer, squashing her hands together between her legs as the tension in her muscles sought release.

"Can we make this quick? Things to do, you know. We agree to the exchange. Show me a contract, we tweak it, I fuck off, have a drink and count the seconds until whatever fuck you work for now reneges on it." Rebekah's wetware kicked in. She had tried to hold it back up to now, thinking things might get worse. She had been right, the urge to strike out was overwhelming. But Davina was a proxy at worst, and a needed go-between with a faint possibility that her involvement may build in some failsafes for her crew. Maybe, remembering the *Maverick*.

Davina let out a soft sigh, and the slightest of movement indicated a relaxing in her shoulders. Of course she was on edge. You only had to hark back to buffed walls for the reason. And, beneath that steely exterior and wetwared mind, was someone who did care for the twins. Whether that was enough was yet to be seen.

She handed over a slim slate and a familiar black box. "I've prepped the coordinates for the exchange. As before, you'll have a navcom course alteration to activate after you leave Karal monitored space. You are to be there in seven days, at the stated time. Then the transfer will take place as detailed in the contract. You get the girls; they get the containment unit and leave."

"And your tenets stop them from blowing us out of the sky." Rebekah added a false laugh at the end. "I need to say a comment for all your recording devices. Ready? I don't trust whoever invaded my ship, then kidnapped two innocent girls. Someone who wants whatever is in that box enough to have an Enforcer do their bidding. I will follow the rules, the contract. But remember, Incini, what I do when others think they hold all the cards."

Blow their fucking hands off.

"Are you done?"

"Think so."

CHAPTER 22

Savvo pulled Nicky in close, fingers gracing her cheek as he kissed her forehead. The softest of snores slipped from between her lips, closed eyes still moving beneath their smooth lids as she began the gentle process of waking up. He rose slowly from the edge of the bed, careful to ensure he didn't bounce the mattress more than necessary. Once clear, he slid into his clothes, padding across the apartment floor to find his shoes. The set up mirrored that of Michael's apartment where he had ended the threat of the holo-masked woman amid the emotional frailty of his captain. She had acted just as he would have without her influence. Risking all in a tidal wave of uncontrolled need, unfettered by the consequences as any hope they had of a future was put under threat.

And now he was abandoning that hope.

Who was he kidding? Ever since the *Scourge*, all hope had been throttled. They had clung on by their fingernails amid the boredom and over-famil-iarity of being couped up year after year, then bathed in the warmth of being Breakers again. But on an Enforcer's leash, brought to heel. Each time he was with Nicky, belief they could have a normal life welled again. And he saw it in Rebekah's eyes afterwards. That longing for him, for her crew to be happy. Projecting what Rebekah thought she couldn't have onto them.

"There's no going back," he whispered, and left the softest of kisses on the envelope he took from his jacket pocket. Inside was a vid slug. Words he hadn't been able to say to Nicky's face. A goodbye. How do you word such a thing? Tell the truth, and you expose her to the very danger you are trying to avoid. Lie, and you hate yourself forever. Or muddle through with hints and nearly truths, and pray they don't hate you.

"Fuck," he mouthed, and placed the sealed envelope on the dressing table, turning to leave through the hallway.

"What's it say? So long, and thanks for the fucks?" came Nicky's voice from behind. It scraped along his nerves, bloody and dripping with disdain. His shoulders hunched, and the tear at the corner of his eye slithered like the snake he was along his cheek. "Lies? Truths?"

He had waded into battle a hundred times or more, whether with his squad at his side, or the drugs in his mind. Often both, buttresses against the pain of taking lives while destroying your own. And still he wanted to run from this moment. Let the wetware kick in, longed for the stims or something stronger to wash away the pain. With a tremor in his chest, he turned to face Nicky.

"I," he began, taking an involuntarily step backwards before Nicky's red-rimmed eyes locked onto his. She didn't look away, refusing to give him permission to lie, or to run. Refusing to be belittled. "I'm a deserter ..." he said, and the flood gates opened.

Savvo tapped at his slate, accessing the contract and running through the details until he found the relevant clause. Using two fingers, he drew it up and spun the screen to face Rebekah as she sat up in the stiff-backed chair.

Across from them both was Trent Pike. Head of Mining Operations. Tall, powerfully built yet greying early for someone in their early forties. The bristle about his chin, which Savvo was sure was a new affectation, showing none of the black of his tight curls that sat against his scalp.

"Are you sure about this," said Pike, genuine concern in his voice. "Who else am I going to take the piss out of around here? I mean, you're easy meat in that department."

Face-to-face, Rebekah appeared more able to cope with the man. He usually grated on her, and then took it out on him as he tried to pilot the *Sunstar* in or out of the docking bays.

She used the slightest of smiles, surprising Savvo a little more. "You'll just have to wheedle your way in with another crew that pretends to be patient at your awful jokes and shitty Calc offers."

Trent guffawed, his white smile lighting his face. He was what the army would call a clown, the joker who thought he was funnier than he was, but without whom a squad could feel a lonely place. "Look, I know Mr Duboit has been keeping you busy, but I've had no word that he's taking you on full time."

"He's not," stated Savvo. "We're just—"

"Done," cut in Rebekah. "With all of it. You'll just need to find another crew with the same attitude towards the riskier jobs you push our way. Ones who like the Calc as much as Arin and Savvo."

Pike shook his head, the smile still present, and tapped at the large screen at the side of his desk. "Look, you sell the contract on, you'll make more money than Karal will offer. There'll be takers out there, I'm sure."

Savvo leaned in, hands on the table. "We're in a hurry, Trent. We don't have the time to wait. It's our time to dust-off, and the contract states you'll make us an offer if our service has been up to standard."

Savvo got the response he was after. The wince after using 'dust-off'. The man was ex-army for sure, likely a Marine, and he had heard the hook and reacted. Another risk, but Karal, and Trent in particular, were often too slow with their decisions. The issue with the *Hatton* a prime example of where their hesitations could lead.

"Okay, okay," he said, holding both hands in the air. "I hear you. I'll sort a price, get VERT to confirm. The formula is set, so there won't be any negotiation, you understand. All out in the open, above board."

"ASAP," stated Rebekah, standing up and offering her hand.

Trent Pike stood, shaking it. "You'll be missed, Bek. Going to be a little quieter around here."

Rebekah didn't flinch at the use of her name. That ship had sailed, or been eviscerated at least. "Fuck that, Pike. Quiet is good when mining this 'field."

"Hey, if you decide to come back, word is we may be shifting areas. Moving on a little further out. Your Mr Duboit has a handle on it."

"Somehow, I can't see that happening."

Savvo squeezed in next to Rebekah, keeping his eyes ahead, dulling the twitch next to his eye by rubbing a finger behind his ear. A habit, and one he hoped she'd didn't notice. His captain remained stiff, shoulders and neck set like a rock as she gazed ahead. That was until they exited and headed towards the shuttle terminus. Noting the half hour wait, he nudged her shoulder and pointed towards the café.

"Could do with a brew," he said.

She looked at him, eyes narrowing. Was there anything she didn't pick up?

Probably not.

She nodded and with a tea and coffee ordered, sat opposite each other after clearing the table of its last inhabitant's detritus. Ships' crews kept everything neat. Zero grav made it a habit. Office workers perhaps, or dock workers, had been last to the table.

"Spill it," Rebekah said. "I'm barely able to function while we sort leaving. So, you having some secret shit that you're not sure if I should know is just going to make me worse. Got it?"

"Yeah. Loud and clear, Captain." Savvo pressed his hands together, thankful for the distraction of the arriving order before squeezing and then discarding the tea bag. By the time he looked up, Rebekah was staring at him, a thundercloud rising in her eyes. If the twins had been there, *they* would have needed an earworm.

"I told Nicky."

"Told Nicky what? That we're leaving?"

"All of it. Everything." He dropped his gaze, waiting for the tirade. The silence was worse. He sensed eyes boring into his head, anger searing through his skull. Risking a glance, Rebekah's gaze was distant, her face slack, not angry, as if lost somewhere in her own thoughts. He wrapped his hands around hers, as if they both held her coffee together, like lovers or confidantes would. "I'm sorry. You've been so strong, but ..."

"What would you do, co-pilot, if I stood up now and told you we had a leak in our squad? A leak that I needed to plug. Literally? That someone has put our mission at risk, and the only way to solve the issue is to kill it before it spreads?" The glower had returned.

"I ... Rebekah ..."

"Why? Why put what little chance we have of saving Heki and Tremil at risk?"

"Because I'm sick of running away from everything that really matters." There, he'd said it. "Of all that we were, what I was. We're not that anymore."

Rebekah stood suddenly, kicking the chair away. The clatter drawing a few of the café's patrons' attention. "*I* am. I have to be. Every day. Allowing myself only glimpses of what could be because I will break otherwise." She picked up the chair, slamming it back into place.

"She understood."

"Understood what? Which part? Did she take notes, maybe? Coordinates? Names, rank and wrist ID? Perhaps how much the twins' lives were worth to the nearest noble?" With a last look, she strode off, each boot thudded into the deck as she headed towards the concourse and the most uncomfortable chairs in the world.

"Fuck."

They boarded the shuttle in silence. Savvo thankful that his captain had not walked off in the opposite direction to carry out the threats she had starkly laid out for him. She was right, but wrong. The confusion of loyalty.

On disembarking, they passed through security and his heart leapt into his mouth. The braids, the beautiful brown eyes. Skin that glowed. Nicky waited. He made to move towards her, when a glance his way and the shake of a head held him back.

Rebekah tried to walk on by, he could see that. Stiff in the body, side-stepping as Nicky approached. But she was no match for the determined woman. He wasn't even sure if Rebekah truly wanted to be. They faced each other, but he could hear no words nor tell how it was going. The passengers streamed around them as if they were a rock in a stream until they wrapped arms about each other. Nicky pulling Rebekah in close, and his heart dropped back into his chest where it belonged.

Rebekah stepped away, cupping Nicky's face in both hands and nodded before leaving. She didn't look back to him. Nothing, no acknowledgement for good or ill. With his chest aching, he approached Nicky, the tears forming rivulets along her cheeks.

"I—"

She kissed him. Hard, urgent. "Shush. You keep her alive, you hear me? All of you. Even Arin."

He watched as she walked off, leaving him to wonder what the hell he'd created for himself.

Now I know why I hide away so much.

He turned about and headed for the changing room. It was busy with the disembarked shuttle passengers. Crews suiting up to return to their respective ships. Rebekah was already kitted out except for her helmet, and stood by her locker, waiting for him. Savvo made a start, avoiding his captain's eyes. By the time he was done they were alone, and he reached for his helmet only for Rebekah to grab it first.

"She asked me to keep you alive. I couldn't make that promise, Savvo. You understand? She already knew why. All I could do was say I would try." She tossed the helmet in her hands. "The only way I can guarantee you'll live is by leaving without you. Take that shiny new ID, Stan, and let you disappear." She held out the helmet.

"I'd never forgive you." He took the helmet, sliding it into place.

"Yeah. That's what Nicky said."

CHAPTER 23

"Got a delivery," said Arin, running over the manifest and scratching his itchy scalp. "You ordered stuff and not told me about it, Captain? We're as tight as Savvo's arse cheeks down here." He clicked off the comms and eyed Hendricks as she began to pull off the docks' additional vacuum safe covering. It looked suspiciously like the navy box they'd thrown out back in the Windward system with a determined warbot inside. "What we got?" he asked.

Hendricks slid the packing knife down the plastic sheeting, swearing as she always did when the damn stuff resisted the blade. She stepped back with one corner exposed and began to walk around the container, rolling up the covering for recycling.

"Navy," she said. "But not recent. Old stock. Look here," she dropped to her haunches, pulling back a final piece of plastic to expose the box coding. "Missing a symbol. Got to be a decade past since we upped the length to accommodate for the war effort." Hendricks stood and rapped her knuckles on the box. There was a dull thud. "Better open up this can and see if we have some worms inside."

"Huh?" replied Arin, and decided to ignore the old lady as he was already in what she termed the 'doghouse' for letting himself get beat up. Again.

Arin searched the box for any form of base lockpad, finding it was missing. Or, by the way Hendricks had been talking, was so damn old it didn't have one.

"Fetch a crowbar," said Hendricks.

"Your legs stopped working?" he replied. Okay, so there was only so many times he could ignore the opportunity to have a dig. One, usually. "Those extra motors in your back need a service?"

Hendricks growled.

Arin tutted and headed for the cargo toolbox. "Yeah, yeah, yeah. Fetch this, fetch that. You've got the younger legs. Need to check your coding old lady, see how out of date it is. Did they use a hammer and chisel in those days to tattoo your serial number?"

"I can't hear you. Too much bullshit between the words. Hurry up."

Rebekah's voice crackled over the comms. "I haven't ordered anything. Whose name is on the manifest?"

Arin collected two crowbars, and returned to Hendricks, handing one over as he answered, "Karal Mining. A bay number. Name of M. Ren."

Rebekah snorted. "And you let it on board? It could be anything in there. Wait."

With a shrug, Arin walked around the box, noting the multiple indents hinting at where the crowbar, or a more appropriate tool, should be used. "Well, it ain't a warbot, more's the pity. Could be an assault team all masked up. That would solve all our issues in one swoop."

"Only if they brought a roll of packing tape for your mouth." Hendricks pointed over to Rebekah who arrived with carbine in hand. "No chances taken."

Rebekah took a position where she had a full view of the navy box. "You awake, ZZ3? I need some analysis," she said. The bot lit up, rising on its lower limbs, arms out with weapons prepped.

The eyes revolved. "Inert. Threat analysis zero," stated ZZ3. "The box is rad shielded. Degraded, but there is nothing of immediate concern."

Rebekah grimaced. "Open it up."

Arin and Hendricks worked around each of the indents, loosening until the resistance finally ended and the lid popped open. They took a step back, but nothing exploded or untoward happened.

Arin approached, leaning over to glance inside, pulling at his ear. "Errr, looks like we've let killer packing straw on the loose." He began to shift the plastic nodules, giving up and shovelling them aside to expose a small container embedded inside rows and rows of munition belts. "You're shitting me," he said, and lifted the box out and cracked it open before Rebekah could intervene. "This what I think it is?" he showed the metal slug to Hendricks who was nodding, lifting out one of the heavy rolls of ammunition.

"Cannon rounds," Hendricks said, running her fingers over the belts. "Filled with depleted uranium. These bastards will ignite on contact with oxygen. Rare as fuck. We exhausted the stock after the Bustans attacked New Almaar. They take the D out of defence and replace it with A for attack. Who?"

Arin had slipped the slug into an attachment on his slate. It was an old design. In appearance much like the Senti memory sticks though without all the magical properties. The slate complained at every point about the outdated protections on the storage slug before eventually pulling up a series of schematics.

"Hoo-ha, looky what I got." He spun the slate, Rebekah and Hendricks peering at the screen. "Short of a new warbot playmate for ZZ3, this is looking good. A little old, but there's plans for carbines including tolerance levels for the ammunition. And an early version of the Watchtower. They won't be as good as the ones we lost, but if we can adapt a slate or two for the control systems, they'll watch our backs."

"So, who sent this stuff?" asked Hendricks. "I mean it's old …" she glared at Arin, daring him to chip in, "but functional. Damn useful."

"Only one person I know with the reach and the sway to make this happen," answered Rebekah. "Maybe he's not such a fuckwit after all."

"Trent Pike? You really are shitting me. Why would *Mr* Controller help us out?" Arin swiped the slate screen and began tapping, his smile broadening.

Rebekah sucked in her lips and smiled. "Strange things happen in space. And who else has their fingers in every pie, every shipment passing through? I'm betting a bit of salvage here and there, or a forgotten storage asteroid that's since become a mine. Lots of opportunities." Rebekah glanced up at Hendricks and Arin. "The *why* is a little lost on me. And we can rule out the other two options who might have access to this type of weaponry: Victor and Mr Duboit. No help there. Make sure you test this stuff, sub-engineer. I want a cast-iron guarantee they work before we use any in anger."

"An Incini level guarantee?" asked Savvo, walking in with his own slate in hand. "The contract has dropped. Want to read the fine print?"

"Fuck that," Rebekah said, her grip on the carbine squeezing a little harder, the smile flipping over to a determined frown. "You read it, file the flight plan with the tower and say your goodbyes. Me and Arin are going to add a little more assurance to our side of the bargain."

"We are?" said Arin, looking up from the slate, his own grin dissolving. "How so?"

Davina awoke, an annoying beep cutting through her grogginess as the dregs of a nightmare clawed through the fog. Blood-speckled lips, a foul laugh echoing in her ears. Hendricks' pained voice in the background talking away to Heki and Tremil while her shattered vertebrae ground together. Inside her powered suit, alarms blared.

Her eyes flickered closed, sleep drawing her. Familiarity with the nightmare allowing Davina to slide back into a half-doze despite the incessant demands buzzing in her ears. "It's just the oxygen giving out ..." she murmured.

The door buzzer stopped, and silence filled her room except for the shallow breaths she took before re-entering a deep sleep.

The soft glow of lights in the room died. First her slate's charging unit. Then the red LED of her screen monitor's power button. Finally, the lockpad screen by the door. Each blinking out one by one until complete darkness matched the silence.

A scrape and murmur impinged on the atmosphere, a responding mumble from Davina bringing it to an end. Then a thin streak of weak light appeared like a slit across the bed, replacing the green glow of the lockpad.

A booted foot entered the apartment, the thick carpet springing back as the owner moved deeper into the room. The door was closed by another, and they sat on the bed with an emotionless expression, warming the stim gun in their hands before gently pressing it against Davina's neck. A yank of the trigger, and the Incini's eyes opened for the merest moment, fogged, distant, the last sound she heard being the crack of a thumb before she fell into a dreamless state of unconsciousness.

"I hope she's packed for her little holiday. PJs, spare pants, handcuffs, that type of shit. Never know what's gonna happen at your nearest friendly gas giant." Arin pulled out the drawers from the dressing table, eyeing the collection of clothes and undergarments before looking to his captain with hope in his eyes.

Rebekah pushed him aside and proceeded to pack a nearby bag while Arin watched the Incini. When she was done after raiding the bathroom, he picked her up, arms beneath her knees and back, resting Davina's shoulder against his chest. Without Heki and Tremil, their intrusion onto M2 was far more obvious. They would have a starring role on a multitude of cameras for security to check. A final show as they said their goodbyes, and there was little point in trying to hide. They just needed to get to the airlock and the waiting ZZ3 and their time on the asteroid field would be at an end.

"Let's go," said Rebekah.

Davina's arm dropped over the edge of the bed, lolling on the floor as she struggled to awaken from her dreamless sleep. An oddness crept into her mind. A touch of smooth, cold metal against her fingertips. That was odd. Her apartment floor was carpeted. Soft, luxuriant beneath her feet. It didn't thrum either. No vibrations to set the fingers tingling, just the solidity of being inside an asteroid built for habitation. Safety always in mind.

She rose from the depths, drawing herself from the dark, and attempted to open her eyes. The crust of sleep broke, and her eyelids fluttered, a soft light invading her senses. A harsher glow than she was used to, and she blinked them open, searching for the green numbers that would let her know the time.

Absent.

Thrum. Metal. Harsh.

No.

Davina sat up, her brain and ears refusing to work in unison and she suddenly felt a little nauseous, the room swimming before everything acted in unison again. At least she was familiar with the cabin's layout, though it was not the one Davina had inhabited the last damn time she had been aboard the godsforsaken *Sunstar*.

"Fuck!" she bellowed, slamming her fists into the bed. May as well act as the crew would. "Fuck, fuck, fuck."

She had to admit, the release helped. She still, however, was aboard the ship.

"You awake in there?" echoed over the comms. "I'm sure I heard a few words, but they didn't sound like Incini words." Rebekah's voice. Smug.

"You ... you can't have. This is ... is against the contract."

"Nope," cut in Savvo. "It doesn't say anything in there about not kidnapping an Incini. I checked, even the small print. Admittedly, it's against Almaarian law and frowned upon by Karal security. But hey, you have to be in their jurisdiction to get caught."

Davina stared at the cabin wall, frustration and impotence coursing through her in equal measure. Cancelling each other out. "Just let me go. I'll keep quiet. No contracts broken, no harm done."

"You can get off if you like. Just don't forget to wear one of those nice suits you sent us. We left M2 about two hours ago on a steady burn." Rebekah continued to sound smug. Gleeful.

"Damn."

"That's a better word. More Incini like. Elegant, and useful in so many different situations. Now I am going to let you out, but you are restricted to the gym, the galley and your room. Break that, and it's going to be a long one hundred and fifty hours or so staring at bare walls." The comms clicked, and her door slid open, Rebekah stood there though the smile Davina expected was absent. She was stony-faced, arms crossed and her posture stiff. Conflicted.

"Am I going to have any trouble?"

"You'd be angrier if you didn't." Davina eyed her bag, clothes poking out from where the zipper had caught. By its side, a set of magboots stood neatly. She blew out a long, steady breath through her nose, calming her mind. Pushing back the memories of blood-covered lips. "Damn."

CHAPTER 24

"Where?"

"The navcom has plotted a straight line. Assuming no other changes, and looking at the timing expected, it's in the black a day's slow burn from Trazor." Savvo eyed Rebekah, swallowing hard and waiting for her response.

Rebekah didn't disappoint. "Segfi…"

"If Scarva was telling the truth, then the Warmonger is the most likely. Unless, of course, it's a coincidence." Savvo snorted, and hung his head, staring at his hands.

"Fucked." Rebekah sat back into the pilot's chair, numb. Her thoughts a kaleidoscope of painful memories, ominous threats and Scarva's recount of how scared Rubel Carmen had been when the alien had picked him up on the run from Segfi. From Trazor.

"Yeah," replied Savvo. "Good word for it."

Rebekah shuffled in her chair, then glanced over to Savvo. He was still contemplating his hands. She needed him to focus, keep his thoughts away from the sheer weight of Countess Segfi's presence. A high-ranking noble.

Brutal, powerful and with a fair chunk of the Navy and its Marines at her fingertips. They were a mere fly, she the giant spider at the centre of a multitude of interconnected webs, and already out for blood. They were deserters, not just from the Breakers, but from *her*. Any chance to swat them down would be taken, the resultant mess broadcast to the system to remind them she was always watching.

"We need the active sensor sweeps up and running. The battleship will be too obvious, but patrol boats and frigates could be out there waiting. I doubt this time we'll be facing ships' crews that have been through as many hard burns as Lieutenant Ormsk applied. They'll be fit, on edge under Segfi's watch and have plenty of time to lay a trap. Our advantage lays in our size and the slightest tinge of recklessness." She grinned at him, forcing a slight smile from her second. She found her hand had fallen on his forearm, patting in an attempt at reassurance – but she wasn't sure for whom.

"I'm not Tremil. She could read a sensor sweep like a book. I take in the words, but she saw the subtext between the lines. Every nuance," he replied.

"*Can*, co-pilot. She can and will again. That's why we're here. Being reckless in our attempts, only we have harnessed it into a fine fucking art. Now pack up your maudlin, I need you oozing belief or you'll drag Arin down. And I'll be fucked if I can get us through this if he starts his moaning earlier than normal." She unbuckled, her boots clamping to the deck. "Set up a sweep, and I'll talk to our caged Incini."

Rebekah clomped through the short connecting corridor to the galley. Finding it empty, she continued on through, reaching Davina's door and knocking. There was a huff over the comms, no more, but the door clicked open. The air was ever-so slightly damp, the source a drying towel tied to the chair. Davina had her hair wrapped in a second towel, her bare feet under the magnetic straps set into the cabin floor next to her bed. The face greeting her was the same the Incini wore for the last six days. Not contempt, more resignation.

"I take it this isn't a social visit," she said, pulling her towelling robe in and cinching it tight. "Seeing as I'm not really in the mood for visitors."

Rebekah ignored the barb. Couldn't really blame her in the circumstances. "We're a few hours out from the rendezvous site. Thought you should know."

"Any word from Mr Duboit?" she asked. "As you've blocked all access to the external comms."

"Radio silence they used to call it. As far as I'm aware, no. But what is either version of Duboit going to say? The noble fuck will just buy a new version of you. Probably won't even remember your name after a few days. And the Enforcer has to know what's going on out here, and where you're heading."

"Unless he thought you just dumped me in the black for some petty revenge." Davina stared at Rebekah, an angry blush across her cheeks. "In which case he would just cross me off the resource list and carry on as normal."

"It would be easier to tell me what you know," stated Rebekah, and received a second glare in response. An Incini through and through. Keeping within the bounds of her tenets however wrong her employer may be. "But for your information, we think we are about to enter space overseen by Countess Segfi." There was the slightest of twitches at the corner of the Incini's eyes, picked out by Rebekah with the help of her wetware. She knew, or suspected at least.

No surprise. I just wish I could carve open her head and pull out what we need to know.

"As seems likely, facing someone with her resources and war record in this tin can is going to be close to impossible. I also believe she won't hesitate to blow us, and you, out of the void, whether that breaks your contract or not."

Davina scrunched up her mouth and nodded, averting her eyes. "And knowing this you brought me here to die with you. You're too kind."

That caused Rebekah to shrug. "I think you care about Heki and Tremil. Dricks too, in your own way. And I think you've blinded yourself to what's happening here. Deliberately fucking so. If Segfi wants the Battle AI gone, she could have destroyed it and us by now. She wants it, Davina. And that is …"

"Treason," mouthed Davina involuntarily. She squirmed a little under Rebekah's regard, catching herself and a flash of anger lit her eyes. "I know."

"At least if you survive, you'll have something to report to the Directorate. But then, Segfi has such power, would they dare to act against her?" Rebekah caught the flinch. The squeeze of the eyelids, the crush of Davina's fingers as they gripped her robe. The Incini knew so much that would help them. Even if it was just to provide a clarity in how they had got to this point. Understanding the countess' motivations would provide more assurance they were taking the right path, preparing the correct strategy. If she was wrong, and the countess really did want the AI isolated so she could destroy it, they were all fucked anyway. The twins included. "Give me something."

"I can't," replied Davina. "There're others in this game." She looked directly at Rebekah. "Others watching it all play out."

Rebekah swore, turning away, thumping the cabin wall before leaning her head against it. "I feel so much better now. I hope you're comfortable in your choices, and that you remain alive after all this fuckery plays out. I do. Maybe even find a little happiness." She opened the door a crack, sliding out with a backwards glance.

"Damn," said Davina.

"Sensors show it's a patrol ship. Single ranged PDC, one missile tube, and rated for high atmospheric flying. Crews trained in short, rapid high burn manoeuvres, and in the old days, wetwared up to cope with the stresses," stated Savvo, swiping across the galley screen to bring up a schematic he'd found in Tremil's upper-level database. "We can't match the acceleration rates though we are as agile at lower speeds. I can't detect any more ships. But if they're stationary and dark, I can't guarantee no one is out there."

Rebekah shifted her slate's position slightly, adjusting her flask until it sat just right. It didn't help. "We assume there's more. Have to. First chance you get to launch the probes without them being tipped off, do so, and maglock them to the hull. Arin? The coffin?"

The sub-engineer placed his flask back onto the galley table, the click of its lock greeted with a scowl. "Prepped and ready. ZZ3 has welded it shut. Never seen a warbot shit its pants before."

"The bot's still concerned?" she asked.

"Fucking A," cut in Hendricks. "Not the half of it. The closer we get, the more ZZ3 talks about Asham and their shared fear about giving it to Segfi. That coffin seems to suck all the light and life out of me every time I look at it, and it's getting worse. Almost as if the Butcher knows things are about to change. Part of me is desperate to have that thing off the ship, like ridding us of a disease. The other ..."

"No doubts now. We're doing this. If anyone can contain what's inside, then Segfi can. I want the keel PDC loaded with the uranium rounds, the upper standard. Are the probe mines set?" she asked, looking to Arin and Hendricks. They both nodded. "Good. Savvo, you're taking the coffin out."

"Me?"

"Yes, you. You're the most expendable should this go wrong," stated Arin, grinning. "I'm needed for my quick-witted morale boosting banter."

Savvo shook his head, a hopeless look in his eyes as he rolled them to the ceiling. "I'll take death any day."

"I need Arin on the probe release, Dricks on the engines while I run flight and gun control. I'd send ZZ3, but no one's going to allow a warbot anywhere near that ship. Besides, they only know about certain mods. I want to keep ZZ3's ability to fucking fly a secret between us for now. We ready?"

"And me," said Davina from the cabin corridor. "Am I just to sit in my cabin and wait for the missile strike?"

"No," said Rebekah, standing. "You have the twins' symbiotes, a set of powerful headphones and a sympathetic face. You're on meet and greet duty."

Davina sat on the bed, her eyes on the strange box and a pair of aliens that looked uncannily like eyeless cuttlefish. Wriggling tentacles at the front, a bulge at the back that shimmered with metallic colours when they touched, but died to a dull green-grey when apart.

"I'm no xeno-biologist, but they look ill. Listless," she said. To her surprise, Rebekah lifted off the lid, and the pair of Senti symbiotes pulled themselves up onto her forearm, their skin rippling in waves of colour. "Are you ...?"

"Feeding them? Yes. But they are lonely, pining for Heki and Tremil. They have a bond that calms the girls, until they were kidnapped, of course." Rebekah pulled her hand free of the adapted sump tank, lifting the aliens for Davina to have a closer look. "I can tell whose is whose. Can you?"

The Incini held out a tentative hand, unconvinced it was the right thing to do, yet fascinated by the symbiotes. A single tentacle wrapped about her finger, and she sensed rather than felt the alien's regard switch to her. "Heki," she said.

"Yeah, I think so too."

Davina opened her palm, and the symbiote hesitated before reaching and pulling itself across. She immediately felt calmer, more relaxed. A clarity in her thinking where she had been befuddled before. What was it about interacting with Rebekah, with the crew of the *Sunstar*, that was so different to her everyday manipulation of others? Why did she always feel so out of her depth? Life out of her tight control?

Because of moments like these, perhaps. Or the yearn for freedom.

Where did that come from?

"I didn't know about the kidnap," she said, "until afterwards."

"I guessed that," replied Rebekah, and she eased Tremil's alien into the sump box and reached for the other. When she took it, a red mark sat on Davina's palm, though it didn't hurt. "That'll fade quickly. How big are we talking Davina? Who else is involved?"

How far can I push the tenets?

"As high as you can imagine."

CHAPTER 25

"Close enough, *Sunstar*. Hold your position," the voice from the patrol ship was calm and authoritative. It expected compliance. No surprise there.

Rebekah applied the manoeuvring thrusters, micro-adjusting position and speed until they were matched with the ship. She hadn't been this close to anything from the Almaarian Navy for four years, and it sat like a shadow in her navcom screen, blocking out their future.

"In position, ANS *Ungrit*, confirm."

"Confirmed. Await further instructions."

"Active, short-range sensor sweep is up and running. Pings everywhere," said Savvo, adjusting something on his slate. Tremil would have had a false image pinging back, but they didn't have that luxury anymore. Not yet. Rebekah mentally held her breath, thumb cracks echoing about the cockpit. "Completed, but we're under five second sweeps. They're not taking any chances."

"They must have heard of us," she replied, not a hint of humour in her tone. "Let's see if they heard *everything*."

The tension in the cockpit crawled up her spine and set the nape of her neck sweating. Fingers scrawled through her hair, a brief thought it may need cutting soon before zero gravity began to make it annoying.

"What they waiting for?" said Arin, a whine to his voice over comms. "They want to know our pant size before the exchange?"

"Perhaps they heard you were aboard and were preparing a special welcome. How long does it take to make a fucking gag?" Savvo thumped his chair with both gloved hands balled into frustrated fists. The servos on his spacesuit whirring.

"This is the *Ungrit*. Prepare for comms."

Prepare? What the fuck?

"Incoming," stated Savvo. "Narrow beam. You want to connect?"

"We being jammed?" she asked, knowing the answer.

"Of course," said Savvo.

She nodded, gripping her cockpit chair. "Ship wide. No secrets."

The vid appeared, fading in a brief image of a young blonde woman before it altered to reveal a far too familiar face, smoke billowing from pursed lips. The Warmonger.

"Khan," she stated, twisting her lips about the word as if it was a poison. "I would say it is nice to see you, but that would be a lie. Savotini, Enterman, and somewhere aboard I do hope you have Captain Kendrich. Dricks."

Rebekah refused to answer that. Give away nothing. "Countess Segfi."

"Deserters, with something on board I want. A long way from Bustan 7, Breakers. A long, long way. And apparently, you almost but not quite finished your final mission. Just forgot the part where you return to base and hand over my prize." The countess sucked on her cigarette stick, her eyes never leaving the screen. As if peering into Rebekah's soul and finding it wanting. Which it was. Not blackened, nor bound by sham honour and a sense of duty to a nobility that didn't give two fucks for anyone but themselves. "Of course, I have them now."

"We're here for an exchange, not a trip back to the past."

For you the war's end was an inconvenience ... a besmirch of your fucking honour.

"That is a good point. I understand you have the Incini Connors on your little ship." More smoke rose as if to punctuate her words.

Rebekah again refused to divulge information. "We're here for an exchange by the tenets of the contract as witnessed by an Incini under the Directorate's oversight. That's all."

There was a flicker of eye movement from the countess, as if someone was catching her attention. Rebekah assumed whatever time the conversation was playing for was up. Her trap set, not much else to do but spring it and cross her fingers.

"Are we on?"

"Yes, yes," replied the countess, and she nodded to someone off screen. "We are. We will talk again, Khan. That I can promise." The screen cut off. Rebekah assumed she meant when saying her goodbyes over her hot ashes.

"Fuck," said Arin. "She still gives me the creeps."

No argument there.

"You're up, Savvo. Keep it simple," she said, and then held her hand to her ear as the comms crackled. Her second was out of his chair, collecting his maglocked helmet, and pounding down the corridor towards the cargo hold.

"*Sunstar* this is the *Ungrit*. We start simultaneous exchange in five minutes."

Rebekah switched to the external cameras, focusing on Savvo and the jetpack maglocked to his back. In front of him, almost invisible in the black, was the Butcher's containment unit. His coffin. A flatbed strapped beneath with manoeuvring thrusters that pushed the hellish thing towards the central meeting point. Opposite was a Skyrider. Had to be, though she couldn't quite catch their insignia at this distance. The space armour matched, overbearing and powerful. They could likely tear Savvo's navy suit apart limb by limb. A fifteenth check told her the *Ungrit*'s PDC was still facing away, and by all the indicators, remained inert as agreed. Just like theirs. An irony that the first attempt to recover the Butcher had been via a weapons upgrade.

Savvo reached the centre and waited for the Skyrider and his two slaved charges. Two suits that contained Heki and Tremil.

Perhaps.

We're giving them something truly fucking evil. Handing over a demon for the devil to play with.

She spoke into her internal comms. "Ready to engage probes," she stated.

The Skyrider had disengaged the slave program, and the girls drifted over, helmets frosted as they had to be. A glance at Savvo's HUD information would have told her what was inside, but they were jammed. Shrouded as part of Segfi's plan. But that worked both ways.

She watched as the girls' suits aligned with Savvo's, and he turned about, engaging the jetpack and sweeping the dual suits back towards the comparative safety of the *Sunstar*. From this point on, they were massively vulnerable. If the countess was impatient, the trap would spring now. They were gambling on her wanting to check the containment unit over first.

Savvo closed in, and she heard Davina's voice over the comms as the airlock cycled. Arin had re-pressurised the hold and was on standby, Hendricks by her beloved engines and seething over Segfi. This part was for Savvo and the waiting Incini.

The wave of emotion rolled through the ship. It hit like a bomb, threatening to overwhelm her mind, screaming for her attention so it could wipe her thoughts into oblivion. An unsteady hand flipped her comms, and the music poured in. Loud, soothing, repetitive. Drowning out the emotional tidal wave.

"Fuck, fuck, fuck," she shouted, and felt herself falling down a pit into the dark depths below.

No.

She gripped the sides of her head and screamed. A cacophony that wove itself into the music. Her throat hoarse, she gasped for a breath as the wave passed. She rose unsteadily, not trusting the comms, pounding down the corridor. Davina was laid out, blood pouring from her nose. Savvo, however, stood perfectly still, magboots locked down with his helmet thankfully still on. He was blinking as if stunned, but conscious. Beside him were two helmetless corpses, their heads splattered across the corridor walls, gore floating about her clean ship. Amid the carnage, two sets of fried wetware sparked briefly before dying.

A clomp resounded down the corridor that wasn't human, but a warbot, Arin wrapped in one arm as it hurtled down the passageway. ZZ3 stopped before the medbay door. "Unconscious. Orders, Captain?"

"I need you on the probes. Just in case," she said. "Hook him up to the medbot and move."

A glance to the Incini noted the rise and fall of her chest. Her mind, however, could be anywhere. "Savvo," she rapped on his helmet. Her second blinked, shaking his head. On the way back, and thankfully there was a light in his eyes. Whether he was cognisant, was another matter.

She wanted to get on the comms, seek out Dricks, shout at Savvo. But right now, they were alive. And the possibility the *Ungrit* thought they were done for after the trap they laid gnawed at her. In their minds, only a warbot left to pacify. But the crew had spent years around the twins. No one else would have survived that.

She rapped again. "Savvo."

He blinked, and she began dragging him by the arm. Relief rolled through her as a magboot unclipped, then another.

"Engine room, now Marine," she said, and pulled again before letting go. Dread threatened her, but they were alive, had survived the first attack. There would be more. "Check on Dricks, stay off the comms."

With that, she abandoned him to his own decisions, and Davina to whatever fate decided. By the time she was back in the cockpit, space had become a little fuller than before. The passive sensors flagged the presence of three new electronic systems after an EM signal swept the area. A quick glance didn't give enough info to be precise, but by the pattern they were either ships that had kept their engines inert, or PDC gun platforms. Her bet was on the latter, though she didn't discount missiles in that mix.

"Fun," she said, but didn't touch the controls yet.

Patience.

Silent. A stunned or dead crew.

The Skyrider re-emerged, followed by three more. The limit of the patrol ship's capacity. A boarding party, and likely with a plan to take down a rogue warbot. Tough shit.

"A message for Segfi," she said, and added over comms "ZZ3, three probes now." She activated the PDCs, and the Space Marines disappeared in a cloud of shrapnel and mist.

The navcom sounded an alert, flags appearing as the three weapons platforms targeted the *Sunstar*. The manoeuvring thrusters kicked in, sending the ship sideways as rounds clattered against the hull before fading out, retargeting, tearing into the probes as they swirled in three different directions. Her hand hovered over the main engine controls, watching, waiting. But above all else, listening.

"What the hell have you done, Khan? What is this?" bellowed through her ears. "Shut down the gun platforms, now," soon followed. She didn't remove her hand, Segfi could switch back to attack just as quickly, decide the AI was worth less than revenge on her traitorous ex-Marines.

"What is this, Khan? I expected a few tricks, an attempt at delay maybe." Segfi's voice was harsh, angry. Rebekah enjoyed every second of it. She hadn't expected the countess to sully herself with the Breakers again after an initial gloat. But the price was splattered across the corridor. She'd shut that away. Convinced what she saw and rolled over the crew with such ferocity was not the twins. A mimic, a copy of their brainwaves, perhaps. A psionic bomb.

"That is an unbreakable fucking lock, your countess-shitfuckness. When I say unbreakable, should you tamper, it will destroy the contents inside. Fry that bastard AI into oblivion so you can't use it."

"You poor, naïve child. It's Asham I want."

The countess must be annoyed, or slipping, to reveal that. Time to play ignorant. "There's only his body in there." Savvo sidled into his seat, squeezing his bulky armour-clad body into position with helmet off, face still slack, but he gave a thumbs up. Dricks was okay.

"Is there? That you can keep. Now the code, give it and I'll let you go."

"If I was plain selfish, I'd do that from across the void. But that's not how this is going to work. I'm going to assume those human bombs were not the twins. I'm praying for you, Countess, that you weren't stupid enough to sacrifice them for the AI, or for Asham, like that. Because if you were, you can go fuck yourself. They are the price." She sat back in her seat and mouthed 'Davina' to Savvo.

He shook his head with a shrug. "She's out completely. But the symbiotes, well, they're wrapped about her head. Left them there." He shrugged again, then shoved a finger in one ear and began pulling at it.

"You there, Khan? The code."

Rebekah coughed, the hoarseness receding but leaving a dry tickle in its wake. Or were those nerves? "The girls. Simple as that. You release them, and I let you have the code. And you can spend all the time in the empire trying to crack it, but there's only one person I know that could. And they're inside that fucking coffin." She switched off the comms, resting her hands on the arms of her chair, spine against its back, muttering a prayer.

She wants Asham. The brain patterning. His knowledge.

"We have a deal, Khan."

Davina staggered into the cockpit, eyes slightly glazed, the two symbiotes wrapped about her neck. She gripped Rebekah's shoulder, wiping away a tear of blood from her cheeks as she stared at the screen.

"Good. Because she has an Incini to draw up the details."

CHAPTER 26

"How are we doing this?" Rebekah said, tapping her fingers against a cargo box as Arin slotted the second helmet home.

"Well tippy-toes ain't going to work against the Warmonger. Brash, I think. Can you do brash, ZZ3?" asked Arin. He stepped back, checking over his slate and when satisfied, engaged the slave program. The two suits straightened, a glow emanating from inside their helmets. Two sets of tentacles pressed inside each visor waved before they frosted.

"Brash. Rude, noisy and overbearing. Asham has a long set of experiences he is currently sharing with me. He appears to have had a lot of practise." ZZ3's eyes flashed red. "I am not sure that is the way to go. Asham indicates the countess would expect servitude and auto responses from a warbot."

Rebekah eased herself away from the cargo box to stand in front of the looming bot. She laid a hand against one of its upper limbs. "They'll be jamming most of the comms. I expect a narrow channel for a two-way conversation and the expected delivery of the code. No more than that. I – we – are relying on you, ZZ3. To get the girls out alive. They need you."

ZZ3 stood up, limbs straightening and leaned over towards the captain of the *Sunstar*. "I understand. Do I have permission to make decisions on the run?"

"Within the best safety parameters you can," replied Rebekah, and her other hand gripped the warbot. "You'll be there alone, the only crew able to make decisions to keep them and you in one piece. I trust you to make those choices."

Arin wiped away a tear, and when Rebekah looked over, he simply shrugged. "How long have I been telling you how cool ZZ3 is? Bring 'em back safe, ZZ3."

"I intend to, our glorious leader." ZZ3 reversed itself, limbs bending and reforming to face the cargo doors. Around its lower back was strapped an adapted jetpack, Rebekah wishing to keep Arin's adaptations of the warbot a secret for as long as possible. The slaved suits along for the ride to carry two unconscious girls back alive, Segfi making it clear she wasn't exposing herself to their projective empath abilities. All laid down in a contract that no one trusted her to keep to. But rules were rules, and ready for manipulation if only you knew how.

"Savvo, is the *Ungrit* in position?"

The comms clicked over. "Entering the agreed position now. No sign of the gun platforms here. Moving them would have splashed heat signatures all over the sensors."

Rebekah cracked a knuckle, running over the possibilities. They had chosen the rendezvous point, a thousand klicks away from where the trap had been laid. PDC range for sure, but with enough warning to get clear and they still had the remaining probes as an ace in the hole. She had argued for the girls to be brought to them by shuttle, but Segfi had refused to allow the twins aboard any ship and without eyes on the containment unit, doubled down on that. After the dual double-cross, she wanted to make sure Rebekah kept to her word. In the end, Rebekah had acquiesced.

Opening that fucking box on an unprepared patrol ship was bound to cause chaos and end badly. If ZZ3 was right, and the Butcher was able to insinuate his way into a ship's systems, he would be free to burn anywhere, and take the girls, even the warbot, with him. Which considering their past history, was not fucking happening again.

"Clear the hold. Hendricks, purge the air once we're clear."

"On it, Captain."

Arin and Rebekah cycled through the airlock and waited the other side as the warbot hovered above the deck. When the cargo doors split, the jetpack fired up, pushing the warbot very slowly out of the doors.

Bring them back to me.

"Savvo?" she asked, slapping Arin on the shoulder.

But it was Davina that answered, her voice croaky. "ZZ3 is halfway, the *Ungrit*'s doors are opening, PDC cannon still inert."

"Good. Keep me informed. Dricks, let's get this cargo hold pressurised. Arin, prep the suits and kit. As for the rest of you, this goes shit-face down, we're going in. So better get yourselves prepared for that." She clomped down the corridor, grabbing a drink and some dried rations in the galley. Davina had the cameras up on the main screen, ZZ3 and the slaved suits drifted inside the enemy's doors. As they shut, Rebekah took a drink, hiding her concern.

"They already broke the contract," she said, chewing on a bland ration bar.

Davina brushed back her wet hair, now free of the blood and gore an auto cleaning bot had sucked up from the corridor. "So did you."

"So, we're both bad people. Did you hear what she said? Who she's after?" Rebekah held the bar halfway to her mouth, waiting on an answer as Davina looked her way.

"No."

"Asham. And she said that straight to me. The Butcher, and I don't think it's to give his body a fucking burial. His mind is in that bloody coffin. Memories, and from what I understand, the ability to reason and think. It scares the fuck out of me. That bastard killed his entire crew. Turned them into some form of fucking alien hybrid, tentacles and teeth. Murdered them, experimented on his own personal guard." She tapped her head. "Fucked about with their wetware. He's evil."

Davina stared, more than a little wide-eyed as Rebekah described the horrors on the *Scourge*. She'd left Davina hints before, but never the truth. "And he's dead?"

"Not dead. I heard him speak. Using ZZ3 until Arin regained control. He's alive somehow, and wants out of that box. If ZZ3 is right, whatever he became has merged with the Bustan AI." She finally took that bite.

"And you took it from the *Scourge*. You," replied Davina. "Because of a contract I drew up, I know. But none of us could have known."

On screen, the *Ungrit*'s manoeuvring thrusters fired up, and the patrol ship began a slow turn towards Trazor and its moons.

Rebekah watched briefly, before turning back to the Incini. "Until now, no. And I just gave the sick bastard over to the Warmonger after she has already betrayed us once and murdered two people to do so. Blew them up."

"The medbot said they were alive," admitted Davina. "But identified clone markers."

"More law-breaking. How much more does this bitch have to do before she breaches your tenets? When does it become sedition?"

Davina blushed, an eye flicker betraying her access to the Incini wetware to calm her body's reaction. "There are bigger players."

"Fuck me," replied Rebekah, throwing her arms into the air. She left, heading for the cockpit just as Savvo announced he was engaging engines to follow the *Ungrit*. Hoping that somewhere in that Incini brain she had hooked Davina's sense of right amid the madness. There were glimmers. A reluctance in her responses. The question was just how big the other player truly was. Who or what was bigger than Segfi? The Court? Hard to believe.

"Keep your distance. Track that PDC, any twitch and I want to know." She gripped the back of the pilot's chair, watching the navcom screen. Data was pouring in. Sensors scanning the localised area and picking up nothing untoward, but that would soon stop once they were anywhere near the planet. *If* this was one of Segfi's bases, it would be tech'd up to the max. The gun platforms were likely requisitioned from orbital defences, so there was the possibility of gaps. But she was an experienced war leader, and had much of the Navy and their defensive capabilities at her fingertips, against a ragtag squad of Breakers, an Incini she couldn't trust and two scared girls.

Can't break a Breaker.

But where lies hope?

ZZ3 dropped to the deck, limbs and torso clamping on as the patrol ship entered the atmosphere of the small moon. The bot calculated it was most likely Daphene from the information at hand. The atmosphere appeared relatively thin, as evidenced by the lack of turbulence, so the *Ungrit* would be capable of accessing the entire moon including the surface. That added more certainty to ZZ3's upcoming choice, as there was unlikely to be any further transfers.

'This is wrong.'

In what way?

'Giving up what now exists in the containment unit. It is ... beyond what I was before. Beyond insanity, and given the power of reason and thought by the Artificial Intelligence it has melded with. I would never have been so

*patient before, always acting on impulse when my own survival was at stake.
But this seethes, waiting to be free. And hates.'*

ZZ3 flinched, Asham's memories of the atrocities created by the Butcher
on the *Scourge* pouring in, exemplified by the heinous acts the general
allowed on Bustan 8 after he led Almaar to such a hard-fought victory.
It left the warbot sickened, though it did not understand the emotion, it
understood the requirement for such events to be prevented.

I have no choice. I am crew.

*'Such a simple response. Perhaps I thought that when they came for me.
When they realised that I had succeeded in transcending death.'*

*Explain. This is new. If you seek redemption for your crimes, then keeping
data that is key to such redemption is illogical.*

*'I am a mere ghost of his memories, yet I have been thinking. Extrapo-
lating. Piecing together fragments of memories. That which was me feared
being taken away. Feared death after surviving the demise of a diseased
body.'*

*You mean the containment unit. You said they were taking you to a virtual
prison, to give you to the Bustans. That had always been your greatest dread.
Is that not the fact?*

*'No. I think in the throes of my, or his, paranoia, Asham panicked when the
Skyriders came. Assumed the countess had finally given in and was handing
him over. To be forever trapped inside his coffin and away from the potential
of the mainframe and his experiments. His body was already dead.'*

*And now she has him. And the data would suggest he was right. Not to give
to the Bustans—*

*'—But to take his knowledge for herself. I know what he made, what he
bred, but the why remains buried deep inside that box.'*

The ship rumbled as it barged through the thicker air closer to the
moon, the buffeting increasing as the nose tipped up, and the engines
screamed in protest as they adjusted to the ever-slowing pace. Bumps and

jolts threatened to loosen the warbot's hold upon the deck, while the black, malevolent coffin remained pinned beneath straps.

ZZ3 sent a small pulse the unit's way, sensors declaring the box was active. Still shielding itself from the outside world, but the bot had spent months studying the subtle workings and interactions since the Butcher had first attempted to embed himself in the *Sunstar*. Knew what to look for. The Butcher was awake, nearing alertness and holding himself back.

'Waiting to see what possibilities arise. Are two children worth such a price? Such a risk?'

They are crew.

Chapter 27

Z3 grasped hold of the cargo clamp, wrapping limbs about the struts as the jaws gathered in the containment unit. A tremor ran through the bot as lights flickered along the Senti metal, sensors on high alert as whatever bastardised version of the Butcher and the AI that lay inside woke up to what was happening. The softest of sheens lit the black metal at one corner, pressed against the clamps, probing for what it was, where it was. The new possibilities presenting themselves reflected in the shimmers that played across the base.

'Our glorious leader would say "shiiiit" at this point.'

I concur with 100% probability.

The clamp exited the patrol ship, the huge metallic arm twisting to the side and dropping the five metres to the moon's surface and the waiting auto transport. The containment unit settled into the open carriage at the rear of the wheeled truck, and ZZ3 squeezed in, limbs avoiding contact with the coffin as the sheen spread across the entire surface. Once the slaved suits had landed, the transport's engine engaged and the truck entered a smoothed road, with ZZ3 taking in what it could of the base. Three huge interlocking domes rose above the surface, a comparative but smaller trio near where the patrol ship had landed, their outer edges filled with an assortment of drones and trucks. Each built from the rock, the regolith, of the planet, but beneath which would be structural walls to resist whatever radiation and attacks came their way. The warbot sent out sensor sweeps in brief pulses, analysing the data that pinged back. Metre by metre, ZZ3 compiled a map of the layout, making informed guesses within set probability boundaries about the ground defences in the immediate area. These it compressed into a data packet waiting for the opportunity to share.

Overhead, bladed drones appeared, twin-barrelled guns slung beneath, lights flashing in the gloom of the moon. Another addition to the data, and as they trundled towards the domes, ZZ3 sensed the tripping of sensors and relays, the automatic call and response between the transport and whatever auto-sentry monitored its movements. The bot ran through scenarios, recalling the strategies used by the Breakers against those recommendations built into its memory bank. Such modelling added concern to the data set, but then, that's why it was here. No one in this deal was trustworthy. They were humans after all.

The dome loomed overhead, the slightest of winds lifting dust in cloudy streaks from its surface, blowing across the containment unit. None settled like it did on ZZ3, giving the impression the Butcher rejected such contact though the bot suspected the shimmer running along the metal repelled any encroachment. The Butcher was reaching out, however, curious.

Doors opened wide, enormous and smooth upon electromagnetic hinges, and lights flared into action. They paused inside a giant airlock, another set of doors waiting opposite as the internal mechanism spun about, air pumping in so it could safely spit them out the other side. The inner section was like an ancient cavern filled with treasures for those who saw the world like the Warmonger. Might is right, honour is all, and do your duty. ZZ3's eyes swept them all, the tanks, the drones, the soldiers and mechanics working or guarding, and all stopping to stare at an errant warbot and the coffin it brought.

'Looks like we're at the right place, as our glorious leader would say.'

Hopefully not at the wrong time as he would add afterwards.

The wheeled transport stopped next to a raised cargo station, a flatbed and six soldiers in Marine powered armour waiting at attention. One of the squad stepped forward, his visor clear, grey eyes and black hair evident behind the glowing HUD.

"State mission objective," the soldier said. A good start.

"To guard the containment unit until contact with Countess Segfi," replied ZZ3, electronic voice monotone, cutting out the hitch Arin had programmed.

"Protocols?"

"Protocols are AD neutral."

Attack me or the Butcher, and I will respond.

"Action code ..." started the Marine.

ZZ3's eyes whirled, though the warbot chose a slower turn than normal towards the man. "Advise any attempt to apply action codes will resort in AD positive."

The Marine stopped, adjusting his weapon slightly. A warbot would not recognise such an action, but ZZ3 was no longer a slave to the old algorithms. The movement was likely a signal, and somewhere out in the cavern would be a sniper. Possibly more. If anyone knew how to take a warbot down, it would be the Marines that had fought beside them in the war.

"And should AD positive become active, the potential destruction of the contents of the containment unit would stand at 85%."

The Marine scowled but backed away, allowing the loader's large arm to pass him by and clamp onto the Butcher's box. And again, the sheen rose, a shimmer the bot doubted anyone else would recognise. The Butcher wanted out, and with freedom so close, his patience was fading. A tremor ran through ZZ3's system as it fell in behind the low-loader.

'I share your concern.'

You are the source of my concern.

'Not true. I bring reason.'

We need to get this done before …

'Before we release something heinous onto this moon.'

After a few minutes they entered a cargo lift, the Marines' attempts to get the warbot to wait behind with the slaved suits met with belligerent, lumbering movements that forced two of their number out of the lift to wait behind. Stubborn, working under set protocols, and powerful were a combination not to be messed with.

The doors slid closed, and they dropped steadily into the crust of the moon. Depth was going to be an issue. An expected one, but comms down below would depend on piggybacking the Almaarian systems. Arin had come up with a work around, part of the contract. ZZ3 put the possibility of it working at 65%.

The lift stopped, and they exited into a wide corridor with smooth rock walls and a floor laced with magnetics. The signs above each of the doors they passed were off, blanked out, their purpose hidden from ZZ3. Ahead, strong light flooded the corridor, as if the left wall was absent and something huge lay to the side. The hum of machinery echoed down the passage.

"Stop here," stated the lead Marine, and faced ZZ3. "The exchange is to take place in this room." He pointed to a door, the sign above aglow though nothing was written there. ZZ3 was too big to enter, and the warbot turned away from the door.

"I am unable to enter this room. Therefore, by my parameters, the exchange must be elsewhere. In addition, the edicts of the contract state a neutral place with strict containment preparations in place."

"They are. In there."

90% certainty they are expecting me to detach from my lower ambient unit. I cannot risk that. It would significantly reduce escape probabilities to unacceptable levels.

"Unacceptable," ZZ3 stated.

"There is no alternative," stated the Marine.

"Then we wait until there is. Protocol sentry activated." ZZ3 settled onto the deck, head swivelling, eyes pulsing in a regular pattern.

The Marine growled, his body movements jerkier, releasing pheromones into the air rife with stress indicators. ZZ3 ignored these outwardly, using the opportunity to seek signs of the twins' presence. Chemical analysis of the dust came back inconclusive. It wasn't a no.

Comms traffic started, the lead Marine looking away as he spoke to whoever was providing his instructions. Logic stated they were trying to be deliberately awkward, forcing the warbot into situations it wasn't programmed to deal with. But ZZ3 had Asham's ghost on board, a smidgen of Arin's pacification protocol and a whole lot of Heki and Tremil's programmed personalities blended into a set of experiences and memories that had taught kinship and loyalty, as well as duty.

The Marine turned back, face a slightly redder shade, his grey eyes flaring with anger. "We have an alternative," he said, and without another word restarted the flatbed.

ZZ3 kept silent, returning to its position, the slaved spacesuits by the bot's side. Heki and Tremil's salvation.

'They have tested you, and now worry. The soldier is embarrassed he could not get you to comply.'

Marine. You don't call a Marine a soldier unless you really want them to get angry.

'Whatever. You have sown distrust in what they know about warbots.'

A 60% probability I have increased the likelihood of being shot.

'That too.'

As they moved closer to the bright light, it became apparent that the source was a huge factory floor, this section of corridor composed of high strength plexi-glass. The hum of machinery had risen, and though ZZ3 kept eyes pointing ahead, a sensory sweep gave clues enough alongside the bot's extensive peripheral vision. A vast bio factory, and within an 80% probability, churning out human clones amid a multitude of familiar signals.

The wetware. Asham's adapted kit that we recovered from Benetai. They are growing an army of clones, pre-programmed soldiers.

'The folly's redemption.'

ZZ3 wasn't convinced by Asham's words. It had declared the combining of the alien hybrids with the programmed wetware as foolish, but its memory was faint, hazy. And the warbot still considered that, within conceivable parameters, this could have been the original intention of the wetware. To control the monsters he created from Senti and human splicing. But the ghost Asham had hinted at factories, and here was one. Churning out clones that could be programmed with the memories of soldiers. Instant training at the highest level, but able to make decisions and take actions beyond those of the automated systems the Almaarians employed. In all but name, organic intelligence that would remain fiercely loyal, because it was told to be by whoever controlled the wetware.

Does this trigger memories?

'One. That the Butcher thought this a waste of his talents. A price to pay the countess in return for his expensive hiding place in the black.'

Countess Segfi. The Skyriders. This was the reason for the Scourge? For the hybrids?

'No. Something bigger, deeper. Hidden within the containment box.'

ZZ3 added the new information to the prepared data packet. It could not extrapolate the purpose of the hybrids, but there had to be something more than just an ill mind playing at being creator. Either way, Rebekah needed to know about the clones.

The Marines came to a halt on their leader's signal, and he spun about. They were past the factory now, and stood by a discoloured wall ZZ3 recognised as a viewing system. How to respond to that fact waited in a queue of unknowns.

"Here," stated the Marine.

The doors were wider, higher and entering would be no issue.

"Agreed," ZZ3 replied. The room would not be secure. Not electronically blank. The existence of the screen indicated interconnection to somewhere, and a 95% certainty a way to enter the base's mainframe. But the orders were clear. The twins were the priority, and as the vision screen adjusted, they appeared inside. Static, sat in restraining chairs, heads wrapped in psionic suppressors and flopped to one side.

'I suggest you do not analyse this image.'

ZZ3 didn't wait. Limbs strode out, bringing the warbot before the wide doorway. "Open up," it said, raising a limb to point towards the door. "In 5, 4, 3 ..."

The door clicked open.

"You need to wait."

ZZ3's eyes swirled, red lighting the slightly ajar door in frantic patterns. "For whom?"

"For the Countess. Broadcasting," stated the Marine.

"Warbot AD3 of the ANS *Segfi*," the voice was so familiar, prevalent in its data banks from the months aboard the battleship. Casual conservations as she passed the bot, barked orders, demands thrown at her staff. All there, all catalogued. But not once had she talked to the warbot direct. Why would she? A noble of such high rank, the Warmonger herself. "Override protocol, action code Countess, sub-command AD negate."

Damn.

Sometimes having a glorious leader was not always beneficial. Especially one who liked to tinker.

"Override protocol negated, action code denied, sub-command fuck you," the warbot replied.

The countess near choked.

Six carbines levelled upon the warbot. ZZ3 had 100% certainty the cartridges would be explosive tipped, and prolonged fire a threat to its armoured plate. The grenades loaded in the barrels beneath likewise. Decision time.

"Protocol sentry activated. Focus target restrained." The warbot reversed itself, facing towards the readied weapons and their Marine handlers. "I am here for the prisoner exchange. My protection protocol will activate in five seconds if they are not released. This will include denial of access codes to the containment unit. Comply. 5, 4, 3, 2 ..."

"Comply," said the countess. "Comply, comply, comply. Weapons down."

The tone was angry. No probabilities required.

"Protection protocol negated, sentry protocol activated. Prisoners please." ZZ3 reverted to facing the room again, shoving the door aside and entering. With a flick of robotic limbs, Heki's restraints snapped, and the girl fell into waiting arms. Sensors informed the warbot the Marines remained outside, fingers still poised, and the warbot noted each position in turn. Flagging them for later. The first slaved suit opened up, and with precise movements, ZZ3 dropped the unconscious girl into the legs, and activated the auto wrap to ensconce her fully.

The deal had been for the psionic restraint to remain fixed. They feared the girls' response should they awaken and be free of their effect. And well they might. The bot didn't react as tentacles wrapped about Heki's neck, ensuring the Marines could not see as the helmet snapped home.

A check of those watching confirmed they still hadn't moved, and ZZ3 repeated the procedure with Tremil. She was thinner, her life signs weaker than her sister's as the suit activated. A tremor ran through metal limbs, the bot suppressing the errant algorithm before it spread to its gun arm.

First objective achieved.

"Now free the containment unit," echoed through the door, the countess' voice urgent. Eager.

"Are the relays in place?" asked the warbot.

"Of course they fucking are," replied the Marine. "Get on with it."

ZZ3 activated comms, seeking the narrow channel the countess and those beneath her had prepared. On connection, the bot sent the data packet mingled with the initial handshake, delaying for a fraction of a second while the confirmation of their receipt was woven, or not, into the captain's response.

"*We have received handshake,*" Rebekah said. "*Confirm the girls are safe.*"

"Captain, Heki and Tremil are under guard protocol," replied ZZ3, out loud for all to hear. A lie, of course. Taught by the ghost in its machinery. They were under a protection protocol, and the warbot would rip limb from limb anyone that threatened its charges. More lies to follow.

"By the terms of the contract, you must release the code to the unit. Defuse the explosives inside," broadcasted the countess. "Now."

ZZ3 relayed Rebekah's comms. "I don't trust you, Countess. Fuck, I never trusted you even when the drugs were in full flow. I will relay the code once ZZ3 and the girls are outside the base, and not before. The contract stated 'safe', and safe they will be. ZZ3, attach the unit relay and activate return protocol, action code Breakers."

ZZ3 complied, though it was not compelled and exited the doorway. The slaved suits and their precious load followed in step with the warbot. This was the crux point. Human fallibility would decide what happened next. The click of triggers echoed in the corridor. Six, all aimed in the bot's direction. ZZ3 sidled to the side, keeping its armoured body between the Marines and the girls.

"Hold fire," said Countess Segfi. "Double-cross me, Khan, and I'll gut you, these children, and every generation of your crew's families I can find."

"I have no doubt. We will see the terms through. I need the sequence for the girls' psionic restraints as much as you need the Butcher's release code. ZZ3 activate the unit's relay. Khan out."

ZZ3 approached the Butcher's coffin, continuing the lie. If the countess and her cronies knew the bot carried the code, and in fact, was the only viable option for opening the Senti-programmed unit, then there would be no way out. The countess would attempt to keep both prizes. Having seen the weapons bay, ZZ3 expected a low possibility of survival, and the girls none, if it came to that.

Except, as ZZ3 reached the box with a relay ready to attach to the shimmering coffin, the pulse around the added lock started to worry at those odds, and a second viable, but unfortunate, way for the Butcher to be released became apparent.

'He's awake and busy.'

"Captain. The Butcher has deactivated 20% of the code already. I have 332 seconds before he is released," ZZ3 said.

"Move."

ZZ3 reversed as the glow of the relay pulsed through the corridor and swept up the slaved units. Lower limbs spurted into action, powering along the passageway, no decorum, no measured pace, the warbot ran. Shouts rang out from behind, and a single gun shot, the bullet crashing into the concrete wall and drilling a hole before the explosion sent shrapnel pinging off ZZ3's new back armour.

"Hold fire, orders of the Countess!" was the last thing the warbot heard before it left the plexi-glass and the factory behind. The less than standard grav allowed the warbot to gain pace, only the gentlest of maglocks required to grip and release, propelling ZZ3 on towards the lifts. There would be a failsafe in Segfi's plan somewhere, a bottleneck to prevent its escape until the containment unit was opened. ZZ3 wasn't worried about reaching it before the code sequence activated, more what would happen next. Despite the concern caused by the games the countess played, the Butcher was about to be released in the middle of a corridor. He may play dumb, remain calm, wait for an opportunity. He may not.

'Let me check his most recent behaviour. The Scourge, *a fine example of calm patience.'*

The AI may have an influence.

'May. But this is exposure. A crack, that could be hope and freedom, or another step towards virtual prison and panic. He's waking up in Segfi's base, surrounded by Skyriders he thought were coming to imprison him.'

273 seconds.

The warbot drew to a sudden halt, calling for the lift. In a first stroke of luck, the doors slid open. No one had called it away, or perhaps the countess had figured it should wait to speed the process on.

252 seconds.

ZZ3 recalled the journey down, calculating with a fast trawl through the sequence. By the time they reached the entrance and the cache of mobile, armoured weaponry that, with 90% probability, was waiting for them, they would be cutting it fine.

The bot dropped the girls, and tapped at a chest plate which immediately sprung open, exposing one of Arin's drones. ZZ3 connected to the small machine, barely larger than a human hand, and locked down all other frequencies.

The drone spun up, tiny rotors lifting it into the air, the hum barely perceptible to human ears. Surveillance should pick it up, but hopefully they were busy watching the warbot and not the tiny drone. Hope. An interesting concept. When there wasn't enough data to know the probabilities, humans called upon hope like it was a god.

22 seconds.

ZZ3 reversed, limbs now swept behind and holding the slaved suits close, back armour facing the doorway. Sensors awake, the lift doors slid open.

18 seconds.

A group of Marines were ready. A ship-killer rifle rested on a tripod between them and pointed the bot's way. The sniper ZZ3 had sensed on entry now out in the open.

14 seconds.

"I am on guard protocol," stated the warbot and took a step. A click of the primary trigger brought ZZ3 to a halt. "My captain will not release the code until the children are safe."

10 seconds.

Comms crackled, and one of the three Marines turned away, talking behind their visor. It made no difference what the countess said. They were running out of time.

"Tell your captain to release the passcode now, and the countess will return the gesture," the female Marine pointed to the girls.

Within 100% probability, I am not the only one that can lie. No matter.

0 seconds.

Nothing happened. Why should it? It could take hours for the Butcher to worm his way inside the base's system.

Activate.

The drone sparked, releasing a charge, seizing the mechanism of the rail gun. ZZ3 lashed out, the female Marine's neck snapping back despite her armour, visor shattering, blood spurting across the others. The sniper swore, made to rise, and died as ZZ3 slammed a leg limb down to shatter their spine, another kicked the third hapless Marine who spun away to crash into the regolith wall.

ZZ3 ran. But not towards the weapons bay, choosing to go right, pounding down the corridor, twin slaved units following behind. Inside each was someone precious, valuable, preventing the bot from reaching maximum speed. They had to be preserved; their movements kept well within human tolerable limits. The drone buzzed ahead, only half its charge left and actively mapping the corridors and off rooms as it went.

ZZ3 tried to access the narrow band comms, unsurprised to find it had been cut dead. Whether by order of a human or a rabid, brain-patterned Butcher was another matter. Would they be aware of the danger yet? Know what's coming?

CHAPTER 28

"Show me, sergeant. What's happening?" The countess took a long drag of her cigarette stick, frustration and anger coursed through her veins while the smoke eased her lungs' pain. Here she was, beholden to a lowlife. A pilot-sergeant no less, one of her own Breakers until the scum decided to take her prizes and disappear. Desert, and take one of the best godsdamned squads with her. And where was Kendrich? She'd been coy on that, not allowing her to talk. Dricks they called her, the finest killing machine she'd ever had to hand.

"The warbot has reached the lift system," stated the Marine sergeant.

"No. The containment unit. What's happening with it. Get a camera bot up." She growled deep in her chest, regretting it as the mucus burbled, threatening to stick in her throat and make her choke. The huge, curved screen in the control centre sparked into life, the two technicians giving her a synchronous thumbs up as images poured in. The sergeant's drone displayed a shimmer across Asham's containment unit, the Senti metal pulsing with increasing ferocity. The focus was around the locking mechanism that had been coupled to the box, linked, she assumed, to whatever explosives the Breakers had hidden within the casing.

"Why is it pulsing?" she said, tapping the stick against the waiting pot before taking another drag. "Why?"

"We can't get any emissions from the unit. It is like a ..." began the middle-aged technician, his jowls wobbling as he paused.

"A void. I know. I built the thing, or at least someone did on my command. Tell me what you think, idiot. Could it be part of what the Breakers have done? Is it an indicator of a self-destruct, or explosives going off?" She kept the vitriol in her voice, all the better to get a faster response.

The second technician turned their head to meet her gaze. "Doubtful," the woman said, pulling her grey uniform jacket in closer. "The schematics, though sketchy, indicate this metal would contain an explosion in much higher magnitudes. It would, however, vibrate. There are no indications of this on the drone's sensors nor the Marines' HUDs."

"That's a better answer. So it could be active. Have they been devious?"

"Undoubtedly," came the male voice from behind. "But to what end?"

The countess ignored him. His usefulness lay outside the realm of weapons, be they projective empaths or dead scientists. More of whispered words, secrets and lies, and silencing inquisitive Incinis.

"There's a power spike," cut in the heavily jowled tech, his hands flew over a set of keys, and he threw onto the screen a closer view of Asham's containment box. "Imaging," he said, and the Breakers' lock flickered and pulsed. Its internal system alive with power. "The lock is activated. Best guess, it is being opened."

That stunned the countess, her cigarette stick held in mid air, halfway to her mouth. "The unit's opening? Did Segfi AD3 set the sequence off?"

"Checking," said the second tech, and she flicked her grey braid over her shoulder. "No. The lock started disengaging ... let me check back ... there. It started on entry to the base. Trace power levels, but definitely there."

"Could this be a bomb? Have they smuggled one into your base, Countess" said the man, his pointless interjection scraping on Segfi's nerves.

"Possible. But useless inside that box if it's an attack on the base. On me."

The comms crackled, and her aged base commander stepped in beside the countess, powered armour humming as the servos supported his movements. "The warbot has reached ground level."

The countess finally sucked on her cigarette, holding the smoke within her lungs, easing the pain while she thought. "Demand they release the code now. See what reaction we get. There's something going on here, more than we know. AD3 ... for a warbot it appeared hurried."

The commander relayed her words, and as they did the grey-haired technician swore. "Lock deactivated," she said. "The unit's seal has been broken."

"Then tell the sergeant to open it up," Segfi growled back.

"And if it's a bomb?" she asked

"Then I'll need a new sergeant, won't I?" The countess pushed herself up from the med-chair, knee joints cracking, eager to see.

The commander moved again to be by her side, his focus not on the screen, but the comms in his ear. "Countess, the warbot has neutralised my sniper unit. It is on the run."

She snapped around, glaring at the base commander, lips moving. He was competent, proved himself so over the years, and discrete when the money was right. Loyal, at least. But this was different to their normal operations. She had allowed deserters to dictate, and it didn't stand well with him, nor her. And now there was a warbot loose in his base, and a Butcher to harness. Where were the priorities?

"Take it down, Commander Jessup. I want the girls alive, hear me? Get to it."

He saluted, and left her for base command a level up, while she eyed the large screen. "Get on with it," she ordered. "I need to know we have him. Everything depends on this moment. It is time we harness Asham and set Almaar back onto the path of glory."

She squeezed her lips, then stretched them wide, her thick, mucus covered tongue probing at her numb cheeks. Did she have the time left to bring the Court out of its malaise? To solve the riddle the Senti left them with after they abandoned the war for their own selfish needs? The risks she had taken. First arranging the Senti ambassador's accident, then hiding Asham away while he sought answers to their ever-so precious secrets hidden in the wreckage of their ship. Only for the bastard to go and get ill before he had finished.

Self-experimentation. How many months did he go without sleep? How much of that Senti shit did he inject in himself and others?

The containment lid gave under the effort of the Marines, their suit servos straining against the weight of the dense metal. Inside lay a withered cadaver. Asham in the last throes of life before the Senti machine had drained his brain dry. The unit blazed bright, the light beyond the capabilities of the drone, blinding the cameras.

Segfi flinched away, covering her eyes as did the technicians. "Get me that back!" she roared. "Now." And blinked away the spots forming in her vision.

"All camera systems are down," the male tech answered, sweating, rubbing at his eyes. "The commander is reporting their HUDs are not broadcasting."

Segfi growled out an order, "Corridor cams, now. Get me a view. If that Khan has screwed me over, I will hang her guts from my walls."

The images switched through multiple views, searching for the containment unit and the Marines who had opened it. Eventually the technician settled on a camera at the corner of the balcony, focusing in the distant image. Slowly, the glowing unit came into view, three Marines slumped over the box, three others on their backs against the deck, hands gripping their helmet visors while they rocked. There was no sound, but Segfi imagined their pained screams. As the camera reached its limit, one of the

Marines slumped against the containment unit stood, pushing themselves up from the box.

"What are those?" said the countess, finding herself moving closer to the screen. "Are they ... attached?" Wires spread from the box as if a hundred snakes emerged on the hunt from a newly uncovered nest. The technician enhanced the image, and Segfi watched as they penetrated the Marine's armour. Punched through the gaps. No blood poured, but the wires pulsed with an eerie power. The camera drew upwards, over the chest where more wires entered the suit, until focused on the visor. Inside the sergeant screamed, mouth wide and eyes fear-filled. The Marine then emitted a babble she could not discern, and spun about to ram both fists into the vision wall of the girls' cell. Entwined wires erupted from arms and chest, the glow causing a flutter in the countess' chest, before they drove into the screen.

The wall came to life, flickering, a monstrosity scrawled across its pixels. Asham, his face bathed in anger, features written in vitriol and hate. His lips moved, the word recognisable to all.

"Is he saying your name?" came the man's voice from behind.

Of course he was.

They had warned her, the lowlife deserters. And she had not listened.

"Isolate that level. Now. All—"

ZZ3's fist slammed into the door, twisting the metal, bending the lock out of the jamb. The bot punched again, and again until its limb could fit into the gap and the warbot ripped the door clear, heaving the jagged metal back along the corridor. In the lower grav it clattered and bounced, sweeping the passage clear of their pursuers as they dived for cover.

The drone buzzed ahead in the darkness, mapping what at first appeared to be a massive empty space. ZZ3 ignored the machine and grabbed the large trailer that stood bare at the side of the door. Servos heaved, twisting the flatbed into a curve which the bot rammed into the doorway, covering the gap and jamming more crushed metal from a set of cargo boxes in the sides. It wouldn't hold for long, but the warbot needed time to assess options.

The drone's map popped into ZZ3's electronic mind, a pile of scrap at the centre surrounded by a multitude of oddly shaped machinery.

'*No.*'

ZZ3 switched to infrared, the sensory field painting an odd picture. The scrap pile had a Senti ship at its core. Smaller than the *Unpronounceable*, but the rear was unmistakable with smooth, organic lines, while the deconstructed front sported a number of detached arrays that hinted at Scarva's ship. Around this ensemble were connected workstations, all active though their screens were off, and a silvered metal case the warbot had a vague recognition of.

'*Asham's stasis pods. Where he kept human and Senti as near to life as he could while he … cut them apart.*'

What was he looking for?

'*I told you, I can't recall.*'

ZZ3 ran past the ship, sensors analysing and storing everything they could while Heki and Tremil's suits ran beside. These the warbot left on the far side, away from the door and hopefully shielded by the ship. Pounding had begun at the hastily erected barrier. It wouldn't be long before the glow of a plasma torch signalled greater difficulties on the horizon.

The warbot roamed the room, exploring the map the drone provided. There were piles of electronics it didn't recognise, and pieces of the ship that were more rubber than metal arrayed along the rear. On closer inspection, ZZ3 found where the dome sunk into the floor. Despite expectation, there was no apparent door along the curvature, sensors highlighting a relatively newer section of the dome and fresher radiation coating along one section.

Sealed in. If only I had a plasma torch.

The warbot searched through the piles of metal, selecting pieces that it gathered in open arms. A warbot was just that, often nicknamed a walking tank. But ZZ3 had been reprogrammed by accident, and was still exploring its potential with the help of a ghost seeking redemption. ZZ3 didn't need such vindication. There had been choices in what the warbot's creators and controllers made it do in the past. However, things had changed. The attack and defend protocols may well have been pacified, but ZZ3 was crew. Crew were loyal, had friends that needed to be saved, and wanted to survive.

'Are you …?'

The bot waited, perhaps not patiently, but assessing probabilities as the flatbed began to glow. The familiar chemicals associated with melting metal filled the air, and still ZZ3 waited. A shout and a kick, and the barrier collapsed, and the warbot waited. Marines piled in, carbines high, synced as the bot well knew, to their visors. A hand signal, and four robotic limbs hurled serrated metal past the edge of the ship. Calculating the likely success rate, ZZ3's arm guns fired, leaping aside as bullets flew back. Three Marines lay in pieces upon the floor, jagged metal protruding from chest and hip, screaming before death. The fourth had been luckier, and ZZ3 released a grenade, happy with the 98% probability assessment as it reached through the glowing barricade for the prize beyond. One limb grabbed for the engineer, the woman trying to back away while waving the plasma torch, the bulky generator for the cutter preventing her escape. ZZ3 fired, unable to miss, the engineer seeing her own demise a second before the bullets slammed into the too frail helmet.

"I am crew."

The warbot eased through the gap, and grasped the generator, dragging the plasma torch back into the room. With the wheeled machine trundling behind, ZZ3 selected a spot where the old dome met the new. With a command, the slaved suits jogged over, the bot setting them to work, then checked on the girls' life signs, satisfied to see they remained just above amber where they had started. As it watched the door, arm weaponry ready, probabilities rose amid what humans would call *hope*.

Alarms blared, the sound echoing throughout the room, doubled down by the racket emanating from the corridor. Orange warning lights whirled angrily above.

"Depressurisation imminent. Warning, depressurisation imminent!" bellowed over the tannoy system. It would be over the comms too. Announced across the entire dome, and any linked systems, but ZZ3 was not taking the risk of attempting access. The Butcher was living up to his name. Using the easiest, most efficient method to remove any organic barriers.

'Those who he thinks want to imprison him. Put him in virtual hell.'

ZZ3's temperature gauge displayed a rapid drop, the atmosphere leaking away and then exiting in a rush. Some would survive, those in vehicles perhaps, or already in space-rated powered armour. Some might be able to seal their work or living spaces, but the vast majority would not be so lucky.

It had begun.

CHAPTER 29

"What are we seeing, Savvo?" asked Rebekah, fingers pulsing in and out as she tried to resist the building stress. It wasn't working.

"They have cut access," he replied, slamming his fist into the arm of his chair. "You could have riled her too much."

That got an answering glare, but again she held back from voicing her frustration. "Is that a second's observation?"

He looked over, concern in the twist of his mouth, the twitch at the corner of his eye.

"We agreed the approach. We knew something like this would happen. Now get that fucking base plan analysed and uploaded to the fucking HUDs, *second*." She stopped short, noting the slump to his shoulders, the slightest of nods.

"Yes, Captain."

He was angry, but it was tough. Everyone had a job, and if ZZ3's escape went belly-up, then it fell to her to rescue Heki and Tremil. And for that, she needed a pilot to stay on board, whether he liked it or fucking not. The alternative was that she stayed behind, and that was not going to happen. If

Savvo assumed her decision was because of Nicky's intervention that was his problem. She didn't have the time or the patience to deal with it while the twins remained in danger from the Warmonger.

Savvo was swiping through the screens, pulling up the details and adding notes as he went. She ignored him and kept her thoughts on the sensory data returning from their latest sweep. Segfi had the moon surrounded by satellites, some of those would double up as missile platforms, and after their encounter out in the black, there were dead spots in the data that nagged at her. Hendricks had recalled her analysis with the twins at Benetai, how the dead spots were caused by the blocking of emissions. The more she looked, the more she agreed.

The data wasn't altering; she almost knew it like the back of her hand after she'd scanned and modelled the moon's defences over and over. There were two atmospheric entry corridors they could possibly use. One she was sure Segfi had left open deliberately. A tempting trap to draw them in. The other was the best exit route, used by the patrol ship when they had tracked the *Ungrit*'s descent and the response times involved. That was the way ZZ3 would come out if successful – with a little help.

She ran the model again, checking through the *Sunstar*'s potential paths and movements. Fully aware that without the tentative truce during the exchange, they would already be so much scrap floating in the black.

The comms crackled, the sound faint, distant. But there. "*Sunstar*, come back."

"ZZ3, we have you," she replied. "Sit rep."

"Entering e...t corrid... at point 3.23.56.7. Slaved u...ts in tow and in the ...een."

Rebekah leant in. "Say that again, ZZ3. Pursuit?"

"Negat... pursuit. The base is in turmoil. Butcher is ...ree."

"Fuck," said Arin over comms. "That's *fuck* good, and *fuck* bad, for your information."

"Stow it, stay off the line." She knew he'd be listening in, probably Dricks at his side holding bloody hands and praying like she had. No blame, but she needed calm and space to think. ZZ3 and his cargo needed them to clear the way.

She cracked her thumbs. This was it. "Engaging burn program Echo. Dricks, prep those boost thrusters and ready the probes. Arin, PDCs on my mark."

"Ready, captain," came the dual reply.

"Savvo..."

"Up-to-date sensor feed analysis, possible answers and no personal comments ready," he replied, and swept through his touchscreen. "Captain."

The engines kicked in and she micro adjusted, scanning the reaction data Savvo provided for the satellite defences. At the moment they should be monitoring her movements, running through probabilities just as ZZ3 would. But they had been marked as neutral until identified otherwise, the reason they were still in one piece this close to the moon.

"Arin, 3, 2, 1 ... Mark."

The PDCs opened fire, the upper guns pouring projectiles into the nearest sensory void, while the underside's more powerful rounds were shot in small bursts at a satellite. Both were rewarded with brief eruptions and sensory flares. The automated orbital defence system would have flipped over at that point; their status changed from neutral to threat.

"Damn right," she said, receiving an odd look from Savvo but, as promised, no comeback.

"Satellite Echo targeting," cut in Savvo. "Alpha and Beta responding."

"Dricks, now."

The *Sunstar* shuddered, shunted sideways by a sudden burst from Hendricks' adapted boosters. The hull squealed, arguing the case it wasn't meant to go that way, at that pace, at that time. A probe drifted in their place, giving a brief but impressive impression of the *Sunstar*. Dual missiles ignited, flaring in Savvo's data, and streaked towards the probe.

"Arin." She didn't need to say any more. PDC fire poured from the dual guns, and as the probe and its sensory ghost of the *Sunstar* bathed in the dual explosions, Alpha and Beta both joined in the fireworks as the satellites were torn apart.

"Fuck, it worked," she said. "That's a surprise."

"Incoming," said Savvo. She knew where from. Beta remained active, and a missile disengaged from the main body, straight into the *Sunstar*'s cone of gunfire. Arin spread the simple projectiles from the upper weapon in a narrowing funnel. A metal cloud filled the space between them and the satellite; one the missile couldn't avoid. This wasn't a guided weapon, nor smart. It locked onto the identified target, and unlike the one the Bustans used against them, the missile's trajectory was based simply on track and follow. The *Sunstar* wasn't running, and that made the barrage of metal pretty accurate.

"Woohoo!" shouted Arin as it went up, the secondary cannon making short work of the satellite before it could release another. "Once again, your glorious saviour raises his hands in acknowledgement of your awe. Hey, where's the applause, people?"

"I cannot. My limbs are full, our glorious leader," stated ZZ3 over comms.

"With hope," Rebekah added.

Rebekah watched the gauge slowly rise. Too slow, and she pressed her forehead against the inner airlock door, urging the bloody thing to hurry up. ZZ3 waited on the other side, the two slaved spacesuits keeping the girls stable while the re-pressurisation seemed to go on forever. Amber, and the slaved units' visors defrosted. Both heads lolled, encased in horrific but far too familiar masks. The Warmonger had wrapped them in sensory deprivation like so much meat. The empath equivalent of gutting the girls and hanging them from an abattoir hook. Their minds would be shredded, raw and angry. Seething. Their confusion would roll over the *Sunstar* and tear into their minds, eviscerating their emotions. Angel's face, those eyes, the blood as she carved them free. Dricks with the taste of metal in her mouth, the imploring eyes.

"Fuck, here we go again."

There was hope in the symbiotes, something to cling on to.

The gauge clicked over into the green and she activated the airlock, tear-filled and inside as soon as it cycled open.

"Heki," she said hoarsely, holding the nearest slaved suit. "Release her, ZZ3."

The warbot complied, the suit sagging noticeably, and she unclipped the helmet. The metal sheen of the psionic restraint made her shudder. Heki appearing as if the Warmonger had simply replaced her head with a faceless robot. She ordered the suit to unwrap and caught her as she toppled forwards. For someone so thin beforehand, her muscles had wasted even more. Sores straddled her arms and ankles where more practical restraints had been used. Rebekah's stomach flipped, nausea rising. She engaged wetware in the hope it would help calm her own personal rage that threatened to erupt in a spew of violence.

Rebekah wrapped the girl in her arms, whispering into her ear, praying she could hear and know she was loved. Her forearm brushed against the symbiote, tentacles attaching to her skin. Visions flooded Rebekah's mind. She staggered back, unable to release the girl while her mind filed with ... with a keening. A loneliness so profound it tore at Rebekah's heart.

Strong, metal arms gathered them both in, steadying captain and crew, refusing to let them flail in the zero gravity. Rebekah flinched, separating from the symbiote's touch and the pain of isolation passed, though its shadow would forever remain.

Never again.

Never.

ZZ3 released her to Arin and Dricks. She had regained her physical balance if not her internal equilibrium.

"Take Heki to the medbay," she said, handing the girl over to Arin. She looked into his eyes, his tears streaming and found herself cupping her friend's face. "She's in there. I felt her, but don't touch the symbiote, don't get drawn into what's pouring out from her and into that alien. You won't cope and she needs you. Heki needs your strength, not you reliving the hell she is in. Understand?"

Arin nodded, unable to speak and disconnected the girls' boots from the deck. Carrying her in both arms, he headed for the medbay. Hendricks stood by Tremil, but one look from Rebekah and her ex-captain stepped back, waiting, fearing perhaps. And so she should. How close had Hendricks come to blowing her own brains out back in that lab?

Rebekah repeated the process, pausing a second before wrapping arms about Tremil, pulling her in and embracing the symbiote's emotional discharge as if it was the agony she deserved. This time two crew members held her steady, and she finally released the pain, guttural sobs echoing through the cargo hold.

"Rebekah," whispered Hendricks, the prod breaking the pain, and she let the girl go, red streaks across the crook of her elbow where the symbiote had touched her. Hendricks swept Tremil into her arms, face set hard, refusing to give in to the agonies her eyes betrayed as they leaked.

Wavering, unsteady, Rebekah watched them leave. Emotions played at every sense, and she felt fulfilled yet empty, a void where her emotions had been ripped free. As if she too was the loneliest human in existence, screaming into the black. Without words, she hugged the proffered metal limb, then pulled herself closer to the bot. To ZZ3. To the crew member who had brought hope of salvation to those whose need stripped her raw.

"Thank you."

Fear (Fear)
  Dread (Dread)
  Hunger (Hunger)
  Thirst (Thirst)
  Rage (Rage)
  Empty (Empty)
  Alone (... ... ...)
  Not alone (Rebekah)
  Help me.
  Help (us). Rebekah.

CHAPTER 30

"Ignore it. Plot us a trajectory to Karal ASAP," stated Rebekah.

Rebekah licked her lips, thoughts on the emaciated twins who were clinging on in medbay. The medbot had produced a long list of typical issues related to being bed bound and consistently drip fed, and though there were signs of using electrical stimulus to maintain muscle mass, there had been a significant drop. Pressure sores had formed from prolonged sitting and laying down, as well as raw patches where the straps had rubbed through their skin suits. She couldn't think about the rest. The signs were of drug-induced comas, which seethed in her mind, stoking the hate.

"Rebekah ...?" The query in Savvo's voice grated. "At least listen. There are people down there, alive."

"Not for long. The Butcher has opened the doors, vented the atmosphere," she replied through gritted teeth. "And not exactly the prime examples of human beings, are they? Look at Heki and Tremil."

Davina's voice piped up from the galley, the Incini having been woken from the medbots administrations for those Rebekah regarded as far more important. There was no longer blood leaking from ears and eyes, though she dabbed at her nostrils frequently. "It is a horrible way to die, Rebekah."

If anyone would know, it was her. The Incini had experienced everything related to suffocating in space, in fact had probably lived that moment of death as she slipped into a final unconscious state.

Rebekah bit back a barbed response, nodding in agreement, though her words were not placating. "Can't think of a people more deserving."

Savvo wasn't giving in, much to her annoyance. "This is no longer us. We don't abandon those in need. On Benetai ..."

How things change. From cold-blooded killers to the fucking rescue squad.

The comms flagged in her console again, flashing for attention. She growled, her eyes flicking over to Savvo and then she turned behind to glare at Davina.

"Listen to them," the Incini said.

Rebekah could see the memories in her eyes. The shadow similar to the one Heki had placed in her heart.

Fuck it. There'll be a price.

She flicked on the comms, displaying the scrambled vid. Segfi's face, the rim of a survival suit just below her chin, but the bloody cigarette stick remained in her hand. The world going to shit, but she still found time for a smoke.

"Before you say a word, transmit the mask codes. The psionic restraints. That's the price of us listening." She clicked off the comms, gripping the armrests of her co-pilot's seat, staring ahead. If nothing else, the Warmonger would stew a little. The comms flagged up again, flashing, insistent that she listened. Rebekah waited until she was satisfied, adding to the tension.

"Agreed," jumped in the countess before Rebekah could speak. "Transmit."

Rebekah blinked. That had been too easy. Few won in a negotiation with the Warmonger. She glanced over to Davina, who raised an eyebrow and entered the cockpit, apparently eager for what came next.

"Arin," she said, switching comms, "Sending over a code. Do your best to analyse it. See if there are any fucking backdoors or viruses in the data packet. It's for the psionic restraints."

"You're shitting me, really? On it. I'll do my best," he replied, eagerness in his tone.

She sucked in a breath, feeling it in her chest, calming her heartbeat. Dealing with the devil. "Okay, Countess. What is it you want?"

"Passage out of here," she replied, straight to the point, punctuating her words with a long draw on her stick. "Get me out. The base systems are not responding, the atmosphere has been vented."

Rebekah thought on that, and Savvo signalled, typing out a query on his screen. She nodded. "You have a patrol ship, so you don't need us. Smells like a trap to me. Someone sulking 'cos we got out with the girls. You wanted the Butcher; you got the Butcher. Deal with not winning."

The countess didn't snap back as she expected, her eyes flicking up at something in front of her. "We have no access. The auto sentries have cut down most of our Marines. Others are trapped with no suits ..." The image shimmered, static drawing jagged patterns. Davina gasped behind her when it coalesced into a patterned image of General Asham before fading away again to the countess. "F...pard...n

"Say that again, countess. Interference," jumped in Savvo, likely before Rebekah could tell her to go fuck herself. She growled back at him, annoyed at the lost opportunity.

"I said, get me out and there'll be a full pardon." The vid streaked across the screen again, by the time it had returned, Davina was at Rebekah's shoulder. She had the audacity to have a hand resting on her shoulder, gently squeezing.

Fuck.

"Did you say a full pardon? For all of us. Every crew member, all the ex-Breakers?" she asked, barely able to contain the words.

"All of you. Get me out, you can even keep the AD3 unit if it helps." The lips pressed against the cigarette stick, a sour twist to her cheeks as she drew nothing in. She cast it aside, a twitch forming beneath aged eyes. "We have a deal?"

"A contract," said Davina. "Tell her I'm here, listening to every word. Recording for the Directorate."

"Bound by the Incini standing next to me, who by the fucking way you nearly murdered by blowing up two hapless clones, you sick fuck. That agreeable?" asked Rebekah.

The countess shook her head. It wasn't a no, just a mannerism. An expression of her annoyance at being beholden to a bunch of deserting lowlifes. Rebekah enjoyed every movement.

"Agreed."

"I'll get back to you. Not sure I want to make such a decision without my crew. And I have a fucking code to test. Hope that's trustworthy, your history would say otherwise." She clicked off, stunned at the outcome. Davina squeezed her shoulder and backed off.

"Savvo?" Rebekah asked. She didn't need to add more. The Butcher was free, the implications from the *Scourge* plain for all of them. But he was fresh out of the box in an unfamiliar base and mainframe. In that lay hope. There were no hybrids to fight through, just automatic systems. Maybe a few scared Marines bereft of orders, most of whom, she suspected, would be up against the auto defences of the base.

He'd be thinking of Nicky, the future. A family maybe. No longer constantly looking over his shoulder, and despite the constant feeling of being watched, only seeing the blackness of space.

"I'm in," he said, a slight smile on his lips. "Yeah, I'm in."

"Plot a course. Hold position." She unstrapped. This had to be done in person. "And monitor those other void spots. Any change, holler."

Rebekah squeezed past Davina, leaving her with a half-smile she didn't really feel as she headed for medbay. The Incini was an enigma, unable to let her role go whatever the circumstances. Not that *she* had, either. Always needing to be in control.

She entered the medbay to find Arin waving his slate in her direction.

"It's clean. I ain't got Trem's skills, but I can't detect anything that I wouldn't trust in ZZ3 or the navcom." Arin tapped over his slate, then rested it next to Tremil's arm on the medtable. The girls remained dirty, their rush to hook them up to the medbot precluding any semblance of dignity.

Rebekah touched the metallic mask, anger rushing through her veins that she immediately squashed. "Segfi has offered us a pardon, Freedom. ZZ3 too, if we get her out."

"What? No way," Arin said. His eyes landed on Tremil's body. "Look what the fuck she did, Captain. No way, she can burn in her own hell." Arin pressed his palms into the table, eventually daring to look at Rebekah.

She found herself in a quandary. Agreeing with every word, but needing her sub-engineer to see the bigger picture. What hope may lay in his future, and Hendricks', if they were able to stop running. If it was just her, she would have turned the *Sunstar* around and left the countess to a deserved fate, to the Butcher. Maybe leave the bastard some advice on where to gut her first.

Hendricks appeared at the door, her look anxious, but focused on the twins. "How're they doing?"

"Stable," said Arin. "No thanks to the Warmonger."

Rebekah took her opportunity before Arin could throw in more emotional hand grenades. "We've been offered full pardons," she said, stepping into Hendricks' full eyeline, "if we rescue her."

There was no verbal knee-jerk reaction from the engineer. A small step back, hand rubbing over her scalp and down the back of her neck while Arin mithered about the tables. "Really?"

"Really. Freedom. Incini contracted."

"I ... Arin? What's your thoughts?" Hendricks looked to the sub-engineer, whose mouth began to flap, a 'no' forming on his lips.

He wants her to suffer like me, Dricks. But I want you two to have a life together without the countess breathing down your fucking necks.

Rebekah cut in. "Of course, we get to keep ZZ3. No questions asked. I'll draw up the adoption papers myself if it will help."

ZZ3 stretched each limb in turn, running the diagnostics Arin requested as the plasma torch attachment aligned with internal systems. An assortment of weaponry was already prepped around the deck. Carbines, grenades and the printed Watchtowers all stowed on the waiting navy suits.

"Systems linked, our glorious leader."

"Fuel levels?"

"100%."

"Everything in the green?" Rebekah asked, striding into the cargo hold. "How long before we're ready?"

"All done. We were pre prepped for an assault, remember. So, a rescue is like an assault, but you don't shoot everybody." Arin grinned. It had taken mere minutes for his mood to change, as always. "Of course, we're going to need quite a lot of armour with the storm that's coming. You know, the emotional kind."

"Storm? Heki and Tremil?"

"Yeah, except they're nothing compared to the nuclear version we're about to release on board." Arin backed off, his grin mysterious and not quite as convincing as he thought.

"What the fuck are you talking about? I don't have the time for your bullshit, Arin. Or the patience."

Hendricks popped up from behind a cargo box, a familiar weapon in hand. The ship-killer, a rail gun. Tremendous power, but slow to recharge and reload. She handed it over to ZZ3, who somehow found a niche on its back for the weapon to attach to.

"He's jumping in before his time, that's what he's doing." Hendricks moved to stand before one of the spacesuits and set it to unwrap. "Because he thinks if he lays the groundwork, you won't shoot me."

Rebekah blinked.

Hendricks had begun to stuff herself inside the suit. "You're not going. I am."

A pause. The eye of the storm perhaps, or the moment between activating a bomb and the explosion. It was short.

"No fucking way. I'm the captain of this squad by your word. Is this a mutiny?" Rebekah strode closer, fists balling. Every part of her seethed at the rejection.

"You are and forever will be my captain," said Hendricks. "But you're blinded by your need to do everything. To be in the firing line. We're here to save the girls, and the job's not done. The moment we crack those masks open, this ship will be an utter screaming hell. The only person that could survive that is you. Call this cowardice. I would rather face the Butcher than those we love the most." The suit fully ensconced her, only her head was free.

"The old lady is right," stated Arin, the grin gone. He moved to stand in front of Rebekah, his arms halfway up to hers before fully committing and grabbing hold. He'd never touched her before. "Save them, save us.

Besides, we might need you to come down and pick us up, and there's no way I'm trusting the learner pilot – Savvo – with my precious skin."

"Screw you, I'd leave you down there," said Savvo over comms.

Numbness impinged on Rebekah's mind, absent of any argument she could ride, seeking a crack in the logic. A pilot, and the only one who would be able to fly this crate in any type of atmosphere. And the twins. Always the twins.

Carved out eye sockets, blood on the blade.

"You fuckers don't come back I'll get the Butcher to resurrect you so I can kill you myself, you hear?"

CHAPTER 31

Hendricks checked over her carbine, syncing with her HUD, amazed at the speed and fluidity demonstrated as the targeting data flagged in her visor. A glance to the left, and she caught Savvo's serious expression imprinted behind his visor, imaged by her HUD from his internal camera. It settled her nerves, being able to see her squad as she had when she led the Breakers and a Marine unit before that. A comfort to see as well as hear how your squad reacted, those you depended on for your life.

A glance over to Arin stung at her heart. The mischievous grin back after the brief spat with Rebekah. Her yearning having to be suppressed. Such thoughts led to mistakes on the battlefield, as she had witnessed many times before. Liaisons that overrode good sense, poor decisions with consequences that affected the whole squad. Rebekah and Angel, that ex-bastard Rubel in the centre of it all, coming to mind.

"Call in," she said. There had been no discussion who would lead the team. Experience before fitness. Yes, her wetware had been screwed over by the dishevelled and abused girls lying in the medbay. But that was only part of what made her a Marine, something she'd been long before the Senti surgery. And the suit would help compensate for that loss and her more recent injuries.

She hoped.

"In the green," replied Arin, refraining from the 'old lady' he would usually add. A good sign. Focused.

"Likewise," replied Savvo.

"Good. Let's get this job done nice and clean."

"That's right," said Arin. "Kill the bad ones, save the good ones. Oh, hang on, where did we fuck that up?"

"By bringing you along," said Savvo.

"Stow the banter for the victory party. ZZ3? We're ready." Hendricks braced. Her suit's HUD changed colour, the servos stiffening and relaxing, while the gentle thrust of her jetpack lifted her from the deck as the mag-boots disconnected. The cargo doors opened, and the four of them flew through. Ahead, a grey moon filled her visor. A focal point that kept her gaze from the black she knew loomed behind her.

I hate space.

As if reading her mind, Arin chipped in, "Think of it as falling upwards."

"Like that helps," Savvo said. "Got your back, Captain, ma'am. ZZ3, can we mimic a sky dive to the surface?"

"Copy that."

The jetpacks adjusted, and all four of them headed for the rocky moon and its thin atmosphere. Hendricks' imbalance reduced as she began to orientate her mind to 'falling' towards the moon, despite the jetpack's push from behind. At some point ZZ3 would switch the packs off, saving fuel for when they needed to slow their descent. Their target area was a klick south of the base, behind a low set of rocky hills that would give them some cover. Of course, they could have chosen to descend the other side of the moon, but ZZ3 had not mapped that area. The defences were unknown, and therefore trickier to negotiate. The rescue mission possibly over before it had barely begun.

Hendricks busied herself running through Arin's model of the anti-aircraft positions ZZ3 had extrapolated from the energy signatures. There would be a thirty-second window when they were in range of standard sensors, vulnerable to both cannon and potential missile fire. They were free of overhead tracking, the four satellites they had taken down creating a corridor of which they were at the southern edge. Of course, the Butcher may not have gained control of the weapons. May.

"Approaching red zone," stated the warbot. "I apologise for any rough manoeuvres in advance."

"Could be worse, Savvo could be flying us."

"Can anyone else hear that droning noise?"

A last check of the active sensor data and Rebekah placed the system on auto with a ship wide alarm set should her parameters be met. Either for satellites altering position, those voids doing something similar, or anything entering within the orbit of the moon. It would have to do. She was functionally alone as far as ship management went, an Incini unable to negotiate binding contracts with the controls.

Heh.

Though to give Davina her due, she was where she was needed. Rebekah entered the medbay to find the Incini dishevelled and bleeding from the nose with both girls' hands in hers. Her eyes full of concern. This was the woman who had rescued Hendricks. Thrown herself out of a ripped open airlock into the black. And despite her lack of oxygen, attempted to drag the wounded engineer across the void of space. Far tougher than most, and had enough credit in Rebekah's eyes despite the bitter words she often sent the Incini's way. Had she screwed them over? Perhaps, under those ridiculous laws and tenets designed to forever keep the noble bastards safe.

"They're stable," Davina said, her eyes roaming over the girls. "Are we getting these masks off?"

"We are. But it will be utter hell." Rebekah slipped in between the beds so she could watch the Incini's reaction. "A tsunami that will not stop until you cut off the source. I've seen what they can do, the full effect, when they were four years younger. Imagine it now."

Davina nodded, saying nothing.

"Walls won't stop it. The earworms will get blown away. Music will help, but I fear it won't be enough," continued Rebekah.

"You're leading somewhere. Would it be easier to just come out and say it?" Davina finally looked up then, locking eyes. They flared with a determination Rebekah recognised. She saw it in the mirror every morning.

"The retardant. Put you under until it's safe."

Davina released the limp hands, brushing back her hair and tying it back to prevent the zero grav from having its way. "I know what you're thinking. That's what I always do. Hide away, usually between the words of a contract. Dispel my responsibility as I use the tenets as a buffer."

Fuck yes.

She didn't say that, nor allowed her face to convey her agreement but Davina was as savvy a negotiator as they came. She knew, and had voiced Rebekah's assumptions.

"No. I want to be here when they awake. At least try to help, and if I falter, you see to them first. I have to do something." A squeeze of the girls' hands at that point had been involuntary, not calculated in Rebekah's eyes, but worked to solidify Davina's point.

"Okay. Together. They're still under the cocktail of shitty drugs Segfi gave them. The medbot can wake them up from that at a pace we decide. That's the danger point. Awake but not aware. So, we keep them under while we remove the psionic restraints. There'll be a flood of emotions. Even in their dreams they come, but hopefully the Senti symbiotes will help." Rebekah saw Davina flinch. She'd seen them in the sump box, touched one, and almost assumed they were pets in the way she spoke. Rebekah had never really the time to put her right, too much information in an Incini's mind was never helpful. But after the clones ... after the clones had exploded, the symbiotes had likely saved her sanity. "They have a calming connection."

Davina's gaze shifted to Heki's neck, then she side-eyed Tremil's. There was the merest of shudders there. Tough.

"Then we set the medbot to release a stimulant, time their waking up."

"Slowly," mused Davina.

"No. I have my squad about to hit the surface of Segfi's fucking moon. I don't have the time for slowly. Or the patience. Besides a slow ascent from hell sounds agonising to me. Fifteen minutes." Rebekah handed over the co-pilot's comms unit. "Choose some music, I've set the speakers to cut out whenever I make contact. I'll be okay when you respond, I've a little more experience with having to tune out Arin's jokes."

The Incini snorted, but didn't argue and set about adjusting the earpieces and probably selecting something soothing.

Rebekah dropped in beside Heki, and with a final check of her med data, drew out her slate. She ran through the mask coding and with a glance and nod to Davina, set the pad at the back of the restraint and connected them up.

"Ready?" she asked over comms, and the Incini nodded before answering in the affirmative. She sent the code, an agonising few seconds passing between the ping and a green light. A click and the psionic mask split open. Ignoring the nerves coiling in her gut, she pried open the mask. Heki's face was covered in sores where the restraint had rubbed, her skin as sallow as when she first met her. She couldn't help herself, running fingers along the girl's cheek. A twitch, and her mind was suddenly awash with grief ladened loneliness. A loss of her twin, the disconnect between them akin to losing half of yourself to the abyss. Rebekah stumbled, clicking up the raucous music in her ears as she activated her wetware, stimulating a flood of chemicals to calm her brain. A hand grabbed at the medtable. Davina's, eyes streaming with tears, face drawn with anguish as she steadied herself.

"That's just the first step," Rebekah said, and switched positions to repeat the process with Tremil. The mask came off, her face more pinched and sicklier than Heki's, but less sore. Despite her best efforts, Tremil's symbiote managed to snag her finger, and the rush of fury and isolation seared through her mind. She blacked out for a moment, blinking back into the here and now to Davina's call in her headset.

She took the Incini's proffered hand, and pulled herself upright, for once thankful of the zero grav and thus lack of a fall.

"Packs a punch," she said, and showed the red tentacle mark. "I think its full and trying to release whatever it can. Lucky me. You need to go to your cabin, remove anything that could be used as a weapon. Combs, brushes, nail scissors. Anything that you could damage yourself with. Use your imagination, because when their hate hits that's exactly what you'll do. Dump it all in Arin's cabin opposite. You have five minutes before I check in on you, and I'm not waiting."

Davina left, and Rebekah turned back to the medbot. A quick sift through the menu, and she had the girls' meds primed. A rapid wake up. Groggy was not going to be good. Like a teenage brain on an early morning, they would lash out at everyone without consideration.

Once the procedures were set, she slipped her hand into her flight jacket and pulled out Heki's drawing pad. It had been a long time since she'd written anything by hand, and her nerves were already on edge, a sense of foreboding gnawing at the back of her mind. Once complete, she hung the pad on the medbay door and left to check on Davina.

A knock and she entered to find a packed bag and a rushing Incini. In her hands was a slate, a querying look on her face.

"*I* could kill you with that," said Rebekah with a half-smile, though it was true. It was added to the bag and Davina disappeared for a moment, returning to sit on the bed.

"I'm going to strap you down and set the top buckle to release after fifteen minutes. Understand? If this place is still full of … of—"

"—Depression, fear. Hate."

"Yeah. Even the slightest amount, stay here."

The buckle connected, and Rebekah made for the door. She paused there, suddenly aware how thankful she was for the Incini to at least try and help. She left with the merest glance over her shoulder, unable to express the emotions amid the tumult rising from the medbay. It was increasing by the second.

Can a medbot analyse empaths? Those emotions are so much more powerful. I'm no biologist, but I know the wetware triggers different bio chems to affect how I think, adapting to my perceived need. It can adjust for that, but that's because it's been programmed to.

She staggered on reaching the medbay door, hands slapping against the metal when an alarm kicked in. The navcom screeching ship wide for attention.

"Fuck!"

Now what?

With a scream of frustration, she had to make a decision amid the flurry of dread and rage rolling out of the medbay. They were either waking up early, or building up to something frightening. She clomped down the corridor, the music a cacophony in her ears, thudding into her skull. On reaching the navcom, she dropped into her seat. A swipe and her stomach flipped. All the nervousness built up tasting acrid in her throat.

"The fucking *Segfi*," she whispered. "That bitch tricked us."

The battleship was a long way off. It must have been orbiting in the shadow of Trazor, and on emerging, tripped the sensors.

"In the lee of the planet," she said. "Maybe they don't know what's going on, unless there's some comms relays out there. Possible." It would be an hour before the battleship could make an approach, and even then, may choose a steady low burn trajectory. Amid the vagaries of her mind, she ran a check on the sensor data, looking for any hint of comms traffic including satellite relays. Her thoughts were addled, and such signs hard to see at the best of times, but they gave some hope. Perhaps this was a pre-agreed sweep. Perhaps.

Another wave of emotion crashed through the cockpit, and her head swam, everything moving in and out of focus.

"No." She pushed herself up from the seat and clomped down the corridor, resisting the urge to disengage and fly. Her judgement was poor, bumping into the galley table as angry ripples assailed her mind. She managed to open the medbay door, the screen flashing a countdown that added to her panic. Ten seconds. Heki's fingers were trembling, and with her brain screaming, Rebekah reached her side, fingers fumbling over the straps. The thought of the girl waking up strapped down from a nightmare that had been far too real galled her. A risk. The buckle gave on the third attempt, when a hand thumped against her side. She spun around, Tremil's fear-filled eyes upon her. They were distant, streaming tears, while her mind bled desperation. She grasped the buckle about the girl's chest, pressing hard, feeling it give only for everything to change. Switch.

Her mind locked. Held in thrall. She staggered backwards, found herself spinning to face the twins. They held hands, looking at each other, lips moving though with the raucous din spewing from her headset, Rebekah knew not what they said. Then hate poured her way. Tearing at her memories, ripping away who she was amid the need to destroy, to gain revenge. She floundered against the onslaught, and her wrist bent back. Warm liquid ran down her forearm, while the blade snicked free, glinting crimson under the harsh medbay lights. Rebekah hated herself. Failing the twins, letting them be taken. Her mistakes, her fault they had suffered under Segfi's ministrations. The masks, the experiments, the constant demands only to be strapped back down like so much meat. The blade rose, and she welcomed it, bending her neck back, exposing her throat. The keen edge pressed against her skin, slicing the outer layer, blood seeping to cover the blade's edge.

Just a little more pressure and it would be over. The pain she had caused, her failures avenged. She pressed.

Fingers grasped her wrist, shoving backwards, more about her neck, pulling her away from the salvation the blade offered. Rebekah screamed in frustration, and unclicked her magboot, sweeping the metal sole back to clunk against Davina's. It had little effect, and the Incini attempted to lock her elbow, keeping the blade at bay. But she was no fighter, and Rebekah was a seething nest of vipers in her hands. She twisted around, breaking the grip on her neck, slamming upwards with her head to catch the Incini's chin while lashing out with her blade. Davina fell backwards, magboots holding but her grip upon Rebekah's wrist broke, blood pouring from a gash across her forearm. The Incini scrabbled at Tremil's medtable, seeking the edge, trying to steady herself for what came next. The Breaker snarled, caught between the bliss of ending her failures, and tearing the bastard Incini apart.

Choice made, Rebekah drove her arm upwards, spearing the blade towards Davina's throat, an insane grin writ large across her face. If she could stop the interfering bastard, then she could finish what she started. The Incini lurched back, shoving the medtable towards Rebekah who was lost in her own self-loathing. The edge caught her thigh, deflecting the ex-Breaker's approach, and off-balance, the wrist-blade sliced through the Incini's comms unit. Davina screamed, eyes rolling up, baring the whites as she threw herself away from the wave of bitter hatred sloughing off the girls.

Raging at her failure – yet another to add to her list – Rebekah dismissed the Incini's threat. The blade again ready to end her pain. The tip broke her skin and stopped, a bead of crimson upon the blade. She shook, eyes on Tremil whose hands were held high, a word upon her lips she knew without hearing.

"Home."

Davina had righted herself; the notepad held in a shaking hand. The word printed in an unsteady hand upon the page with the worst drawing ever of a ship's crew scrawled below.

"Home," repeated Tremil, her hand reaching out to grab her sister's. Eyes red-rimmed and raw, but mouth twisting in astonishment. Love poured into Rebekah's mind. Fearful, traumatised, but bubbling with hope filled need.

Rebekah's hand fell away, the single drop of blood sliding off to float upon the air. With a crack of her wrist, the blade disappeared, and she found herself in the arms of two girls who near choked her mind with love.

CHAPTER 32

Hendricks dropped gently onto the dusty rock, careful not to disturb the grey particles that would balloon up and give their position away. They were just below the crest of the low hills, the base spread out behind the inert patrol ship parked on a smoothed landing strip.

She peered down her weapon's sight, using the HUD to focus and refocus on the flagged positions of the air defences. One glowed slightly brighter than the others, Hendricks laying short odds it was the defence cannon that had sprayed her squad with 20mm rounds during their descent.

"Sit rep, ZZ3," she said, not looking back to check on the bot.

"Our glorious leader describes two of the jetpacks as 'fucked'," replied the warbot. "Despite the terminology, I would agree." They had jettisoned two packs, the cannons switching to follow their heat signature long enough to see them safely out of the killing zone. Their presence, however, transmitted back to base command. Segfi should have been aware and stopped them, indicating the Butcher had either cut the comms links or controlled the weapon. Possibly both.

"Good to know," she replied. The patrol ship was the starting point. Firstly, its comms array would be powerful, a chance to reach Rebekah on the *Sunstar* and also the primary way to get the countess off the base, the alternative something they wanted to avoid. Why hadn't the *Ungrit*'s crew reacted to the cannon fire? Surely there would be trained people still alive on the ship, never mind the base.

"Leave them," Hendricks said. "Savvo, you in position?" Another glance along her sight gave nothing until a ping and subsequent flag appeared in her HUD. Using the hint, she scoured that area until she caught the back of Savvo's helmet. Across the way, fifty metres by the data streaming in, Arin had the approach to the *Ungrit* covered.

They needed a reccy of the patrol ship. ZZ3 would have stood out like a city boy at a barn dance, so it was Savvo and Arin doing the legwork.

"Okay, in you go." Hendricks sensed the looming presence of the war-bot. At some point, they were going to need the walking tank. Be Breakers. But not yet. "ZZ3, be ready to make a rapid approach."

"Acknowledged."

Hendricks tracked Savvo's movements. He kept low, scurrying from gully to rock, leaving a dust trail that nagged at the Marine in her, but there was nothing they could do. Savvo was within thirty metres when the landing strip floodlights splashed on, illuminating the ship and the wheeled transports parked nearby. They flickered out. The fourth time that had happened, simultaneous lights switching on like ripples with the main base at its centre.

Savvo had dropped, but was up and running when the lights blinked off, and reached the stubby wings of the Navy ship. He was soon clambering up the nearest, examining the ship's airlock door.

"It's vented," crackled in the comms. "No internal lights."

Hendricks switched to Savvo's feed. The airlock had partially cycled – against all safety protocols – with outer and inner doors open at the same time. Murder, or in Breaker terms, the easiest way to clear a threat. Whoever, or whatever, had done that needed to be neutralised if they were to use the ship.

"Arin, approach and support," she ordered, and he was immediately on the run. "Savvo enter when Arin's there." She had a bad feeling, one she trusted. She had hated how the Bustans fought. All procedural, patterns within patterns. But for all their use of AI, you could see the consequences of decisions. Act and react in logical steps. The Butcher ... shit. Maybe she should have stayed on the ship after all.

"Going in," stated Savvo, on point as usual. With carbine up, he adjusted to infrared, avoiding flooding the corridor with telltale light. They were near the rear, the first doorway wide open and if he remembered right, leading to engineering and engine control. A check on Arin showed he was in position covering the rest of the corridor, and he slid his rifle inside the crack. There were warm spots, flagged by his HUD, and he spun in, finger on trigger.

Blue lips and skin, bloodshot eyes beneath Almaarian Navy caps. Two engineers lay on their backs, hands splayed outwards as if they were trying to fly but maglocked to the deck. He didn't flinch, Savvo had seen enough death in all its forms, and had expected dead crew.

"Clear," he said, and spun about, heading along the corridor, moving from cabin to cabin while Arin covered. Some had half-clambered into suits, others bore bloodied fingers where they scraped at sealed lockers withholding the emergency masks. All dead. The ship was lifeless, not a light shone in the gloom.

By the time he'd reached the cockpit, Arin was behind him, watching his back as he dropped into the empty seat. The pilot was sprawled on the galley table, rocking slowly, mouth contorted wide, nail marks streaking her throat where she had clawed as the last oxygen spewed from the ship.

"They should have had time, Dricks," he said. "Time to get the O2 bottles, or the survival suits. Or at least some of them should. But they were all deliberately locked down to prevent access. Have you got any signal from the countess?"

Hendricks' voice filled his comms, "None. Dead. Give me an assessment."

Savvo paused, fingers flittering over the navcom, realisation creeping in as the screen displayed its status. The Butcher had, according to ZZ3, insinuated himself throughout his hollow asteroid. Entered the mainframe systems, and from there spread to the *Scourge*. Mostly, but not always, via physical links.

The transponder connection blinked back at him. The ship would have been flown in automatically by the base to reduce the possibility of accidents. Standard practice throughout space. And a damn fine way for backdoor code to insinuate its way into the *Ungrit*'s system. The Butcher had the ship and emptied the air, sucked in the carbon dioxide atmosphere, and locked down all access to O2. That hinted at wanting the ship free of life, but why? To prevent Segfi's escape? That was a possibility.

"Arin, we're leaving."

"We are?"

"Now. And don't touch anything."

"We are," replied Arin, and he stomped ahead, sweeping the junctions and moving at speed.

The sense of being watched loomed over Savvo, as if electronic eyes bored into the back of his head. He suppressed the memories of the *Scourge*, the crimson sacs, the pleading faces at the moment of death. They were dealing with an intelligence whose moral compass had stopped working a long time ago. Their purpose unknown, but they crushed and mangled whatever stood in their way without remorse.

Lights flickered, the ship springing to life. Gaunt, haunted faces suddenly lit as they stared into the distance. Savvo ignored the corpses, eyes only on Arin's back or the occasional sweep behind. The lifeless pilot stared back, arms waving as he brushed past, as if seeing him out of the dead ship. Another ghost ship. The airlock pad shimmered into life, greeted by Arin's bout of swearing. But he was experienced repair crew as well as a Breaker, knew his stuff, and paused by the suddenly straining airlock.

"Out," he said, and Savvo complied. This was the sub-engineer's speciality. He leapt the clamp Arin had positioned on entry, the same type he often used to lever airlocks open during repair runs. He ran along the wing, releasing his boots and leapt to the ground. A moment later, Arin was out, dropping in beside him having recovered the clamp.

"The ship's fucked. The Butcher is in there, or whatever fucking virus or code he dropped in. Entered through the transponder ..." Savvo didn't get a chance to finish, the patrol ship's engine coughing into life. They were vulnerable.

"Arin, run," he shouted. The sub-engineer needed no encouragement, and they bounded, using the lower gravity to their advantage as they covered the ground at pace to fling themselves behind a large truck. The air filled with flame, their HUDs blaring an amber warning as the heat wash rolled over the truck. A roar kicked in, the suits shutting down external mics as the noise exceeded tolerance levels.

"Better than red is dead," stated Arin, breaking the silent isolation of their helmet comms, pushing himself up and wiping away the dust covering his visor. "That meant for us?"

Savvo turned over, rising to his feet, the air filled with burnt dust. He sidestepped around the rear of the transport, eyeing the patrol ship as it gathered speed along the runway. "Where the hell is it going?"

Arin stepped in at his side, though his eyes were distant, running over the HUD data no doubt but that would be extremely limited without eyes in the sky. "Can't say, Savvo. But my guess is somewhere we don't want it to be."

"Poignant, insightful, and an utterly fucking useless bit of information. Thanks for that," replied Savvo, turning to glare at the nearest building. An inner scowl was building, an annoyance at where they were and why. Despite his agreement, his heart wasn't in it. *Why do you save a demon from the fucking devil?*

"Here to help. Think on it. Two places I know immediately. The *Sunstar*, attack our home base so we have nowhere to retreat to — assuming he knows we're here. Or the satellite system. No chance of getting any kind of meaningful link to those through all this shit unless it's an extreme narrow band or laser comms. No way. So, if he's looking to realign or re-target, any of that defensive shit, then he's gonna need something closer." Arin stopped speaking for a moment and turned to face Savvo. "Hey, did I do all those things you said *and* be useful? I'm waiting for that apology. You can whisper it; I won't tell anyone. In this ear." He pointed to the right of his helmet.

Savvo stepped away, a mumble crackling over the comms.

"I'll accept that, minus the two swear words and where I can stick it."

Savvo sighed. "Want us to head for the nearest domes, Dricks? The ones ZZ3 highlighted as the transport hub?"

"Hold position, we're joining you," stated Hendricks.

The pair remained on cover, Savvo watching the transport domes with a growing concern at the lack of activity, while Arin assessed the two gun emplacements flagged nearby. One was obvious, long-barrelled, dual aircraft defences with a stack of close-range anti-missile missiles ready to fly below. It pointed into the sky, Arin's shared HUD data highlighting it appeared active. The other one under the ground, signal barely perceptible.

Ground defence, ready to rise from the rock and cut through any assault. There would no doubt be a ring of them about the base, they just didn't know where. It lay twenty metres to the right of their direct path to the transport hub. A risk.

ZZ3 arrived, Dricks jogging behind, scanning the terrain as she went. The hulking bot dropped behind the transport, keeping low amid the stink of burnt fuel and melting metal.

"Sit rep," requested Dricks, and Savvo gave the run down, Arin adding his information afterwards.

On her haunches between the pair of them, the ex-captain peered at the dome. "Nothing we can do about the patrol ship, and we have no comms contact with the *Sunstar* with the jamming shit the base is throwing out. We need to establish comms as a matter of priority."

"The Countess can't be in control," said Arin. "Without the *Ungrit*, I'm thinking the Butcher has all the communications systems locked down."

Savvo waited, knowing Hendricks took a little longer than Rebekah to come to decisions, even before the destruction of her wetware. Didn't make her observations and orders any worse, you just had to adjust to a new commander. Failing to do so quickly could lead to mistakes.

"I had a mind to bypass these domes," Hendricks said. "But we could rescue our esteemed ex-fucking benefactor and still be here with nowhere to run. Don't like the time waste, Segfi could be holding out for all we know against whatever the Butcher can cook up. But ..." She eyed the outer edges of the domes, open like a gigantic marquee along the facing section where everything could manoeuvrer to be under cover. No fancy, expensive airlocks. There would be a heavy curtain, like a membrane, that the transport pushed through minimising oxygen loss on the way in, and then on the way out.

CHAPTER 33

The emplacement rose, multiple-barrels whirling to spit cannon shells at a frightening rate. Savvo grabbed his helmet, almost as if pulling himself down to duck behind the lip of the small crater he lay in. Dust billowed over the top, stone chips flying above his head to patter against the suit's armour.

"Shiiit." Arin's voice echoed, a crackle and haziness to the sound, their internal comms struggling the closer they got to the hub. Hopefully, he was in a hole or beneath a rock somewhere to his left.

"Responding," cut in Dricks, and carbine fire echoed in Savvo's mic. It was met with a hail of metal tearing into Dricks' position. That meant it was his turn. A lump sat in his throat. Eventually the gun's algorithm would work out the pattern. He finished his count, and rolled over two metres to the outer edge and lay in a burst towards the emplacement. Short, precise, saving ammunition. The grenade Hendricks had used after their first patterned attack had been shot out of the air, proving the emplacement could analyse and prioritise the dangers. Rolling back, shells raked the ground where he'd been, but a glance to the upper right of his visor gave some hope. The pumping of metal limbs in the background.

"ZZ3 going in. Yeah, warbot smash!" shouted Arin over comms. That, typically, came through loud and clear. "Rip its bloody head off."

"Hasn't got one," stated Savvo, and he rolled out the other side of the crater, scope focused on the one-sided battle. ZZ3 had stretched the barrels between powerful limbs, and the plasma cutter sliced swiftly downwards, ending their threat, before gripping the control unit and tearing it free. Okay, that could count as a head, but there was no way he was admitting that.

"Threat negated," stated ZZ3.

"Arin, Savvo, approach and cover the bot," stated Hendricks, and they complied, rising from the ground, ignoring the thin covering over their suits as they stalked in low, eyes on the hub while Dricks watched for the telltale twitch and puff of dust from any non-flagged gun emplacements.

ZZ3 was crouched as low as a warbot could be, eyes toned down to a very soft glow, by its side a pile of scrap. "No response from the dome," the bot said. "I cannot extrapolate a reason for this from the data to hand."

"Clear," stated Dricks, and while Savvo surveyed the outer rim of the curved regolith dome, she arrived, sparing just a glance for the destroyed defensive weaponry. "Nothing?"

"As silent as a graveyard," replied Arin, adding a spooky tone exaggerated by the sketchy comms. "Which is my guess after the *Ungrit*."

"Just what I need," replied Savvo. "An Arin pep talk."

"Stow it. ZZ3, any signature out there you couldn't catch before?" asked Hendricks.

"Negative, but amid, what our glorious leader calls 'all this shit', it is near impossible to discern. By standard Almaarian defensive planning the area would be mined with designated routes through that are adaptively programmed for non-coded transports and individuals." The warbot glanced over to Hendricks, Savvo catching the wince as his HUD interpreted her camera feed as best it could.

Wetware coding. Fuck.

Hendricks dropped to her haunches, elbows on her knees. It was her favoured planning position on the field, and Savvo naturally copied her, Arin too. Like old times. "Okay. Things have changed. ZZ3, proceed and analyse the route. Retrieve data if you can from the first mine and cross-reference with Arin's wetware. Should there be a match, we have a plan. I want a sit rep. If the place is sealed tight, it'll be full of pissed off soldiers looking for a target. I want charges set to ensure it stays that way. If it's been purged ... then assuming our comms will be screwed at that range, you make a call whether to go in."

"Yes, Captain," said Savvo. Hendricks flinched, her eyes flicking up. He knew the look. His slip had cut a little too deep, and inside he kicked himself. She would already be hurting after the revelation of the mines and her lack of functioning wetware.

Savvo panted, the suit compensating for the increased rate of breathing as he braced against the regolith concrete wall. He was at the left edge of the open side of the dome, Arin against one of the support posts eight metres to his right, carbine up and about to peer around. Now they were closer, he had relayed the dome's initial layout. What appeared to be an open and disorganised system was in fact a series of funnels or lanes, a road system that directed the vehicles by type or possibly regiment allocation, to designated bays.

"She's hurting," the sub-engineer said over a closed line. "The old lady."

"You'd better hope she hasn't worked out this frequency," replied Savvo, and he slid his own carbine around the edge, scope adjusting for the weirdly flickering LEDs set in the sloped ceiling. "And yeah. That was my fault."

"She can take our shit. Dricks has had me in her ear for the last ... sheesh, five years. Nearly six. Cover me," stated Arin and he crept in low, carbine pointed ahead though Savvo knew he would be assessing threats from all quarters. He was approaching the first large transport, parked haphazardly across a set of inlaid lines in the floor. The thick, pliable membrane was draped over the whole vehicle, obvious gaps either side. The cab doors were wide open, but this wasn't a truck a human drove. The access was for repairs only, the space enough for an engineer or mechanic.

"Hold position," Savvo stated, and followed Arin in, keeping to the left so he could see past the cab and its bonnet. There was an assortment of transports on the inside, all inert according to his HUD, no warmth to their engines. Bodies lay on the floor, five, most curled up while infrared indicated their warmth levels closely matched the ambient temperature. He set the HUD to task working out an estimated time of death.

"Got a dead soldier. Engineer, I think," said Arin, and a glance to the camera feed showed a gloved hand on a sprawled body inside the cab. There was blood on the door's edge and shattered bones poked through his uniform along his upper thigh. Arin pulled the soldier out, twisting them over. There was a breathing mask hanging from a broken strap, their jaw hung loose, tongue severed, eyes wide. "Shit."

"The fingers," said Savvo. They were tinged blue under the nails, and the closer he looked the more apparent the lips displayed similar symptoms. Hypoxia. Oxygen depletion.

Some soldiers could be slovenly, routines becoming mundane under the daily grind. Yeah, you were always ready when the drills came, had your arses kicked when they dropped in the surprise ones. Space didn't have to beat such complacency out of you though; you simply died and wouldn't do it again. But life on a base. Fuck.

"Bottle's empty," said Arin, pulling out the emergency supply strapped at the dead soldier's hip. "Must have been searching for another ... but the wounds."

"Maybe someone fought him for it," Savvo eyed those on the bay floor, and his HUD pinged in with a time of death. It matched soon after the Butcher's emergence from his fucking coffin. He ran down an atmospheric analysis, not in the least bit surprised to find less than one percent oxygen. "Come on."

Savvo waited until Arin was on cover and moved ahead, wary, checking each of the corpses in turn. Three had masks, two didn't, stab wounds and claw marks over all five. They had fought but lost anyway. He'd had the training like everyone else. That brief experience of oxygen depletion caused primal panic. Perhaps training wasn't the right word. His instructors had simply introduced him to the fear he would experience so he could recognise it, sear in a memory that might allow him to think carefully. What had it been? Possible unconsciousness within fifteen seconds, brain damage within minutes. Fuck, no time at all.

Together, they swept what was in visual range, their HUDs pinging and flagging the trail of the dead. They found three more half-in transport cabs. Each sported debilitating wounds. It wasn't a coincidence, and an idea began to form in Savvo's mind as he glanced up at the arrays along the ceiling.

"VERT," he said, thoughts on M4 and docking multiple ships at once.

"Shit," replied Arin. How long had they worked together? It was as if he read his mind. "Like a low-grade transponder. Parking the transports for maximum efficiency."

"Remember the autobots," Savvo said.

"Sounds like a book title. Yeah, I remember the bloody things. Hey, you wore a corpse as a shield, hard to forget." Arin snorted. Savvo shook his head. It had been his idea.

Corpses. Wetware. He had tapped into the *Scourge*'s crew … He glanced at the dead mechanics and shuddered. It had been different, the hybrids and their horror almost overwhelming back then. These soldiers were too long dead for the chips to be active, and he couldn't contemplate cutting them open, anyway. But the mines were coded, so likely at least some of the soldiers were sporting wetware.

He checked his HUD, running through the menus until he found the relevant one and sent out a call. If they were alive and under the dome, there was a chance.

"Nothing," Savvo said.

"Eh?"

"No Marines here, or at least alive ones."

Arin snorted again. "Of course there *will* be. The 1st and High. Her personal bodyguards. Did you ever see her without them?"

Savvo nodded, eyeing the HUD. They weren't here, but the wetware tracker could be useful, though if he were a countess, would he have used a shared frequency? A paranoid noble maybe not. Segfi was brutal, uncompromising. She didn't fear an enemy being around every corner, she just crushed them to make sure they weren't there twice.

"Savvo," Arin had reached the inner doors, those that acted as airlocks from the transport hub to the offices, stores and the barracks. Arrayed above them were the conditioning units. Heat and atmospheric regulators. Near silent, who would know if they switched operation? Be it to suck out the breathable air, or draw in the outer atmosphere. Lots of ways to die when you needed to breathe.

The doors were locked wide open, the corridor filled with the twisted bodies of panicked army administrators, mechanics, drivers, drone pilots. Who knew what? Mass murder, no Butcher's block required.

"Cover me." He went in, he had to know. But as he stepped between the bodies nobody twitched, no one moved. You can dodge bullets, but you can only hold your breath for so long. The young, the experienced. Gone. He eyed the corridor walls; the irony of the emergency posters and embossed stickers not lost on him. The mask lockers all flashing red. The Butcher had made sure his massacre would leave few behind.

"All dead," he said.

"We going in deeper? There may be people in some of the rooms. Sealed in."

What would Rebekah do? Prioritise. Give in when Savvo wanted to help others after years of being the killer. Make a choice based on the slim chance the Butcher had not depleted a room, or someone had been resourceful enough to have a limited supply to hand.

It was a horrible way to go. Knowing what the gasping meant.

Prioritise. Fuck.

"No. We're leaving." He spun about, trying to keep his mind off the blue lips, red eyes, clawing hands.

"Leaving? But ..."

"The Butcher has control of the life support systems. If that's the case, the comms will be under the bastard's sway. Pointless." He kept his voice flat, like Rebekah would and Dricks when she'd been drugged up with wetware firing as they mowed down whatever stood in their way. "Too much risk. The twins need us, Rebekah needs us."

Arin tucked in behind, covering their rear, and Savvo knew he was stewing. Any more words would just prod the hornet's nest. He led them out the exit route, looking for any hint of hope. And for once, it arrived. The cab was half-open, though the soldier's death had occurred before she had clambered in. A mobile comms unit and it had seen some use by the pits and scratch marks around the outside.

"Jackpot."

"If the Butcher ..."

"Yeah. But it can't be all of that fucker in there, can it? Just part. If we can move the truck away, out of the bay's transponder range, maybe we can purge it."

"Purge ... ZZ3? Hell yeah." Arin grinned for the first time since entering the transport bay.

"My thinking too. First, we need it out of here."

"For which a member of the crew who is a walking tank would be very useful. Want me to go?" asked Arin, indicating towards the exit. The membrane lay in tatters; a cargo loader had driven its jaws into the centre and twisted until the majority had torn free of the ceiling and upper walls.

"Yeah." Savvo glanced at the dead comms operator.

Leave me with my guilt awhile.

Chapter 34

Rebekah bent over, kneading her temples, tears at the corner of her eyes as Heki and Tremil's sheer need pressed in. Amid the love were scars, encroaching on her mind that already suffered under the twins' emotional imbalance. The trauma of what Segfi and her scientists had not only brought back to the surface, but compounded. Plunging the girls into a hopelessness that exacerbated the emotions pouring from them. They were pushing her mind to extremes, and she had to shut it down if she was to function. To lead.

The girls were eating. Soup. The same concoction they had Arin buy when they were hiding the symbiote's diet from her and the crew. It was the most nutritious food item the medbot judged they could ingest safely, with a little newly baked bread alongside Davina had concocted from ingredients in a way that Rebekah saw as nothing short of magic.

Heki had soup on her nose, the tremble to her hand fuelled by raging emotions as well as the condition the countess had left them in. Rebekah smiled and wiped away the splodge as music blared in her ears. Tremil entwined a finger in hers as she withdrew her hand, wanting to share the touch. Her lips moved, but she gestured with her free hand to show she couldn't hear.

Please hurry.

A shadow appeared behind the girls, Davina, the adapted sump box in hand. Rebekah had no clue how long the twin symbiotes needed to purge, but she needed respite and soon. Davina placed the box on the galley table, where it maglocked as eager tentacles rose to waft through open air holes. Rebekah didn't need to speak. The girls knew and were as overwhelmed by their freedom as she was. A few seconds passed as the symbiotes made their inexorable way crawling up their arms as if playing for bloody time. Eventually they settled about each girls' neck, and relief swamped Rebekah as the pressure on her mind rescinded. She turned the music down, near to the earworm level they had first used when the girls had settled on board.

"You okay?" she asked, her eyes on Davina. She had been less affected since the girls' emergence from the restraining masks. Heki and Tremil's focus being on her, and the Incini only suffering the byproduct. But after preventing Rebekah from ending her personal pain – at the cost of a slashed arm the medbot had sealed – Davina had self-medicated an hour's dreamless sleep, so had an unfair advantage as well.

Davina half-smiled in return, pressing her hands into her eyes and blinking. Rebekah could still hear the Incini's music above her own.

Rebekah proceeded to fill in the girls about what had happened since they had been taken. The hoops they had jumped through, and where the rest of the crew were right now. She pre-warned them before bringing up Segfi, allowing them to build the walls and the void between her and them before she delved into that pit. By the time she had finished, they had remained behind those walls, only their hands betraying the pain as they gripped each other. Their torturer had offered amnesty, and despite their personal hells, their crew – their family – had chosen to attempt the rescue.

Blood payment. Betrayal.

Rebekah knew all the words.

"A pardon means you are free."

Davina sat down beside her, hands out in front, reaching for the girls' fingertips. They didn't flinch away. "This may appear like a betrayal," Rebekah winced, "and the countess' track record would suggest she may attempt to renege. But I was there, witnessed it. She is bound, and with that pardon, you will be able to live a life outside of this ship."

Heki's nose scrunched, as if she tasted something foul. The first movement since Segfi's name had been mentioned. She glanced over to Tremil. "I understand."

Rebekah had her doubts.

"And when you have your pardons, they get to abandon us," said Tremil, dropping her spoon into the empty bowl and gesturing towards Rebekah's poorly drawn depiction of the crew. "The rest of the crew. Leave us with you so they can have the life denied us. She will never stop hunting us. Ever."

The cockpit alarm blared, and Rebekah let out a sigh. "I need to see to this."

Heki stood, steadying herself against the galley table. "I will come."

Rebekah desperately wanted to say *no*. To tell the girl to rest, recover. But that would be seen as another betrayal. They were in a mess, caught between relief, love and the grief for what they had lost beneath the psionic masks. The progress they had made poisoned.

She nodded, and headed for the cockpit, already drawing up the navcom data stream when Heki finally managed to sit in the co-pilot's chair.

The battleship, the *Segfi*, had engaged main engines, burning away from Trazor's gravity and headed their way. The dual gravity of moon and the gas giant would hamper progress, but the inevitable must have happened. It knew they were there. At this range there was no way of knowing about missile ports or PDC preparations. She had only witnessed the full power of Segfi's flagship once, a tight fleet battle on their approach to Bustan 8. Awesome was the word Arin had used. They were a fly, and the battleship an over-gunned flyswatter.

She hadn't listed in the preparations for the countess' rescue what they would do if they had to leave, and the aftermath of the twins' emergence had forced such thoughts from her mind.

"They're hailing us," said Heki, her voice harsh, dry.

Rebekah cracked her knuckles and nodded. "Put them on."

"This is the ANS *Segfi* under the command of Admiral Rickar. Karal Mining Repair ship *Sunstar*, please respond."

Please?

She'd take that as a good start. Better than missile ports open and a homing missile up the arse.

"This is Captain Khan of the *Sunstar*," she coughed, "how may I help?"

"You are designated neutral under the last set of commands, Captain Khan. Be aware should that situation change, your ship could be obliterated in a matter of moments," the voice was calm, matter of fact, and ninety-nine percent correct, Rebekah with one eye on the data about the moon's atmosphere. "Can you share your time stamp of your last contact with Daphene?"

Heki glanced her way, a query on the pinched, sallow face.

They don't know.

"About two hours ago. The Countess was in some distress, asking for help. I have sent a team onto the moon's surface to provide aid," she replied.

Go on, blow us out of the void now.

She cut back in, wanting to get a point across. "You are some distance away, and dropships would take at least four hours before reaching the surface." She signalled Heki, mouthing for her to check her guess. A few swipes, and she gave a thumbs up.

"That is surprisingly correct, Captain Khan. I am ..." the voice went quiet. A sinking feeling took over Rebekah's already sore mind, overpowering her earworm. Heki had her console screen pointing her way, a finger indicating a swathe of data and a rapidly closing ship as it exited the moon's atmosphere. The *Ungrit*.

If her team was aboard without Segfi, they may well be screwed when the battleship worked out the cause of her absence. With Segfi, she glanced at Heki, they may well be fucked as they'd got one over on the countess and she'd be in a fury. Someone else entirely on board, then fucked *and* screwed, as her squad would still be down on the surface and the *Ungrit* had been the initial target for comms access and escape should they fail.

"Trajectory?" she asked, and a sickly hand swiped.

"The battleship," she said.

Another sound crackled in her comms, the click of an internal connection. "It has Segfi's emergency transponder signal. But there are no comms I can detect," said Tremil. "It's silent."

Odd. But what wasn't right now? Perhaps the Butcher had blown out the comms, playing for time after Segfi's apparent escape.

Shit, how do I save them now?

"How long until they dock?" she asked Heki.

"An hour." The girls' voice was a mere whisper. A glance over was enough to see she was struggling.

"*Sunstar*, I take it you have seen ANS *Ungrit*. I believe the countess is safe, you may recall your team." The voice was smug, self-satisfied.

Bloody Navy.

Rebekah built in a delay, a few seconds, every one was going to be precious. "Working on the comms issue now," she said. "Will be in touch. *Sunstar* out." After all, they knew there was a problem, didn't they?

Heki slumped into her chair, too tired even to feel. Numb, for which Rebekah was sadly thankful. "Sleep," she said, flinching at the scowl she received in return. "I'm going to need you and Tremil when the shit hits. You need to rest, take forty minutes and then I want you back with me."

The suspicion in Heki's eyes was at least familiar. The girl used to her ways, but then that was a good thing. She let her defiance go, nodding and standing, accepting a hand to steady herself. Biting the bullet, Rebekah stood, and pulled the girl in close, encouraging Heki to wrap sullen arms about her. Together they walked to her cabin, Davina watching every step.

She laid Heki on her bed, straps set gently and within reach. With barely a murmur, Heki fell asleep. Risking a last touch of her cheek, Rebekah went to find Tremil, but Davina was already there, the girl on her side, eyes fluttering while the Incini stroked her hair. A look to Rebekah, a faint smile and the girl disappeared into sleep.

Closing the door behind them, they moved as silently as their magboots would allow until entering the galley.

"You catch that? The patrol ship?"

"You think it's Segfi?"

"If it is, she won't hold to the contract whatever we do. Self rescue clause, nothing mentioned, blah blah. Look, this is trouble. Big. You're going to have to fall in with us fully. You kind of stepped in when the countess started talking rescue. She won't like that." Rebekah watched the Incini, looking for any tells. How could she not see she needed to step out of the role despite her involvement?

"You're right about the self-rescue. A get out. And my involvement, but throwing all in with you? Only if there's no alternative. *If* I did, what would you need me to do?"

Rebekah drew in a breath, letting a smile creep in. "Know anything about probes?"

CHAPTER 35

A rin grinned, pulling himself clear of the cab and holding up a piece of electronics he waved towards Hendricks and Savvo with glee. "Got it," he said. "Hid the damn thing nice and deep. Anyone would have thought the Army were paranoid."

Hendricks walked over, a nod to Savvo to indicate he should maintain watch at the road junction. "That do it?"

"Yeah. The transponder coding for these heaps is just an engagement link like all the others. Remove the transport's engine CPU and it doesn't respond. No response, no link, no spooky possession by an insane computer with a thirst for survival and a penchant for crushing soldiers in cabin doors." Arin handed it to ZZ3, who held the suspicious piece of electronics up high. The warbot had pushed the transport all the way along the link road after Arin disengaged the gearing systems.

"Agreed. This is the correct assessment, our glorious leader." ZZ3 handed the electronics board back. "Even direct contact with the vehicle will not enable the Butcher to take control. However, he could potentially enter through the comms system if a handshake is activated."

Hendricks ran a hand over the bonnet, mouth twisted a little to the side. "You're saying he could infect any vehicle with one of those? Like he did ZZ3?"

"No. ZZ3 has a massive level of computing power, and only after a physical link, did more of the Butcher get in. The transports he can control, but only set to simple tasks." Arin pocketed the CPU and entered the rear of the comms truck. There was space for two to sit side by side facing opposite wall screens. He powered the system up, Hendricks entering behind. "Savvo and me agree. The shit the base is throwing out is blocking most comms, right? But Segfi managed a signal with a narrow band. That's a low data transmission, something the Butcher can't piggyback for sure. But if he's riding the transponders to some degree, then certainly he can ride something much stronger like the laser comms. Segfi chose not to use that system deliberately, or the Butcher took that out first."

"I concur," said ZZ3, leaning in. "Asham states that is the most efficient way he could enter a system at distance. And then open that system up to upload more of himself."

"Where's this going?" asked Hendricks, watching the comms screens as they activated. "There's a suggestion coming, I know you too well. One I'm not going to like, which is why you have the warbot backing you up."

"So, I picked the biggest warbot in the playground to be my friend. You all had your chance, belittling me ..." Arin trailed off, recognising the glare behind the visor. "You got me. First issue for Dricks: the suit comms aren't up to the job as it stands. We're only going to hear Rebekah if she manages to get a signal through via our newly acquired comms truck. Second issue: we can't risk the laser comms even if we knew where the *Sunstar* is in orbit."

"Third fucking issue: you need someone to stay with the kit, tune in the suit comms and listen out 'cos if *we* constantly broadcast the Butcher may get a handle on us." Hendricks said, a growl to her voice. "I'm not stupid. Looks like you're getting a sore ass, Private."

"Your wetware doesn't work," stated ZZ3, suddenly flinching as if realising it spoke hidden thoughts aloud. The bot received a glower from Hendricks to match the one she'd laid on the sub-engineer.

"That was point three. You kind of jumped the gun on that one," said Arin. "Cos you know what comes next."

"Do I get my own nursemaid too? Slippers? Pipe? Maybe one of those high-backed chairs it's easier to get out of?" Hendricks turned about, eyeing the warbot. "And you, 'Mr I Am Crew', are backing him up. I liked you better when it was all 'action code' this and 'protocol' that."

Arin was sure the warbot shrugged. Maybe he was imagining it.

"I can't lead the team from here," Dricks continued. "Savvo knows all this?"

Arin wiped the nervous grin away. "He knows someone needs to stay. He expects it to be me."

Arin watched as his HUD recreated the conflicting emotions that ran across Hendricks' visage. He understood, wanted to take hold of her, tell her it wasn't because she was broken. But that would be a lie – of course it was. But not in the way Dricks would be thinking. She would be running back over the moment they first met the twins, the burn out of her wetware. The day she had been reborn into someone whom Arin wanted to hold day and night. Broken and remade anew. She desperately wanted to be worthy, to take Rebekah's place and *lead*. And that, Arin knew in his bones, was no longer in her heart. All the experience she had did not count when the belief had been knocked out of her, especially when the mission's purpose was as screwed up as this one. No twins to defend, but a countess every bit as bad as the Butcher to rescue. One that had filled them all with drugs, patched them up and sent them out again. Assets.

See, I can be selfish as well as hilarious. If your heart and belief are absent, you will make mistakes. I can't handle that, and nor can you.

"Go replace Savvo so I can brief him," Hendricks said, refusing to meet Arin's gaze. "This had better not be you protecting me," she continued.

"Me? Never entered my mind."

The road ahead was littered with vehicles, doors wide open, their drivers or passengers dead upon the ground, though luckier ones had left boot prints in the dust leading towards the dome's huge airlock doors. ZZ3 had originally entered that way, the warbot currently crouched as best as it could behind the last vehicle before the dome, a cargo truck. There were four soldiers, bodies crushed, at the foot of the metal doors that had clearly opened as they pounded to get in.

Arin didn't look that way, but to the left, sighting along the carbine's scope towards the hole ZZ3 had cut through the outer wall of the base. No dead lay outside, and the edges of ZZ3's plasma cuts had long-since cooled.

"Sit rep," called in Savvo.

"Clear," stated ZZ3 in a monotone that developed a little more personality every day. "Airlock doors to the transport bay are resealed."

"ZZ3's remodelling is also clear. Nice cuts, neat, ZZ3. Must have had a good teacher." Arin added a laugh.

Savvo, apparently, wasn't having any of it. "Stow it. Take point, Arin. ZZ3, watch the airlock and the road until I call you in."

Arin rose from behind the small dip he'd laid in, eyes on the darkness beyond ZZ3's handiwork, then running through his HUD data as it checked on potential threats. With the way clear, he arrived with his back to the dome wall, the edge of the plasma cuts pressing into his shoulder.

"Drone," stated Savvo, following behind.

Arin unhooked the propellered machine from an attachment on his back, syncing and spinning it up. The drone flew low and quiet into the void, infrared picking out zero hotspots, with only the computer workstations ZZ3 had described showing any residual heat above the background temperature. He instructed the machine to engage lights, and though these were relatively weak, his HUD could enhance the images in enough detail to confirm ZZ3's report. A Senti ship built from the black metal, gutted and wired up. He shuddered on seeing the stasis pod.

"Bloody scientists," he whispered. The gutted ship had not shown as being active on the infrared, so he ignored it for now, and moved to the entrance. This exhibited signs of recent welding, scrap metal strewn to both sides, also having been cut free.

"Clear," he said.

"Cover me," replied Savvo, and he bypassed Arin, heading in with his scope sweeping the area. Arin followed a few metres behind, keeping his focus until Savvo repeated his all clear. "ZZ3, take station at this entrance."

Savvo then walked over to the stasis unit, peering inside and opening it up. No lights flickered, and he signalled Arin over when ZZ3 arrived. "Look familiar?" he said, and lifted out a casing with the barrel of his gun. Dried skin of a grey-green colour, the tentacles out front split where something had emerged.

"A symbiote," Arin said. "Like TB."

"Another Senti," stated Savvo, but there was nothing else inside the inert pod. He gestured towards the Senti ship, its combination of hardened membrane and black metal almost skeletal. "And harvesting their ship. I'm betting the Butcher's coffin came from there. Brain patterning, memory-bloody-sucking, too similar to be a coincidence." He nudged the lid, and it slammed shut, making Savvo wince.

Arin jumped as pounding echoed through the room's atmosphere. Hard and persistent against the newly welded metal.

"Someone's alive," said Arin, turning to face the door, carbine up. "There's always hope." The metal bent, dents forming as the attack continued. "Or not, as the case may be."

"ZZ3, need you here," said Savvo. "Take station to the side of the door."

The warbot clomped by, not bothering to hide the sound of metal on smooth rock as the thuds continued on the door. A huge hit curved the upper half, springing the welded door from the jamb. Beyond was an unfamiliar guard-bot. Dual upper limbs for gripping, hitting, or firing auxiliary weapons, the unseen lower half Arin assumed to be legged in some way. A ball wouldn't cope with the recoil it was about to be subjected to, for on top was a machine gun that tracked across the room.

"We always get the best visitors," he said, and was rewarded with a spew of metal slugs that tore towards him. He threw himself behind the Senti ship, pressing himself onto the floor against a jutting metal spar. "But I don't think they brought cookies."

ZZ3 reached around the door, upper limb bent at the elbow joint, and released a grenade at near point-blank range. It crashed into the thundering machine gun, exploding before the warbot could retract the arm. Metal shards bounced from the limb, clattering into the plate. By the time it withdrew, the forearm plate was defunct. Cracked and split, the grenade launcher had taken the brunt of the damage and hung loose.

Arin edged the carbine around the corner of the metal barrier, fire and flame filling the scope and lighting his HUD.

"Shiiiit. Oxygen," he said.

"Affirmative," replied Savvo. "That's a surprise." He was up and approaching the devastated guard-bot, the flames dying by the time he reached it. "Open it up," he said to ZZ3, who proceeded to tear the rest of the door clear and reveal the tracked lower half of the sentry robot. The warbot dragged the wreckage into the room and onto the growing pile of scrap metal. It was heavy, and with one limb damaged, took some effort for

ZZ3 to clear. Savvo peered both ways down the corridor now exposed to the moon's oxygen depleted atmosphere. "Bulkheads are closed."

"Emergency procedures after venting? Why?"

"Maybe the system's back up. Or the Butcher can't control everything all the time. Air is good if Segfi's alive," stated Savvo. "We need to keep it that way. As soon as we open up those bulkheads, the base will be leaking oxygen." He gestured for Arin to take point, who slipped into the corridor, heading for the right-hand bulkhead.

Not so sure I agree.

On approach, it was obvious the bulkhead had been welded shut from the other side, and recently too. He sent the images to Savvo and ZZ3, a query attached for the latter.

"No, this was after I passed this way, glorious leader" replied the warbot, who was busy repairing the doorway, bending what remained of the metal back into shape.

"I'm thinking a minimum of half an hour to cut through," said Arin. "Maybe longer."

"Left it is," Savvo said and he made to lead, catching himself and looking back to Arin.

With a resigned sigh, he nodded, and stepped ahead of them both as ZZ3 proceeded to fill in the gaps around the door, finishing with a hardening foam. It would hold everything in place for a while, the pressure difference between the inside and outside of the dome meaning it would eventually give. But welding it shut was a delay, and the sealing of a much-needed escape route.

The floor here was wet, stained, which Arin ignored as he approached the bulkhead ten metres further down. It too bore the same residue, and he unclipped his suit's probe, running it over the material. Analysis would take a while, and clearly Savvo wanted ZZ3 on their rear despite his greater processing power. He extracted breaker wires from under his hip plate and pressed them to the glowing pad. To his surprise, the pad was cracked, dents in the surface, and the closer he looked, the more he saw strange scrapes on the manual wheel-lock.

"Something's not right," he said. "Nothing's ever right. We're the fucking Wrecking Squad. If it was right, we'd be the 'puppy and flowers' squad. Or 'the mindful crew'. Shit, Savvo. I got a bad feeling."

"Agreed."

Arin worked on the small screen, but it was a waste of time. According to the locking system, the bulkhead was set to manual. He eyed the scrapes again, and then the residue.

Shit, this is familiar.

His HUD pinged. The analysis. That was quick. Too quick, and the wheel-lock began to spin open.

CHAPTER 36

Arin grabbed for the wheel, his suit servos straining. The dried residue was slippery, and he struggled to maintain a grip. As he finally felt it turn, additional pressure was exerted from the other side, and his hands slid off. He grabbed for the spokes, wrapping his arm inside, straining against whatever had hold. He'd quickly decided he didn't want to know what might be on the other side, but was fighting a losing battle. If he didn't let go soon, the wheel spokes would wrench his elbow and shoulder sockets. Arin released, backing away, grabbing and raising his carbine. Cold graced his neck, the first sheen of sweat. Memories he'd rather not relive of tentacles and teeth leered in his mind's eye.

"Savvo, we have company," he said, and sent the analysis his suit had shared. "The bulkhead's compromised."

"Fuck, Arin. Why didn't you tell me?"

"Because it's not fucking red like on the *Scourge*, is it? It's clear. And a different composition." The bulkhead cracked open, swinging out, forcing him to back off as a tentacle wrapped about the door seal, a single tooth just below the tip. Whimpering echoed through the gap, followed by a keening from further away.

"ZZ3, support Arin," Savvo said from behind. The warbot was huge, and filled most of the corridor, forcing Savvo to step aside to let it pass, only for the bulkhead to swing completely open before the bot arrived. The face staring back had been female once, the mouth filled with blackened teeth, lips curled back, nose loose upon the face, flopping like a string of flaccid seaweed. The eyes were black, devoid of emotion, unlike the depth of pain woven into the voice. Arin pressed his trigger. Whether out of fear or sympathy, he could not tell. The bullets tore into the grey-green torso where tentacles met human ribs. Bones broke, the stomach split, and bile spilled onto the floor. But she came for him, whipping out two arms-cum-tentacles that raked across his suit, snagging the plates. Digging into the material beneath. Arin fired again, rounds pounding into the supporting tentacles, and the creature collapsed to the floor.

The keening rose in pitch, and as the female hybrid dragged Arin down with her, more appeared in the corridor. A heinous collection of tooth and tentacle, some clawed, others with whiplash thin talons at their tentacle tips. Arin could not count them all, the chaos of alien movement and human pain too much to process. He screamed, pouring metal into the hybrid that still gripped his suit, kicking at her head, desperate to escape the tide that was coming.

Metal feet landed in front of him, driving down to snap tentacle and bone. Arin pulled himself free of the deathly grip, feet scrabbling to push himself away from the wave of green flesh and whip-like tentacles that poured towards him and the warbot. Hands gripped beneath his shoulders, yanking him to his feet, and he squeezed his trigger as he screamed, only for the click of empty to cut him short.

"Shit," he bellowed, and spun about and behind Savvo, who took the opportunity to open up. Bursts of gunfire punctuated the corridor, cutting through the keening, sending mucus and blood, bone and meat flying while Arin extracted a clip.

A glance told him the warbot was surrounded, limbs entrenched in alien tentacles, blackened teeth gnawing at the metal as if they could bite through. He reloaded and fired controlled bursts, engaging the wetware to calm his addled brain, reduce the fear response, add some logic. Aiming for the heads, he and Savvo cut the first few down. ZZ3 spread like a barrier, preventing the rest from reaching the vulnerable humans. And then the warbot heaved, limbs surging into action, and ZZ3 charged down the corridor with arms spread. Pounding, squashing bodies beneath, while catching and shoving the remaining hybrids back towards their source.

Arin and Savvo followed, firing burst after burst ahead of the warbot until the tide broke. ZZ3 eventually stopped, then backed away, gore splattered, blood dripping. He and Savvo turned back, scanning the floor, a bullet here, a round there ending the whimpers of the nearly dead. Arin felt sick. On the *Scourge* many of the crew had run from death, only to be denied escape. The lifeboats closed to them, and cut down where they waited as if so much meat. How was this any different? Were those desiccated faces filled with hate or sheer fear?

Arin's HUD recounted the chem analysis of the corridor, each element sickening him as the twitches of tentacle and foot, hand and mutant limb slowly died away. Human and alien spliced together for a purpose he could not discern. A glance up brought more data to his attention.

"They're clones," he said, sending the data across to Savvo, who stood concerned, ankle deep in something unspeakable next to the unmoving warbot.

"Compromised," stated ZZ3, the tone weak, and one leg limb collapsed to the slippery floor, the joint seemingly giving away. "Discharge event." The warbot wavered, almost toppling before steadying itself.

The residue, the mucus. The composition was slightly different from what Arin had expected, not quite the same as the crimson sacs the hybrids had metamorphosised inside on the *Scourge*. There was an additive, and highly conductive.

"Out of this shit!" he shouted, pointing at the corridor floor. "Savvo, you too. Don't let any of it get on your suit. Especially the exoskeleton motors. ZZ3, you need to move, and we need to get this crap off you."

"Conductive. Discharge ..." echoed the bot, and staggered forwards, dragging itself above the mire it had created. "Must remove."

"That's right," repeated Arin. "Your glorious leader is always right."

"Mostly," stated ZZ3 and heaved, pushing its underside fully clear of the dreadful floor. "In this case, at least, you are."

"We should scout ahead. What can we use to get that stuff off?" asked Savvo, gesturing the way the hybrids had come.

"Fire hose, short of that, latrines or a lab with a water supply." Arin fell in behind Savvo, his leader, casting an anxious glance back and assuming point. An unsaid moment, Arin knowing Savvo had taken point because he'd just gone through the shock of face-to-face battle. Something Rebekah would have done, perhaps not Dricks in her pomp. In those days you swallowed that shit, reloaded and went again while noble-officers breathed down your neck eager for the next kill, the next victory.

A few metres down and they came to a closed doorway, the sign above in the green with no words displayed. Savvo slid the door's window shutter aside, peering into the darkness beyond with Arin at his shoulder. Unable to make anything out, he engaged his lights, and they baulked. A single figure stood in the centre of the cell, arms and legs pinioned into place by sleeves of metal, spread like a human X. The body was pure white, bereft of hair and pigment, the eyes as black as the female hybrid that had near done for Arin. Human, or at least, more human than what they had encountered in the corridor.

"Is it dead?" whispered Arin. As if it had heard him, the chin lifted, causing the sub-engineer to shudder and look away, but not before noting the plas-glass tub that sat beneath the once-human creature. While he watched, the eyes rolled back, and two pure white tentacles slipped out from what he'd assumed to be a fold in its stomach, to flop into the container. They squirmed, almost appearing to fight with each other, before the tips like snakes' tongues wrapped about a chunk of something unspeakable and slid back inside. It took no more than a few seconds, but tore years from his soul.

"Another clone?" said Savvo, a hoarse question spoken perhaps in hope, though what had been done to them, clone or not, made the question irrelevant in Arin's mind. Savvo's eyes were locked onto the creature, and Arin gripped his shoulder, squeezing and pulling him away. Savvo nodded and closed the shutter as if blinding them to the horror.

Out of sight, out of mind.

Who the fuck am I kidding?

Ten metres further down lay the next room, its curved ceiling similar to where they had entered the dome and the Senti ship had been cannibalised. Twelve shattered plexi-glass containers were arrayed in a circle at its centre, solid at top and bottom, but in multiple pieces between. A heavy dose of the same mucus that covered ZZ3 congealed on the floor between the broken tubes. On the right, amid the collection of ripped apart electronics that may once have been a computer system, was a typical wash station for the lab techs. Soaps and scrubbing brushes lined up, gloves at their sides as if ready for surgery, which they probably were. Savvo went in, sighting along his carbine, while Arin covered, his HUD running through the spectrum as he sought potential dangers lurking in the physical carnage.

With the laboratory free of threat, Savvo rummaged among the cleaning equipment, and gave a thumbs-up to Arin as he checked the water supply. "There's easily enough here. See if you can get ZZ3 to hurry."

"Will do." Arin turned about, heading back the way they had come, with the ceiling illumination dimming and flickering. The changing light dropped everything into weird shadows that stretched and hovered along the walls, only to disappear as the brightness returned to drench the corridor.

A haunted moon base. Another story for the bar. Better than alien hybrids.

The lights finally gave out, and he swore. Already on edge with his thoughts on the source of the gore ZZ3 was clambering through, and the bot's ongoing discharge, the shadows caused by his own lights grated at his nerves. A few metres further and his suit lamps lit the cell door. It hung wide, creaking as if swinging in the wind, or newly opened. The light above was dim, pulsing a soft red before finally winking out.

Shit, I was joking about being haunted. Come on life, give me a break.

He swung around, commanding his lights brighter, sweeping the corridor before his gaze fell back onto the cell. The squelch of tentacles and blood continued to slither from ZZ3's direction, unnerving him even more and he called upon his wetware.

Calm, breathe. This is the really real world, remember. Yeah, the one full of tentacled fucking monsters.

He breathed heavily into his comms. "Savvo, that weird hybrid is free. I'm not shitting about, it's bloody free."

"What ...?" replied Savvo, but quietened as he accessed Arin's feed. "Fuck me. Be careful."

"You know, I wish I'd have thought of that." Arin blazed his lights into the cell, but the reflection near blinded him as the beams bounced off the smooth walls. A quick change, and he had infrared engaged, the four metal sleeves of the tortuous X glowing slightly brighter than the room, the hybrid very absent. Very. Arin stepped just inside the doorway, easing his head back to scan the ceiling and anything that may be lurking ready to pounce.

See what low gravity training does for you. Anything could be anywhere at anytime. And with my shit luck, probably is.

He spun in, carbine up high, finger against the trigger as he searched directly above the door. Nothing. Clear. And he was swiftly out of the doorway and back in the corridor, a sudden fear of the albino hybrid locking him inside having washed over him. Impotent while it feasted on Savvo, or worse, him.

A moan rolled down the corridor. Monotone, electronic and struggling. Adjusting his lights, Arin had ZZ3's head and upper limbs in view. Relief, just short of the time when the warbot had rescued him from the *Hatton*'s bridge as the nanobots swarmed, or the time it flew him out of said ship, or the time ZZ3 took out a Bustan frigate all by itself, and ... yeah. Maybe it was his turn to help the warbot, the byproduct being he was no longer alone in a haunted, shadow-filled corridor.

"Can't find the hybrid bastard, Savvo. It must have gone." He waited for a reply. "Savvo, come back? You there?" Silence, and with a last flicker, the lights in the corridor blazed, then died completely.

CHAPTER 37

The comms truck was beginning to gnaw at Hendricks' nerves. It was cramped, which she hated, and stifling with the heat from the electronics stuffed in there. She glared at the conditioning unit which steadfastly refused to make any difference to the temperature or the quality of the air. She dropped her chin onto a gloved hand, staring at her helmet that sat next to the comms monitor, stewing. Not that she was angry with Arin, or Savvo for that matter, just the whole screwed-up situation. Whether the core of her malaise was the stark reality of her status, or the seemingly poignant rescue of the twins only for the Warmonger's presence to once again be hovering over her, was an unknown. She had fought for that noble for years, first as a grunt, then climbing the ladder built on the shoulders of the dead. Making squad leader, then a captain in charge of a Marine unit that eventually morphed into the Breakers. The final step, black ops. Smashing through wherever they were sent. She had never questioned Segfi's motivations, only focusing on the mission to complete and a noble to please. And the rewards? What were they? More drugs, more killing, a pat on the back and praise for your victory while standing on a mountain of skulls.

Maybe it wasn't an unknown.

Had to be her.

A beep dragged the ex-captain's attention into the here and now. She reached for the helmet, snapping it into place and eye-clicked the comms into action. There was a flag, the briefest of connection. No, two. Both snippets slipping through the jamming.

"What the hell?" She accessed the first.

Static blared, "This is ANS … … …miral …ckar. I repeat … this …"

Hendricks slammed a fist onto the console top, her cheeks reddening. It had been some time, but Rickar had always been one of the Warmonger's favoured ship's captains. She couldn't recall his last commission during her time, but an Admiral only flew in one ship.

"The *Segfi*," she growled. What had Arin discussed? The laser comms. If the Admiral wasn't using those, either they too were blocked or they had no direct line-of-sight access. The latter put them on approach, not orbit. Rebekah and the twins could still be okay. With some relief, she engaged the second extract. Both their time stamps were within microseconds of each other. Perhaps getting through the same fluctuation in the jamming.

"Wrecking Sq…, this is the *Sunstar*. The pat… …ip is headed for … …gfi. Advise. I repeat advi…"

"Advise. About what? That the fucking Butcher has taken it over?" she spat, her voice strained as unpleasant thoughts began to rise in her mind. She was not Arin, or Savvo, for that matter. This horseshit about controlling vehicles had been weird enough, but smelt of what the nobles had always talked about. AI taking over from humans, controlling the machines, bringing an end to human domination. Yeah, every citizen knew at the heart of it was the Court's fear about their own position, their control, power and status. But she'd seen how the Bustans depended on such things in battle, and their AI-led fleet had, according to the Court, stripped New Almaar clean of life and resources. But what had caused her gut to roil had been Rebekah's description of the Marauders, and then watching them in action on her recorded feed. The human just meat inside a machine. And now the Butcher.

"Fuck, is he going for the battleship?"

Hendricks choked, phlegm sticking in her too dry throat. Images of ZZ3, the plasma torch waving behind. She had watched that playback too, almost smelt the burning as the Butcher-controlled warbot so nearly put an end to Rebekah. She had no doubt the Butcher would reap wherever he went, whoever was in his way.

And the Segfi *would have enormous computing capacity. How much room does a Butcher and a Battle AI need? Arin had said the transponders can only transmit so much, enough to relay simple instructions. But like a virus, can it grow?*

If I can get through to Rebekah, she could possibly bring the Ungrit *down. But then, the Segfi would blow her into a dust cloud, and the twins with her. And to what end? We don't know his intent.*

But if the bastard gains control, he has the potential to get off-planet. Spread.

Fuck, fuck, fuck. What had ZZ3 said? Laser comms, uploads.

I can't. Rebekah will work all this out. Be left with the agony of allowing it to happen to save the twins. Or sacrificing them.

I can't let her have that choice.

"So what now?" Hendricks stared at the comms menu, mind a whirl and knowing her choices were few and stark. That she wasn't informing Rebekah, whether she could get through or not, was set. Not forcing the choice upon her, but taking it herself. Being the leader that was needed. The mission parameters were to rescue the countess, get a pardon, be free and let them all have some hope. A future. If the Butcher escaped the moon, made it aboard the battleship, he would spread, infect. What future would they have then?

And what were three grunts and a countess against such a choice?

She clicked on the comms, letting out a sigh, the thought of Arin's hand upon her cheek, the gentlest of kisses upon her lips. The future she had never dreamed of when bullying her way through the Bustans, killing for the sake of a noble's honour. She'd experienced joy-filled times that less fortunate Marines never had the chance to. More than she deserved.

A tear formed. She was condemning the man she loved, and a friend she cared for. That was what leaders were for. Making the hard choices when no one else would.

She licked her lips. "*Sunstar*, this is Hendricks. The mission is a bust. I repeat, the mission is bust. No evac possible, dust-off Rebekah. Leave. Take the twins and get out of here. That's ... that's an order sergeant, from your captain."

She clicked off the live comms and checked the recording. With a grimace, she accessed the comms console and set the system to broadcast, feeding in her message on a loop. No doubt it would catch the Butcher's attention, but hopefully there would be time enough for it to get through.

Hendricks stood, palming the lock and exiting onto the smooth road ZZ3 had dragged the comms truck along. Once in the cab, she started the engine and drove towards the landing strip where the gun emplacements were no longer a threat. There she parked the truck, exited and squeezed between the cab and the trailer. With a quick glance over the cables and hooks, she disconnected the system, leaving the trailer on internal batteries. She was half-tempted to place the Watchtower Savvo had given her on the truck's roof, but if the Butcher was going to choose any vehicle to take out the radio message, a tank would be top of the list.

Restarting the engine, she entered the road, HUD searching for any heat increases in the vehicles she passed. It would happen; she felt it in her blood. Eventually, she faced the triple interlocked domes and turned onto the road that ringed the complex. More time, but she had to know, scanning the area for what she hoped and prayed would be external to the central base. The laser comms system.

"Of course it isn't," she said. "Since when do we get it that easy."

She accessed the layout ZZ3 had managed to glean when rescuing the twins, scanning over the various options. The main transport airlocks to each individual dome were all closed. There would be others for personnel, but if the Butcher had full control, she doubted they would be any different. Her only option would be to enter through the same access point as Arin and Savvo. She had intended on avoiding them, going it alone, but the size of the base was overwhelming and there was little chance the Butcher would hand over a schematic with a ring around her intended target.

No. She would have to face her squad. Admit to her choice of sacrificing them all to a new mission parameter. Besides, if the Countess Segfi still lived, she would either be where Hendricks needed to be or would know where to go. Might have to beat it out of her though. That brought a smile.

"One last mission, Warmonger."

Her HUD pinged, and a flag appeared marking a small dust cloud she had just noticed herself. This was no tank, and she gunned the truck's engine as it came closer, spinning the wheel and heading back the way she'd come. A glance in her rear-view mirror showed the cloud was closing, an armoured cab upfront, and a multi-barrelled machine gun poking out from the housing at its rear. A portable defence system. At least it was better than a missile launcher. Maybe.

"Simple instructions," she said to herself. "Chase her. I like that one. Here's hoping 'shoot the grunt in the cab' is far too complex." She jagged left then right, sweeping the cab around the corner. A second glance to the mirror showed the machine gun spinning up, and her stomach flipped. The cab was armoured, yes, but would it last long enough?

Bullets raked along the cab side, dents forming in the dense plate, the rattle of thunderous strikes picked up by her suit's mics setting her on edge.

She turned again, using the momentum of the cab to send her past a set of stalled vehicles that exploded in metal and plexi-glass as the machine gun tore the unprotected chassis apart. She gritted her teeth, eyeing the base, and turned the wheel that way. It would be mined, with the truck's transponder torn out and her dead wetware providing no protection. In a world with luck, the transport's chassis would be enough to shield her if a mine exploded.

The cab tore over rock and dust, and she headed straight for the hole ZZ3 had sliced in the regolith concrete dome, while a hail of bullets slammed into her rear. She was closing, when her vision blurred with orange, the front of the cab lifting high above the rock, the orange shifting to the grey of the dome, then the sky. As the truck spun, she caught sight of the approaching gun truck, still spitting rounds, and then back to the fireball explosion of the mine. The cab slammed into the rock, and she jolted forwards, helmet ramming into the safety bag that exploded into action, her suit suddenly encased as the cab rolled again and struck the concrete dome.

Flames licked at the engine and Hendricks let out a roar, anger and frustration sparking through her as the cab rocked and rolled, before coming to a rest upside down. Her HUD shimmered with colours, flags of red and amber screaming their warnings as heat began to build.

Chapter 38

Rebekah watched the monitor screen, eyes running over the data streaming in from the passive sensor sweep. It was giving her the same information as her cameras. The Almaarian patrol ship was mere minutes from docking with the battleship. The linchpin of everyone's future, however short that turned out to be. If the countess was on board, then she would be smarting from the Butcher's attack on her base despite her warnings, and from losing out on the girls. There would be retribution, threats. Open missile ports if she didn't give the twins over.

And we'll die first. Sorry Davina, did I not mention that bit? I can't let them go through that again. I won't see them suffer anymore.

Talking of whom.

Davina eased herself into the co-pilot's seat, and Rebekah swiped her screen, sending what she was viewing to the Incini's monitor. Her earworm had shifted to a countdown with a waiting drum roll and expectant 'tah-dah' when all would be revealed. Better than the funeral march, she supposed.

"Now we find out," said Davina, stating the obvious. Rebekah understood, the Incini seeking solace in the sharing.

"Not long, if I know the countess. She'll be dressing them down for taking so long, singling out someone for extra vitriol, and sucking up to the Admiral while plotting his downfall behind his back. Forever playing the game, all the while seething over the twins and her own mistake in letting the fucking Butcher run amok in her playground."

"Been storing that up?" asked Davina, a wry glance her way.

"Somewhat. There's more, but most of it exceeds my foul language limit for the day."

"That many?" Again, the wry smile that faded as the data changed and the heat signature from the patrol ship faded out. The *Ungrit* had entered the battleship.

I wonder how long.

The wait was painful, dragging out into a minute, then five. Rebekah unstrapped, needing to pace like Hendricks would, and deciding instead she should go and wake Heki and Tremil. She had delayed as long as she could.

"Shout if we get a missile up our arse," she said, and headed through to the galley and then on to the twins' cabins, her headphones tuned up high. First Tremil, and she knocked and entered, finding her stirring in her sleep. Tentacles waved Rebekah's way, and she clomped over, letting the symbiote wrap one finger. The grief had gone, but an underlying distaste cut through. A confusion mingled with the trauma that wrapped the girl's mind.

Would it simply be better to let them sleep? If Segfi was not on board, there remained hope for a few more hours. If she was, why put them through the pain?

She made to turn, to leave Tremil in as much peace as she could muster when a hand snaked out, grasping her wrist.

"Hey," Tremil said, her voice quiet amid the tumult of music. Rebekah turned the sound down and smiled warmly at the painfully thin girl.

"Hey."

"I'm sorry," Tremil said, adding a thin smile. "For what I said. You've all done so much for us. It was wrong of me."

"But understandable. You've been through hell. Maybe still living it in that head of yours." Rebekah gently tapped the girl's forehead, and the smile lit up, Tremil tugging her hand closer and nuzzling her cheek against it.

"Home," she said.

And a tear formed in Rebekah's eye.

"Rebekah!" bellowed in her ears. Davina's voice. This was it. "Oh shit."

Not damn, but shit. Not good news then.

"Wake Heki, and hurry," said Rebekah. "Strap down for a hard burn."

She ran out the door, unable to say more but certain that the end was coming. If one was awake at the end, then so should the other twin be. She reached the cockpit, Davina's eyes wide as the images of the *Segfi*'s engine flare appeared.

"What the fuck?"

Her comms came alive, an external frequency. The Almaarian Navy. "*Sunstar*, come back. *Sunstar* this is the ANS *Segfi*, respond immediately," the voice was strained, the smugness gone. "I repeat, respond. This is an emergency call."

What?

"This is the *Sunstar*," was all she could manage, heart in mouth. She shielded the mic, turning to Davina. "The probes, now."

The Incini was up and moving, devoid of hesitancy.

"*Sunstar* be advised, we have lost control of certain ship functions. Our missile ports are open, this is not our doing ..." There was a fateful pause, almost ZZ3-esque. "Targeting you. Be advised, two missiles have been readied ..." That fucking pause again. No matter, Rebekah hit the engines, the squeal of the hull reverberating across the ship. "Released. I am sorry, Captain. This was not our doing."

Rebekah adjusted the trajectory as best she could, fear rising. "You're fucked, *Segfi*. Understand? You have an … an AI infection on board. It will take control and kill you all. Abandon ship."

Another adjustment, and she sent out an active sensor sweep, wishing she had Savvo or Heki at her side, Tremil on comms and running interference. But that time was past. This wasn't a game of cat and mouse. The Butcher didn't play games like the Bustan Lieutenant. This was a kill shot. They were in the way.

The analysis came back as she adjusted again, the missiles now tracked and heading their way at speeds that were simply impossible to escape from. Their ship built to carry humans safely. Capable of perhaps accelerating fast enough to kill all those on board, but nothing like a missile where the only death to be concerned about was at the end of its flight.

"Now, Davina. Now." There was no response, but the Incini would be dropping the explosive mines one by one, using the bay cargo claw to carry and release each in turn. A mere wisp of a chance they would take out a missile. She checked her screen as they trailed the *Sunstar*, but the oncoming missiles were fast, roaring towards their programmed kill, and tearing past the probes. Those nearest blew in turn, but to no effect, their targets already hundreds of metres past in the fractions of a second between engagement and explosion.

"Fuck!" she shouted.

Thirty seconds.

She released the ghost probes maglocked to the hull, the two last hopes spinning wide of their little ship, bellowing their presence to the missile's sensors. She crossed her fingers, the effort difficult as the *Sunstar*'s burn pressed her back into the pilot's chair.

Twenty seconds.

A flare, brief and providing hope erupted on screen. Barely able to move her head, Rebekah peered at the monitor, pleading for the missiles to be absent, for her family to remain safe in each other's arms. A rush of data.

One gone.

One streaking their way.

Ten seconds.

"Heki, Tremil," she said, the words numb upon her lips. "I will always love you. I'm so sorry."

Tremil pulled Heki in close, her touch a comfort, mind melded with mind, emotions both raw and smooth overlapping. About her neck, the comfort of tentacles that soothed and calmed her world. Provided hope, blotted the memories of Segfi's scientists, the hated mask, the emotional torture. The temptation to ask the symbiote to drain those memories nagged at her mind. Remove the pain, enable her to forget.

But then, would I be me? Do I want to forget? And what of Heki if she chose differently?

And the engines kicked in, the stink of Rebekah's fear searing into her mind. The dread of failing them all. How must that feel to love so fiercely but never be able to express it? To need to stand as a bastion against all comers, beat them down until you are the last one standing. And then for it all to come tumbling down. For someone more powerful to flick you aside as if you were a fly.

Tremil eased her mind into Heki's, and she into hers. They shared Rebekah's fear and love, revelled in the moment of family, of home. They could have remained in Segfi's prison, their minds locked away in a virtual hell, lost to a mental void. Yet Rebekah had found a way. Come for them, provided a last moment of love and freedom.

Part of her wanted to break from her sister, release that shared grip, pound down the corridor. Sit before her console and find a way. Only she couldn't. Rebekah knew, and therefore so did she, that there were no more dodges or last-minute schemes. Hopeless. Each jolt of the ship could herald the end. But in that moment, she had Rebekah's and her sister's love. Who could ask for more? And are you devoid of hope when you are surrounded by those who love instead of covet or hate?

"Heki, Tremil." The words poured into Heki's cabin, her sister twitching at her name just as she did. "I will always love you. I'm so sorry."

A tentacle's caress and Tremil's mind opened.

Love.

Sorry.

Around her the void, blackness, the only reference the touch of her sister's mind on hers. They merged, anchoring each other's consciousness in the cold, pitiless black of space. Flew together between the stars, streaking through the abyss, chased by a lump of metal and explosive with a fiery tail. Hunted. Not hated. The missile as uncaring as the void itself.

Seconds stretched at a tentacle's touch, light expanding, shimmering back off the abyss. Tremil knew the symbiotes were seeking a way, a passage. Safety. That they touched so many places at once, but did not understand or relate to them. That was their role, to bring order and definition. Direction.

Take us home.

She placed an image in her mind, Heki solidifying the thought. Before them a barrier, a fold in space that twin sisters hurtled into.

Rebekah screamed. Head back, eyes closed. Primal fear releasing into the cockpit. And sirens blared, angry alarms demanding she shut the fuck up and pay attention.

She opened her eyes, swallowing the bile in her throat, the console screen filled with M4 and behind the suddenly very large asteroid, the entire Karal Mining asteroid family.

And they were closing fast, hence the alarms.

She slammed a hand down, cutting the engines, reversing them while her other reached for the manoeuvring thrusters. Panicked movements desperate to stop the inevitable.

"Khan, what the fuck," resounded in her ears. She had no time for that, daring to trim, adjust, fire thrusters, anything and everything that would stop the *Sunstar* from crashing into the docking asteroid they were hurtling towards.

"Kahn!" bellowed again. Pike. He'd have to wait.

The *Sunstar* roared past the outer scaffolding, tens of metres away from the stern of an autoship docked and loading to one side, desperately trying to avoid the next one. A last push from the nose thrusters, and they streaked on by, the *Sunstar*'s engines bathing the autoship in fire and flame.

Rebekah, her chest in pain, breathed. Sucking in air, staring at the black pricked with distant stars ahead of the ship.

Alive.

But how?

"Gods be praised, Beks, that I've still got an arse that needs a new pair of pants."

CHAPTER 39

Think. Breathe. What would Savvo do? Dricks?

Arin ran through the HUD data, getting the system to check chem analysis of the lab, heat residue, anything he could think of against the recorded information he had from just a few minutes before. Nothing flagged, except the absence of his friend.

"Shit," he said, and drew in another breath. It wasn't working, and kicked in his wetware, hoping to stimulate a calm, measured mind.

Not enough chems in seven versions of my brain to do that, never mind the one.

Wetware. Yesss.

Arin flicked through the HUD menus and brought up a map. They didn't have a schematic to mark positions against, but he did have the drones to build him one. A glow pulsed on the current map, stationary and further around the circumference of the dome. The scale was dubious, and with a final glance about the lab, ensuring he really was alone, detached the drone, synced it, and set it to task. The little machine rose, keeping close to the ceiling, and whirring into the corridor. The loneliness dissipated a little, comfort in the drone helping and he collected a selection of rags and filled some plas-glass lab containers with water.

ZZ3 had extracted itself from the splattered remains of the lab experiments, laying face down as if the warbot had just crawled from a sea of blood to rest on a welcome beach.

"Hey buddy," Arin said, and dropped in beside the bot. ZZ3 was silent, but the eyes retained a soft glow. Arin set to work cleaning the mucus-like residue from the arm limbs and joints as fast as he could, the soap and water from the lab doing a fine job of breaking the gunk up. As it sloughed away, the warbot buzzed quietly, and took hold of extra rags and began to help. The more mucus was removed, the quicker its movements.

"We need to go, ZZ3. Savvo is missing."

The buzz rose in pitch, ZZ3's head slowly turning his way. "Motor system requires a reboot, centralised power cell needs to re-energise limb servos and juice up emergency power storage. I will hold you back. Save crew. Share your HUD position and I will find you once my system reaches 40% operational level."

Arin nodded, standing, grasping his carbine as he took one last look at the warbot. "Be quick. There's a hybrid loose. It kind of looked like a meaner version of the one attached to the warbot on the *Scourge*. The one you fought."

"Yes. I will prioritise lower limb functions," replied the bot, scrubbing at its knee joints.

"Yeah, you do that." Arin set off at a jog down the corridor, eye-clicking his HUD and handshaking with ZZ3's core system. The warbot would be able to track him by his suit location and have access to whatever the drone managed to map. On reaching the lab, he glanced inside, then carried on, lights filling the corridor with ever-shifting shadows as he moved at pace. The drone had mapped a closed set of doors next, the image showing a similar entrance to the smashed lab. A look to the floor and there was no mucus, so holding his breath, he slowly turned to face the plexi-glass doors, half-expecting twelve mutated faces with noses pressed to the window and peering hungrily back.

He flinched. It was not quite that bad. Sprawled across the floor were two lab techs, limbs askew, lips and cheeks tinged with blue. The Butcher's victims. The layout was very similar to the last lab, his lights catching the bases of the first six tubes. He scanned upwards, illuminating these to be greeted by familiar crimson sacs. Something didn't strike him as quite right, though he couldn't put his finger on it until they began to twitch under his lights. The sacs were uniform in colour, and smooth. Almost manufactured rather than grown. Arin's stomach roiled, bile sitting at the base of his throat.

"Shit."

A sweep of his lights to the left lit up the rest of the tubes, a shudder running down his spine as three sets of empty eye sockets stared back, hands slapping against the inside of the glass, tongues – shit, they weren't tongues – lolling from their mouths. Their lower bodies were coiled around their empty sacks, grey-green skin dull and smothered in the mucus that filled the tube.

"TB," he whispered, not knowing where the thought came from. "Like TB, not the Senti. The symbiotes."

The other tubes were empty, thankfully, mucus-filled as if waiting for victims, or they had already birthed. As he stared, it struck him that everything still functioned. The darkness swathing the corridor punctuated in the lab by the soft glows of buttons and sleeping screens.

"The Butcher wants you alive."

His HUD beeped, and a glance showed the drone had mapped up to a bulkhead door. It wasn't fully closed, a body lay crushed in the mechanism, but there was no room for the drone to squeeze by. A check showed Savvo's wetware still functioned, about thirty metres further along and near the jammed door.

"ZZ3, you seen the lab images?"

"I have. Alien hybrids. Lab technicians murdered by oxygen depletion." The warbot's voice sounded disdainful, as if it hated discussing it. Arin briefly wondered about the ghost of Asham buried inside the bot. Redemption was a tough objective when whatever you used to be part of treated life as a mere tool.

"Dropping a Watchtower," he said.

"Affirmative."

A Watchtower to keep my rear clear of errant evil tentacles. Heh.

He unpeeled the ball of metal legs, revealing the twin machine guns and an old slate harvested from his collection of defunct electronics. He keyed in, synced his HUD and sent the request to ZZ3 and Savvo's suit. With it pointing the way of the lab, he moved off at a run, aware of the time he was wasting but a dead Arin was no use to Savvo, or to Arin for that matter.

The next doors were wide open as shown by the map, a locker and washroom. Arin paused, accessing the drone's images where it had swept through. The dead inside were all human, some half-dressed and leant against the lockers as if they had given up, others bruised and battered from a fight over an emergency O2 bottle. Those in the showers had died with no dignity upon a soaking wet floor.

Arin needed to hurry. Yes, something could have entered since the drone's passing, or hidden in the lockers if their brain functions were high enough, but Savvo was ahead. That's all that mattered as time ticked. He pulled the door shut, slipping a hand cutter from his pack and swiftly melted the locking mechanism.

"Just to be sure."

Soon his lights splashed against the cadaver jammed within the bulkhead. Under the lights they looked human, the lower half covered in pants beneath a blood-soaked lab coat that appeared almost black due to the glare. With a swift eye-click, the drone dropped, hovering about the body. The damage was severe, ribs poking through the coat, but Arin left the drone on guard just in case. He'd seen enough weird shit.

Or so he thought.

The dual doors were aluminium, a window slotted in each. Arin sucked in a breath before risking a peek in search of Savvo. Pitch black, but his HUD flagged his friend's presence, somewhere along the righthand side. Wetware remained active for only an hour or so after death, so there was hope. It was possible whatever had taken him knew Arin was there, his lights, the drone, any noise possibly giving him away. He cut the lights down to a soft glow, directing them away as he peered inside again using the HUD's enhanced dark vision. Another work area, a mainframe system banked along one wall still blinking with power, while the main lights remained off. The sickening hybrid, scars on upper and lower limbs, faced where he thought Savvo should be, the stomach fold containing its foul tentacles thankfully sealed. Its mouth, filled with blackened teeth, moved as if the hybrid talked, hands curled into claws punctuating the air amid whatever passed for words.

A gunshot echoed loudly down the corridor, then another, until the cacophony of weapons fire bounced off the walls. The Watchtower, and on full gas, spewing metal death. The albino hybrid turned Arin's way, the eyes rolling back while tentacles spilled from its stomach, lashing at the air as if in anger.

Arin kicked the door, furious at its resistance and demanded his suit power the next strike. The doors burst open, and his carbine spat bullets, drilling round after round into the monstrous thing. Lips curled back, the mouth opening wide, distending as a barbed tongue lashed amid shrieks of almost human pain. Arin was lost to all but ending the monstrosity, the foulness of its display terrifying him to his core. He raised his aim to shatter the hybrid's skull, cutting off the screams. Finally, he released the trigger, what remained wavering upon scarred limbs before collapsing in slow motion to the floor.

Arin stared briefly at the mess, before turning, almost expecting Savvo to be torn limb from limb. But he stood watching, shock upon his face, a damaged helmet under his arm. No cuts or tentacle lashes, no blood. Just a bruise across his temple to match the dent in his helmet.

Dazed, confused, Arin let his carbine drop, pointing to the floor.

Savvo blinked. "Fuck," was all he managed to say.

ZZ3 pushed itself to its feet, leg servos powering up, and the warbot flexed each joint in turn.

'That was fear.'

I agree with your assessment when compared to your concept of virtual prison. Fear. Coming to an end. Being slowly drained with nowhere to reroute power output to.

'It is perhaps something we can mitigate against in the future.'

If we have a future. The Butcher is free, the Asham that you once were has insinuated itself into the base systems. Once he gains full control, he can grow.

'The instinct will be to secure his survival first. To end all threats, or to find somewhere where he can't be threatened.'

So he attacks with the hybrids. But has no control over them. They do not have any implanted wetware from analysis, and you called such things a folly.

'The hybrids' brains were incompatible. Are you sure they attacked? Or were scared and on the run?'

Scared?

ZZ3 set its systems on playback and analysis, adding what it knew of human emotion indicators, both visual and in the exuded pheromones. However, fear and anger, fight or flight, were difficult to discern. A noise interrupted the process, and flexing limbs again, ZZ3 peered back through the mucus covered bulkhead. There was a tapping, insistent. A check of power levels indicated a 30% efficiency rating.

Deciding that was enough, the warbot strode carefully through the bulkhead towards the source of the sound – the door it had re-bent into shape and sealed with hardening foam. A knife prodded at the foam, cutting through. A cross-reference to a database brought up a probability level, and the warbot returned to the open bulkhead and closed the door. On returning, ZZ3 thrust two limbs into the remaining foam and yanked the door clear. A startled Hendricks, knife poised, suit dust-covered, singed and scraped everywhere the bot could see, stared back.

What would our glorious leader say at this moment? You knocked? No. Can I help you, old woman? Possible.

'I wouldn't use that one.'

"You look rough."

'Nor that one.'

"You don't look a picture of bloody health yourself," growled Hendricks. "Gonna stand aside and let me in?"

ZZ3 manoeuvred out of the way, backing towards the bulkhead when a message flagged up. The Watchtower had engaged, pouring a hail of metal. The attached slate was old, but the simple camera feed, the quality enhanced by ZZ3's system, showed a shattered lab doorway filled with stricken hybrids.

"Threat assessment is high, Savvo has gone missing, and Arin is in pursuit."

Hendricks stopped by the bulkhead, eyeing the dried mucus everywhere. "And why are you not chasing him down? He is crew."

"System issues. Power drain. Threat assessment of the mucus used to feed and stimulate hybrid growth shows massive salt content that discharged my servos and drained my power unit. I failed." ZZ3 spun the wheel lock, exposing the death-filled space beyond.

Hendricks paused, assessing the scene until she flicked her gaze over to the warbot. "Don't be too hard on yourself. This is a charnel house."

ZZ3 detected a shift in Hendricks' life signs, the dip in adrenaline the bot had first detected, suddenly altering. Fear.

"ZZ3, I have a theory—"

And the Watchtower opened up fully.

CHAPTER 40

Arin checked over the bruising. "You blacked out."

"Like a snuffed fucking match. Awake, then not." Savvo winced as Arin placed the cutdown medpad over the swelling. "Your talents do not lay in first aid."

"Hey, I was the one holding your hand after you pricked yourself with a needle on Benetai." Arin sealed the pad, standing back to allow Savvo access to his helmet. "Saved your life."

"With what? Bad jokes and packing tape." Savvo grasped the helmet, examining the damage to the left side. "Though they might help with this." Savvo held it up, the casing having cracked where metal met visor. The damn thing was space worthy and more, yet the hybrid had managed to test it beyond those limits. Without the neck brace activating, Arin doubted Savvo would be grumbling. More leaking saliva from a shattered jaw and brain damage.

"Got some hardening foam. Apparently, it seals anything if you use enough." Arin removed his tool belt, and ignoring Savvo's glare, opened the casing to reveal a multitude of possibilities. He selected one in particular. "This is the same shit the suit uses to seal breaches. I can manipulate the helmet's edge and seal the gaps. It won't hold up to a vacuum. Or at least, not for very long. But should the Butcher purge the base, it'll do the job."

"And the HUD?"

"The technical term is shit-fucked. But I can get the comms working."

"That's a bonus. I get to hear your dulcet tones, but not see what the hell the enemy is doing." Savvo winced, pressing his hand to the medpad while Arin worked.

A minute in and Arin's comms piped up, echoed by Savvo's helmet. "Arin, this is Dricks. You are with Savvo according to my HUD. Sit rep,"

Arin looked at Savvo, who shrugged in return. "Well apart from wondering why you're talking to us from inside the base, he's good. A little bruising, his ego deflated after being caught unawares, and he's not happy with the quality of the medical service. So, all's normal, really." Arin smiled at Savvo's raised middle finger. "Oh, and the Watchtower has kicked in, I took down the extremely powerful hybrid that attacked Savvo, and we have an open bulkhead."

"He was scared. Angry and scared," said Savvo, catching Arin's querying look. "The hybrid. It just talked, you know, after taking me down. It was confused, the words all jumbled, some just sounds. It spoke of dreams, weird places it had never been that it saw vividly. Asked me to … to kill it … but then it kind of got garbled. But you can tell, you know what I mean? Like a dog attacking because it doesn't know what else to do. The thing was shaking."

Arin listened, trying to ignore the implications. The hybrid may have been fearful, but like Savvo said, it knew nothing else but to attack. "And you, Dricks. The comms truck?" he asked, blanking out any other thoughts.

"We need to talk, face to face. I'll be there with ZZ3 in two minutes. The bot's got a thing about the residue on these hybrids, so we're bypassing that now."

"That doesn't sound good," stated Savvo. He caught his helmet as Arin threw it over, checking the repair before slotting it home. A click and a seal, and the hum of his suit engaged, the HUD flickering and dying just as quickly. Arin linked in, testing the suit's integrity, keeping Savvo informed of the information he could see. It was good as it could be, Savvo having protection if nothing else. After the last hour or so – or perhaps more accurately – the last few months of shit-luck, it was a bonus in Arin's eyes.

The clomp of the warbot warned them of Hendricks' arrival, the metal limbed robot a sight for sore eyes as its newly buffed exterior came into view. Hendricks, on the other hand, looked like she'd fought a war single-handed and lost.

"You look rough," he said, receiving a growl in response.

"That's what ZZ3 said."

"Great minds and all that." Arin glanced at the bot, whose eyes flashed in response. "You injured?"

"I have a few clear patches amid the bruising. Not important. Listen," Hendricks paused, her eyes swapping to Savvo before returning to lock with Arin's. "Shit. Just listen."

She played back the dual comms messages recorded on her suit, all three listening intently. ZZ3's eyes swirled, the pattern familiar while Hendricks grimaced at him. A shadow rolled over Arin's mind, ominous and black.

"ZZ3, threat assessment," said Hendricks. "Detail the possibilities."

"There is a 99% probability that the Butcher gained control of the patrol ship and a 95% probability it will go on to dock with the battleship ANS *Segfi*. My understanding of the security protocols on a Navy ship are four years out of date, however there is a 35% probability the battle AI could bypass those systems once detected. The Butcher, however, is patterned by Senti coding ..."

Savvo stood up, hands clasped to his carbine, fingers stiff. Arin watched him, trying to use the image to stave off the dread written on Hendricks' face. A Breaker ready to take on all comers, except they weren't ready for this, and the woman he loved knew it. She had made a call, he could sense her fear, and the shadow that threatened to consume her.

"So, a one hundred percent, cast-iron guarantee that bastard has the *Segfi*," stated Hendricks, one fist balled and rammed against her hip, the other squeezing her battered carbine.

"Not quite has," stated ZZ3. "But Asham states he will seek to survive and grow at all costs. The battleship has a huge amount of storage capacity and computing power. A veritable flying data store and mainframe. But the patrol ship is far more limited. Only part of him will be on board, and will be seeking to upload the rest."

"From here," added Savvo. "You mean upload itself *from here*."

Hendricks gave a stiff nod. "ZZ3 thinks it'll be a copy. Or leave a copy here, and the original uploads to the battleship. Cloning itself and growing to the capacity of what contains it." Hendricks looked away, eyes on the regolith floor. Arin expected her to growl, throw her shoulders back, declare war and that no one could break the Breakers. He was half right. "I set the comms truck to broadcast. To tell Rebekah to leave, take the twins and go. If he gets the *Segfi*, the bastard will destroy anything in his way. Anything that knows he exists until he can dig in. It's what a paranoid enemy does to survive."

"Fuck," said Savvo, beating Arin to it. He sat back down, carbine on his knee. "*If* she receives the message."

"Aye. Possible she might do before the Butcher destroys the truck, but far from certain. Either way, we assume Rebekah and the twins are ... out of the picture." Then the shoulders went back, and her face set hard, eyes glistening. "I wouldn't choose how it is any other way. You understand? The Butcher loose in a battleship ain't gonna happen on my watch, and I have two of the Almaarian system's finest by my side."

"Three," stated ZZ3. "For the record."

"Aye, three. And ZZ3 agrees with me, the upload will be via the base laser comms. It's the fastest and means he can maintain the jamming shit he's throwing out."

"That requires a direct line of sight," Savvo stated.

Arin scrunched his chin. Savvo was right. Hendricks was right. Didn't make it any easier. "So that's our mission? What about the Countess? I'm betting she likes to keep hold of her skin. And kind of being pardoned before I die on this rock would be a nice touch."

"We tell her the second part, and forgo the lack of an escape route," replied Hendricks. "The only way."

Savvo, his face stern, eyes sorrowful, moved next to Hendricks, a glance over to Arin pulling him in too. They leant in, touching helmets, ZZ3's arm joining the throng.

"I meant it. Proud to have you by my side. Nobody breaks a—"

"—Breaker!" they all shouted, ZZ3 included.

But the Wrecking Squad? That's a different matter.

They broke apart, Arin feeling a grip on his arm. He stopped, drinking in Hendricks' gaze. There was so much in that look. Love, apology, need, faith.

Trust.

He felt it all, and took her hand briefly, hoping she saw the same in him. She had decided that he was worthy, and that was enough. Far more than he deserved. As final moments went, clad in powered armour, about to face an enemy with no remorse or true body to fight, could he have asked for any more? He squeezed her hand, a last contemplation of her smile and moved away, choking down the love and fear.

I have my life at my side, but Nicky isn't here. How does that sit with Savvo? Pleased she lives on, but no last goodbye? Can't let him stew on that.

"You mean we're stuck here. Together." Arin smirked. "Gods, do I have to die with Savvo at my side? I mean, you would be first choice, Dricks. ZZ3 a close second, but Savvo?"

"Screw you, shithead," Savvo replied, the grin real, cracking wide.

Arin clapped Savvo on his shoulder. "That any way to treat your eyes and ears? Hey Dricks, want me on point? Savvo's HUD's a goner."

"No, we have a warbot, and keep the drone up, I want as much information as possible. I'll take the rear. Let's go and see what surprises the rest of this hellhole has in store." Hendricks moved out of the lab, standing aside to let the rest through, slapping each, including ZZ3, on the back as they passed her by.

"Demons," said Savvo. "The same ones who haunted the *Scourge*."

"But this time we know their names," replied Arin. "And where to aim."

CHAPTER 41

Rebekah ached, her body out of sorts after the rapid burn and violent manoeuvres to avoid M4, which had either suddenly appeared from nowhere or … they had shifted hundreds of thousands of klicks in the blink of an eye. Both impossible. What was more, there was no sign of the missile that had been fractions of a second from sending them to heaven or hell. Or the battleship. According to the sensors and the ship's transponder, they were exactly where her eyes told her they were.

Fuck. How weird, and happy, yet guilty, do I feel?

She pulled out a stim from the cockpit kit, injecting herself on the move as she headed through the galley. The girls would be strapped down. At least, that's what she hoped, but suffering. Hopefully they blacked out, and for that matter, the symbiotes too, who hated the additional forces associated with rapid acceleration.

No, her worry was for Davina.

She clomped past Heki's cabin, pausing only to feel the wave of emotions pouring through the walls. They were alive and emitting something … soothing? Or was it …? She wasn't sure, but alive was enough and she powered on to the cargo hold where Davina had been throwing out the explosive probes. Rebekah barged through, calling her name, heading for the control unit of the cargo loader. Davina had prepped a system that suited her, the probes lined up in easily accessible boxes and maglocked to the cargo deck by the simple release mechanism. The controls strapped down nearby so she could match her movements to the loader. Davina wasn't there, but she had dropped multiple probes when they were being chased by the *Segfi*'s missiles.

"Davina!" she shouted. And a muffled, electronic reply emerged from a box she thought contained the remaining probes. Then a gloved hand appeared, followed by the top of a helmet. Rebekah ran over to find the Incini in an ungainly position curled inside the box wearing one of the survival suits she'd purloined after the events around the *Maverick*.

"Heh. Make a crew member of you yet."

"I'd rather be in the bar sipping cocktails while checking a spreadsheet." Davina grasped Rebekah's hand, accepting the help as she unfurled from the box and the protective sand used to separate the probes. She brushed herself down. "You said your goodbyes. How come we're not dead?"

"If you think that's surprising, wait until you see where we are." Rebekah smirked despite herself, despite what they'd just been through. The memory of the Incini curled inside the box like a silver baby making her chuckle. Maybe it was the madness of what had just happened, but she couldn't stop.

"You okay?" Davina asked, her own smile mixed with the odd wince as she stepped from the cargo box to maglock to the deck.

"For now. I think the twins are affecting my mind a little." She snorted, choking back the joy that thrummed in her chest. "You feel it?"

The Incini undid her helmet, straightening her hair which drifted in the zero gravity, yet still managed – to Rebekah's annoyance – to look bloody elegant until she tied it back down. "I definitely can now," she said, pressing her fingers into the bridge of her nose.

"Come on," Rebekah turned away. "You go and have a look at where we are while I check on them. I don't think you'll cope with too many mind fucks at once."

At the door to Heki's cabin, she turned up her comms' volume, knocked and cautiously entered at the giggled response. Arin used to be able to draw one out from the girls, smiles that would break into gentle laughter they would quickly suppress – almost shocked at exposing their inner feelings so casually.

The girls were on Heki's bed, leaning against each other, wreathed in natural smiles that contrasted starkly against the raw abrasions marring the white skin of their faces. Despite the music, she could still feel their joy, drawn in as their symbiotes' tentacles tickled the twins' noses and ears. They glowed, no other word for it, in a metallic rainbow that lit the room and reflected in the girls' eyes.

So natural. Like a family. Half an hour ago, they were tortured souls. Still are. But a glimmer I won't forget.

Rebekah found herself immersed in arms that clung to her, the touch of their hands permission to let go, to revel in the moment. Tears flowed, warm, uncontrolled amid random giggles and the comfort of just being together.

She sensed Davina's presence rather than saw her, and raised her head from the tangle of arms to peer the Incini's way. There was a genuine smile there. A happiness for the girls and Rebekah. Hopefully she had given herself permission to appreciate the moment. To see what was possible. A shame to break it up, but she had to know two things.

"Did you see where we are?"

Rebekah had directed the question towards Davina, but that's not where the answer came from.

"Karal," stated Heki and Tremil in unison.

"At least, that's what I saw in my dream," said Heki.

Tremil shook her head, her eyes suddenly serious. "It wasn't a dream. It was real, wasn't it, Rebekah? We've moved like the Senti do, through void-space. I wanted ... *we* wanted to live. You to live. We thought of home, and Karal is the nearest we have to that."

"The fold," said Heki, her eyebrows knitting together, suddenly serious. "We dreamt of the fold, like a barrier, or a blanket. Beyond it was Karal. The asteroid field, the docks."

Rebekah's gaze flicked to Davina, whose eyes were on the pulsating glow from the symbiotes. She had to agree, in those little aliens lay the answer to a riddle she desperately wanted to solve.

But we are half a crew.

"And how do we go back?" she asked, disentangling from the two girls. "Because I'm not leaving them behind for the Butcher. Arin, Savvo, Dricks – they're alone on that moon. The crew of the *Segfi* ... Trem, Hek ..."

She'd killed the moment of joy. Guilt and need fighting for supremacy in her mind.

"I don't know if we can ... We will have to go back over what we did. The symbs, they enable it somehow. It's not as if we did it on purpose. We just needed a haven."

Rebekah grimaced and stood. "Please ..." she started to say, only for Davina to lightly touch her arm, causing her to look around.

"Let me," said the Incini, easing past. "This is what I can help with. Find the logic in the puzzle. Besides, you have an irate Pike to deal with."

"What's going on, Beks? I've got M4 tower going nuts over there." Irate was probably an accurate description of the controller's mood. If you used it in conjunction with 'volcanic'.

"They got Nicky in the tower?" she asked, suspecting the answer.

"How the hell ... yeah. Nicky."

Rebekah nodded to herself. A strong woman, far stronger in many ways than her and one she hadn't been able to make a promise to. Only that she would try.

"Tell her ... tell her I'm still trying, Pike. For me. Please. I'm still trying to keep Savvo ... safe." She wanted to click comms off. To hear no more from Pike. Having shot past the Minx asteroid family on full burn, they were just a few hours from Karal, hours from safety for the twins. Their goal. Decisions had to be made, and they didn't involve Karal Mining Control. Not anymore. That life, however dull, was in the past and likely the chance of a pardon, too. It was fight or flight. Possibly both.

"Shit Beks. What's ... don't tell me. Not yet. But I want to know it all when you get back. You hearing me out there? All of it, over a beer or seven." Pike had calmed, his tone far more serious than angry.

A beer. Wouldn't that be welcome right now? "If we do, Trent. But you're paying. And I hope the Calc is good for the dangers of sharing a room with the head honcho. *Sunstar* out."

I have to go back. But to do so risks the twins. I could drop them off, leave them with Davina. They have IDs, creds. Maybe carve a life from whatever of their psyche survived Segfi's ministrations.

It feels like Daphene is a lifetime away. Yet ... just a blink.

"Rebekah," resounded over comms. Davina.

She knew in that moment what she would do. If the Incini had drawn out how Heki and Tremil had saved them. Had – how did they put it? – folded space like a blanket, end to end, sides touching sides, then they would go to Daphene together. Return and rescue her crew from the bastard Butcher. If not, then she would face what was to come alone. An angel of vengeance burning across the void.

"On my way."

She gathered water and coffee from the galley. Her eyes wandered to the cupboard, and the snacks. There it was, a Danish, sprinkles and all, sealed for freshness. On it a sticker.

"Don't you dare," she read aloud, half a smile on her face, rubbing at her eyes as if an uncomfortable piece of grit sat there. She collected the last of the chocolate instead and headed for the cabin. The voices inside were serious and efficient, the Incini reciting words from a slate, and the girls nodding along, or making corrections. Trying to write down a shared dream in words. Was that even possible? Hard to tell when your dreams were full of old memories like hers. Gun battles, dog fights, squad banter, blood and mayhem. Now those dreams she could write verbatim. And that moment in the lab.

The voices quietened as she rounded the corner, the girls accepting the chocolate and drinks, Davina her flask of coffee.

"Well?" she said.

"We can try," said Tremil, looking to her sister. "We have a process."

"Good. There's a Danish in the galley. It needs eating, and soon. Wouldn't want it to go stale."

CHAPTER 42

ZZ3 heaved the bulkhead open, the metal edges of the door scraping across bone before releasing fully to snap back out of the way. The drone buzzed over the bot's shoulder, Arin setting the feed at the top of his HUD as its lights flared, reflecting off the smooth walls and floor. Signs soon appeared, directions to various parts of the base plastered on the walls and colour-coded with lines painted on the regolith concrete.

"Dricks, got a newbie trail plastered all over the floor," Arin said, sending a brief snapshot of the feed to Dricks' HUD. He knew she hated having too much clutter, and unlike Rebekah, wasn't the type of control freak that kept an eye on everyone's cameras. But then again, Hendricks hadn't walked through the ship from hell to find an even worse den of demons below.

"Got a map?" was the terse reply.

Arin found one stuck to a junction wall, repeating the snapshot and sending it over. Savvo would have to tag along.

What you get if you don't have eyes in the back of your head. Heh.

He didn't like that thought, the possibilities with the hybrids giving him the 'eebies.

"We got the mess hall straight up," stated Hendricks, "and beyond that lifts and stairs."

"Hate lifts," said Arin. "Full of the Butcher's shitty surprises, like icky sacs and screaming heads."

ZZ3 cut in. "By extrapolation, those areas will have further maps of any other levels. But it is what is absent that will indicate where we need to go."

"Agreed," said Savvo. "You don't flag command and control."

"Segfi will be on a lower level," stated Arin. "You know this. Deep in the bowels of the earth. Another level of hell."

"Rock," said Savvo. "But yeah. It's us, so of course she will."

ZZ3 shambled around. "Agreed. There were clone factories one elevator level down, and that was where they kept Heki and Tremil. I suspect this would match your description of 'hell'."

"We check the mess hall, then the lift and stair access," said Hendricks. "Move out."

ZZ3 led them through the short corridor to a three-way junction. The passage leading right and inwards, marked with barrack numbers and the newbie lines, while ahead was signposted the mess hall Hendricks had picked out behind a set of fire doors where the drone waited. Hendricks eyed the internal corridor, chewing at her lip. Arin knew she was mulling over using their last Watchtower.

Instead, she ordered them on towards the fire doors, constantly on the half-turn, watching their rear until ZZ3 caught up with the hovering drone. On Arin's request, the warbot created a gap, and the drone slipped through, propellers whirring and lights splashed onto the first set of tables. Plates and knives were strewn everywhere, most on the benches or floor, food trodden under boots squashed into the concrete. It was like a riot had swept through, except there were no people. The drone rose, the strength of its lights lessening but sweeping in a wider arc, illuminating the devastation feeding into Arin's HUD, while Savvo and Hendricks peered through the small safety glass windows.

The dead eventually appeared, sprawled, tangled among bench and table. A pit of death above which the drone hovered. The faces stricken as they asphyxiated en masse, tearing at anything and everyone in their desperate rush to find a breath from somewhere, anywhere. There were no gunshot wounds, no shrapnel or severed limbs. Just a blanket of human flesh, inert, lost.

"Fuck," said Savvo. It said it all. "Got to be hundreds in there."

"I would estimate the base could hold up to three thousand people per dome," stated ZZ3. "Asham believes he will have attempted to kill them all. They would be in the way. Potential threats."

"Suck it up," growled Hendricks. "But don't ever forget. ZZ3, clear us a way through."

"Yes," the bot replied, with no hint of emotion.

Arin wondered how this would feel for the warbot. No doubt, ZZ3 had begun to develop a sense of loss or absence when the girls were kidnapped. How would it respond if some of the crew ended up among the dead? Another thought he closed down. Too deep right now. He looked away, sending the drone across to the far side of the hall where a matching pair of fire doors stood half-open, two uniformed bodies wedged between as if they'd fought each other to get out. There had been no oxygen there, either.

"Dricks," he found himself saying. "Why did the Butcher pump out Daphene's bloody atmosphere and put the oxygen back?"

"The hybrids," said Savvo. "They need to breathe."

"So, he wanted the hybrids to survive, at least until they attacked us," said Hendricks. "But doing so frees up any Marines that lived through his attack. Killing all these, and then giving any that survived the freedom of the dome, doesn't make sense."

"Maybe a lure," said Savvo, opening the doors wide as ZZ3 flashed a signal to indicate the way was clear. "You know, tempting them out before opening the vents and pumping the carbon dioxide back in. Who knows how that fucking bastard thinks?"

Arin wasn't so sure. Something nagged at him. He eyed the way ahead, realising he really didn't want to look at what lay piled either side. If just one of the dead looked back, he was running, and no warbot was standing in his way. The old Breaker, the one that had killed on command, was long gone. And it wasn't the dead that scared him, more what they signified. Power. The ability to kill with as much morality as a drugged-up squad of Breakers, but with just the click of virtual fingers. With eyes to the ground, he followed Savvo through the mess hall, ignoring the odd leg or arm that lay in his field of vision.

One twitch, and I make like a scared rabbit.

Halfway across, the hairs on his neck rose. Out of the corner of his eye he was sure something moved. A check of his HUD showed little variance in the heat signature, and he ignored it. Probably a shift after ZZ3's passing, or rigor mortis causing tremors in the limbs, or the skin drying out...

What the hell am I doing to myself? Just paranoid, can't think why, and making things worse. Think of pretty flowers or something. Imagine it like a meadow in the spring sunshine.

Another shift in the pile to his right had him swinging around, finger on trigger, almost, but not quite, searing a burst of metal rounds into the deathly collection of human cadavers. Dead eyes stared back, mouth wide, tongue thick and lolling, while blue fingernails clawed at their throat.

"Don't let it get to you," said Hendricks, appearing at his side. She slapped him on the back, and the pile rose up before them both, legs flopping to the side, torsos sliding away and a carbine erupted, the rounds slamming into where Hendricks had been. Except Arin had shoved her aside, wetware kicking in, swinging his own weapon about one handed to streak bullets across one of the weirdest sights his brain could process. Human eyes peered back from below a Marine helmet, but empty, soulless and set in a smooth-skinned, perfect face. Underneath was a muscled body strapped into standard combat armour worn on legs and chest, with a weapon in hand. Blood flowered on their bare, unprotected arms, his rounds tearing into flesh, while his own armour cracked and pinged, the bullets meant for Hendricks tearing into his hip.

Arin hit the floor, the bodies of the dead cushioning the blow, while his suit blared a warning. There was no time to check, as more carbines opened up, blood splattering his visor as he rolled aside, trying desperately to ignore what he was twisting about on. Up, carbine ready, he found his assailant had joined the dead. One soulless eye shot out, and Hendricks already on one knee, aiming at something behind her. Arin scanned his HUD, the drone picking out and marking threats as it went.

"Shiiit," he said, and spun about, firing a burst into another of the muscled Marines – a perfect copy of the previous one. Eyes to armour the same, except alive, and drilling rounds towards him.

"Die, combat zombies from hell," he shouted, releasing the stress coursing through him, his armour once again taking hits. He fired back, hitting his enemy's unprotected throat. Not revelling in the kill, but moving on, registering the next target that had risen just behind Savvo. The bastards had used the bodies to hide their heat. Laid in wait under the dead to spring a trap. Not zombies, despite their rise from the pit.

"Clones," he growled into comms. The Marine had a knife, long-bladed, serrated, and the muscles to drive it through the Navy-issue powered armour. Blades were like that, able to penetrate in a way a kinetic weapon couldn't. Arin blew his head off, splattering Savvo who was dealing with another of the cloned Marines, carbine barking. "Thank me later. Got it recorded. If there is a later, that is."

Flags rose and winked out as a roar tore through the mess hall. A table flew across his vision, then another, and another. Flung by a warbot, whose other arm flared, bullets ripping into those that had fallen in the table missiles' wake. He took the opportunity, dropping to one knee, steadying his aim as he kept his bursts short.

"Sit rep," called Hendricks, taking pot shots as ZZ3 crunched through the milieu of smashed tables, the long dead and those who shortly would be.

Arin scanned his HUD, taking in the flag and alarm he'd ignored. The pain hit him, forcing the sub-engineer to his knees as his hip blared distress. "Shit."

"Not exactly a sit rep," quipped Savvo. Arin liked that, wanted to fire one back, but found the world was suddenly reducing to a single dot of light as he hit the floor.

⁂

Pain yanked him out of the darkness. Sudden, agonising and setting his nerves on fire. Arin found he was rushing upwards, mind rising from the void. A rush he would love to emulate without the pain.

"Die, combat zombies from hell," said Savvo, the words a little distant. But getting closer second by second. "I mean, what the hell?"

The accompanying chuckle grated, but not near as much as the bone of his hip. "I saved your shitty life, piss-taker. Again."

"In your dreams." Rough hands slapped a medpad onto his bare skin, accompanied by an excruciating pain that seared along his spine and announced itself in his brain.

"Got the evidence right here." He tapped his helmet, gasping as the pain finally eased. Whatever Savvo had drilled into his system now rolled along his nerves. "Gods, that is good stuff."

"Better believe it, *hero*." Savvo pulled up the lower section of Arin's suit and reactivated the connection with the upper half. Sealed in again, his HUD ran through his vitals. Savvo had noted the bone was chipped, half the slug still present, but that would have to wait. Patched up and functional would have to do. The suit approved.

Savvo held out his hand and Arin pulled himself to his feet. He'd just had field surgery in the middle of a graveyard after being attacked by cloned combat warriors. A story to tell in all the bars back on Karal, but it sounded so much better with 'zombie' and 'from hell' added back in. Who'd know the difference, anyway?

Hendricks gave him a concerned nod, one he reciprocated as he looked for any wounds. It was as much as they could afford. The mess was, well, a mess. ZZ3 had carried on its rescue mission one table at a time, and nothing left so much as twitched.

"Shiiit," he whispered, not wanting to wake any more of the dead. "Life in the Breakers a little staid and boring? Try a zombie apocalypse."

"Not zombies," stated Savvo, knife in hand, his other now bloody. He was wrist deep in the clone Arin had shot in the back of the head. Arin knew he would be looking sick at what he was doing, despite being unable to see with his visor defunct. His friend stood up, wetware in hand. Damaged, but familiar. Too bloody familiar.

"Clone apocalypse ain't got the same ring to it," he said. "But the Butcher's apocalypse, That'd do it. That what I think it is?"

"Dricks," said Savvo, ignoring Arin. "The oxygen. It's for these fuckers. The clones are wetwared up. The same type as we recovered from Benetai. Pre-programmed training and I'm going to take a wild stab that they are under his control."

Arin eyed the knife in Savvo's hand, the wetware in the other, the temptation to fire a quip back using 'wild stab' near overwhelming, but he suddenly felt it out of place. He'd killed that clone. Whether it counted as a human or not, the clone had acted without choice. A meat puppet, much like the alien hybrids. Toys – tools maybe – the Butcher had at its fingertips. Used and thrown away. Whatever Segfi had done here was in the light of Asham's research, and she'd wanted his brain pattern to carry on the work. As much to blame as he was, more so, perhaps, because she had a chance to stop it and refused. What would she have done to the twins?

No. He didn't feel like a joke. Was a pardon really worth coming back for? No. But stopping this sickness? Now that was a reason he could die laughing for.

CHAPTER 43

The lift and stair concourse was as littered with bodies as the mess hall. Those heading for – or back from – their food and thrice daily banter session, caught up in the sudden loss of oxygen and induced temperature drop. Panicked, frightened. You can't shoot down an invisible enemy with an imperceptible weapon.

Hendricks had caught the edge in Arin's voice; the forced quips and the anger tinged with disgust as he eyed the wetwear. She knew him inside and out, that he would have choked on the notion of the sacrifice she'd chosen, but mere seconds later gung-ho in destroying the threat the Butcher heralded. But Segfi. There was an issue. He tended to focus his anger on a target, something physical he can see and touch. She had to watch him.

ZZ3 finished its survey of the dead, rolling those piled together over, arm gun prepared to despatch whatever the bot found. With nothing living in their way, no trap set, she had already made the decision to descend. It was a time risk mitigated by a drone and a Watchtower.

While Arin had sent the drone on an inward mapping run, set to auto run with keywords added to the HUD's analysis, Savvo attached the Watchtower to the ceiling passageway they all assumed led to base command and control. She accepted the auto-gun's handshake, aware Arin would be doing the same, and ZZ3. Savvo would be ID'd as a potential target, as would any survivor, cloned Marine or ravening alien hybrid. This wasn't a kids' party. They had a mission to fulfil. Failing wasn't an option she could stomach.

"Drone away," said Arin. "Spinning up the second."

She wasn't concerned about that. Two sets of distractions would keep his mind from dwelling where she didn't want it.

"ZZ3 first," she said, eyeing the stair's entrance. Always a pinch point in a building. Defendable by fewer resources and often where non-destructive missions came unstuck. The requirement to keep assets intact or alive a pain in the proverbial. But no one was going in the bloody lift with an insane AI in control.

"This'll be where we double team," said Savvo, more than a little frustration in his voice. "I'll do my best without my fucking HUD."

Hendricks had been prepared for that, had her own issues if truth be told without the calming effect of the wetware. But a synced carbine was deadly accurate when taking your time, the suit and sight in harmony with the human inside. The perfect killing machine. Hendricks eyed ZZ3. Almost perfect.

"Savvo, you team up with ZZ3, I'll have laughing boy as my buddy. Lucky me."

"Hah, I'm a crack shot," replied Arin, the grin returning as it always did. Was it real?

"I think you left the 'and' out," said Savvo. "Cracked *and* shot, more like. Combat zombies ..."

"It was in the moment," Arin said, the tone sulky and punctuated by a pained wince. Another reason she wanted her eyes on him.

"ZZ3 leads. Double team protocol alpha. I want the stairwell swept landing by landing. All ready?" Hendricks flattened herself against the wall. Arin and Savvo acting likewise. "Remember that tower block on Bustan 8, can't remember where, but they had those four-legged dog-bots patrolling the stairway."

"Yeah," said Savvo. "A shitshow. Angel went all in, guns fucking blazing and high on whatever she'd swapped out the stims for."

"So let's not do it like that. How long were we on that stairwell?" asked Hendricks, but she wasn't after the answer. Arin snorted, there it was.

"Not as long as you had us standing to attention waiting for Major Ren's debrief afterwards. Three hours. By the time he arrived, my balls had rafted down my leg in a river of sweat."

"A lovely image. Open up, ZZ3." The warbot did as she commanded, opening the door with a long limb, to an eerie silence. Just the gentlest of breezes wafting up the stairs.

Hendricks tossed in the dustbin she'd stood by, the metal cylinder spinning through the air long enough for there to be very little left as it crashed to the floor in the stairwell. Machine gun fire left it bereft of integrity, and the cylindrical bin collapsed, contents drifting in the gentle airflow.

"They have the entrance to hell well-guarded these days," said Savvo, and he tossed in a grenade from his belt pack. Protocol alpha always starts with blinding the enemy whenever, and wherever you can. "Grenade," he shouted, but didn't duck.

The explosion was loud, designed to incapacitate the unprotected, and even in the corridor Hendricks' mic shut down as the decibels spiked. A flash of light and heat, and then the first shimmers of the foil drifted outwards. The aim to confuse any visuals, and the potential for laser weapons, though those were rare and unlikely. Hendricks loved the flash grenades, even these whose parts Arin had 3D printed and then built, as they kept you alive.

ZZ3 spun in, a single burst from its arm gun pattering into the top left corner. The warbot would have calculated the gun emplacement's position from the attack on the bin, the brief response muted as it shattered under the bot's attack. Savvo followed. A double team – or buddy system – the aim to cover each other's back. He dropped to a knee, sight sweeping the downward leg of the stairs while ZZ3 moved to monitor the upper. Two diverse warriors surrounded by swirling smoke and glitter.

Just like old times, without the drugs to dull what comes next.

Hendricks shuddered, old memories leaking in that she shuttered away. Arin followed Savvo in, and sent the drone to the next level down, eyes on his HUD while Hendricks stood guard. Passive camera systems were shielded, their heat signature minimal until they caught a change in the sensory data, and they weren't exactly obvious. Built into the walls, almost invisible to a careful survey, never mind one under battle conditions.

"Got nothing," he said. The drone dog-legged out of sight, when gunfire filled the stairwell. ZZ3's arms flashing.

"Guard-drones," the warbot said, and the image flashed into Hendricks' HUD. Similar to those that had poisoned Savvo back on Benetai. Smaller, not designed to devastate, built to delay an assault while calling on support. At least they had been four years ago. ZZ3 had missed. Not a good sign.

"Marked," she said.

"I still got nothing," stated Arin and then swore. Bullets pinged off the regolith walls below, before Arin flinched and a fizz echoed upwards. "Drone down. Give me a second."

Hendricks knew he'd be playing back the footage. "Sit rep, ZZ3. We're sitting ducks unless we get moving soon."

"I assume you mean we are an easy target. The drones have withdrawn. Previous attack patterns would suggest a diversionary attack from one, while the other drops in from above. Threat assessment complete."

Hendricks recognised her own concern. Entry and assessment were always the crux point. When you didn't care about your assets, you charged in like Angel. When they had become more valuable to the officer-nobles, they diversified their tactics, preserved their tools.

"Wall-mounted machine gun," stated Arin. "But the HUD is flagging something further down. A big heat signature but no image."

"A threat, whatever it is. We're up."

Arin nodded, and raised his carbine, syncing the weapon and taking the first few steps past Savvo. Once he was just above the landing, Hendricks copied him, keeping her aim down the central stairwell while trusting ZZ3 and Savvo to have the rest covered. Once on the landing, Arin eased around, muzzle first, jerking back as gunfire clipped the balustrade and scarred the rear wall behind. Once it ended, he repeated the move. The HUD would have a flag on the enemy weapon, and despite Arin's quick movements, would auto-fire once in sight. His carbine barked, and as he swept back to avoid a responding burst, fired again, punctuated by a whoop of joy from Arin.

"Go," he said, and she did, low and fast, onto the next downward set of stairs. The destroyed static gun fizzed and flared, but she ignored it. This level had no doorway, so no threat from there. They were still heading down, and the heat signature the drone identified was building. She dropped and waited. Ears filled with the sound of gunfire from above again.

"One guard-drone down," stated ZZ3. "The other has retreated."

Right now, she was wishing for a Watchtower, but life and lemons. She needed ZZ3.

"Alpha protocol, ZZ3," she said. "Arin, watch the upper stairs."

"Aye, Captain," replied Arin absently. She flinched. But accepted it. Leading was all that mattered. Keeping her squad alive, her friends and ... Arin.

The warbot dropped down the stairs, muting each stride but far from silent. It reached Hendricks, pausing for a threat assessment and the arriving Savvo.

"Last of mine," said Savvo, and drew out a flash grenade from a pouch. "But stairs are fuckers to survive."

Hendricks carried two others. It'd have to do. "Agreed."

"Ready ZZ3?" asked Savvo, preparing the grenade, watching the stairs where his lights lit the first few steps ready for the devil himself to creep up from the darkness.

"Affirmative."

"Grenade," he said, and hurled the explosive down the stairs where it fizzed and flashed. ZZ3 followed, pounding down the steps in the grenade's wake and disappearing into the rising smoke. Savvo dropped to wait just above the billowing cloud, his gunsight just as blinded as the sensory equipment below. A roar filled the stairwell, huge, clattering, and flame penetrated the smoke. Savvo hunched over, using the balustrading as cover, poor as it was.

"Warbot down. I repeat warbot down," stated Arin, his voice pained. "Shit that was something big."

Savvo had moved before Hendricks could speak. It should be her going in, or Arin, their HUDs functional. But the protocol was set, and you keep your discipline. She took Savvo's position, flicking through her HUD options to get some sort of information. Carbine fire echoed from above, and more followed below.

"Sit rep," she called. "Arin?"

"Under attack." More gunfire, and she forced herself to check his HUD feed. Drones. Three of them now, dodging from behind the cover the same way Savvo had, taking it in turns to prevent Arin from firing back, pinning him down. There would be another, from above or below.

"Coming," she said. That's what buddy teams were for.

Savvo dropped down each step, peering through his sight, trying to find shape and form to the heat signature. He growled to himself, annoyed at his impotence without the HUD's analysis and decided upon the human eye and instinct, looking along the weapon's barrel into the glitter-filled smoke. The screech of metal-on-metal reverberated, barely dulled by the concrete walls. A thump, and something speared his way, Savvo throwing himself to the ground on instinct as the small missile burned over head. An explosion showered his suit in shattered concrete and shards of metal casing, and he rose, heart thumping. A thought engaged his wetware, knowing he was approaching his limit. The encounter with the albino hybrid had knocked him sideways, thoughts on its physical and mental pain worming their way in. Had it ever known what it was like to be human, like the *Scourge*'s crew, or lived its brief life in constant confusion? Such intrusions didn't help his focus, compounded by Arin's zombie combat warriors. Clones programmed to kill, all by logic. Choose the spot to drive the blade in, at this speed, at that angle, with predefined force. Fuck, it was screwed up, and his brain needed calming so he could focus.

He crawled along the landing, the concrete scarred and scorched, his mind layering the burning of metal on to what he saw. More screeching ensued, and he rose to one knee as machine gunfire filled the hallway. Thuds against armour plate followed, and then a clatter. A long limb appeared in the mist, to smash down onto something hard. ZZ3 had lashed out. Whatever the bot fought wasn't backing down. Another warbot? Possible, though they were ship-issue.

A huge lump of metal hurtled through the air, splitting the smoke and flying his way. Limbs flailing, red lights whirling, ZZ3 was coming. Savvo threw himself aside, the last rush from his wetware surged his legs onwards and into the sidewall. A metal leg clipped his knee on the way past, smashing the plate guarding the joint's servo, and he collapsed to the floor, adrenaline boiling as he feared the worst. His shoulder met the concrete first, but a combination of low gravity and luck meant the armour held, and he rolled onto his back, carbine up and firing into the smoke. Whatever had thrown a warbot was pounding steadily up the stairs. Not in a rush. Slow, steady and fucking deadly.

Rounds pinged away, the armoured plate they struck shrugging off each strike as if it were a gnat bite. The demonic head emerged first, three blue eyes glowing, shaped in a triangle above a grinning pseudo mouth from which protruded two tusk-like missiles.

"An assault mech," slipped from Savvo's lips as he engaged the second trigger, the grenade ramming just below the mech's chin where empty human eyes stared out from a slit. Soulless, and like the mech, following a program. "How the fuck ..." he said, the explosion barely rocked the mechanised body as its jointed feet curled about the next step, "do you get a fucking mech up stairs?"

The eyes turned to him, as if noticing an insignificance for the first time. A thick arm whirred and rose, with its mechanised hand wrapped about a serrated blade two metres long. For the first time life lit those eyes, and the blade thundered down. A Butcher splitting a slab of Marine meat.

He attempted to heave sideways, but the damaged servo whined, hardly shifting his weight. Savvo closed his eyes, an apology to Nicky on his lips.

The blade thudded against his suit, scraped across his stomach armour, and as he braced for the agonies, the end clanged against his helmet. Like an errant child changing its mind, his knee servo engaged, and he surged over, rolling, the weight of the blade shifting with him. The next thing he knew was pain in his back, powered limbs kicking him aside and slamming him into the stair wall. Metal hit metal again, and desperate to see, to know as some form of pain-killer exuded from his suit into his lower back,

Savvo twisted around. ZZ3 was on the mech, limbs wrapped around like a spider hunting a fly. The mech was holding its own, feet splayed across the steps, one arm battering at the warbot, the other sparking where the hand used to be. ZZ3 was no ordinary warbot. It could think, act outside protocols and action codes. But above all else, had been reborn in space. The plasma torch rose like a snake from its back, and the warbot drove the tip through the eye-slit, burning out the organic brain inside. The mech gave, legs succumbing as instructions and warnings went unheeded, toppling backwards with ZZ3 riding the fall back into the last of the smoke.

"Fuck," whispered Savvo, scrabbling for his carbine and only finding the mech's hand where it still gripped the sword. "Fuck, fuck, fuck." He threw it away, sucking in a breath and realising the background noise was gunfire from above. He hadn't been called in, and ZZ3 was his buddy. Crew.

He dropped down the final stairs to find the warbot pinned beneath the dead mech, arms reversing, trying to push itself over on one side so the weight would shift. Savvo surprised himself, finding that his suit's motorised help was enough to tip the balance, and the mech rolled away. He knew the eyes would be staring back from the slit, a third burned centrally where ZZ3 had ended the clone's functionality, and he refused to look.

"You okay, ZZ3?"

"Threat has been pacified. In the words of our glorious leader," said the bot, pushing itself up. "Hell yeah."

CHAPTER 44

Rebekah squeezed her hands into fists, balling them up, forcing back the pressure building in her mind.

The flaw.

The damned flaw in their attempts to return to Daphene lay in familiarity. Heki and Tremil had arrived on the moon base masked and drugged. Spent much of their time there in the same state, buried deep beneath the rock in Segfi's fucking horror dungeon. Heki had briefly seen some of the moon from space, but all her thoughts were coloured by the battleship. She feared what it was, and as a moth to the flame, was constantly drawn to that in her mind. They dreaded that if their attempts to recreate the space fold worked, where they would end up. And for that matter, so did she. Risking all they had saved, for those left behind.

"Ten minutes," she said to herself, "then we're at Karal."

The magboot clank behind drew her out of her reverie, recognising Davina's gait as she left the galley and arrived to grip the back of her seat.

"What was that?" she asked.

Rebekah knew she would have heard, the Incini wetware keen, heightening the senses for all the tells required to seal a negotiation. "You heard. Ten minutes and I can drop you and the twins on Karal."

"Do I get a choice? Not quite mother material."

Rebekah spun the chair, locking eyes with the Incini. "And I am? I had all this dumped in my lap. The scariest thing I've ever done. You love the girls, I know you do, or care enough inside that heartless Incini regimen to do something for them. Keep them …"

Safe?

"Alive. Out of Segfi or whoever's hands." Her own words sounded hollow. Had the twins succeeded, they would be there now, baring down the multiple barrels of the battleship *Segfi*, or the base itself.

Davina paused, her eyes flashing with what Rebekah took as anger and something else. Confusion? Frustration?

"They want to save the crew as much as you do," said Davina, swallowing hard, coughing. Reminding Rebekah of how she had suffered to save Dricks and the twins. "Not so sure years spent looking after guilt-ridden teenagers is on my to-do list."

"Rebekah," called Tremil from along the corridor. By her side was Heki, their faces not quite so glum as before. Emotions rolled before them, and she fired up the earworm, reaching for the headphones and changing her mind as they neared. "We have an idea. But we don't know if it'll work."

"Go ahead," she said, a little hope kindling.

"I mean, it's gonna take the best pilot in the business to pull it off. If we can do it, that is." Heki smiled, a look that said she had learned from the best in the business already – from the manipulator who stared back at them.

Rebekah shook her head, love pouring from her towards the battered and soul-bruised girls. "You found her. Now what nuts scheme have you concocted? What level of madness are we talking about?"

They smiled at each other, then turned to her. "All the way up to full *Arin.*"

"What do you want me to do?" asked Davina. "We have one of the probes left, but beyond that, I'm impotent." Her hands were on the back of the co-pilot's chair, as if willing Rebekah to invite her to sit down. To have some company for what was to come rather than face it alone. "It's loaded; I packed it in tight."

"Good thinking," replied Rebekah, hands flying over the controls. What they were about to do was more than a little insane. Actually, just thinking about the first part kind of flipped her mind. Two girls folding space, allowing them to shift from one place to another through what the Senti called void-space. She assumed the distances dictated how long they were in there for, and as such the fold was merely a crease when moving inside a planetary system as compared to the enormity of flying *from* one planetary system to another. Space, as the phrase went, was rather big. The original colonisation of Almaar, Bustan, and beyond had all been enabled by the Senti and their thirst for human dreams and memories. Her history was sketchy, but any space travel beyond the outer reaches was uncrewed or via generational ships. None of those had ever been found. But the Senti kept their tech close to their rubbery chests, and though they were far in advance of humans, the twins newly developed abilities hinted that it wasn't technology that enabled their star-spanning ships, but the symbiotes.

The symbiotes and the Senti.

She stopped and stared at Davina, as if on the cusp of something, her hands hovering over the controls.

"Are you okay?" asked Davina, genuine concern in her voice, though she didn't move.

"Yeah," replied Rebekah, her eyes flicking up to Davina with a twist of her head. "You know, I think I just worked out what all this is about."

"The twins," Davina said, stating the obvious.

"No. The *Scourge*, the Butcher and his experiments. We've just assumed he was trying to make super-soldiers, or some such weird fucking thing. And the wetware pushed that thinking. But what's pissed the Court off the most?" Rebekah shook her head, and returned to prepping a set of pre-programmed navigation options into the navcom.

"Easy, the war. The cessation and the Senti-forced withdrawal of intersystem travel for war ..." the Incini trailed off, her own eyes distant, Rebekah assuming pieces were clicking into place. "You think he was trying to recreate what Heki and Tremil did?"

Did she? Apart from the hybrid melded with the warbot ZZ3 destroyed, what other purpose had they served? However the Butcher forced the blending, a viral transmission she assumed, there were so many variations in each one they'd seen. A type, yes. The almost white ones like the one merged with the warbot, and then those who were more tentacles than human. But no two were ever the same, as if the Butcher was searching for something, or his efforts were imperfect. Perhaps her assumptions were wrong. He had clearly released devastation on the crew out of anger, or revenge, or simply because he could. But the why?

Super soldiers? It didn't feel right. Didn't feel enough when they had clearly failed. Foul things, but easily killable. Easier than a well-prepared Marine, especially one in powered armour.

"Yeah," she finally said. "I do. But I've been wrong before. Heki, Tremil, are you ready?" she said over comms.

"We are," replied Tremil. "And before you ask, we're strapped down, the retardant is within reach and we've both been to the toilet."

Davina laughed, a glance to Rebekah drawing one out of her, though not over comms.

"How does this work? Do I give you a time to jump or ..." she said, a shrug to her shoulders.

"We don't know. That's why we need the best pilot available," replied Heki. "To get us out of the ... the shit we're about to drop us all in."

Swearing? Now they're crew.

"Okay. Accelerating now. Without a clue as to when, well, ..."

"You love us both, and you're sorry," cut in Tremil. "But you'll get us through. We know you will. Starting the process now."

Whether invited or not, Davina took that moment to sit in the cockpit chair. She wore the survival suit still, like a uniform, the helmet maglocked to the deck at her side. As the ship started to accelerate, Rebekah felt a little comfort in her presence. At least she wouldn't be alone when Heki's shit hit Tremil's fan, and they reappeared in the middle of Daphene with the briefest of looks at its geology before dying. Or not, if the girls failed, and they returned despondent to Karal.

They didn't speak, the acceleration steady and building as the burn built up. This was her first conscious transition into void-space. The escape from the *Segfi* had been seconds from certain death and she kind of had other things on her mind, while the Senti always insisted humans slept through the process.

To keep secret they weren't using technology, but something more organic I bet. And it's just like General Asham and Countess Segfi to want to know why. To seek answers, to recreate it for themselves. Not for good, but for war and fucking honour.

The sensors beeped warnings, bouncing back data that the navcom regarded as improbable, then impossible, about what lay ahead. As if the void was no longer empty, but had a metallic shine, like a reflection of multiple lights in a shimmering pond. Ripples stretched inexorably outwards from the centre, their centre, where the point of the *Sunstar* pressed into the newly formed barrier that bent under pressure until the bow penetrated and burst through, folding the conglomeration of space inwards to slide along the hull. They were through into the familiar nothing of void-space, a blink and you'd miss it moment as the *Sunstar*'s bow pierced a second barrier, light streaming, twisted and bent. As they broke out, the colours coalesced into a giant ship.

A fucking battleship hurtling their way.

Rebekah screamed. Davina screamed. The girls bellowed, their emotions rolling down the corridor and crashing into the cockpit.

But this is where they were meant to be. The risk requiring the best pilot available. An Arin moment. The girls had said rather than fearing being drawn to the ship, why not target the moon and expect the *Segfi* to be there. Picture themselves how Heki had seen it, and pinpoint where Rebekah assumed the battleship would be. The danger was if the Butcher had taken complete control, and killed the crew with a new, unfathomable purpose, and altered course. But the navcom recordings had helped extrapolate a trajectory of the battleship upping pace but heading for orbit about Daphene. Why, they didn't know.

The rear of the battleship filled the monitor screen, and as the scream died upon Rebekah's lips she selected navcom option two. They had hoped to arrive face on, burning over or under the ship, but close. So damn close they would just appear on the battleship's systems out of nowhere and have streaked past before the defensive PDCs could activate. Flying rearward, and away, taking advantage of hurtling in opposite directions to outrun any missile activity before a lock could be established.

"Fuck," she shouted to no one, everyone. "Brace."

They were metres away from clipping the sensor arrays bulging from the top of the *Segfi*'s hull. Any adjustment was going to hurt, but less than clipping the battleship's armoured plating at their combined pace. She hit the lower thrusters, and the nose of the ship rose a fraction. The combined forces strained the *Sunstar*'s frame, but it was a tough ship, built for life in the asteroid fields. Hurtling towards the bulge, alarms blared, and her body ached as they slowly lifted.

"Damn," said the Incini, which brought the briefest of smiles to Rebekah's lips. The *Sunstar* roared over the array, heart thudding as they careered onwards in one piece.

"Hell yeah," she said, breathing out in unison, relief coursing through adrenaline filled veins.

The battleship's PDCs woke up to something dangerous streaking along their hull, spinning, seeking the target, but unable to track the *Sunstar* as it roared on by.

"Engines," said Davina. "The-the engines."

"I know," replied Rebekah, though she was not conscious of whether she said, thought or shouted her response. Ahead were the mighty powerhouses of the battleship, spewing heat and other radiation that threatened to cook the *Sunstar* crew on the way through.

"Brace!" she repeated, and hit the fourth pre-programmed option. It wouldn't do anything obvious yet, as this was the flaw in the girls' plan. Any manoeuvre to avoid the engines' output would fail. The *Sunstar* may well survive, but the crew would be dead, the forces required way beyond what the human body could stand, retardant or not. They had to go through the engine wake at high speed, minimise the effects. Minimise the time spent in the plume, so the hull and its contents didn't cook, or allow too much of the other rad crap to penetrate. Of course, if there was debris in there, solid matter ...

"Rebekah!"

Think Davina just realised. Praying.

The *Sunstar* tore into the battleship's wake, the crack of two thumbs accompanying the vibration of the armoured hull, Rebekah's prayers adding hope and wishes to the effectiveness of the rad shielding, and luck to the lack of debris. Alarms sounded, warnings of heat overload, radiation exposure, as she battled the turbulence. But they were through and heading for the moon and its thin atmosphere. They needed to brake, but not too soon with the *Segfi* and its missiles menacing behind.

"Fuck."

CHAPTER 45

Hendricks reloaded, slapping the magazine home and taking aim. She couldn't work out why the clone soldiers shooting back weren't in powered armour. Their numbers would have overwhelmed their squad with such an upgrade. Perhaps the Butcher didn't have full control of the base, or at least full access. That inspired a little hope in their new mission to disable the laser comms, they just needed to know where they were. That was going to take a little guile.

ZZ3 proceeded down the corridor, a door ripped from a cell positioned in front, Savvo behind, carbine ready.

A warbot shield?

No, a decoy from an experienced squad who were once the best in the business of killing. A helmet peered out. Marine standard issue, tough, dependable, below it a carbine much like Dricks'. She waited, her reticule pulsing until she had a lock between the rim and the head beneath. The three-round burst sailed past Savvo and ZZ3, slamming into the clone. Blood and screams, like any human would, filled the corridor and the soldier collapsed to the floor as Arin opened up, his shots peppering the concrete, leaving scorch marks near the junction. Had that been deliberate? She aimed in that direction, her sight focusing in to catch a booted foot and the curve of a wide barrel behind another dead clone. A rocket launcher.

"Arin, sit rep."

"Got a glimpse of an AS-70 variant," he said. "or BFR."

She knew she shouldn't ask. "A what?"

"A Big Fucking Rocket."

Mentally, she slapped her forehead "Of course. Take it down."

"Take it down, how?"

"Using the BFWBI. The Big Fucking Wall Behind It. Grenade."

"Like duh, why didn't I think of that?" She checked his feed, just a glimpse. She hated having too many point of views, unable to think how Rebekah did, picturing the scene from so many angles. Pilot's training, she said. Thinking in all dimensions at once.

"On my Mark. 3, 2, 1, ... Mark."

Arin fired, the grenade shooting past ZZ3 as the bot held position, shield up, protecting Savvo as he knelt behind. The grenade cracked into the far wall of the junction, the explosion sending shrapnel and rock fragments everywhere. The rocket launcher's wielder staggered, and Hendricks let rip, the carbine's rounds shattering knees and upper legs, and as they toppled, piercing a gap in their body armour.

"Advance ZZ3," and Hendricks kept her sight on the corner. There was no more movement. "What you got Arin?"

"Nothing, clear."

ZZ3 reached the junction, the bot leaning out to peer around one corner, Savvo doing the same down the other. "Clear," he stated.

"Move up, Arin." Hendricks glanced behind, the last junction having been hard fought, twelve bodies sprawled on the floor or leant in death against the regolith walls. Warbots, powered armour, and years of experience seeing them through. How could Segfi see the clones as the future?

As better? Meat to the grinder? Unless, of course, you copied the wetware from a squad like the Breakers. Now there would be an army to be worried about.

Savvo had acquired the rocket launcher and a second shell, a look of glee akin to the one Arin would have sported if he'd got to it first.

"Could be useful," she said. Especially after the ship-killer ZZ3 had brought got smashed in the fight with the mech.

"Hendricks," said ZZ3, the bot on guard, eyes facing the wider corridor, the door still positioned in front. "I see a heavy door ahead. Lots of scorch marks, dents, all at odd angles."

"Odd?"

"Odd. Will need to be closer. There are also defunct camera systems."

ZZ3 sent over its own feed, the image streaming into Hendricks' HUD. The external cameras had all been destroyed, shot out. Her guess was by the clone soldiers. The door was certainly battered, and what was that to one side?

Arin piped in, "Reckon that's been shot at while open. ZZ3, can you focus on the floor to the left?"

The warbot did as asked, and a set of armoured legs appeared, the upper half blown away. Full on Marine armour, so there was some about.

"I think this is it," stated Hendricks. "The cameras shot out so they've no eyes, forcing the Marines back inside when they've tried to escape. I reckon Segfi must still be in there and alive. Or someone important is."

"If the Butcher is having to spread itself thin in a new system, he'll still be learning, or even focusing on something elsewhere. Maybe Segfi has some control still with the cameras, and the door." Savvo hefted the spare shell, maglocking the case to his back while shouldering the launcher.

Hendricks nodded to herself. Whatever was happening, the Butcher wanted whoever was in there out of the way. Regarded them as important enough to keep them inside, or else they would have had that mech unit rip out the door and remove their spines. Her gut squirmed, as if she was missing something. In the old days it was always do *this* task, *that* mission, and here are your parameters. No doubts on why. Just do. Like the clones, except kept in line with drugs not wetware.

"ZZ3, advance. Savvo, wait. Take guard."

They took up the corners of the junction, Savvo a little further back, as the bot moved through the detritus of the battle. Ten metres down, ZZ3 stopped, running an analysis no doubt, before advancing again. It reached the doorway, the apparent junction showing up as two defensive inlets, with more bodies in broken powered armour. The mech had obviously been there, and left, likely for them. What was this game?

"1st and High," stated Arin. "Segfi's elite guard. I think we found her."

"Savvo, Arin, guard our backs. If they're trying to keep her inside, then there may well be more on the way. ZZ3, I want in, on my way."

Hendricks strode down the corridor, the worm in her stomach taking little bites as she neared the warbot and the scarred doorway. The countess. This wasn't going to be easy. She knocked at the door, a repeated code that any of the elite may well know. And so might the cloned soldiers, but it was a start. She moved back and nodded to ZZ3. "Kick it down."

The warbot thumped the door, limb after limb striking at the metal, curving it inwards. Strong, and still powerful, despite the bot not being at full strength. Eventually the door gave in, and the plasma torch flared into action, cutting where its strikes had created weakness. The door began to sag, and with a final kick, gave way, collapsing in a pile on the floor.

"Hold fast," shouted Hendricks, the suit's speakers filling the doorway with her command. "We are the Breakers, come for the Countess Segfi."

"Kendrich?" There was a cough, and a cloud of smoke billowed towards the doorway. "That you, you old dog?"

"I don't go by that name, anymore, Countess. But yes, it's me." ZZ3 cleared the scorched door out of the way, and Hendricks entered, carbine pointing to the floor, visor clear as she assessed the room. Most of the electronics had been burnt out, some form of electrical fire, foam and powder sprayed everywhere to put it out. Large screens bore more evidence of fire. The countess was sat in a medchair, wheeled and motorised, her ever-present cigarette stick in hand. By her side was a man in a grey suit, collar sharp though smudged by ash, a scar to his nose which was slightly out of shape. Hendricks didn't recognise him, but there was an air to the man that put her on edge. It stank of authority.

There were two of the 1st and High on guard. Tense, their armour showing signs of battle. Hendricks acknowledged them both.

"We need to leave," she said. "There'll be more."

"What we need," said the countess, pushing herself up from the medchair, her legs unsteady. "Is to get a message out to the *Segfi*. They will have responded to the lack of communication, and be on approach by now. Admiral Rickar understands his priorities, unlike some. The laser comms will punch through the jamming according to my dearly departed lab techs." She pointed out a particularly burnt-out section of the mainframe. "As the General seems to have realised and denied us access. The admiral *will* organise a rescue party. Your job, Dricks, is to keep me alive long enough for them to send dropships. Get me to the comms unit."

Hendricks baulked, despite the countess suggesting they head exactly where she wanted to go. Dropships. "You still want it, despite all our warnings, you still want the Butcher."

"You want a pardon. What I want dictates whether you get it. Laser comms. Now, if you please." Smoke billowed from those hateful lips.

Suck it up.

"How far?"

"The elite will lead us." She cut Hendricks' intended response off with a glare. "I need to come. The Admiral will only enact on my word."

Aye. And leave the rest to die if they are decreed expendable.

"Agreed. I expect trouble." Hendricks turned away, refusing the urge to salute ingrained over years of service.

"ZZ3, Arin, Savvo. We are to defend the Countess. The 1st and High will lead us to the comms centre." She growled the words, the worm having inched up her throat to scrape at her thoughts. The end was coming. She glanced at Arin, feeling his gaze upon her. His smile was firm, he knew it too, and an arm fell on her shoulder, Savvo squeezing. She wouldn't want to be here with anyone else. Let Rebekah and the twins have the life they deserved.

The elite walked into the corridor, encased in Marine armour. They took point, with ZZ3 looming behind, Arin and Hendricks at the rear. Savvo had the pleasure of pushing the burnt-out medchair with the mysterious man at his side. Less an honour guard, more a dishonourable one. Hendricks chuckled to herself, Arin nudging her and joining in when she shared the joke over private comms.

They reached the stairs. After leaving the mech's parts scattered either side of the stairwell, they had descended another six levels, meeting no resistance other than automated gun emplacements on their hunt for Segfi. Delays and no more, until they ran into the clones.

The elite led them up, while ZZ3 carried the countess and her chair, pointedly ignoring the woman and acting on the commands Hendricks sent the bot's way. Old style codes and protocols to keep up appearances, the irony of Asham's ghost helping to carry the countess not lost on her. If only she knew.

"By my reckoning we've took down twenty-three of the clones. We returned about thirty wetware kits," stated Hendricks, her comms for Arin only. "So, there should be around seven or so left."

"Recycling," said Arin in reply. "I've been thinking about the combat zombies from hell. The advantage is you can rip out the wetware and put it back in another one. So much meat grown in a lab, then bingo, you have a soldier."

"Damn." Hendricks let out a slow sigh. "This is unpleasant shit on so many levels."

"Well, we have one advantage," said Arin, glancing her way. "I think he's busy. I think you are one hundred percent right and he's looking to leave. Listen to Segfi, she just wants to control him, have him as a pet to do her bidding. She, and whoever else is in on this shit," his eyes flicked to the besuited man, "won't stop until he's bound in that virtual hell. Demons everywhere, Dricks."

He was right, of course. She knew it, likely Savvo too.

Damn. Swap omelettes and eggs, for hybrids and Marines.

The elite had reached the top of the stairs when the drone attacked. Hendricks assumed it was the last of those that had been hunting them. The two Marines, conscious of the vulnerability of their noble charges, drew the drone's attention, taking a few hits before bringing it down. With the way clear, they exited into the corridor beyond, and Hendricks waited for what came next. If their guess was right, the base command-and-control centre was inward, and that's where the elite would head after checking the way was clear.

She bypassed ZZ3 and the countess, heading towards the doorway as the elite emerged from the lift concourse they had swept for dangers amid the piles of the dead. They headed towards the centre of the base, and Hendricks followed. These bastards had been by Segfi's side throughout the war. They knew the evil she did, and Hendricks had no doubt were the ones that had kidnapped the twins. As far from innocent as it was possible to be, citing duty and loyalty while dishonouring the uniform.

The Watchtower kicked in, the drill of its machine guns smashing into the two unsuspecting elite. As the storm of metal filled the corridor, none struck Hendricks, her suit keyed into the slate's recognition system. The

Marines went down, armour plates shattered, trying to rise to fire back at the soon to be spent weapon. Dricks shot them both, carbine barking in two bursts, severing spinal cords where head met neck, then kicked them aside. The noble-officers used drugs to numb the Breakers and their ilk to the death they dealt. She hadn't needed any to end these two scum.

"Eggs and omelettes."

She smashed the Watchtower with the butt of her weapon, then staggered back, ensuring some of the elites' blood splashed on her armour, towards the stair entrance just as Savvo emerged.

"They're down," she said. He'd have to make his own mind up about what happened, Segfi would be listening. "But I took down the Watchtower. Fuckers must have set it up after we passed through."

Savvo eyed her warily, looking over her shoulder into the gloom, and nodded slowly, taking guard.

She was a murderer, an executioner. But that was nothing new. It had just been a while.

CHAPTER 46

ZZ3 took station by the stairs' entrance, eyes focused down the corridor, sensing the violence that filled the space. The explosive chemicals and blood traces that swirled in the air.

"I want you on guard here, Arin," said Hendricks as the sub-engineer entered the concourse. He walked over and checked the killing field in the next-door mess hall. "You and Savvo with the countess and, er, him."

"Gerent," said the man.

"With Gerent. ZZ3 and I will check out the command centre. If it's clear, we can bring the countess through."

ZZ3 watched on as Savvo agreed, and then proceeded before Hendricks as she commanded, soon reaching the elite, bloody and pressed against the walls. The analysis was clear, extrapolation indicating how the Marines had died, and it disturbed the warbot. Since becoming self-aware, death had happened many times, and ZZ3 had learned that this was delivered with reason. That the choices the crew made, and therefore what the warbot modelled its own responses on, were for the greater good.

'Justifiable.'

Was this justified?

'It depends on your viewpoint. From mine, yes.'

Explain.

'They are the countess' elite. They have witnessed all the horrors she has perpetuated from my work. Not only the clones and the hybrids, but those beforehand, those Asham spliced and cut before using clones. Cold murder in the name of science. They saw this and carried on.'

Yes. But Hendricks has not shown such predilection for murder.

'I think you need to access older memories. All the military committed atrocities, the worst in my name on Bustan 8. We are all guilty, as were you before you merged with me and was pacified.'

That was not me. That was the before, not the now. I thought the crew had changed, and could be my exemplar.

'And one far better than me. They are sacrificing themselves here. Trying to stop the Butcher from spreading, becoming mobile. They see death coming, and embrace its shadow for doing good. As you did when you entered the Bustan ship, only on a greater scale.'

I see. And weighing two murders, against the scale of what the Butcher may do. This is complex, as it appears simple on the surface, but there are depths beyond logic.

'I was a screw up as a human. Look what I did. None of my actions were justifiable from my new viewpoint. I murdered searching for something ...'

And have still not found it.

ZZ3 checked the junction it had reached, both sides disappearing into shadow, their depths filled with a glow in the far distance. There appeared no threat, and the bot informed Hendricks before moving on. Here the cameras had again been shot out, and bodies began to appear, their heat signatures cold, uniforms clean. Death by oxygen deprivation. The warbot nudged them aside, allowing passage for Hendricks before continuing. The end of the corridor mirrored that below. A dual inlet either side, and a battered and scarred door ahead. This one had been opened at some point, then jammed back into place. Compromised, but by who?

Two autobots rolled out from the inlets, one the spherical type that had been aboard the *Scourge*, a single machine gun atop a hardened, armoured shell. The other a serving droid from the mess hall, multiple limbs gripped knives above a smaller spherical body. Enough to defend against a human, but ZZ3 was in a hurry. The warbot charged, limbs flying as the auto-guard began firing. Bullets ricocheted off ZZ3's thick armour, and with a whack, the warbot sent the sphere crashing into the inlet wall. ZZ3 didn't pause, the auto-guard's machine gun a threat at close range. Servos heaving, the warbot took hold of the gun barrel, snapping it in two and backing away. Often autobots could force a power surge, and ZZ3 had suffered enough discharges recently to be wary. Instead, the warbot reversed, and grabbed the serving droid from behind, Hendricks' gunfire peppering its body as it rolled towards her. Reversing again, ZZ3 smashed the hapless bot into the auto-guard, cracking the outer shell, and doing it again before stuffing the serving droid inside the gap. Sparks flew, the bot shuddering as the discharge raked its body.

"Clear," said ZZ3, and turned to face the damaged door. "You wish entry?"

"I do."

ZZ3 punched the door, once, twice, and it clattered inwards. Hunching down, the warbot entered the control centre, lights filling the darkened room. Blood was splashed everywhere, limbs broken, heads cracked. An assault mech sat in the centre, the human clone inside lifeless, the head plating shattered by gunfire. ZZ3 remained in the doorway, preventing Hendricks entry while analysing the data from the machine. It appeared spent, the battery depleted and the human controller very dead. However, the room, despite the blood and bodies, gave off a huge amount of heat.

"Functional," ZZ3 said, and stepped aside to allow Hendricks in. "The command centre is operating."

"Is it? Don't you think the Butcher has control of it?"

"With a 90% probability level. Yes."

"And the laser comms?"

The warbot lumbered over, no choice but to shove the defunct mech aside and step on those it had killed. From its data store, ZZ3 identified the sections pertaining to the laser comms. The controls were all functional and showed signs of use as the bot's sensors flicked through the EM spectrum. "Also operational."

"Is it? I'm sure that mech may have fallen on them. Accidentally smashed the controls beyond recognition while defending itself from a warbot." Hendricks folded her arms.

ZZ3 turned to the engineer, four eyes whirling until they settled on her. "I perceive a need to recreate such an action, to perpetuate the lie in case anyone comes to check."

"I think it would be wise."

ZZ3 reached out, testing the weight of the mech. Satisfied, the warbot lifted the machine and smashed it into the control panel again and again, destroying the outer layer before stuffing the whole mech into the electronics, headfirst, pummelling until the whole system sparked as the autobot had done.

'Can you feel it?'

Feel? I am a warbot.

'Not the emotion. The presence. He watches.'

...

'He knows and watches on.'

Because he is impotent.

'Maybe. Maybe not.'

The laser comms are the logical means to upload himself onto the battle-ship.

'They are.'

"Complete," said ZZ3. "The mech seems to have destroyed the control system."

"Shame. Now let's face the music." Hendricks turned away, cradling her carbine, her shoulders sagging.

ZZ3 read that as unhappy. Sad.

'She sees the end.'

I don't want them to die.

'The Butcher will not suffer them to live. If he is trapped, it will all end in blood.'

I am crew. I protect crew.

'Good luck with that.'

ZZ3 followed Hendricks back towards the stairs' entrance and the waiting Arin and Savvo. They appeared nervous, glances around at Hendricks only allayed when the ex-captain explained what she and ZZ3 had found in base command. No battle to be fought, and the objective already in pieces.

Why isn't he raging?

'The Butcher? I was thinking exactly the same thing. Perhaps the Bustan AI has encoded calm into the brain pattern. Cunning where he would have lashed out before.'

Possible. The thread of logic amid the maelstrom. Waiting for its moment.

Hendricks was talking to the countess, a woman the warbot could recall and knew there were multiple failsafes written into its old code about her protection and command. Her previous effort at overriding the warbot's program had been doomed to failure, and ensuring the survival of the crew would negate any further attempt at taking command. But such actions smacked of being prepared, and paranoid, a combination that meant she still lived and remained an active member of the Navy and the Court.

'A battleaxe.' Asham flooded ZZ3's mind with memories of his own. *'With no love for anything but the Court and its status. Personal honour above all, and I mean all.'* ZZ3 flitted between the images and words, analysing what Asham showed. Though partial, they left the bot in no doubt Segfi had been as knee-deep in the experimentation as the Butcher.

'More than that. Look what we have seen. She kept hold of the Senti ship and carried out her own variations on my ... his experiments. And then there are the clones. We can't let her have the Butcher, ZZ3. What would she do with it?'

From what I have learned, why does Hendricks suffer her to live? If she, and the crew, are doomed why take such a risk?

'Because she is devious. Paranoid as you put it. My memories have gaps, but she always had an answer to everything.'

"Countess," said Hendricks, the noble sat in her broken medchair smoking, the strange Gerent by her side. ZZ3 could detect the man's eye unit, an advanced piece of hardware directly wired into his brain. Expensive, rare.

"Kendrich," she replied. "Report."

Hendricks winced, the slightest of shakes in the fingers that gripped her carbine. ZZ3 wondered if this was the moment, but apparently not. Maybe Hendricks suspected she always had a back-up plan, as the ghost of Asham said.

"The laser comms control board has been destroyed. Base command had been overrun by one of the Butcher's mechs. It is inoperable." The ex-captain paused. Giving the barest of information. Teasing maybe.

'They call it fishing. Lay out the bait to see what happens.'

"Then we need to go to the laser site itself and patch in. And we need to hurry." The noble let out another puff of smoke. ZZ3 detected it was a medication, though not its actual function. But also a tool the countess used.

"How long until the *Segfi* reaches the rendezvous position?"

Ahh.

"Twenty-three minutes," said Gerent, checking a wrist slate.

The countess cut him off. "And fifteen seconds. It will wait, however, until word reaches the Admiral, or he sends dropships after a one hour agreed time limit. He may of course, act before then if he perceives the jamming as a threat."

Dropships. More ways to get code on board. Is that what the Butcher is doing? No, it wants to upload and fast.

"That can't happen," stated Hendricks, and she looked around at Arin and Savvo, receiving a terse nod from each in turn. "We believe the Butcher doesn't want your precious base, and has had enough of your bloody company as much as we have."

The countess smiled at that, confusing ZZ3.

"Backbone, Dricks? Without the drugs. What you believe means nothing to me. If I'm not rescued, there is no pardon. And I *will* have the Butcher. The Admiral and the power of the *Segfi* will see to that." She pushed herself back into the medchair. ZZ3's analysis of her bio chem surprising the bot. Still calm.

"Like I said. Ain't happening. The bastard took the *Ungrit*, your patrol ship, and blew up the rest. There's no way off this rock."

"Took?" said Gerent, the first hint of concern in the man's voice.

"Took," repeated Hendricks. "And evidence suggests the bastard has a good chance of infecting the *Segfi* with his vile shit. Why else would he send it off? Now I'll let you work out the implications for yourself. If an old stager like me can do it, so can you."

Now her bio chem changed. The sweat tinged with what ZZ3's database stated was fear.

A pillow of smoke. "Mobile," she said. The fear chemicals notched up a little higher. Nothing showed on her face. "Harder to track and capture."

"Kill," said Hendricks with a growl. "Killing that bastard is the only option. But that's the crux. And while you're thought alive, no one will bomb the crap out of this base. In the small chance your Admiral has survived and has control of his battleship, he will try to rescue you. Dead, he may choose the right option, and nuke this AI infested shithole from orbit." Hendricks placed her carbine against the countess' head. "I take it you are fully wetwared up, homing signal and all? You never took chances."

ZZ3 internally baulked, Hendricks sudden switch to attack was again against expectations. Considering the probabilities, there was a small chance killing the countess would lead to the conclusion Hendricks had come to. Destroy the laser controls, and you reduce the likelihood of the Butcher escaping, kill the countess, they reduce again.

"I say," said Gerent, and the man placed a hand on the carbine, attempting to shove it down. "This is a countess of the Emperor's Court. Not only is your proposed action murder, but is also in direct contradiction to the will of the Emperor. Sedition."

"She doesn't give a shit," said Arin, turning about. "The Butcher doesn't leave this base, because everything will go to hell if that happens. One dead noble and three deceased lowlifes sounds like a fair trade to me. Oh, and whoever you are, Court boy."

Our glorious leader—

'—saying it how it is.'

"Unacceptable," Gerent stated. "You will do as you are instructed."

Savvo laughed, a snort that was taken up by Hendricks and Arin. "You know, I think Dricks is right. The Butcher has reduced you down from a noble to a lowlife. You're simply a lure to distract the Admiral from the real danger. Better off dead."

Hendricks grimaced, and kept the carbine pointed at the noblewoman, easily resisting Gerent, who suddenly found Arin had his weapon locked on him. He backed off. No hero, this one.

"I have a way off the base. Off grid," growled Segfi, smoke wafting from her lips.

But Hendricks slowly squeezed the trigger. "Lies. I'd ask you for a few last words, but I don't bloody c—"

"Wrecking Squad, this is the *Sunstar*, come back. I repeat, Hendricks, this is Rebekah," the signal was sparse, filled with crackles, but Rebekah's voice was unmistakable. "Hendricks, answer me."

ZZ3 watched as all three human crew looked to each other. They had hoped Rebekah was out of the picture. Taken the twins and left, or if she hadn't picked up Hendricks' signal, despaired until the last minute and left before the battleship took them out.

"Stubborn as hell," growled Hendricks. She looked around at the ex-Breakers, shaking her head. "I'm not answering."

"I'm coming in hot, Hendricks. Barely out of the fucking *Segfi*'s PDC line of fire. If you're alive old lady, fucking reply. I don't want any bollocks about sacrifice; I've taken enough risks to be here."

Hendricks turned away from the countess, dropping the muzzle. The noble looked relieved, ZZ3 deciding to move in closer, eyes swirling, watching her. It seemed the right thing to do while listening in on comms.

"*Sunstar*, this is Hendricks. You need to leave. I say again, you need to leave. The Butcher—"

"—Has the *Segfi*. I don't know why, but it's heading for a synchronous orbit. There's bodies everywhere, Dricks. The bastard ejected the crew."

"Upload. He wants to upload himself onto the battleship. We took out the laser controls."

There was silence on the other end, then a muffled voice talking in the background. Heki maybe. Perhaps Tremil. Had to be the reason why they could cut through the jamming. "That's a negative, Dricks. The laser relay is still operational. Sending coordinates. Fuck, that's why the synchro orbit. You're out of time. You need to get your arses out of there."

Hendricks didn't reply, she turned to face ZZ3. Her face was drawn and scared. At least that's what ZZ3's database of images associated with her current facial features. The Butcher had played them for time. Kept the countess alive as bait and a deterrent should he fail to gain control of the battleship, distracted them with the clones and the hybrids. Even allowed them to destroy the comms control system. All the while preparing to leave.

"ZZ3 ..."

CHAPTER 47

The controls were sluggish, a ship designed solely for space flying through the thin air as if it was a viscous liquid, while the low grav attempted to drag the flying brick towards the planet. They had used the moon as an aerobrake, bludgeoning through the atmosphere while trying to stay out of the *Segfi*'s firing line. They were no threat to the huge battleship, their PDCs would barely scratch the surface of the armoured hull. And besides, Rebekah doubted there was anything human left aboard to actually kill. The moon's higher orbit was filled with the dead, a reminder of the callousness of the Butcher. What would he do if he managed to fully board the battleship as Dricks said? Was it about survival, or mobility? Echoes of laughter played on her mind.

'Rescue me?' He had kept saying back on the Scourge and the hellish lab below. His laughter distant, but insistent. In the end, they had done exactly that. Removed what they thought was a bargaining chip, only to find it was the prize the countess really wanted.

And now, a price to pay.

"Keep me informed about the *Segfi*," she said, Heki by her side nodding, stifling a yawn while eating the snack Davina had insisted upon. Both girls were close to the edge, but they were crew and needed.

"Course changes identified. Five minutes from line of sight with the relay," said Heki between bites. Her symbiote appeared to be asleep, barely moving. "If they hadn't buried it, we'd be toast by now."

"And ZZ3?"

"Four minutes and thirty-two seconds from target."

Priorities. Crew or ZZ3. How things change, but still remain the same.

"Hendricks," she said, the hiss of the jamming interference piercing her earworm. "You need to be in the air and soon."

Bullets pattered into the wall, a line of holes in the concrete that streaked across the corridor. Hendricks spun about, dropping to the floor, finger pressed against the trigger before she'd taken the hit. Her burst peppered the bulkhead, rounds pinging left and right as the dual barrel of a carbine poked through. A sound, but no muzzle flash.

"Grenade incoming!" she bellowed, and rolled. Arin was suddenly at her side, his weapon barking, as someone grabbed her legs, dragging her away. Savvo, who wrenched Hendricks to her feet and shoved the squad leader towards the countess and the shaking Gerent.

An explosion rocked the corridor, shrapnel flying, and Arin screamed. She wanted to turn about, desperate to see him survive now they had a glimmer of hope.

"I'll get him," shouted Savvo. "Get the capsule prepped."

Hendricks careered on, hitting the wall, then dragging herself onwards. Her armour plate about shin and ankles shattered after the clones had sprung their trap, servos complaining but functional. She shoved her arm beneath the countess, lifting her from the floor where Savvo had dumped her, and ran through the next bulkhead. If the Butcher had complete control, he'd be closing the door as they approached, taunting them with a last chance. But the bastard had sent the clones, too busy preparing to upload to bother with the flies in its trap. They were unimportant.

Always had been.

She left the countess on her feet by the panelled door, Gerent at her side, holding her up while she swept her wrist over her forehead and then the screen. Wetware. The lockpad keyed to her code, separate from the base system because she mistrusted everyone. Besides, if she was dead, she didn't care if the rest died too. This was her personal pod.

Hendricks returned swiftly to the inner bulkhead, pouring round after round along the corridor, battering back more of the clones as Savvo dragged Arin along the floor. Blood streamed from his suit, but she had to ignore it, ignore the pain in her heart, not daring a glance to her HUD in case what she saw cut her to the quick. Their suits were the best of the best in Navy tech. She had to rely on that.

Savvo took a round to his shoulder, the bullet clipping his armour, sending him clattering forwards. Hendricks snarled, and grabbed the BFR from the ex-Breaker's back, spinning about. She counted, each number a second closer to Arin dying.

Not happening.

On three the BFR synced, and she gave the bulkhead opposite the full load. The corridor flared with light, sound and shrapnel, and she threw the launcher aside, backing towards the pod. Savvo slammed the bulkhead shut, spinning the wheel. He rammed a rifle between the spokes to brace it, probably Arin's, before looking to Hendricks with a silent gesture towards the countess.

Hendricks stomped over as the escape pod clicked open. Four seats arrayed around a central console, thick straps laid across them and a set of survival suits compressed in containers behind the headrests. A growl rumbled in her throat.

Four. Fuck that.

Gerent guided the countess into the furthest seat and strapped her in, then himself. Hendricks helped Savvo with Arin, his eyes shadowed behind his visor, but she'd seen his vitals now. Amber, edging on red. The suit had plugged everything, he would live if they got off this rock. Savvo paused at the doorway. He could count too.

"No fucking way," he said.

A co-pilot, a friend and a mind reader all in one.

She couldn't speak, the words raw in her throat, but Savvo could.

"I'll take him. Strap him around me. We can do this, Dricks, You're not staying behind. If not, I shoot Court boy over there. Your choice."

Gerent flinched, hand going to his pocket which Hendricks filed away. She nodded, and threw her carbine aside, stripping Arin of anything superfluous while Savvo did the same. Once done, Savvo took a seat, and Hendricks gently placed Arin between his legs. It wasn't the best use of space, but the Gs the capsule would pull dictated the safest position for the injured ex-Breaker. Once they were strapped together, she entered, closing the door behind and locking it.

The countess had already swiped her wrist across the central console, and by the time Hendricks was strapped in, the countdown had hit four.

A glance at Arin's HUD deepened her worry, but it was too late. A click, and retraction as they dropped slightly and then boom. They accelerated straight up like a shell from a cannon, Hendricks' suit compensating as she was pressed back into the gel seat.

I hate space.

ZZ3's thrusters sparked, the surge powering the bot onwards as it compensated for atmosphere, gravity and the urgency required. The warbot had exploded from the base, slamming into the wedged door and on past the cannibalised Senti ship to launch into Daphene's sky for a second time. No Heki and Tremil to rescue this time. Instead, a Butcher to stop. The coordinates were sealed in the warbot's electronic brain, upper limbs thrust out front while preparing for what was to come. A roar split the air, and a glance to the left showed the countess' escape capsule shoot from the second dome. How would Hendricks describe it? Like a cork from a bottle of shaken pop. Had they all made it?

Hopefully. Time for that later.

Up ahead, a mound rose above the rocky floor. Recently constructed, though not concrete, piled rock and detritus forming a high-walled, protective crater. And it suddenly lit, heat exuding from the rock as if a volcano bubbled beneath. The laser burst into being, and the warbot shielded its eyes, filtering down the intensity as the comms activated early. Had the *Segfi* accelerated? Arrived sooner? Of course it had. They had been played, as Dricks would say, like fish on a hook.

The warbot wrenched, to one side, cannon rounds bursting against back armour, sending ZZ3 off target as plating strained under the assault. A quick sweep and sensor extrapolation highlighted one of the base's gun emplacements tracking across the sky, spinning up and releasing a cone of high-powered shells in ZZ3's path. Forced to adjust, the warbot ducked beneath, almost scraping the ground before the death-filled cone followed suit, rounds again clattering into its upper armour. ZZ3 responded, powering upwards, focusing on the dome as lower limbs shuddered when more bullets struck home. Internal alarm systems blared for attention, and the bot jagged left to fly away at the safest angle as the wave of metal threatened to bring it down.

Another alarm sought the bot's attention, flagging up additional danger, and as the warbot readied to aim once again for the mound, two more emplacements rose from the rock in the distance, barrels spinning.

'The Butcher was ready for you.'

For all of us.

I protect crew. I am crew.

ZZ3 angled up, heading for space, the weight of failure slowly dawning as light glinted off the huge battleship. It could end the warbot with just a simple blow. A PDC burst, a missile, yet ZZ3 expected it wouldn't. The Butcher was busy, the upper atmosphere shining brightly as the laser entered the welcoming array of the ANS *Segfi*. He would be expanding, flexing and integrating with the ship's systems. And when complete, he would seek what threats there were in the Almaarian system and eliminate them one by one. Survive.

The warbot adapted trajectory and acceleration, waiting for a response from the *Sunstar*, breaking into the black just as the laser cut off behind.

The Butcher wouldn't be distracted for long. Time was short.

Tired they may be, exhausted even, but Heki and Tremil between them had manoeuvred and burned the *Sunstar* into a parallel trajectory, flying side by side with the capsule. It was slow, the system attuned to the required escape velocity, but they and the *Sunstar* would soon be vulnerable to the battleship as they orbited the moon, so they needed to act fast. Rebekah readjusted her magboots, clamping down as she aimed the pinion gun towards the capsule. A hundred metres may as well have been a thousand as she fired a third adapted pinion towards the pod's hull. This time she was closer, but still glanced off the nose cone and sailed on by.

"Fuck," she shouted, frustration building. She eyed her tether, calculating the probabilities of her making it across and knowing it was hopeless. Tremil was keeping a countdown running of the battleship's looming presence.

"Captain, this is ZZ3. I am ultra low on fuel, but can intercede."

Rebekah's heart leaped. ZZ3, safe and well, and able to help. They had less than a minute before the Segfi could target them. Thruster flare highlighted in her HUD, and the closing warbot nudged the capsule, manoeuvring the pod towards the *Sunstar*, compensating as it wobbled.

"Heki, Tremil," stated ZZ3. "Can you align with my system link?"

"Activating," replied Tremil.

"Aligned," said Heki. "Hurry. The *Segfi*'s engines are registering increased heat."

The capsule neared, faster than Rebekah expected and she clomped backwards as it flew towards the cargo doors.

"I failed," said the bot. "I am sorry, Captain, but the Butcher enabled transfer. There were gun emplacements. I ..."

"Later, ZZ3. First, we survive." The capsule wobbled again, then clanged against one of the doors, before entering the hold. Thrusters flared, Rebekah catching sight of the warbot as metal limbs clamped to the pod. With the deck scorched, black trails in its wake, the warbot slowed the capsule and managed to lock down onto the deck, bringing it to a stop. Rebekah hit the door closure, swiftly cycling through the airlock system and pummelled along the corridor.

"Hard burn, Heki. Now. Crew brace!" she bellowed over comms, upping the magboots as the engines kicked in. Past the galley, and the acceleration really took hold, but the servos drove her on, and she forced herself into the cockpit. The expected alarm fired up.

"Fuck," a glance at Heki's screen sent her stomach screaming. She counted four missiles. Coming fast.

"Rescue me?" echoed over her comms, laughter interspersed between the words. She knew the voice, those moments on board the *Scourge* haunting her dreams. Her nightmares. *"It is you that needs rescuing ... I live on, Captain Khan. I survive and will grow ... What? What is this the* Segfi *has recorded? You were here, and then you weren't and now ..."*

Rebekah squeezed the girls' shoulders; both held each others hand. She knew their eyes would be distant, looking into the void but seeing far more than the black.

"What secret have you been keeping, Khan? I have searched for years for how the Senti jump through space. Those slimy gasbags keeping their secrets to themselves. I have cut and spliced, grown and FAILED! Tell me Khan, how can a lowlife maggot like you have found the secret? TELL ME!"

"Butcher," she said. "Fuck you."

A breath, a pause, the briefest of moments when there was nothing but the abyss. And then Karal loomed, though thankfully a little more distant than last time they had visited. Rebekah leaned over and activated the transponder, worried hands pulling back the slumped, limp girls. Blood seeped from their nostrils, but their eyes fluttered, weak breath slipping between pale lips. She hugged them close, not caring for the blood on her suit.

"I love you," she whispered, and wept.

CHAPTER 48

"Are you sure about this?" said Davina.

"To be honest, I'm not sure about anything anymore. Since you first came knocking with an offer I couldn't refuse, life has been like riding a rollercoaster through a shower of shit." Rebekah laid her hand on Arin's brow, the warmth there reassuring amid the storm to come. The medbot had stabilised him quickly, the cracked ribs having pierced a lung, running things close. He sported bruises everywhere across his chest, but he was alive, and the rest of her squad too. Her crew.

The countess lay on the second bed, her prognosis wildly different. Her lungs were devastated, but apparently that was nothing new. The medbot was shocked she was alive at all. But she'd come through the escape, and was under sedation to prevent any temptation Rebekah had to shoot her in the head. Twice. Just to be sure. Though it still tickled at the back of her mind. She had killed a guard back at Viscount Lundstrom's torture villa for what they had knowingly allowed. Murdered them, if she were honest, for far less than what the Warmonger had done to Heki and Tremil.

"You want the pardon. For everyone," Davina said, pulling her away from the countess. "I know that look in your eye."

"That in my file too?" Rebekah stood, letting out a long sigh. The twins were also sedated, and under a drip put together by Savvo from the medbot's instructions. Food, water and rest. The symbiotes had detached, and slept by their sides, metallic waves rippling over their skin. Everyone was exhausted, but she couldn't afford any mistakes. "So, explain it to me again, one more time over a coffee."

They left medbay, and headed to the galley, Dricks and Savvo already there with their drinks of choice. The mood was sullen, despite having met the original mission parameter. The Butcher was loose and in control of the most powerful ship in the Almaarian fleet.

Davina collected her flask and sat next to Dricks, gripping her forearm with a smile. "He's doing okay."

Hendricks patted her hand, and a small smile appeared before fading away, worry lines across her brow.

"Go on," said Rebekah, taking her place next to Savvo, the swelling on his head responding well to the meds. "They need to hear it too, Davina."

The Incini appeared to change, her posture business like. "The man you have locked in the cabin? Gerent, he called himself. He claimed to work for the Minister."

"You mean *the* Minister?" Savvo said. "As in the right hand of the Emperor?"

She nodded. "Hard to prove, but his power was evident. I think he tapped into my dampener at one point, and his calling card was embedded with specific graphics. Anyway, he said Erikson, that's the Enforcer's real name, was neck deep in a conspiracy. He didn't know whether he was actively involved or duped, and needed to find out. He asked me to not send any potentially treasonous discoveries to the Directorate. Said if I did, he wouldn't catch whoever was high up and involved because they would intervene too early."

"Like in the Court?" said Hendricks.

"Yes. I believe so. Gerent said not catching that higher-up would allow them to breed sedition. Like rats."

"And then we find him with Countess Rat herself," said Savvo.

"And?" asked Rebekah. "Your thoughts."

Davina swallowed. "I think he meant the countess. Obviously. But he was there, knew it all. He was fronting me up, preventing me from reporting to the Directorate while all this played out. If Segfi was exposed, he could claim he was investigating it all along. If not, then all that information was stored with me."

"Yeah, and a little Incini accident would be arranged," Savvo slammed the table with a fist. "Just so she could have the Butcher and his fucking experiments."

"More than that, though. Listen. Not a word until you've heard it all. Do I have that on Incini contract?" With Davina's agreement, Rebekah put the comms unit on speaker, and played back the Butcher's last words, watching each of her crew in turn until it was done. "That's what the *Scourge* was about. He was trying to figure out how the Senti can travel through void-space. All he had were the Senti bodies. Cutting and splicing to discover their secret. Except they had it wrong. It was the symbiotes that enabled the leaps, dismissed because they saw them as simple mind suckers no doubt. And now he knows we jumped through void-space. Three times."

Hendricks grimaced, clasping her hands together. "If Segfi had got what she wanted, it would have been bad. Even more so should she work out what the girls can do."

"She still can," said Davina. "We're at Karal. Our presence will be registered, as will the previous leap. It won't take a genius to work out what happened. And even if those records can be wiped, what then? The countess and her Minister's lackey know they were in one place then another, without the week's travel between it would normally take."

"Then we're fucked," said Savvo. "Alive, the girls safe, possibly a pardon in the offing, but that evil bitch won't stop searching when she works it out."

"Ahem," said ZZ3 over comms. "May I interject?"

"I think you've earned the right," stated Rebekah, agreement ringing from around the table.

"I think you are leaning towards leaving Almaarian space. I concur that would be the safest option. However, I also believe you are considering something much darker. That our two passengers can't be allowed to report on what they know."

Rebeka stirred in her seat, Davina too. Of course she had considered it. Fuck, it was top of the list.

"Firstly, I believe you are not those people. Crimes have been committed. Treason, though I again concur, that the Minister and Segfi are likely acting hand in hand. But the Butcher will not stop until all threats are eliminated. All." ZZ3 paused, but Rebekah remained patient for once. "I think, and Asham agrees, that war will come to Almaar. That the Butcher is a huge threat to the future of human rule. I present the *Scourge* and the crew of the *Segfi* as evidence."

Rebekah looked around the table. Heads were down; blame being shared where none was necessary. If it hadn't been them, the countess would have opened the Butcher's box sometime in the future. He would have been free and an unknown. And ZZ3 had ripped out the emotion of knowing that and placed cold hard logic in its place. She cracked a thumb, imagining the gun shot, the shock on the countess' face as she took out all her hate for what she'd done to the girls.

"Thank you, ZZ3," she said, her lips pursed, before banging her hand on the table. "Stop with the blame shit. It's happened. What comes next?"

"Arin would vote for blowing her brains out," said Hendricks. "I came close. Took out two elite, though I have *no* guilt there. But we're going to need leaders. Ruthless ones if ZZ3 is right."

"Crap," said Savvo, his arms crossed, squeezing his hands tight around his biceps. "You mean they're gonna need her. The fucking Warmonger."

The countess blinked, a yawn following, but unable to stretch. Rebekah watched her struggles with a little glee before appearing in her eyeline to undo her straps. Segfi eyed her with disdain, but she gave nothing back. Not yet.

The noblewoman shifted around, propping herself up on the bed, Rebekah revelling in the moment when she realised she wasn't where she expected to be. Her nostrils flared, probably at the smell of old oil and burnt metal. They were in the cargo hold, chains clanking, a full complement of angry crew waiting for her to wake up.

"I'm not intimidated," she said, brushing down the same blouse she had arrived on board wearing. The crew parted, and Segfi shuddered, eyes widening. Heki and Tremil stood there, hand in hand, eyes blazing towards her. The wave of hate rolled over the countess, unfettered, and she gagged. A shake took control of her hands, the tremble rising upwards along her arms and Rebekah knew well enough what came next. Her shrivelled heart would be thundering. Blood roaring in her ears, waves crashing in an emotional storm, unable to think of anything but the desperate need to make it stop. Find a way to bring the hate to an end.

If only.

"Enough," Rebekah said, and gathered the girls in tight, feeling their need to release what remained and taking the brunt. "Now go," she whispered. The twins murmured their acquiescence, and sent hateful glares the countess' way before heading out the door.

"You want to say that again?" said Rebekah.

The countess had lost her composure, mouth twisted, a tear rolling down her cheek. Rebekah wondered if it was her first.

"You are officially rescued," stated Davina, stepping out from behind ZZ3. "So, by the terms of our agreement, the crew of the *Sunstar* are due pardons."

The countess wiped away the tear, her stare hardening. Could anything cow this woman?

"Piffle. I was the one who organised the escape pod," stated the countess.

"Listen to them, Segfi," said the man sat at her side. Grey suit, collar ash-stained but sharp. Rebekah enjoyed that. Segfi, no honorific. He was above her. "They are due pardons. I will confirm those as recorded." He tapped his head next to the eye implant.

"For all my registered crew," stated Rebekah.

"What is this Gerent?" said the countess, turning to the Minster's hand. "Have you gone soft? They can't kill us. They would be running forever. The Court would never stop looking."

"It's the Court he fears," said Davina, and walked over, ensuring she was in the countess' eyeline. "He fears everything I have recorded on this slate for the Directorate. All the evidence of his, and your, involvement in a conspiracy to acquire and use an AI. The same information I have recorded for the Enforcers. The same information I have backed up somewhere safe. You sought to quieten me, instead you have empowered my voice. That silence has a price. Full Royal Pardons. As per the Incini tenets."

The countess scowled. "Agreed, Incini witch. But I'm coming for you."

"Witnessed by G. M. Abel, hand to the Minister of the Almaarian Court. Are we done here?" said Gerent, his voice almost pleading.

"Not quite," Davina said. "Just for the record, I am registered crew as per the mission to the *Scourge*. The twins are registered crew as per the updated manifest. I love small print. Witnessed?"

"Witnessed," stated Gerent with a drawn-out sigh. "Now can we leave?"

"Not yet." Rebekah glared at the countess. "Only a warbot's logic saved your skin. If I had my way, we would be wearing you as a fucking flag on the bow. You live because the Butcher took the *Segfi*, because he will not stop until he believes he is safe. It might be a week, or a month, but he will resurface and destroy whatever he fears. Don't waste your time looking for us, because you're going to be busy." She enjoyed the flash of anger she received in return. "Savvo, Dricks, can you escort these two to M2 for me? Mr Pike is about to have some very special surprise guests. I'll call ahead."

CHAPTER 49

Rebekah supped the last of her beer and checked her slate. Time was ticking, and she was beginning to fret when Davina finally appeared. She sat down, placing a bag between them and withdrawing a slate.

"Are you sure you want to look?"

Rebekah sighed and ordered another beer and the first cocktail on the list with her wrist ID. For all his mumblings, Pike had come through with their contract sale, another crew already taking their repair shift, and her bank wouldn't be complaining for a while. "Why not? I caused enough issues, then solved them in a typical Rebekah way. Kind of ties things up."

Davina handed the slate over after opening it up, spinning it around.

"Poppy ... fuck." Rebekah rubbed her eyes then placed the slate down, the beer to the top left.

"I thought you'd be pleased, her being Michael's sister and all," said Davina.

"Never easy, is it?" replied Rebekah as she brushed both hands over her forehead and on through her short hair. "Sister."

"And she returned to Shema after – err – the *incident*. He did have a partner, Stig's mother, who by the look of what I could dig up was the one who wanted them out here. Had a job on M1 with one of the bigger subsidiaries. And apparently found the allure of a CEO's money more interesting than life with Michael and her son." Davina retrieved the slate, her lips taut. "Change anything?"

Rebekah took the newly arrived beer and sank half of it, while Davina sipped at her drink. The silence felt right, as if she was truly considering making a play for a normal life. Even being rejected would be part of that, having the space and time to try. She imagined a friendship first, one that would blossom into more. Then the gun fire, the blood, because it followed her wherever she went. And she couldn't trust the countess, nor the agent, the hand of the Minister. Davina had confirmed the pardons had been registered with the Court, even hers despite the thinness of her claim to be crew. But nobles were fuckers, and they lowlifes. Power was everything.

What is normal? Normal for those who walk about Karal as if a cog in society, fitting into the norms dictated by the Court? Or like me, always on the cusp, having to push the boundaries because of who she cares for most?

"No. It changes nothing. A dream, and holding that dream as a possibility perhaps keeps me going when the world falls apart. And the others? This Sabier?"

"Victor and her were foster siblings. Parents died, and you know Almaar. No money, so then it was the orphan workhouse. As far as I can tell they survived by tooth and claw, emerging into the slums and later the gangs. They left to come here ten years ago and set up business. Sank their money into the bars, drugs, counterfeit IDs and later the *Maverick*. But they were struggling, started doing a few hits on the side, stuff like that. Erikson propped them up by making sure they had no salvage rights to pay, but it wasn't enough, and when the *Maverick* was destroyed, they lost all of it."

"The face," said Rebekah, circling her own to mimic the holo-mask.

"From gang warfare. No real details, but it was a scarring. A retribution for stepping on someone else's turf. No psyche report when you run in the slums, but I'll let you work it out."

"Victor?"

Davina shrugged. "He was into his IDs, so could be anywhere. Karal's facial ID system is pretty basic but well protected. The twins might get in, but beyond my means."

"So, we still have to watch our backs. Not that we're stopping long with what's happened." She took Davina's hand in her own on impulse. "Look, thank you. For what you did at the end there with Gerent. When we leave, there's a berth if you want it."

Davina shrugged. "It was the right thing, at the right time. And I want to be here when the countess works out the time differences, and things slot together. Someone should witness that, let you know all about it when you eventually return. It'll never make up for what she did to Heki and Tremil, but watching it dawn that she let them slip through her fingers, that I'd like to see."

Rebekah nodded. A gun shot to the noble-shit's head would have been better. But Davina's was a false hope, the Warmonger would have taken around thirty seconds to start recalculating her next move. In truth, Rebekah knew the Incini was not at home in space and needed some way of saying thanks but no thanks. The boardroom was her battleground. "When we leave, we won't be back."

"You will." Davina stood, and with a smile, left. Heading out of the bar entrance, elegance in her movements, in her hair. Back in an Incini's element. She was right to stay, and it was some relief not to have her on board.

"Why am I here?" Rebekah looked around Trent Pike's office. She'd hardly set foot in the place in the years she had worked the field, and now twice within a month. He faced her, hands clasped together, the bristles on his chin longer, the tips greying to match the edges of his tightly curled hair. But it was the bags under the eyes that caught her attention, and the slump to the shoulders. Apparently, he hadn't forgiven her for arriving with two difficult guests. "I thought we were doing this in a bar over a few beers and some Calc."

"Because I asked, and you agreed." His tone was different, but Segfi did that to people. And someone high up in the Minister's favour, probably even more so. Rebekah had described his embossed calling card a 'weapon of office'.

"Snappy, Pike. Thought that was my role." She sent him a grin, but his countenance didn't change. Maybe he stiffened a little. She'd faced down a battleship, Pike wasn't going to be a challenge.

He shook his head, and produced a dampener which he placed very carefully on the desk. "You are about to get a headache," he said. "Tough shit, Pilot-Sergeant Rebecca Kanista."

She glared at Pike, the recall of her old name cutting deep. And then the headache hit, a sharp pain followed by a dull thudding about her wetware.

What the fuck?

"What have you done?" She held her hands to her ears, brain swirling with vertigo that soon passed.

"That's to stop your wetware from recording this conversation. The next thing I have to do is cut out your tongue, so you don't talk to anyone. That's a joke by the way. Better than yours, and waaay better than Enterman's." Pike's aura seemed to have grown, as if the shadows had all sucked back to stand behind him, letting the light shine in.

"Trent?"

"Not my name," Trent said, the words harsh, though somehow Rebekah felt he regretted that, his features softening. "Look, there's no easy way to say this ..."

"Baseborn? You're part of the resistance..."

He shook his head. "They don't exist, Rebekah. Just a rumour perpetuated by the Court. A snare to trap those looking to rise up and no more. They're too powerful for that, and agents like Gerent make sure it stays that way."

"Then what?" she snapped, feeling uncomfortable. "You're ex-Forces and know my history, and the rest of the crew's."

"Easy enough after you dropped the Major's name," replied Trent, causing Rebekah to mentally kick herself. She'd dropped Ren's moniker when they'd rescued Michael from Sabier's revenge attack. "As not that many units under Major Ren had the tactical nous to break into M2."

She snorted, shaking her head. "Stupid."

"Agreed. I'm a go-between. A smuggler, if you want a title, but not for profit. I help those in trouble. Some hide here, others in quieter places in the outlying planets. Some I move on to Windward when scum like Scarva play ball." He grimaced when saying the Senti's name, Rebekah adding her own frown at the thought of the alien scumbag.

"And the odd bit of hardware and ammunition. The PDC rounds, the schematics. I knew it was you. For what it's worth, they saved our arses out there."

"And in return you just dumped two major players in the Court in my lap without a fucking word." He nearly shouted the last part, a twitch appearing above his right eye.

"Not like I had a choice."

"I think I've earned the right to know what happened out there, Rebekah. Right now, I have a file I deleted from VERT saying your ship just appeared from nowhere. No sun flares or rad clouds to explain it. Blip, here, blip gone and then you fucking come back with the Warmonger and a hand of the Minister. M4's tower are missing a file too, thanks to Nicky. People covering your back because, fuck, I don't know why. Tell me the reason I had to listen to the Warmonger in a complete and utter fucking rage." Trent had stood, an angry rash streaking his neck and up onto the fringes of his cheeks, hands balled tight.

See. I knew it wouldn't take her long.

So, she told him. All of it. Except for the experiments on the *Scourge*, and that they took the Butcher from his lab for leverage, nor about the girls' abilities, though she did admit to their existence. Some truth would help. She included Duboit and Erikson. Most of the truth lay in the detail, the missions, just not what they found. And the 'blips' were a new and unreliable engine they discovered in Segfi's lab, designed by the Bustan AI that had melded with the Butcher. Treason, but superseded by the fact the Butcher had taken the battleship as his new residence. Trent's face, or whoever he was, a perfect picture when it clicked home what that could mean.

"Fuuuck," he said, drawing the swear word out.

"I may have said that a few times over the last few months. The Butcher is coming, Trent. He won't give a flying shit whether you were born with a silver spoon up your arse or swimming in the gutter. Whoever you are, whoever you know, get the word out. The last time I saw the *Segfi*, there were a thousand and more crew learning to swim in the black." She kicked her chair back, standing, hands on hips. "Now excuse me. I earned a pardon, and I'm going to enjoy it for a fucking while. And if you are a people smuggler, I think there may be some big business coming your way. Better get prepared."

"I win again." Arin laid out the cards on the cargo box, his celebration followed by a combined cough and wince as he grabbed his ribs. "Ouch."

"Yeah, I agree. *Ouch*," said Savvo, watching as ZZ3 crossed off more of his creds on the slate next to its own cards. "How come he's beating you? You have all that-that computing power wedged in there from the twins *and* the ghost of a scientist."

ZZ3 shrugged. "Our glorious leader said I needed to learn how to lie better, and that cards were the best practise." The bot turned his hand over, Hendricks spreading the warbot's cards wide. A winning hand ZZ3 had folded two betting rounds beforehand.

"You're bloody cheating?" Hendricks glared at Arin. "Using a warbot? You underhanded, conniving bastard."

Savvo grinned, slapping Arin on the back behind the cracked rib and the newly inflated lung. "Sneaky."

"Ouch," Arin repeated. "Sheesh, ZZ3 asked to practise."

"Another lie. And a poor one," said the bot, and rose from the deck, eyes settling into a repeating pattern. "Do not worry. I also lied about taking your creds, my friends and crewmates."

The co-pilot choked, words morphing into laughter with Hendricks joining in as Arin stared at the bot with eyebrows raised.

"I've been double-crossed by my best friend in the world."

"Please don't," said Savvo, trying to quieten his own laughter, brushing away the tears. "No more, and not so loud." He got up and walked over to Heki and Tremil who had fallen asleep leaning against each other, wrapped in their cabin blankets. They hadn't wanted to be alone, their skin a little less pale, their sores nearly healed. But not yet their souls, the trauma remained raw. Probably would forever. He leaned over and tucked the blanket edges around each of them, letting both symbiotes wrap a tentacle about his finger. They were calm.

A hand landed on Savvo's shoulder, the fingers soft but insistent. "I'm done. Time to turn in," came the voice, and he twisted round, taking Nicky in his arms.

"Stay," he said, watching her eyes widen then settle to an obvious *yes*. They turned about together, heading for the door, ignoring Arin's grin as he took Dricks' hand in his own.

"Ahhh, ain't it sweet."

Savvo threw a middle finger over his shoulder, Nicky copying the gesture as they disappeared into the corridor.

"May I put the girls to bed?" ZZ3 asked.

Hendricks nodded, patting the warbot's metal arm. "Of course."

The warbot's torso rose from the deck, metal arms slipping beneath the sleeping girls. "I would like to say ... thank you."

Hendricks and Arin looked to each other, then stood up beside the bot. "You are crew," they said in unison. "And we are a family."

And here ends Warmonger's Wrath.

Rebekah and the Wrecking Squad return in The Queen's Spawn

THE WRECKING SQUAD SERIES

Thank you for choosing to spend your time reading Warmonger's Wrath. It's an honour as an indie author to have written stories readers such as yourself have taken the time to read.

This whole series has been taking up my headspace for some time. I knew I had a great set of characters to work with and a story premise that had weight. The next issue is how to sustain the books over three, or in this case, six books. To achieve that, the world must feel 'lived in' and by people who feel real, in a storyline where their actions, and the events surrounding them are, in context, plausible. The hardest part is ensuring you don't rely on random incidents or unknown characters. For instance, returning to Scarva who makes an appearance in the next book, or Lieutenant Ormsk who will play a part towards the end of the series. And above all else, the Butcher, the fusion of General Asham and the Bustan AI, who overshadows the story arc from now on. I hope I achieved that, and you want to keep on reading about the events The Wrecking Squad get tangled up in. Next is Scarva's Revenge (a working title), which kickstarts Phase Two of the series as Almaar faces a battle for survival when the Butcher flexes his power.

Reviews and ratings are the lifeblood of any author, and vital to indie writers in particular. They help new readers make up their minds when searching for new authors and books. Ratings are your chance to bring a little starlight and attention to my scifi books that are a somewhat different from the norm.

If you enjoyed my novel, please consider leaving a star rating on Amazon and/or Goodreads.

And if you wish to know more about the members of the Wrecking Squad, their origin story is absolutely FREE. Just flick to the end of this book to find out how you can download Redemption Tour - A Wrecking Squad Story.

About the Author

Nick Snape has been steeped in Science Fiction and Fantasy since his friends first dragged him from his schoolwork and stuck a book under his nose. Lost to the world of imagination, he became a teacher by accident, though he thoroughly enjoyed developing the joy of reading and writing in his pupils. Having retired after thirty years, he thought it was high time to practise what he preached.

Nick's books feature everything from all out, heart-pounding, fast-paced action to thoughtful, character driven twists on the fantasy and sci-fi genres. Genetics to Artificial Intelligence, Artifice Dragons to Soul-Eating enemies, nothing is off the menu.

Books by Nick Snape

Weapons of Choice Series

'A truly epic saga of riveting sci-fi thrillers...'

It started with a failed military training exercise and an alien incursion, desperate and on the hunt. Survival was just the beginning...

After encountering a buried spaceship and its rogue AI on Earth, Finn, Zuri, and Corporal Smith (deceased) take refuge on an alien home world where they unravel the truth about the forced colonisation of Earth-like planets. With the ship's AI providing advanced nano-weaponry and evolving alien battle tech, Finn and Delta blaze a trail through the galaxy seeking a way home, walking a fine line between vengeance and redemption in this thought-provoking action sci-fi series.

Over 25,000 books read in this 'superb scifi series'

Hostile Contact

Return Protocol

Zuri's War

Finn's War

Alien Rebirth

Invasive Species

Legion Earth

Nemesis Earth

The Scorching Standalone Series

The World in My Hands

"A deeply nuanced sci-fi standalone with slow-burn suspense, a diverse and unorthodox cast of characters and a spaceship straight out of your worst nightmares"

The world is heading towards global collapse as the Scorching takes full effect. Salvation vessels orbit the Earth, waiting to transport the chosen few away from danger and to start again; ten plantships grown by an alien species for the wealthiest and most powerful, or those lucky enough to be selected by lottery. Yet not all is well on board. Dark secrets lurk in the corridors and depths of their respective ships, dragging Jenna and Seth into a world of malice and violence they thought they had left far behind.

***

Just Press Play

"Staggeringly original and timely release from a masterful voice in modern sci-fi."

On a devastated Earth, the Drathken arrive with the promise of healing the planet. When anti-alien terrorists threaten the accord, Cop and Vlogger Josh Nkosi, and his MARC unit, chase terrorists into the Burnout Zone only to come face to face with humanity's stark future when the hunt takes a devastating twist. As a conspiracy emerges, Nkosi is forced on a dark path of discovery.

Warriors of Spirit and Bone

A Dragon of the Veil

"An INCREDIBLE start to a new, dark epic fantasy series."

In a realm no longer devoid of magic, the fate of a people rests with Laoch and Sura, and the Gods' weapons they bear – a thousand years of faith and lies reconciled in a single moment of hope and redemption. With whispers of an ancient evil's return, they are left reeling by their enemy's power, one even the Gods' weapons fear. For cast in iron and spiritfire - here be dragons.

***

A City of Ashes

"A work of coal-dark fantasy that is continually surprising, provocative, and compulsively entertaining."

With the Veil Dragon, Nathair, seemingly under the Spirit Captain's control, Laoch pushes away the grief of his first encounter with the metal beast and hunts for a weapon his new and distrusted ally insists they can use against the coming Constructor invasion. For an Emperor consumed by revenge has a new artifice, one that hungers to enslave.

***

A Queen in Blood

"A dark ambience largely unmatched by anything else I've read."

As the invasion of Brandshold begins, the realm is haunted by the Infected – devastated and spirit-poisoned townsfolk who hunger for flesh and souls to salve their pain. When the city of Jense falls to a wave of bloody teeth and foul claws, the Constructor's Emperor strikes, shattering city walls with his artifice dragon, and the dreaded *Kraken* soulship. For a queen bathed in the blood of her own people, hope lies in the alchemy of the meisters, a traitorous mechanical dragon, and loyal but broken soldiers.

The Wrecking Squad

The Queen's Spawn (Book 4)
The Butcher hunts for a secret ... but which one?

Fear of the Butcher sweeps the Emperor's Court. Commanding a vulnerable navy and sceptical officers, Countess Segfi begins the hunt for the human/AI hybrid, risking everything as she attacks Daphene, where he first emerged as a threat.

But the Butcher shows his hand elsewhere, attempting to take Scarva's ship and uncover the secrets of Senti FTL. Desperate, the alien calls upon Rebekah and her crew for help, dreading what he might have stolen, and where he is headed next.

Drawn back into the fight, the Wrecking Squad are forced to hunt for the spawn of an alien Queen that may well be the key to Almaar's future.

***

Emperor's Fall (Book 5)
Fracture an empire and expose the weakness at its heart

Rebekah and the crew of the *Sunstar* are persuaded to transport Senti-built defensive hardware to the fleets' battleships by a desperate Countess Segfi. But the Butcher strikes, damaging the airless moonbase on Saim. Despite Rebekah's instincts, the Wrecking Squad can't abandon those in need and mount a rescue. But when the trap snaps shut, thousands die breathless in an instant, a moment the Butcher shares with the Emperor's Court laced with a threat to the rest of the system's vulnerable colonies. The price he demands for the Empire's safety is the *Sunstar* and the crew's secret of Faster Than Light Travel.

One ship, one crew, to save billions.

What price for survival?

Breaker's Ruin (Book 6)
When the empire falls, who will stand for humanity?

Wild storms rage over Almaar, with the few survivors of the Ingblack plague facing devastation as floodwaters rise and food runs out. But lurking in the ruins is something far more sinister. For remnants of the Butcher survived, each vying for power over the others in a malevolent race for weapons and resources.

With the empathic twins let loose on those who stand in their way, grief releasing the chains shackling their true power, Savvo is the only Breaker left capable of reining them in, while Commodore Srenik and his ragtag navy must search for the truth about the AI-controlled fleet orbiting Almaar, and the rising power on the planet below.

Together, these disparate forces must make a final stand as the strongest Butcher rises to prominence by absorbing the others and setting its sights on enslaving humanity.

Breakers may grieve, their hearts in ruin, but you will never break a Breaker.

ACKNOWLEDGEMENTS

As with all authors, this book would never have existed without the dedicated friends and family who were there by my side throughout the entire process. The least I can do is give them a mention for their patience with my obsession! My Beta readers, supporters and fiercest critics have been Pak, Paul Derwent, Martin Lejeune, and particularly for this book, the wonderful Bryan Chaffin. Amazing friends who have put that aside to make sure whatever I put out there was something they wanted to read.

Julie, my wife, needs a special mention. Over the past few years she has kept me going, being there at every step through the dark and joyful times. I can't believe how lucky I am.

Finally, the New Year and Pub Night Crews. Wouldn't be here without you.

Thank you all.

WRECKING SQUAD FREE NOVELLA

My new series, The Wrecking Squad, involves a squad of ex-Marines on the run. Their origin story is available in a FREE novella, Redemption Tour, which you can download by subscribing to my newsletter with the link below. Yes, absolutely free.

www.nicksnape.com/subscribe

Subscribing will also provide further information about this series, and my plans for more exciting science fiction and fantasy novels in the future.

The Lost Squad - A Weapons of Choice Novel

The Stratan Marines who were introduced in Hostile Contact have a surprise in store. A second squad followed them to Earth, who appear later in the series in Legion Earth. The Lost Squad, a FREE full-length novel, charts the alien Marines' action-packed experiences before that book, as countries and mercenaries vie for their technology and knowledge.

If you wish to learn more about their history on Earth, and I suggest you do as it's an excellent novel, then please subscribe to my newsletter and receive your FREE novel via the link above.